APB: Artists against Police Brutality
Collection Copyright © 2015 by Rosarium Publishing
Content Copyright © 2015 by Attributed Authors and Illustrators
Cover © 2015 John Jennings
Book Designed by Jason Rodriguez and John Jennings

Rosarium Publishing
P.O. Box 544
Greenbelt, MD 20768-0544

ISBN: 978-1-4956-0752-3
LCCN: 2015950995

1

# APB

ARTISTS against POLICE BRUTALITY

# TABLE OF

# CONTENTS

# INTRODUCTION

## BY: BILL CAMPBELL

There are so many ways to sugarcoat this, but I'm going to be honest with you: this project was borne out of anger.

It was the night when a Staten Island grand jury decided not to put the officers responsible for killing Eric Garner (and the coroner did rule it a homicide) on trial for his murder. It's not that that decision was extraordinary or particularly surprising. We black folks have known, since the first slave masters organized posses of white indentured servants to hunt down black indentured servants, that we "enjoyed" a special legal status on this continent. This can be loosely translated as, "We're gonna do whatever we want to you." In fact, it was the utter predictability of that non-verdict that enraged me, that spurred me to call Jason and John and to, that very night, create the anthology you now hold in your hands.

This special legal status to many communities of color closely resembles an undeclared war—a "police action," if you will (Huey P. Newton once likened the police to an "occupying army"). It hides behind such slogans as "tough on crime" and "law and order," and is reinforced daily by the overrepresentation of black crime by the media. These slogans are wholeheartedly believed by most, because these same officers act quite peacefully within white communities. While, to many, this may seem a bit overly dramatic, some of us can feel totally justified in feeling that our "justice system" acts more like a war machine—ending over 1,100 American lives a year (far more than Iraq ever did), killing nearly one unarmed black person a day (far exceeding the rates during the lynch-crazed days of the Jim Crow South), brutalizing countless others (no stats), and currently holding 2.3 million POWs (no, I'd never claim these folks are innocent—but almost half of them are nonviolent drug offenders).

I've been lucky in being relatively unscathed in this conflict. My first encounter was when I was fifteen, walking home late from editing my school newspaper. The police stopped me a block from my house in my 99% white neighborhood, said I "fit a description" (a common refrain), and made me spread 'em for all my neighbors to see (probably prompting some of them to say, "Honor student, my ass, I told you he was a criminal"). The last time was a few years ago, coming home from work, when I was stopped for running a red light on a street I hadn't driven down. It was the same officer who stopped me previously for going 30 mph in a 30 mph zone (I wish I were making this up). I wanted to yell, "What about a middle-aged, overweight black man driving an 18-year-old car with a baby seat screams, 'Drug dealer?!'" Instead, foolishly, I refused to even look for my registration. We both knew he was lying, and he let me go. See, lucky.

I have, so far, always been lucky, and I know it. But since I was 15, I have been stopped, frisked, and questioned more times than I can count while walking, while driving, while about to fly (in the pre-TSA days). Pleasant experiences with the police, for me, are rare. And why wouldn't they be? No matter what I do, how I act, I know I am still a black man and am viewed by the police as a potential suspect, a possible enemy combatant.

Coach Darrell Royal once said, "There are three things that can happen on a forward pass—and two of them are bad." I know, as a black man in America, when I am confronted by the police, there are five things that can happen—and only one of them is good. I can be ticketed, beaten, jailed, killed (or all four), or let go. No matter how it plays out, everybody knows the cop can act with impunity. After all, how many soldiers are ever put up on murder charges? Even if I lay for hours in my own blood, their supervisors and your average American will say, "They were just doing their duty." You know it when you're stopped. The cops definitely know it. They have carte blanche. You know you're utterly exposed, totally vulnerable, and you can't help but feel a certain amount of anxiety, apprehension, and even fear—and, ultimately, anger.

That was the anger that flooded me the night the Staten Island grand jury made their decision. Because I—like most black people, whether male or female, whether gay, straight, and especially trans—knew I could've very easily been Eric Garner. Any of us could've been minding our own business, could've been angry or "respectable," could've resisted or complied (the report would say we resisted either way), and we still could've ended up dead. Or worse yet, one of our children could one day end up dead as well. I was angry because, once again, I had concrete proof that these "civil servants" who are sworn to "serve and protect" can do whatever they want with my black body, that I was once again justified in feeling that they are a menace to my society, and that I can never tell my child that she can go to the police if she's ever in danger because they may very well view her as the enemy and endanger her even further.

Throughout this brief essay, I have likened police interactions with communities of color to war. Well, much like Vietnam, this is a war that is being brought into your living room every day—and on your computer, your tablet, and your phone. If there were a memorial wall constructed in the nation's Mall here in DC to this war, it would be an ongoing project that would in a very short time become a life-sized maze encompassing the entire city.

Like the Vietnam protestors back in the day, nobody involved in this project thinks that when *APB* is released, the justice machine will suddenly see the error of its ways, things will be reformed, and we will all live happily ever after. This ain't no Tom Cruise movie. However, what we desire is to simply further the dialogue, make some people see this debate in a different light, perhaps change a mind or two, and, most importantly, exercise our freedom of speech in honor of all those who have had their voices silenced.


Bill Campbell
Washington, DC
July 2015

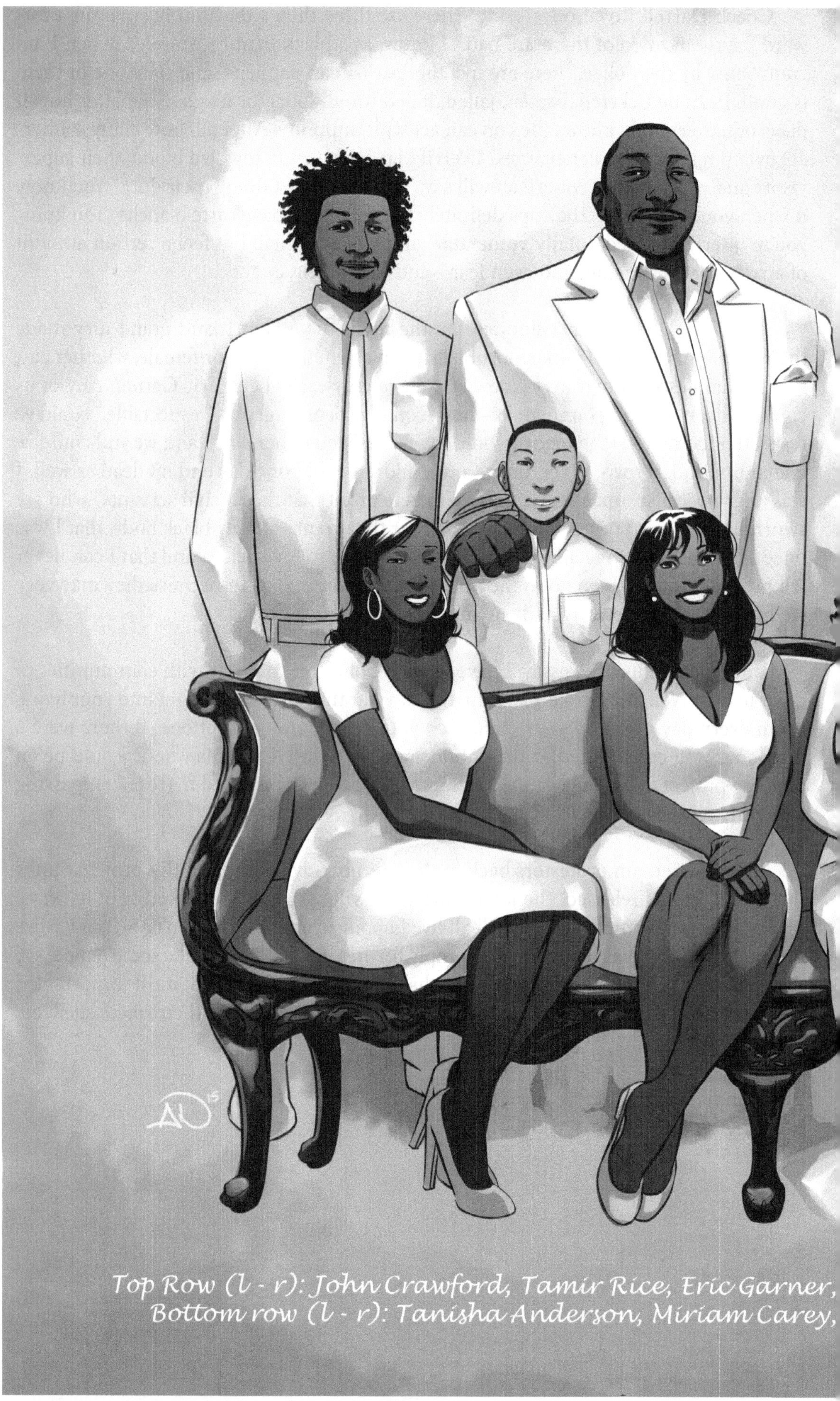

Top Row (l - r): John Crawford, Tamir Rice, Eric Garner,
Bottom row (l - r): Tanisha Anderson, Miriam Carey,

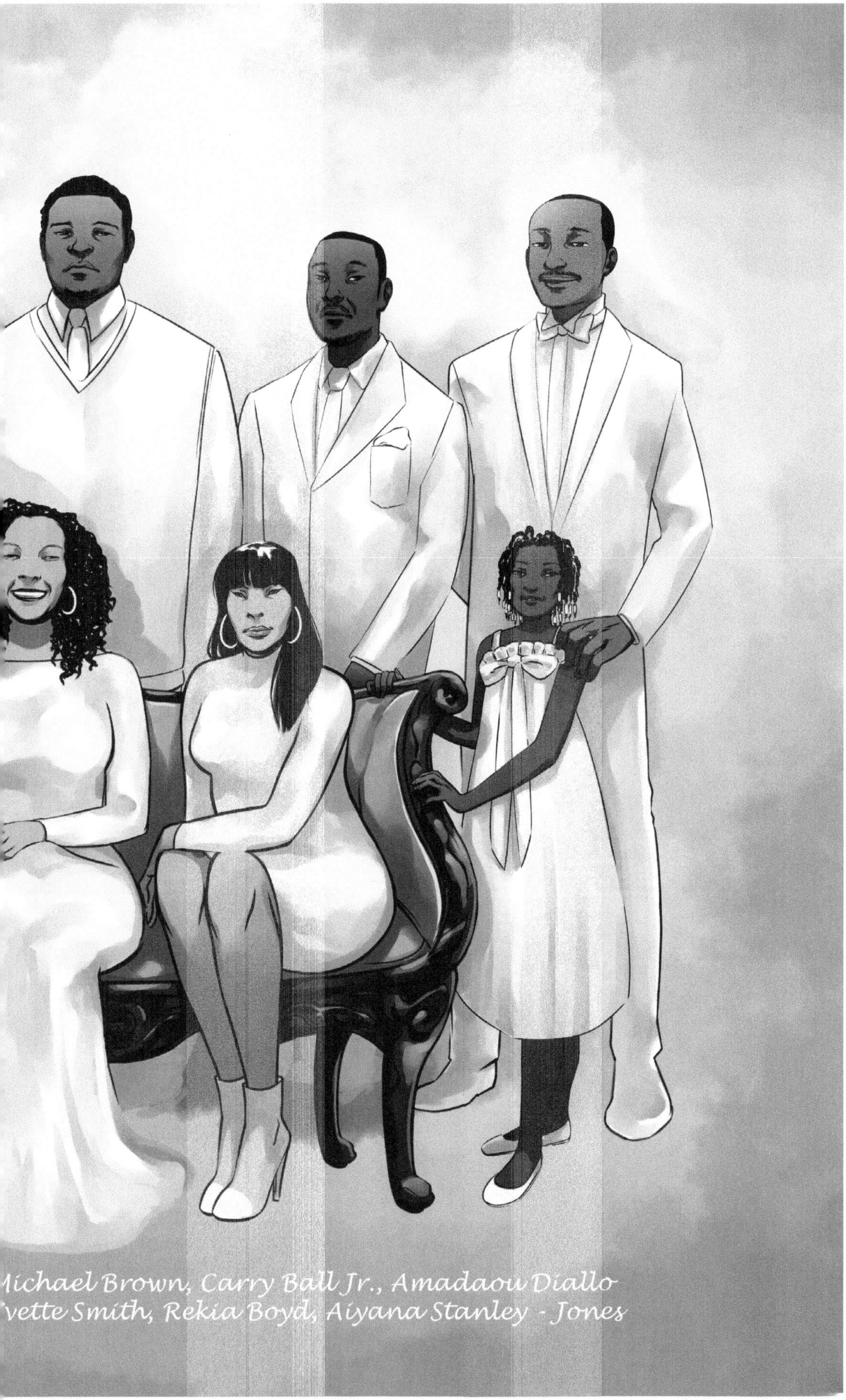
ichael Brown, Carry Ball Jr., Amadaou Diallo
vette Smith, Rekia Boyd, Aiyana Stanley - Jones

# Shame

by David Brame

Grimace and disdain
Jaw clenched
silence seeping out
'tween scissor teeth
crushing muscle
visible through skin
pulsing pulsing
quiver and pulse

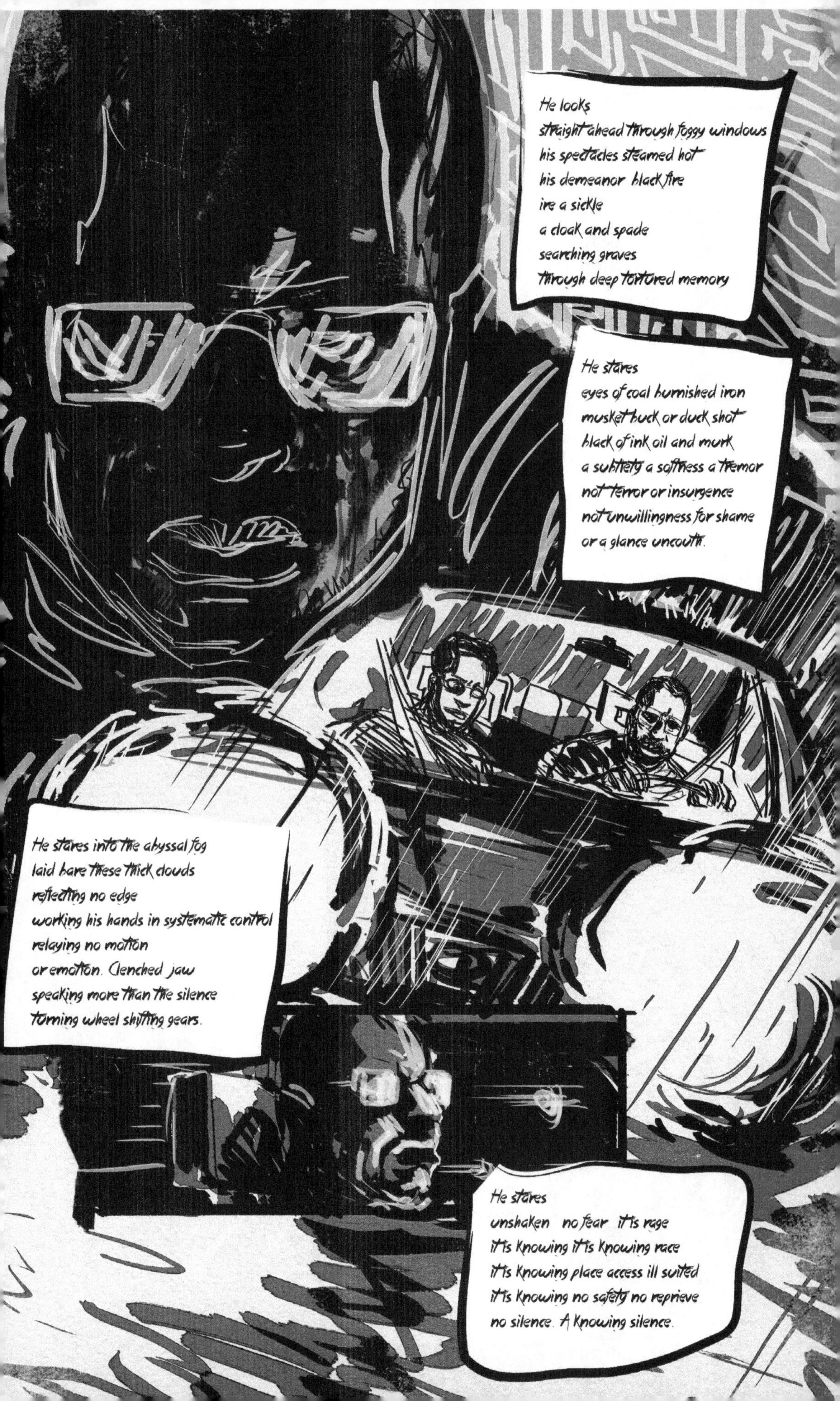
He looks
straight ahead through foggy windows
his spectacles steamed hot
his demeanor black fire
ire a sickle
a cloak and spade
searching graves
through deep tortured memory
He stares
eyes of coal burnished iron
musket buck or duck shot
black of ink oil and murk
a subtlety a softness a tremor
not terror or insurgence
not unwillingness for shame
or a glance uncouth.
He stares into the abyssal fog
laid bare these thick clouds
reflecting no edge
working his hands in systematic control
relaying no motion
or emotion. Clenched jaw
speaking more than the silence
turning wheel shifting gears.
He stares
unshaken no fear it is rage
it is Knowing it is Knowing race
it is Knowing place access ill suited
it is Knowing no safety no reprieve
no silence. A Knowing silence.

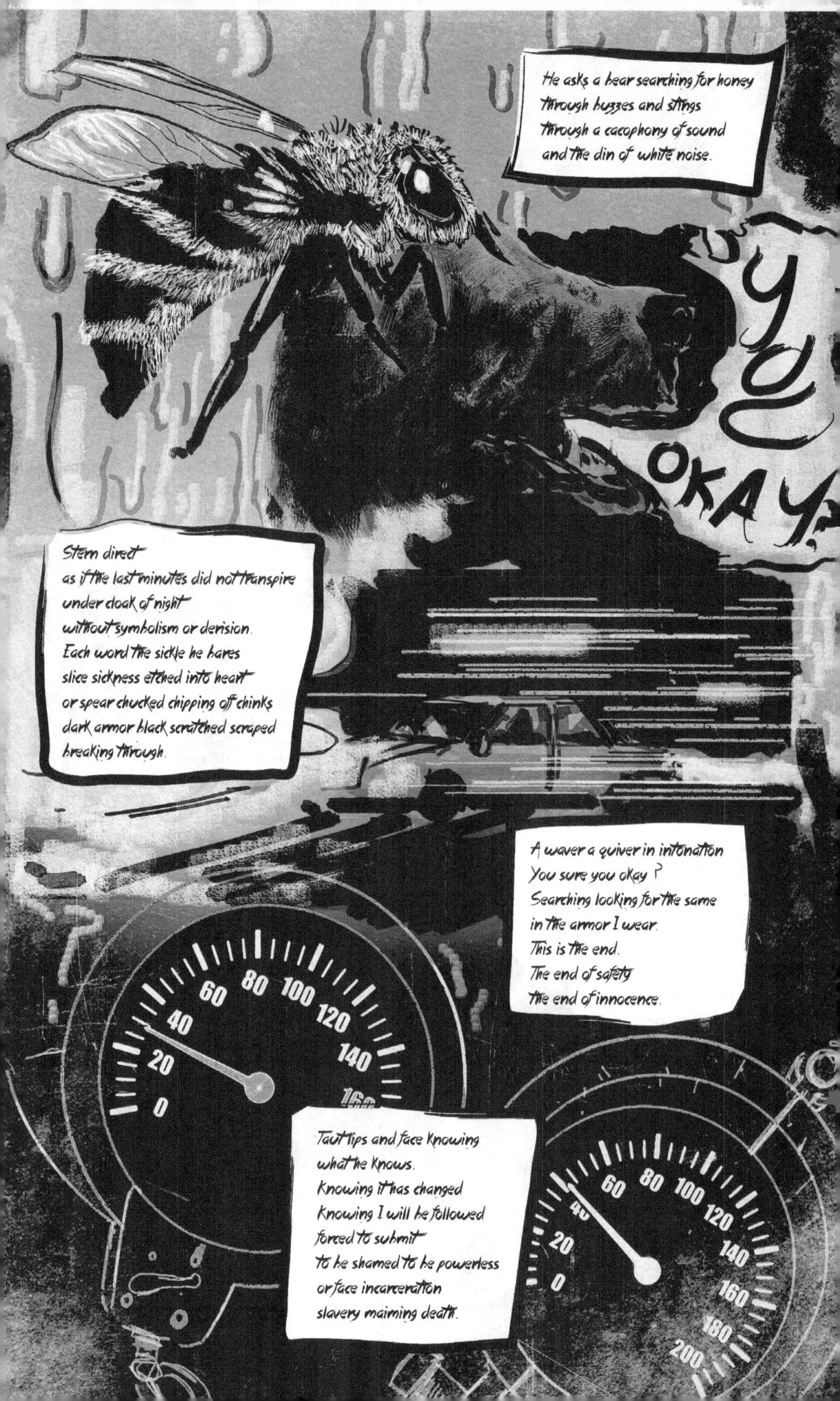
He asks a bear searching for honey
through buzzes and stings
through a cacophony of sound
and the din of white noise.
You OKAY?
Stern direct
as if the last minutes did not transpire
under cloak of night
without symbolism or derision.
Each word the sickle he bares
slice sickness etched into heart
or spear chucked chipping off chinks
dark armor black scratched scraped
breaking through.
A waver a quiver in intonation
You sure you okay ?
Searching looking for the same
in the armor I wear.
This is the end.
The end of safety
the end of innocence.
Taut lips and face knowing
what he knows.
Knowing it has changed
Knowing I will be followed
forced to submit
to be shamed to be powerless
or face incarceration
slavery maiming death.

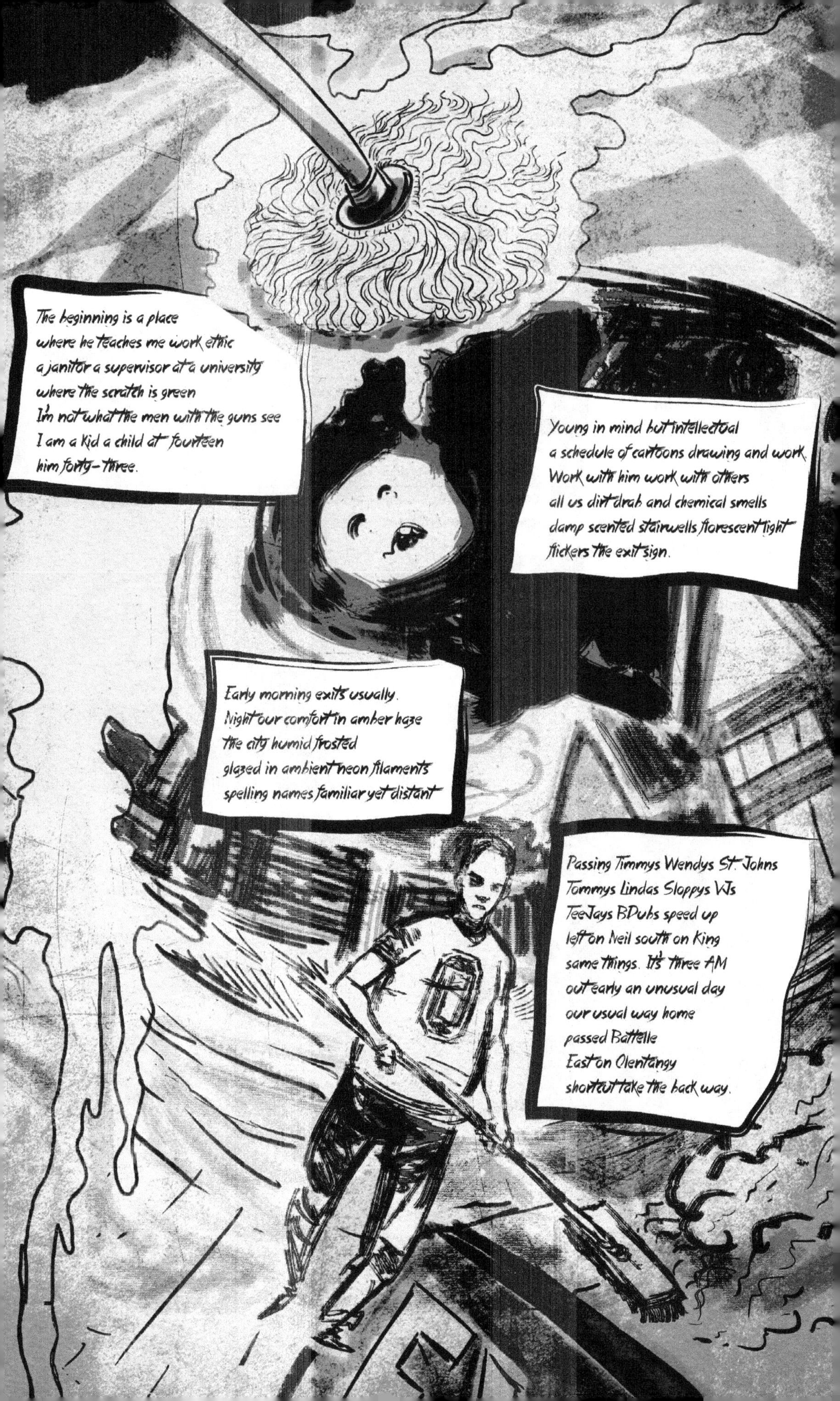
The beginning is a place
where he teaches me work ethic
a janitor a supervisor at a university
where the scratch is green
I'm not what the men with the guns see
I am a kid a child at fourteen
him forty-three.
Young in mind but intellectual
a schedule of cartoons drawing and work.
Work with him work with others
all us dirt drab and chemical smells
damp scented stairwells florescent light
flickers the exit sign.
Early morning exits usually.
Night our comfort in amber haze
the city humid frosted
glazed in ambient neon filaments
spelling names familiar yet distant
Passing Timmys Wendys St. Johns
Tommys Lindas Sloppys VJs
TeeJays BDubs speed up
left on Neil south on King
same things. It's three AM
out early an unusual day
our usual way home
passed Battelle
East on Olentangy
shortcut take the back way.

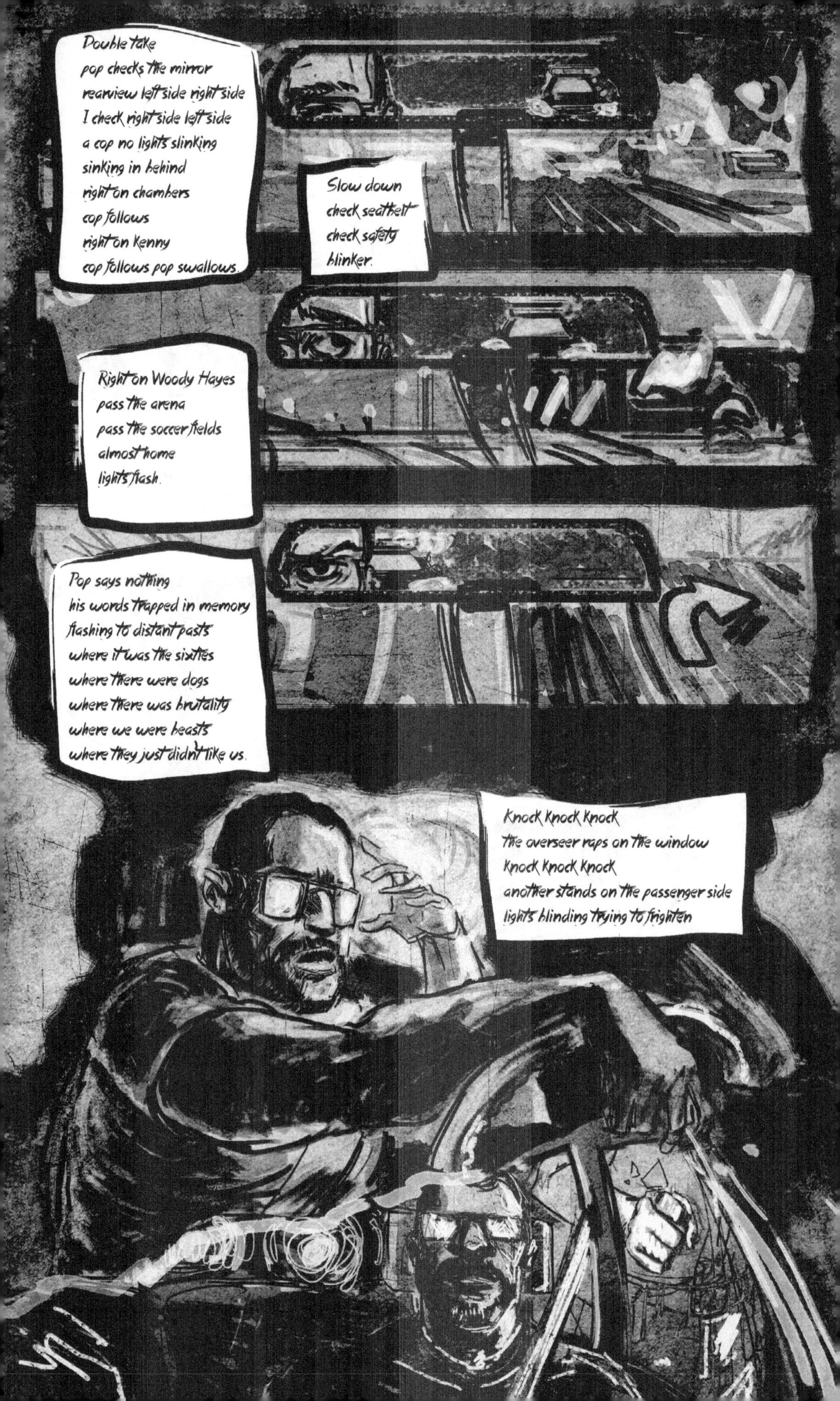
Double take
pop checks the mirror
rearview left side right side
I check right side left side
a cop no lights slinking
sinking in behind
right on chambers
cop follows
right on Kenny
cop follows pop swallows.
Slow down
check seatbelt
check safety
blinker.
Right on Woody Hayes
pass the arena
pass the soccer fields
almost home
lights flash.
Pop says nothing
his words trapped in memory
flashing to distant pasts
where it was the sixties
where there were dogs
where there was brutality
where we were beasts
where they just didn't like us.
Knock Knock Knock
The overseer raps on the window
Knock Knock Knock
another stands on the passenger side
lights blinding trying to frighten

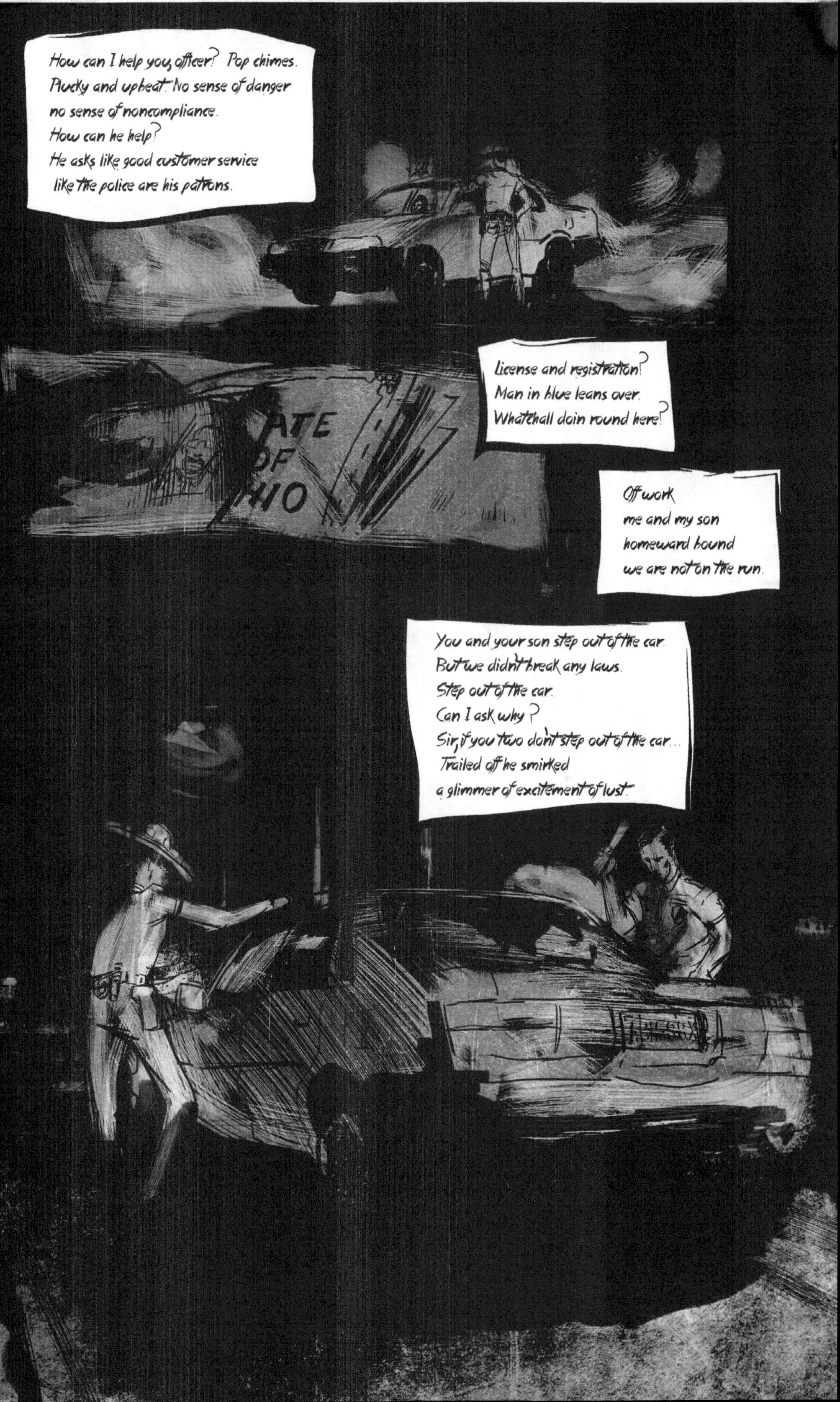
How can I help you, officer? Pop chimes.
Plucky and upbeat. No sense of danger
no sense of noncompliance.
How can he help?
He asks like good customer service
like the police are his patrons.
License and registration?
Man in blue leans over.
Whatchall doin round here?
Off work
me and my son
homeward bound
we are not on the run.
You and your son step out of the car.
But we didn't break any laws.
Step out of the car.
Can I ask why?
Sir, if you two don't step out of the car...
Trailed off he smirked
a glimmer of excitement of lust.

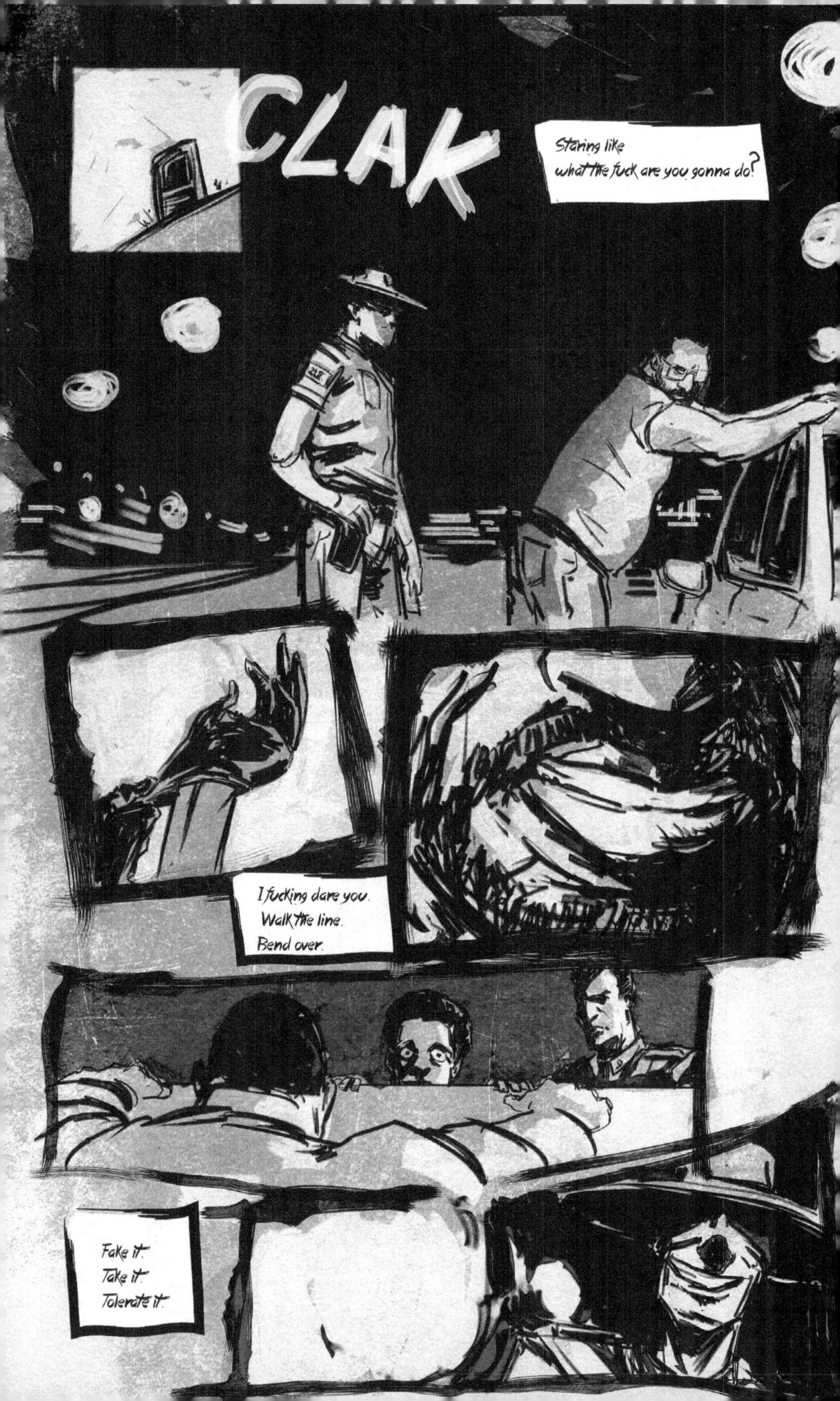
CLAK
Staring like
what the fuck are you gonna do?
I fucking dare you.
Walk the line.
Bend over.
Fake it.
Take it.
Tolerate it.

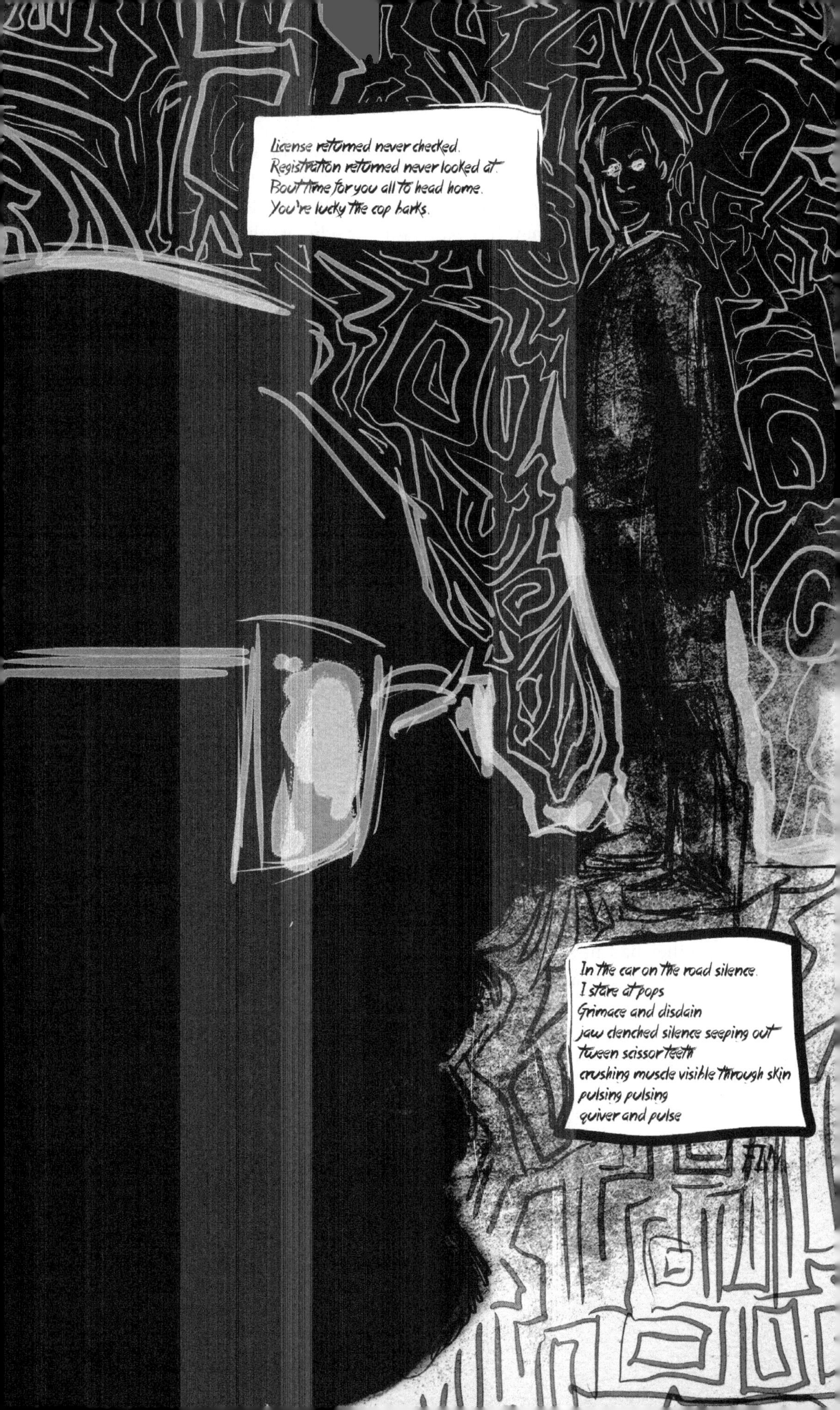
License returned never checked.
Registration returned never looked at.
Bout time for you all to head home.
You're lucky the cop barks.
In the car on the road silence.
I stare at pops
Grimace and disdain
jaw clenched silence seeping out
tween scissor teeth
crushing muscle visible through skin
pulsing pulsing
quiver and pulse
FIN

# INNOCENT BYSTANDERS

## BY JENNIFER MARIE BRISSETT

She'd taken the train all the way home from school, the second in her family to attend college (hopefully the first to finish.) The end of a phone call said not in words but in the shaky goodbye that she should skip her class that night and check on things. The family of three had little money. If it wasn't for her scholarship, college would be all but impossible. The few dollars they could spare went to their current problem.

A flush and moments later her mother emerged from the bathroom, slumbering down the hall, wiping her nose and sniffling.

"Help yourself to some dinner there," her mother said waving slightly in the direction of the kitchen.

Cooling on the stove lay a Dutch pot of stewed chicken. She could dish herself a plate of rice & peas, lay the warm meat on top and ladle on the salty sweet curried gravy. She didn't want to even though she was hungry. Instead, she followed her mother to the darkened living room and watched her ease into the chair in the corner. Heavy red curtains pulled closed over drawn down blinds entombed them, the air thick with the rich scent of the cooked meat. Time ticked in the glass encased clock, the polyester butterfly-tipped second hand circling.

The plastic covered couch squeaked and moaned as the daughter sat down, placing her backpack on the floor beside her. She held vigil with her mother with no words of advice or useful skills to offer. Only her presence. And even that seemed like a bit of a waste. Still, she had come.

"Dey beat 'im, yuh know," her mother said looking at her daughter, wiping her nose and sniffling loudly. "Dey tumped 'im in de face. Dey made 'im say he did what yuh and I know he could never do."

Her brother had never been in trouble before in his life. Sure, he could be a jerk sometimes, but the reported story sounded like no one she knew.

"Every time I think of 'im in prison—" her mother stood up and rushed to return to the bathroom.

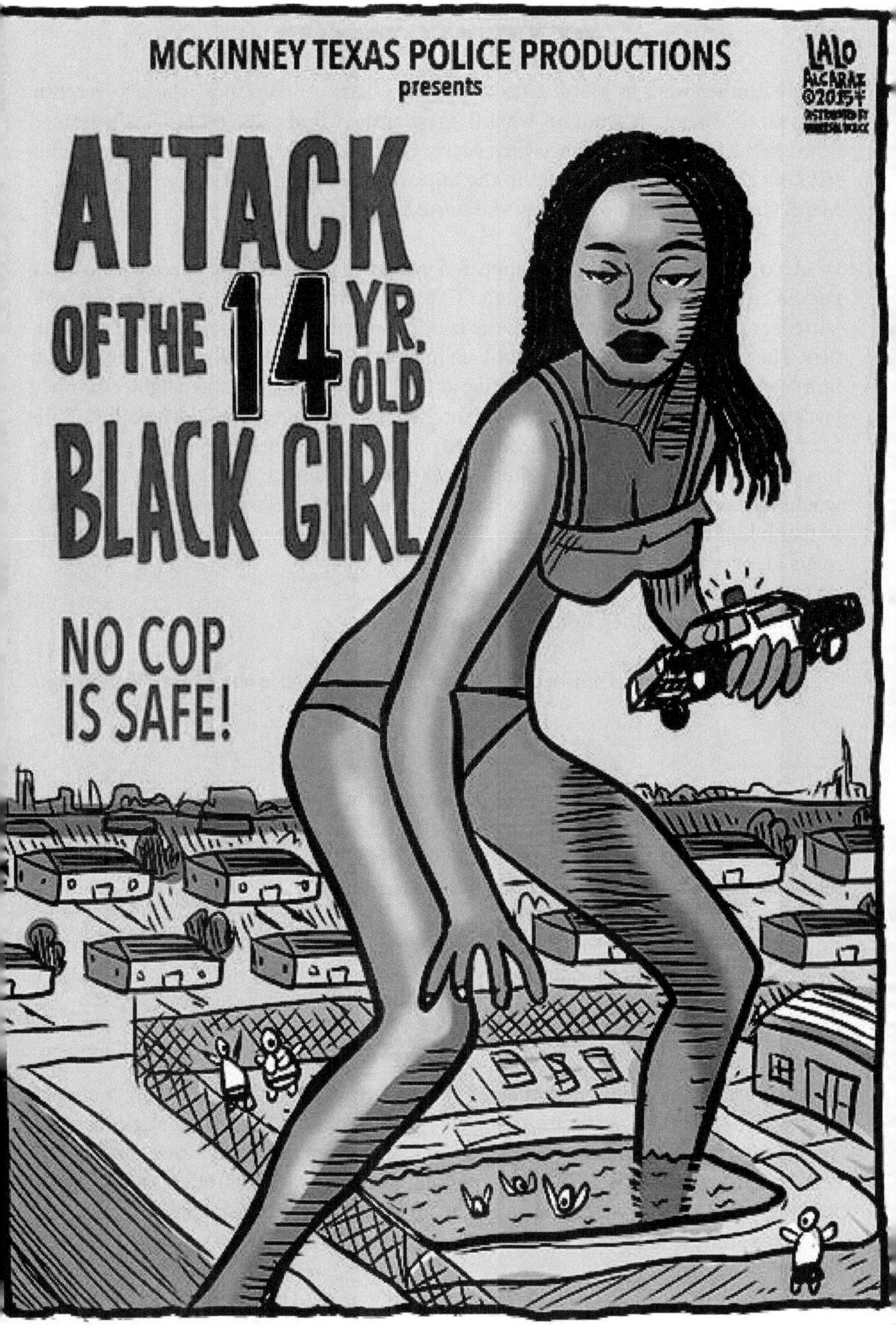
MCKINNEY TEXAS POLICE PRODUCTIONS
presents
ATTACK OF THE 14 YR. OLD BLACK GIRL
NO COP IS SAFE!
LALO ALCARAZ ©2015

# A SPIRIT IN NEW ORLEANS

## BY YTASHA L. WOMACK

My mother went to Mardi Gras a few years back. An educator who was recently "revitalized" (her code word for what the rest of the world calls "retired"), she headed down to the Crescent City to see what Mardi Gras was really about. At one point, while trekking along the lavish parades in the thick of the mugginess, a shopping bag full of Mardi Gras masks and boas in tow, she started hyperventilating.

A young man, late 20s or so appeared, took her hand, cleared space through the packed crowd, and snaked her through. "Get back, get back," he yelled. The sea of people parted, and he ushered her through the tangled weave of holiday regalia and drunkenness. The guy seemed familiar. He took on his role as protector easily. Something about him seemed like he could be her son. She got a glimpse of him. He was a lighter-skinned black man, toned, six feet or so, with tightly-curled hair, but she couldn't really see his face. Sweat was in her eyes and she focused on regaining her breath. She was grateful for this guy, whoever he was. The sweltering feeling of the familiar overcame her. If only he would turn around so she could see his face. He ushered her to a bench. She motioned to thank him but he vanished in the crowd. Then the reality of this mysterious young man's identity hit her like a ton of bricks.

"That was my brother, Ronnie," she recounts.

Ronald Williams was murdered in New Orleans by a police officer over 40 years ago.

§

Age three was a big year for me. I had a major birthday party in a record-breaking snowstorm. I watched Roots with my babysitter and discovered much of my family was kidnapped off the shores of Africa. I also discovered that I had an uncle I'd never met who was shot in the back by a plainclothes police officer in a New Orleans steakhouse.

Family lore revealed that whenever one of the men in the family had a mischievous twinkle in their eye and Cheshire cat smirk, it was my Uncle Ronnie they were invoking.

My family talked about him all the time.

With kid eyes, I envisioned him as being still very much alive but acting more like a fairy and resembling a 50s era civil rights worker of sorts with black slacks, a white button-up shirt, black skinny tie, and big wings. My mom and aunts swore that his eyes resembled Prince, who was the closest they could get to explain the effervescent sparkle in Uncle Ronnie's eye. When Prince would come on TV, everyone stopped and watched to catch a glimpse of their beloved relative.

Growing up, I would look at his pictures and wonder. He had the same smirk from childhood to adulthood, and his charisma poured out the photos like a fountain of spells. I never met him, and yet he, through my families' stories and tales, felt present. His photos emanated a liveliness that was ever-now. My little sister, Rahni, was named after him, and his name in one form or another resounded throughout the memories of my life. As a kid, I would piece together these tales to get a fuller picture of his life.

My mom recounted stories of him teasing her as a kid. He teased most of his siblings, it seemed. Even his high school friends talked about his relentless teasing. On the other hand, Uncle Ronnie was also extremely protective of his family and loved ones and thus the rescue mission from the other side when my mom was in need.

He had a stack of love poems he'd written that was in our attic. My cousin Jimmy says that Uncle Ronnie, at one point, owned a baby monkey. One day, the monkey escaped, and my cousin Jimmy and Uncle Ronnie were running up an alley on the Southside of Chicago trying to catch it before anyone noticed. He was a high school wrestling champion. In high school, he was the first black full scholarship winner at the grocery story he worked for. He got a kick out of challenging his brothers physically and with biting words. He was quite the savoir faire character, too. He asserted that he was the best dancer in the family, the most attractive, the most athletic…yes, as the middle boy, he was a bragging king. Ladies loved him.

There's even a larger than life story of him as a kid climbing into a lion's den at Lincoln Park Zoo. The staff had to rescue him.

So what happened?

The story goes something like this. Uncle Ronnie had recently moved from Chicago to New Orleans. The year was 1973, and he was looking for a fresh start. Nearly seven years prior, while a senior at a midwestern college, he was in a car crash. He was the only survivor who still had use of his legs. The passengers in the colliding car were young and white. One died. The judge couldn't determine who was at fault. The town, according to one relative, "wanted his head." Although he received two years probation, largely for his clean record and being from a "good Negro family" with a "father who worked at the post office" (the judge's words, not mine), the survivors' family chose to file a civil suit against him. He lost and was ordered to pay $1 million. He countered by filing for bankruptcy and never returned to that town again.

He didn't finish school, either. "He dropped out of society," his younger brother, Clarke, recalled. Any dime he made for the next seven years would have to go to the family in the crash. In defiance, he opted not to work. "He wasn't antisocial. He just wasn't striving for that piece of the pie anymore."

At some point, Ronnie decided that he wanted to work and live off the land. He adopted more of a hippie take on life (hence, the monkey). He loved children, often playing the painted clown at birthday parties. He took up playing his dad's guitar. This search for more in life took him to New Orleans.

A few months after his move, Uncle Ronnie was eating at a steak house chain on his lunch break. He had recently landed a city job with the motor vehicle inspections department, his first job in years. He'd been working out a lot and was more muscle-toned than usual. Two white plain-clothes cops were dining in the steakhouse and started to harass him. The conflict was totally unprovoked, but it seemed to be something about Ronnie's sheer confidence that irked the officers. New Orleans was still desegregating and these "we-have-overcome" stances were not welcome.

"I don't feel like getting shot today," Ronnie quipped to the officers. Those were his last words.

When he got up to leave the restaurant, the officer grabbed him by the shoulder. My uncle shrugged it off. The officer shot him in the back.

The officers asked all the black patrons in the restaurant to leave. They concocted a story with the white patrons, asserting that my uncle attacked the officer. This story went into the police report.

The officer (like most officers who murder unarmed men) claimed my uncle had a gun. It was a stamp puncher from his new job. He also wore a holster, much like the bus drivers of old to carry the puncher. It was the gig uniform.

The story made the news. A civil rights group investigated. Someone (the officers, perhaps) tried to smear my uncle's character, but the news clippings from his scholarship winnings countered their narrative.

Some of the black patrons said they were willing to testify, but my grandmother opted to drop the case. She was from Mississippi. She knew these stories all too well. Her own father was a land-owning farmer when the white citizens in his town set him up and accused him of stealing cattle. He killed himself, preferring to die of his own hand than have his family watch him be destroyed.

It was best to move on, she said.

So no charges were filed, no trial took place.

It's this forward motion that many families with unresolved deaths at the hand of police officers who are never charged are forced to do—they "keep it moving." They move on for peace, they move on for inner solace, they move on because, short of setting the world ablaze with their seething anger, moving on seems to be the only "acceptable" thing to do.

Moving on ensures that in a system where justice hangs in the balance that your rage won't become vengeance and that vengeance won't get everyone killed. It ensures that you can look at your child in the morning and still expect the best for them without fearing every second of the day that a flippant cop will be threatened by their manhood. Moving on, in its many facets, asserts that justice is divine, that matters will be handled. If you keep walking in faith all will be fine.

A few short weeks after my uncle's murder, his brother Clark recounts hearing his son laughing in the middle of the night. He walked in and saw the toddler having a grand ole time. He asked his son what was he doing, and the child remarked that he was playing with his Uncle Ronnie. The incident happened again and again. My uncle even swears he once felt his brother in the basement with him and finally had to ask Uncle Ronnie, who apparently was hovering in the supernatural, to leave.

"You have to move on," he said.

I'd heard this story many times, too. I wondered where my Uncle Ronnie went? Did he stay earthbound? Did he go back to New Orleans? Did he go to a dimension where he didn't have to deal with the three-dimensional?

One day, I asked my Uncle Clarke why he wanted his brother to move on.

 "He was scaring people," my uncle said. "He didn't need to hang around the living anymore. He needed to go to wherever you go to next."

"I discovered that the people who pass away literally just go to another plane," one of my cousins once recalled. "But they appear to know everything we're doing and they're around."

A decade after my uncle's murder, my mother took an astrology class. She had just had her third child, the one named after her brother, and she wanted to try something different.

One day the astrology teacher instructed the students to write the name of a person on a sheet of paper. The teacher claimed that she could read the energy of the name and would share the person's history. My mom wrote "Ronald Williams."

The teacher read the name, put the sheet down, and said she'd return to it at the end of class. She went around the room, reading all the other names for each student and finally returned to my mother.

"This person isn't alive," the woman said.

"No he isn't," my mom affirmed.

"This person had a violent death," she said.

The woman went on to recount the story of his death. My Uncle Ronnie and the officers clashed. These men who'd never met before had so much opposing energy when they connected, something explosive was destined to happen.

But the killer, according to the psychic, was never the same. Shortly after the murder, he lost all that he had. He descended quickly. He lived a tough life and lived out his days in a mental institution.

This is the only information anyone had received about the fate of the officer. My mom called up everyone in the family and shared the story. No one denied its plausibility. No one double checked to see if it were true. This astrologer's insight was enough. The revelation swept a sense of peace over everyone.

Justice, it seemed was imminent.

I don't know what family moments your family likes to pass on, but this is a treasured one from mine.

When I think about the astrologer's revelation and Uncle Ronnie's occasional spottings, I think back to those countless photos and the Cheshire cat grin, that ebullient glow of his eyes and wonder. I think about his legendary knack for teasing, and I wonder. I think of the undercover officer and his tragic end, and I wonder. I think about my cousin remarking that people who pass on are always around. Let's just say I wonder and end it at that.

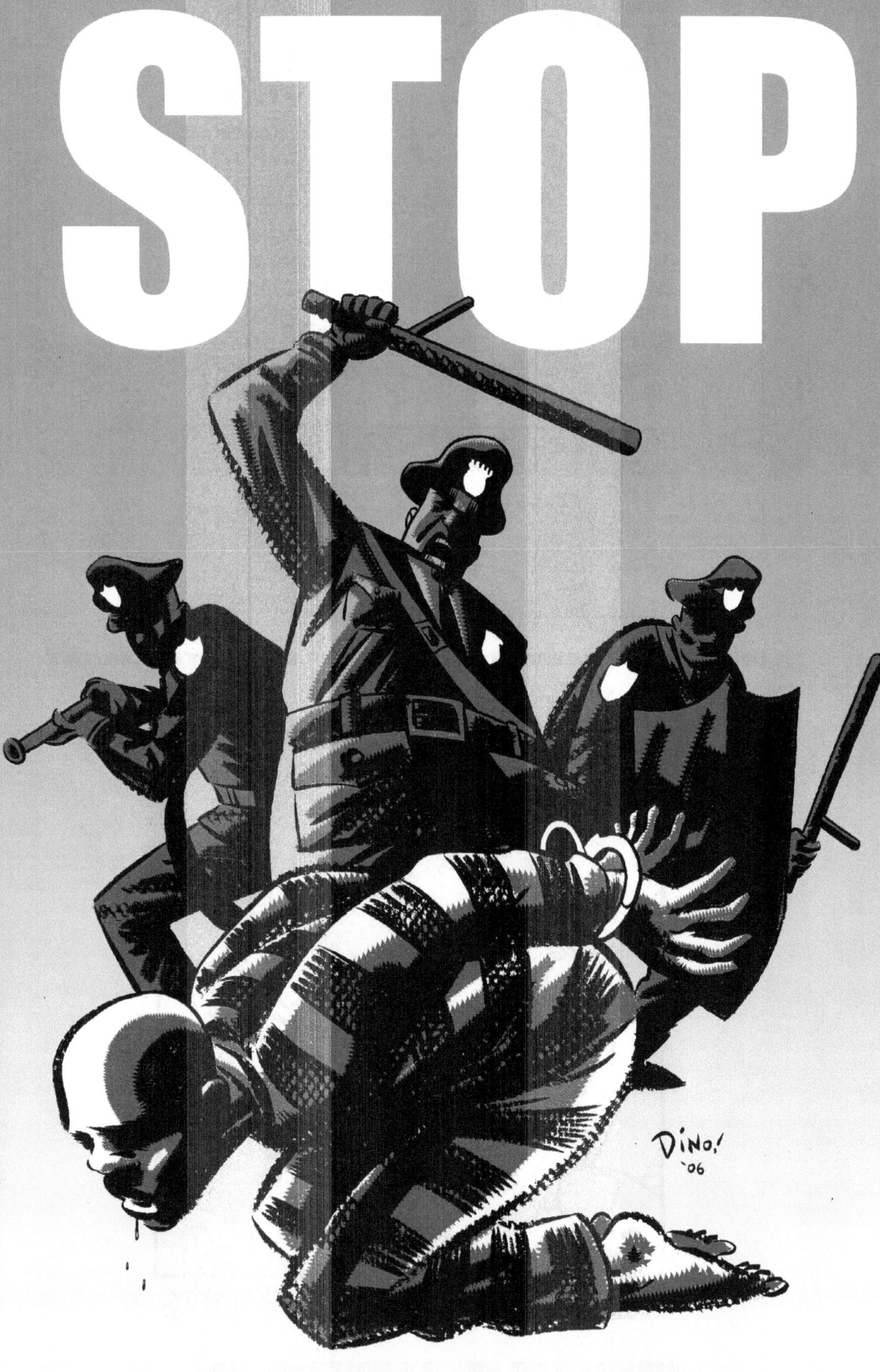
STOP
DINO!
'06

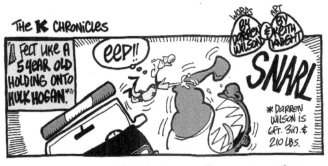

The K Chronicles
Words by Darren Wilson
Art by Keith Knight
"I felt like a 5 year old holding onto Hulk Hogan."*
eep!!
SNARL
*Darren Wilson is 6ft. 3in. & 210 lbs.
"When he stopped, he turned, looked at me.. made like a grunting noise..
..and had the most intense, aggressive face... it looks like a demon."
SCHNORT..
..GRUNT
"It looked like he was almost bulking up to run through the shots."
"The reason I have a clean conscience is because I know I did my job right."
©2014
keef@kchronicles.com
www.patreon.com/keefknight

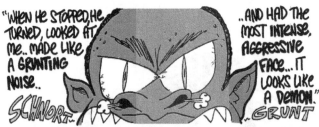

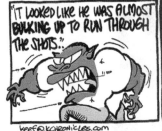

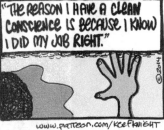

WORDS BY DARREN WILSON, ART BY KEITH KNIGHT

(th)ink
By Keith Knight
©K.Knight
What do you see in this picture?
Sons, brothers, fathers, human bei
Target practice
POLICE OFFICER APPLICATION: QUESTION #6

WORDS AND ART BY KEITH KNIGHT

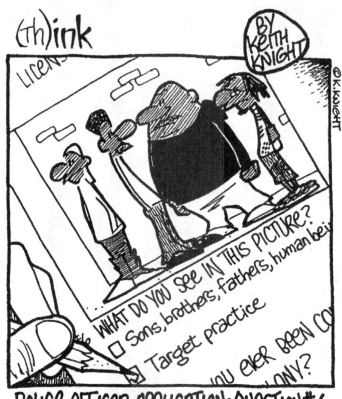

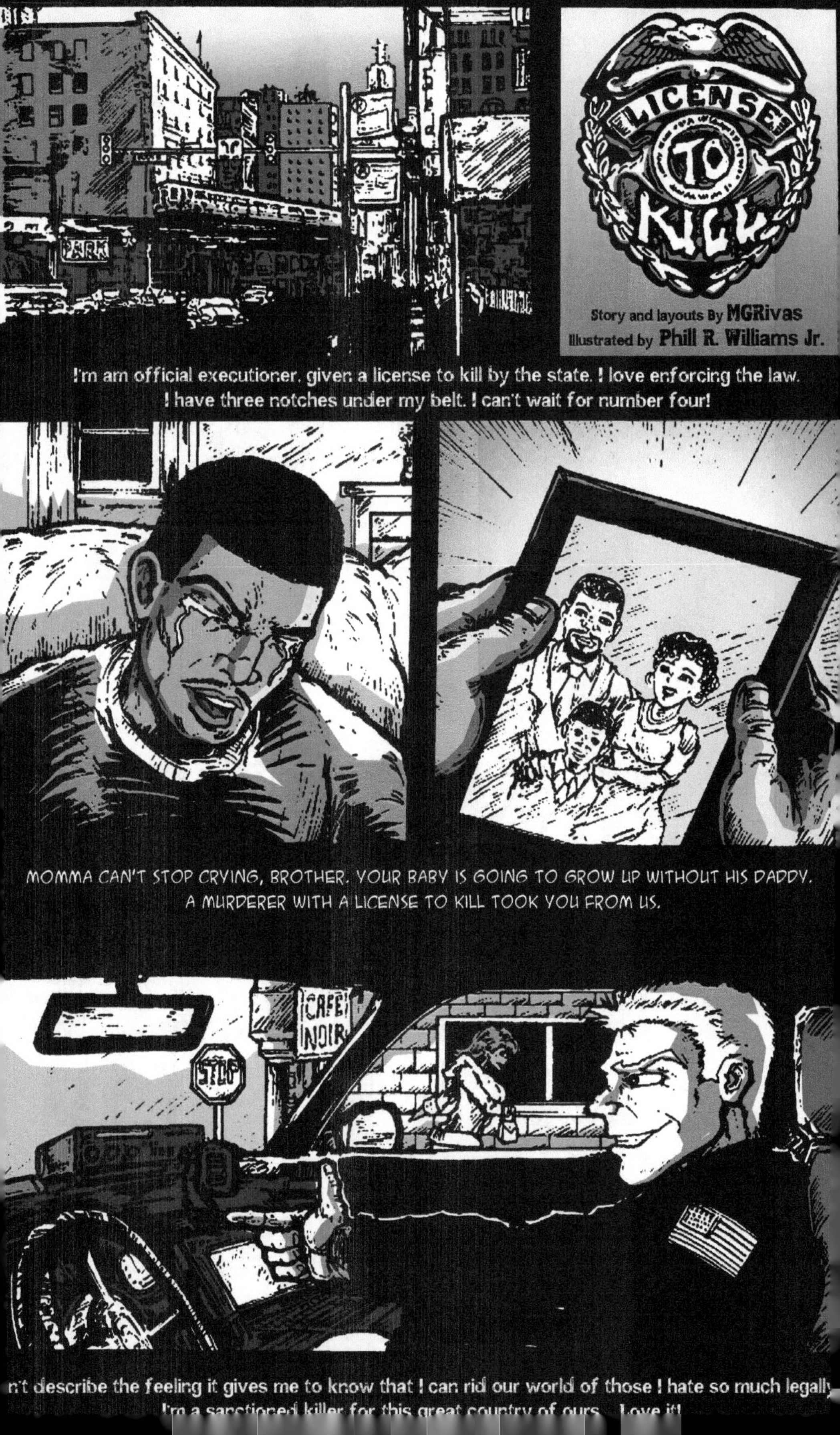
LICENSE TO KILL
Story and layouts By MGRivas
Illustrated by Phill R. Williams Jr.
PARK
I'm am official executioner, given a license to kill by the state. I love enforcing the law.
I have three notches under my belt. I can't wait for number four!
MOMMA CAN'T STOP CRYING, BROTHER. YOUR BABY IS GOING TO GROW UP WITHOUT HIS DADDY.
A MURDERER WITH A LICENSE TO KILL TOOK YOU FROM US.
CAFE NOIR
STOP
n't describe the feeling it gives me to know that I can rid our world of those I hate so much legally
I'm a sanctioned killer for this great country of ours... Love it!

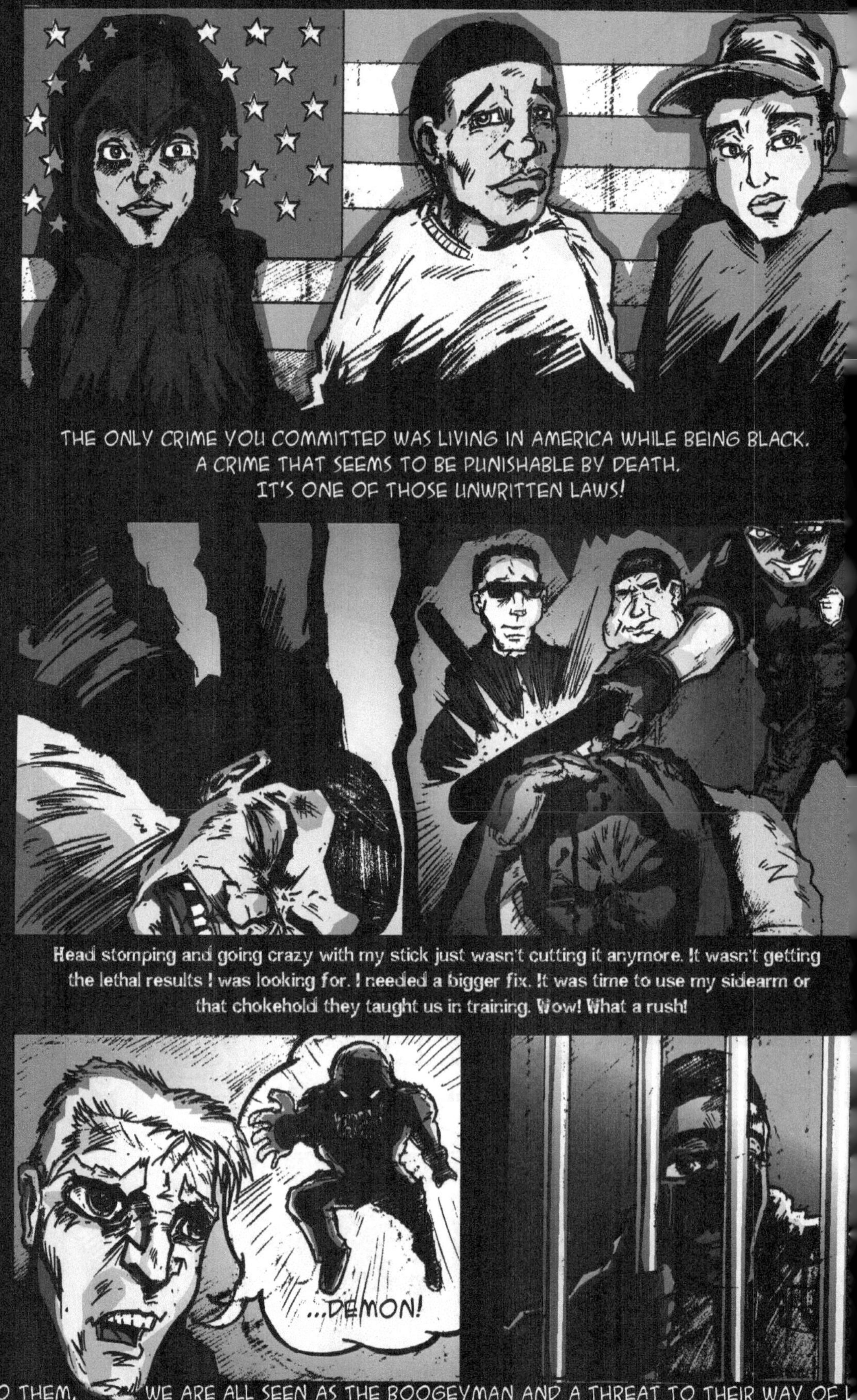

THE ONLY CRIME YOU COMMITTED WAS LIVING IN AMERICA WHILE BEING BLACK.
A CRIME THAT SEEMS TO BE PUNISHABLE BY DEATH.
IT'S ONE OF THOSE UNWRITTEN LAWS!
Head stomping and going crazy with my stick just wasn't cutting it anymore. It wasn't getting the lethal results I was looking for. I needed a bigger fix. It was time to use my sidearm or that chokehold they taught us in training. Wow! What a rush!
...DEMON!
TO THEM, [redacted] WE ARE ALL SEEN AS THE BOOGEYMAN AND A THREAT TO THEIR WAY OF L
FUNNY! IF THERE'S EVER BEEN A THREAT TO ANY PEOPLE'S WAY OF LIFE,
IT'S COME FROM THEM."

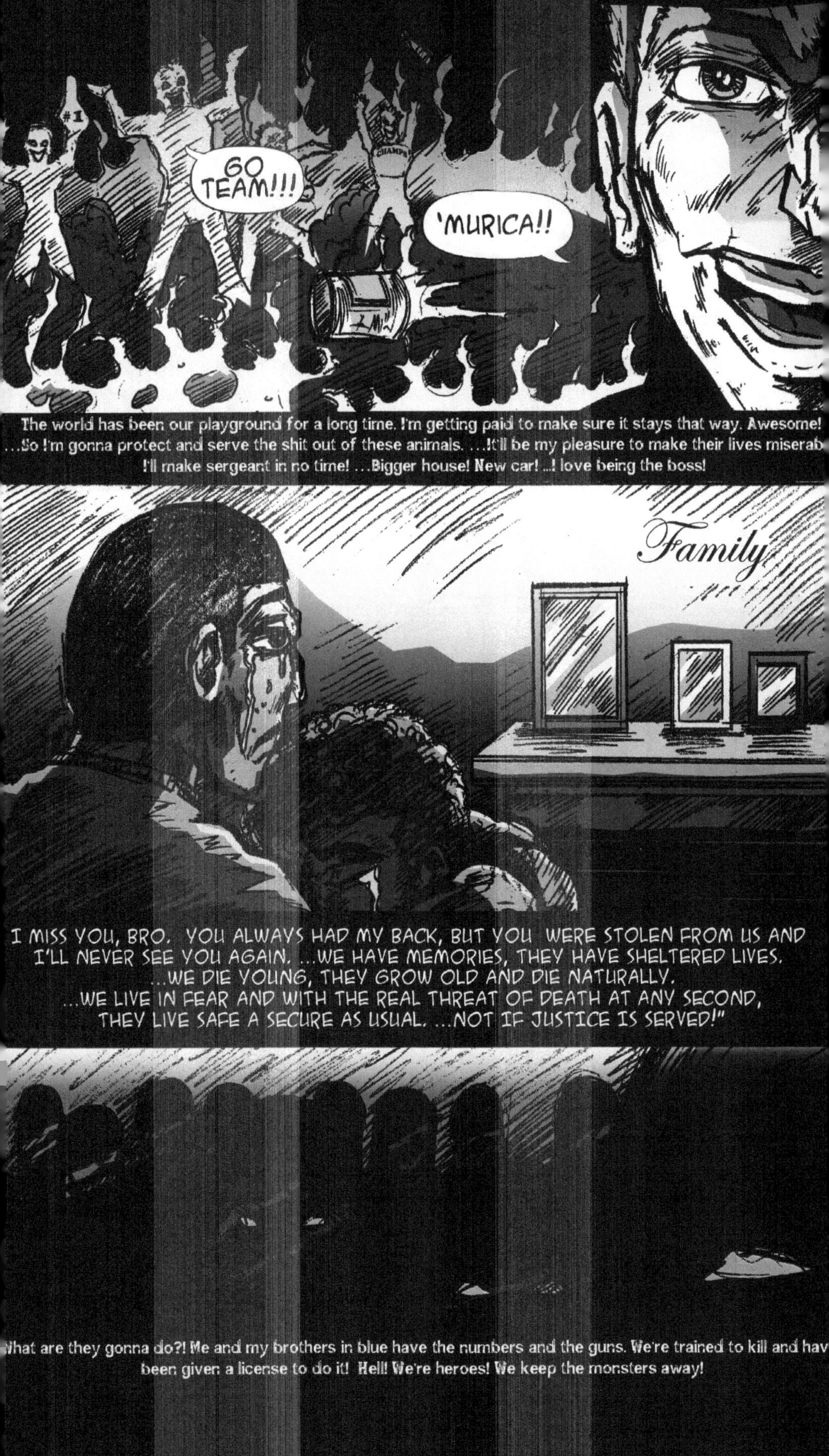
GO TEAM!!!
'MURICA!!
The world has been our playground for a long time. I'm getting paid to make sure it stays that way. Awesome!
...So I'm gonna protect and serve the shit out of these animals. ...It'll be my pleasure to make their lives miserab
I'll make sergeant in no time! ...Bigger house! New car! ...I love being the boss!
Family
I MISS YOU, BRO. YOU ALWAYS HAD MY BACK, BUT YOU WERE STOLEN FROM US AND
I'LL NEVER SEE YOU AGAIN. ...WE HAVE MEMORIES, THEY HAVE SHELTERED LIVES.
...WE DIE YOUNG, THEY GROW OLD AND DIE NATURALLY.
...WE LIVE IN FEAR AND WITH THE REAL THREAT OF DEATH AT ANY SECOND,
THEY LIVE SAFE A SECURE AS USUAL. ...NOT IF JUSTICE IS SERVED!"
hat are they gonna do?! Me and my brothers in blue have the numbers and the guns. We're trained to kill and hav
been given a license to do it! Hell! We're heroes! We keep the monsters away!

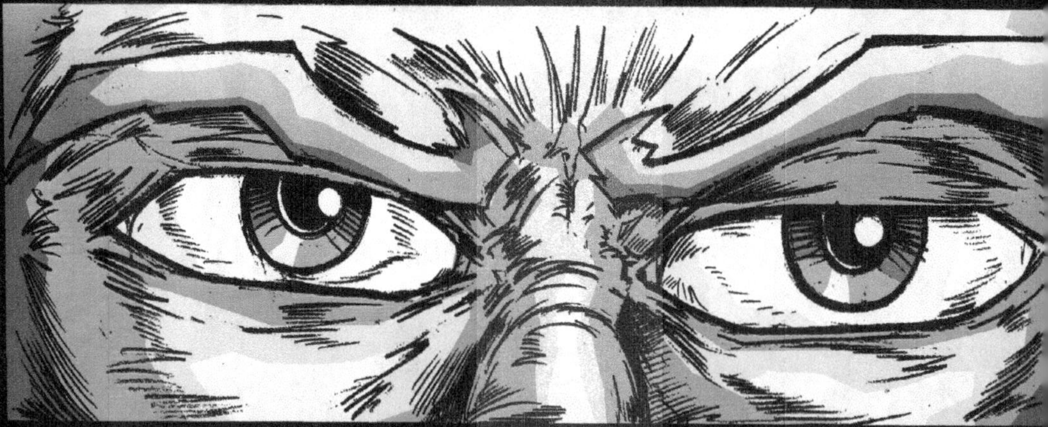

Granddad and his granddad would be proud. I'm carrying on a legacy and doing my duty t
keep the Commies. Liberals and savages from taking what's ours. The license is just a perk. .
I'm gettin' all choked up…. God bless America. Dammit! We own the world and
I get to take out the ones who say we don't!

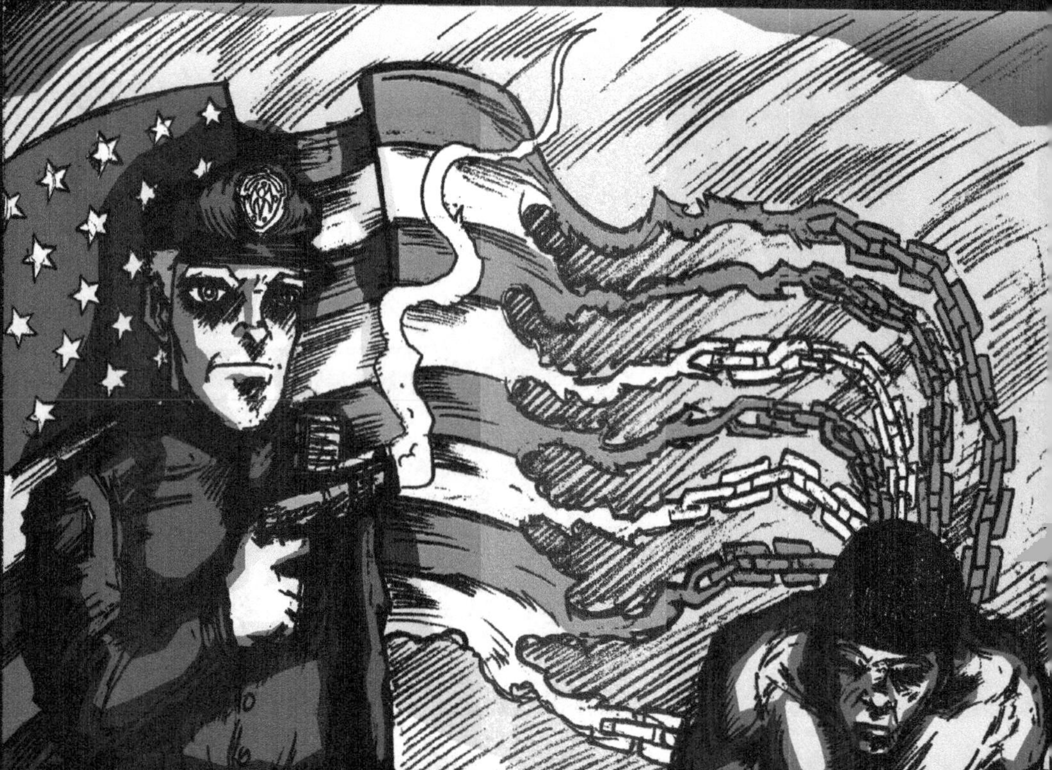

I HEAR PEOPLE SAY WE NEED TO CHANGE THE SYSTEM FROM THE INSIDE
IT'S TOO LATE FOR THAT! ...THEY CAN ASK YOU, BROTHER, IF YOU HAD
TIME TO ASK THE SYSTEM TO CHANGE OUT OF THE KINDNESS OF ITS HEAR
...ASK ERIC GARNER IF HE HAD TIME TO WAIT FOR LAWS TO BE PASSED T
MAKE THE MURDERERS MORE SENSITIVE! ... ASK MIKE BROWN IF HE CAN
GO BACK AND ASK FOR THEM TO BE LESS RACIST. IN THE NEXT FEW
MINUTES, MORE THAN LIKELY, WE'LL SEE ANOTHER BLACK OR BROWN MAN
KILLED BY THE ONES WHO ARE DOING WHAT THEY WERE CREATED TO DO

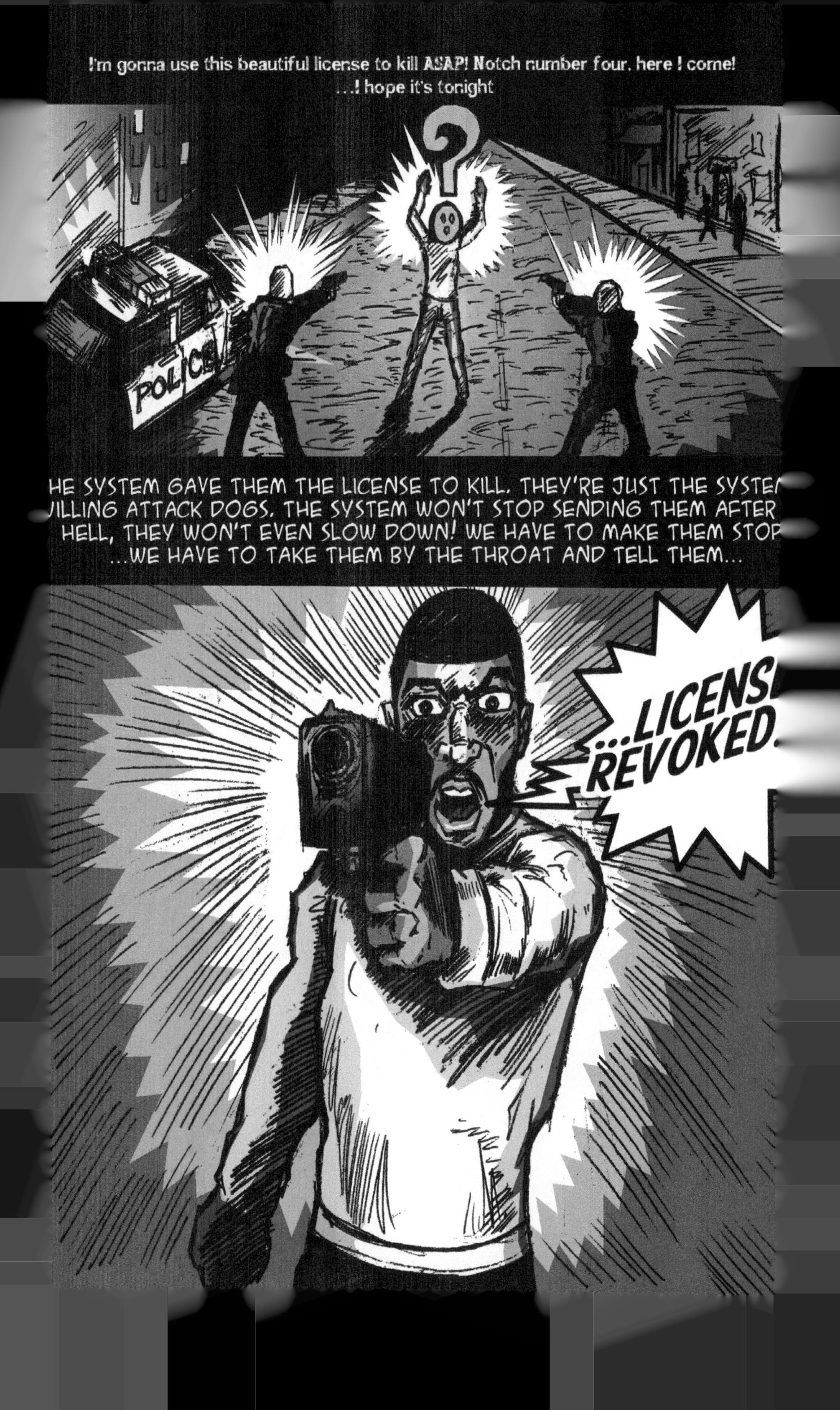

I'm gonna use this beautiful license to kill ASAP! Notch number four, here I come!
...I hope it's tonight
HE SYSTEM GAVE THEM THE LICENSE TO KILL. THEY'RE JUST THE SYSTE
ILLING ATTACK DOGS. THE SYSTEM WON'T STOP SENDING THEM AFTER
HELL, THEY WON'T EVEN SLOW DOWN! WE HAVE TO MAKE THEM STOP
...WE HAVE TO TAKE THEM BY THE THROAT AND TELL THEM...
POLICE
...LICENS
REVOKED.

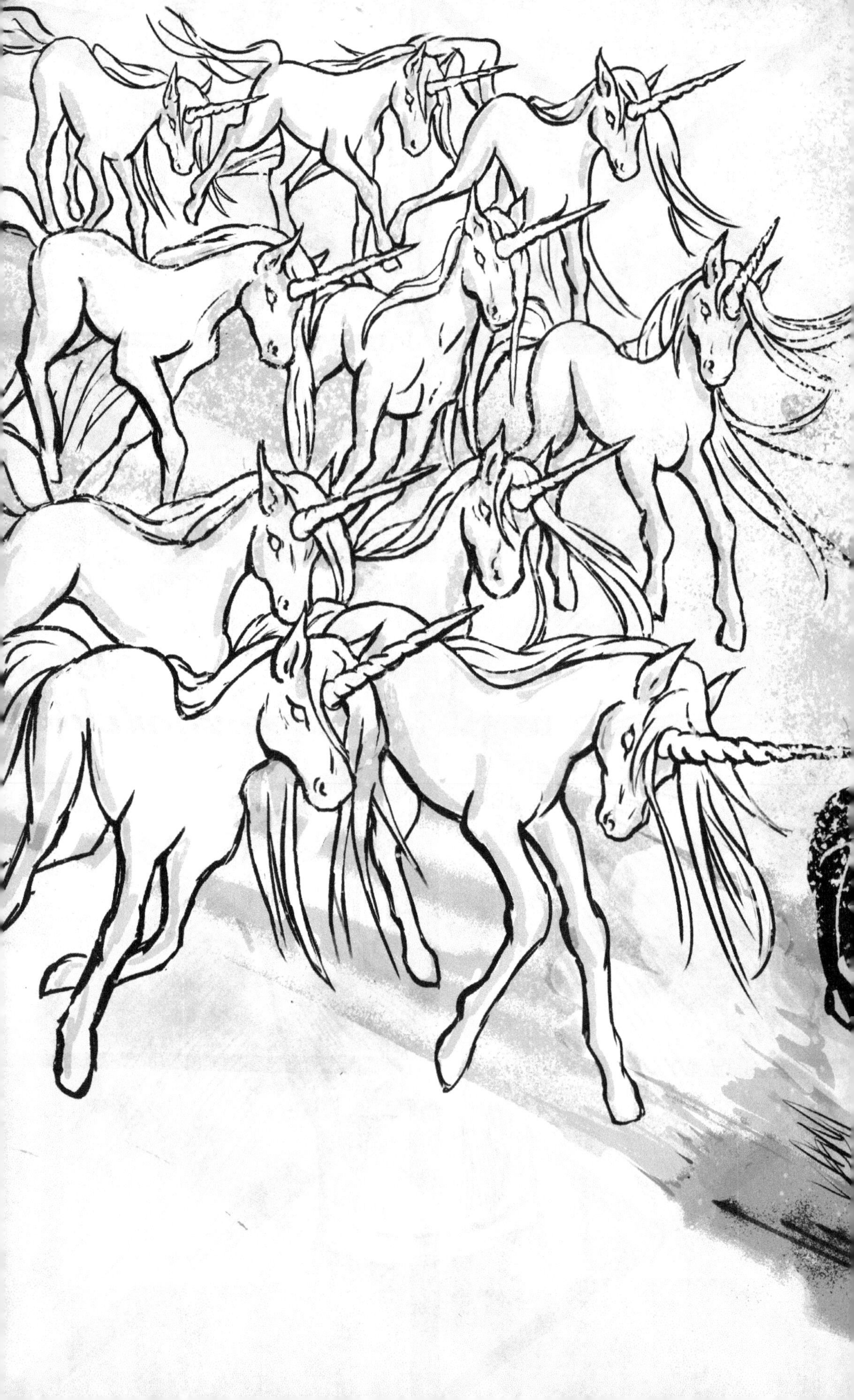

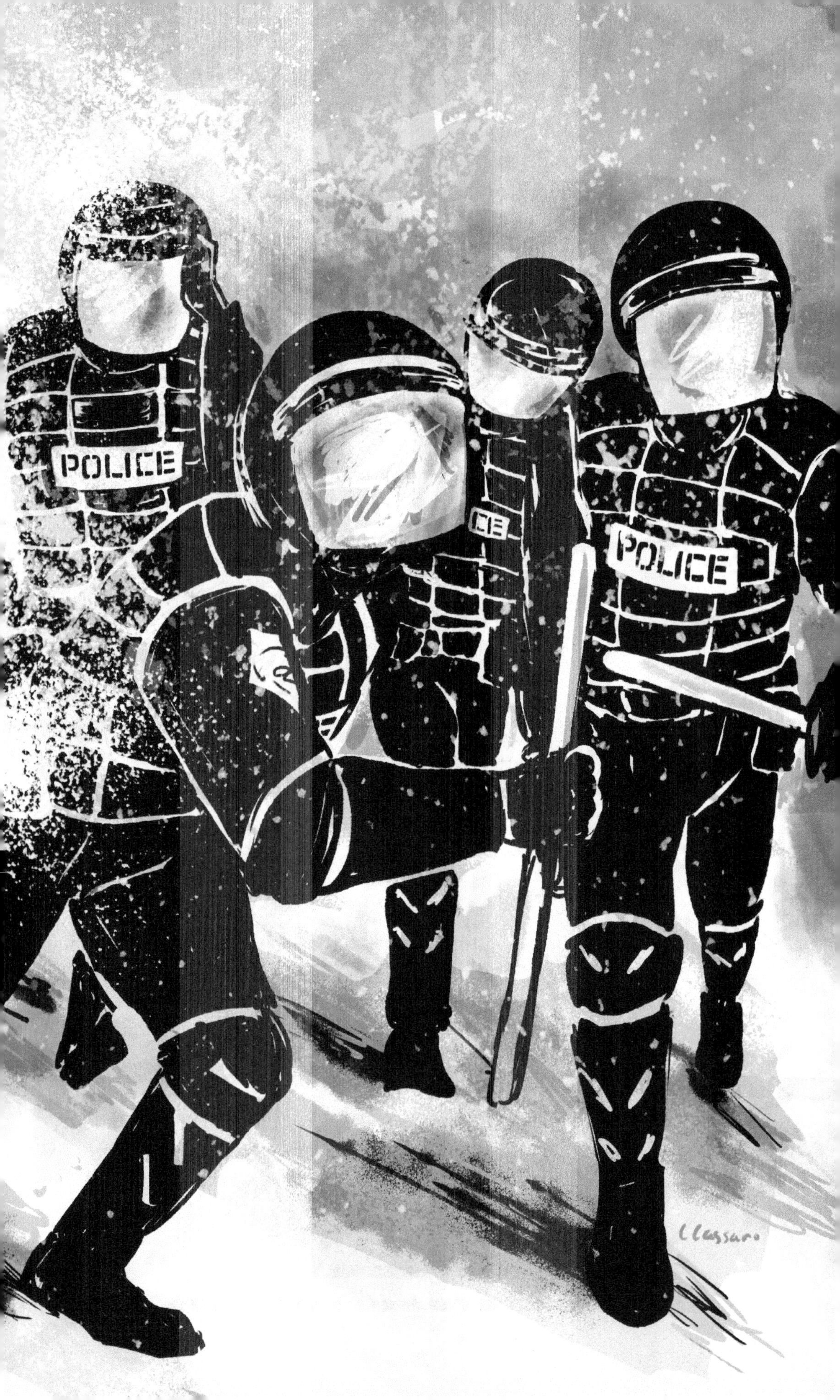
POLICE
POLICE

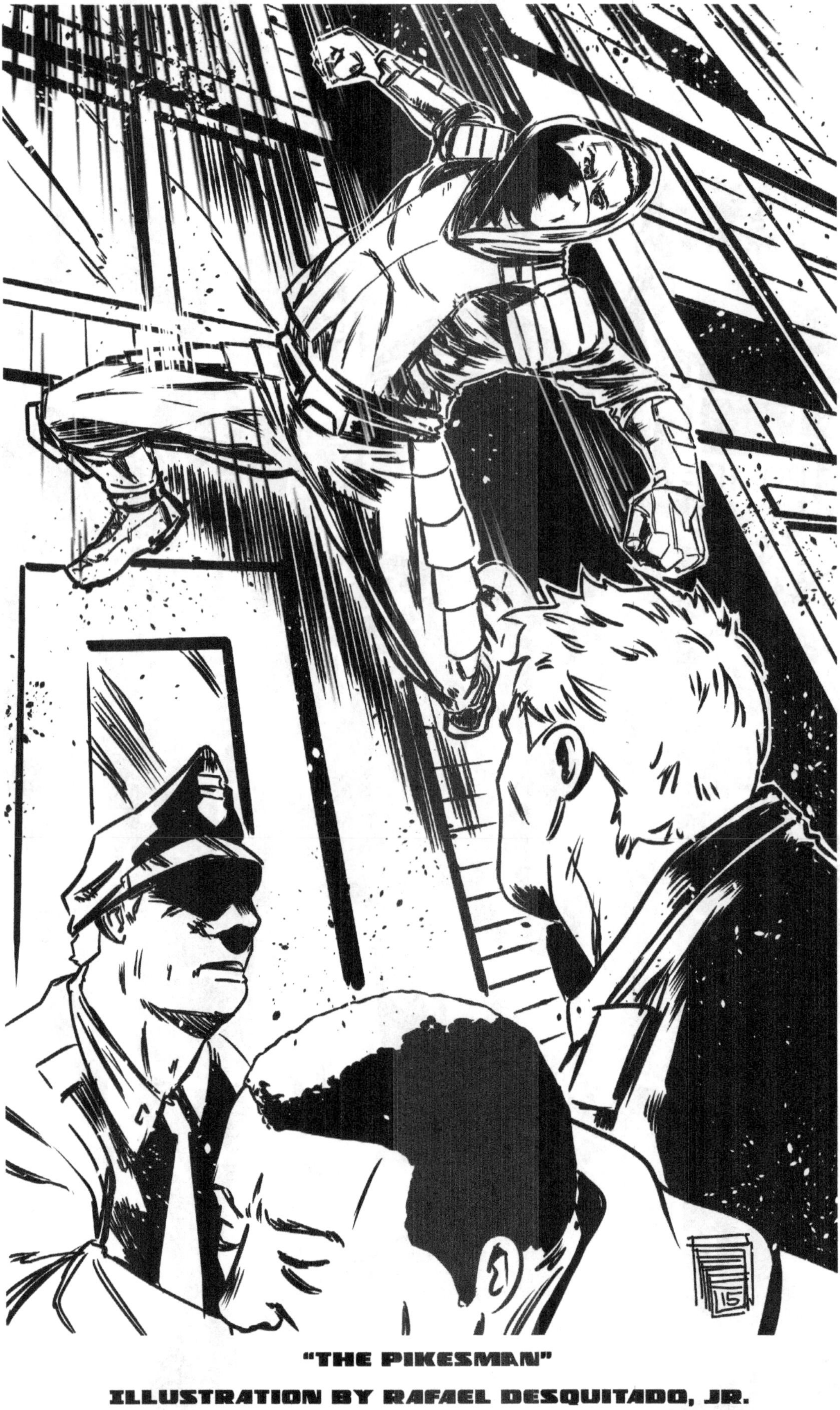

"THE PIKESMAN"

ILLUSTRATION BY RAFAEL DESQUITADO, JR.

# THE PIKESMAN'S PATROL

## BY GARY PHILLIPS

The Pikesman came to the roof's parapet and, looking down, saw the huddled figures in the passageway below. There was grunting and grappling; indirect lighting shimmering along the shafts of the alloy batons as the instruments struck their blows with brutish efficiency.

His flat, emotionless eyes in the dark cowling revealed nothing of the cold fire that burned within him. Unlimbering his high tensile strength line as he simultaneously leaped feet-first into the night air, he swooped down on the three beating the man on the ground. His suit's micro-processors were functioning correctly, so his shoulder wasn't pulled out of its socket.

Twenty feet from the earth he released his grip, and his momentum carried him into one of the figure looking up at the sound of his approach.

"The hell," he said, blasting at the intruder with his semi-auto sidearm.

The bullets bounced ineffectively off the Kevlar and carbon nanotube blend of the Pikesman's black-and-gray costume. His calculated descent drove his boot straight into the shooter's jaw. The man blacked out, his nose broken in two places. The vigilante turned his attention to the other two officers.

"You're interfering with a lawful arrest, asshole," growled one of the others. He swung his T-handled nightstick, clipping the masked avenger behind his calf.

He dropped to a knee, and the two had their guns out.

"We're gonna teach you a fatal lesson, Pike dick," the stockier one growled.

In a fraction of a second, before either he or his partner could squeeze their triggers, the Pikesman—trained in parsing time by the most beneficent one, Tal Ul-Rahn—set off one of his mini flash grenades. It was the size of a lipstick tube, but it delivered a deafening roar and disorienting burst of light.

The Pikesman had particular bafflers in his hood that allowed him to hear yet also canceled a large portion of the sound effects of his device. He'd shut his eyes too, so was not blinking furiously as the other two were as they stumbled about.

"You goddamn—" one of them began but didn't finish as a roundhouse kick caused him to sag. The Pikesman followed up with several blows to the man's head using the cop's baton.

The third uniform, eyes tearing, flailing about like a wind-up Frankenstein, got his arms around the dread knight.

"Now you're got," the officer enthused.

Rather than try a get him to loosen his grip, the Pikesman ran forward and, pivoting his body, drove the policeman into the wall of a building. The cop gasped but still held on. The street defender repeated the action and this time the cop's arms lost their tension. The Pikesman turned and, raining a series of hand-edged strikes at the man's upper shoulders and neck, keeled him over unconscious with a broken collar bone.

As this only took seconds, the cop who'd been struck with his own baton was coming out of his daze, reaching for his radio pinned to his upper chest.

"This is Adam A Nine Four, requesting back up at—" But he didn't finish as the Pikesman was on him and, using a choke hold on his carotid artery, put him out—but not dead. He walked over to the suspect they'd been working over. He wasn't more than twenty, the people's crusader estimated.

"I don't know how to thank you, man," the kid began.

"What they stop you for?"

"Expired tags."

"You got a cell phone?"

"Yeah."

The Pikesman handed him a business card. "Call this lawyer now. Tell him what happened and he'll handle the rest."

"I ain't got that kind of money."

One of the cops groaned from where he lay on the pavement. "Don't worry about that, the Pikesman said in his reassuring baritone. "It'll all be taken care of...it'll all be taken care of..."

...The doctor had said when they wheeled him into the ER. That was what, three years ago? Four years now? Whatever. The sun felt good on Johnny Beck's face. Able to use his index finger, the quadriplegic toggled his electric wheelchair a little closer to the window. The policemen's fusillade of bullets had penetrated his hoopty and his body. His spinal cord had been severed and part of his larynx destroyed. In court, he was a heartbreaking sight but his garbled testimony, lacking eyewitness corroboration, resulted in no criminal convictions.

Johnny watched the grade school kids walk home from school and a small smile animated his semi-paralyzed face. He began to compose another tale of the Pikesman in his head. A story in which he saves a school bus laden with happy children...

# BOYZ IN A HOOD

MAMA'S BOYZ BY JERRY CRAFT WWW.JERRYCRAFT.NET

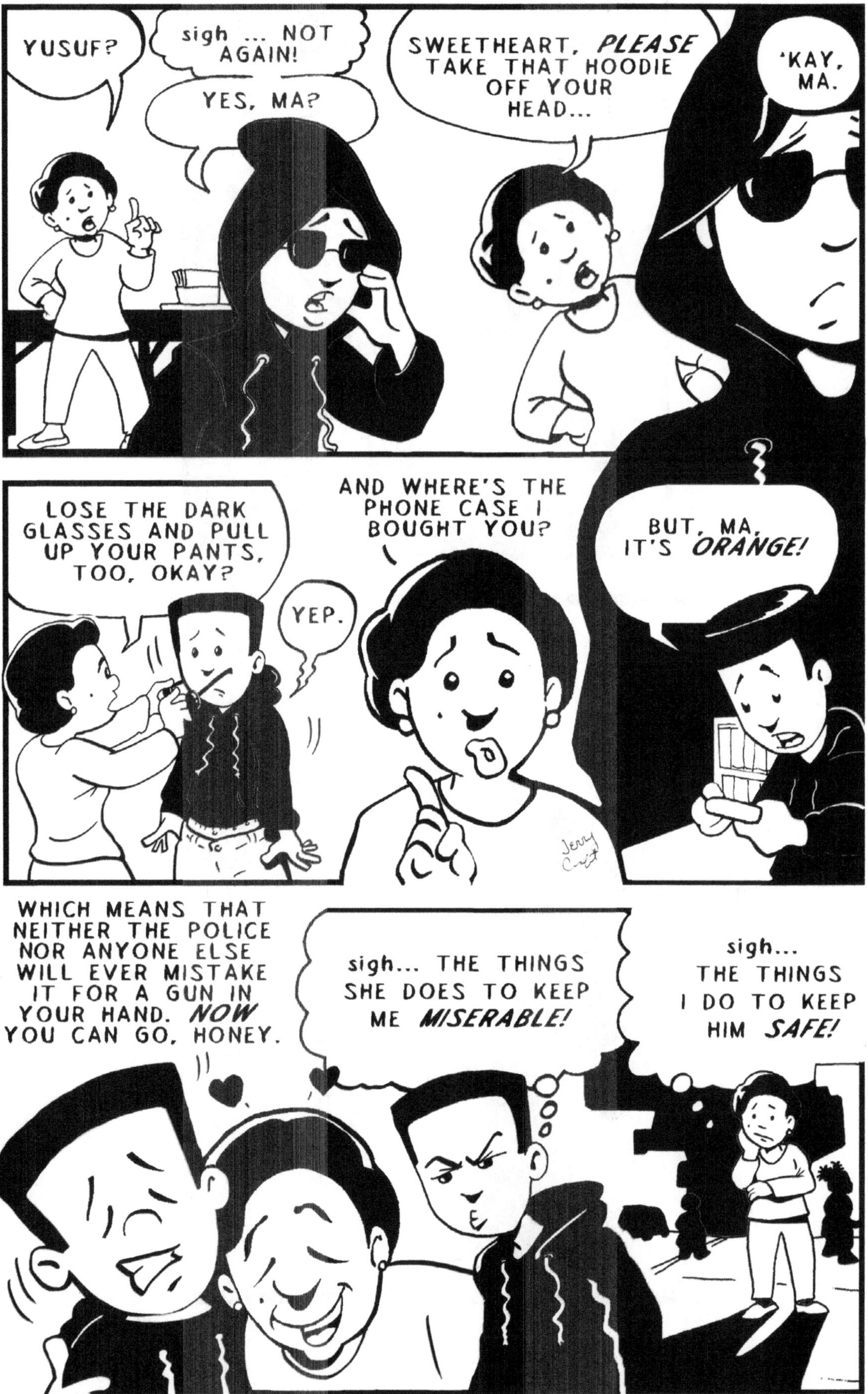
YUSUF?
sigh ... NOT AGAIN!
YES, MA?
SWEETHEART, *PLEASE* TAKE THAT HOODIE OFF YOUR HEAD...
'KAY, MA.
LOSE THE DARK GLASSES AND PULL UP YOUR PANTS, TOO, OKAY?
YEP.
AND WHERE'S THE PHONE CASE I BOUGHT YOU?
BUT, MA, IT'S *ORANGE!*
Jerry Craft
WHICH MEANS THAT NEITHER THE POLICE NOR ANYONE ELSE WILL EVER MISTAKE IT FOR A GUN IN YOUR HAND. *NOW* YOU CAN GO, HONEY.
sigh... THE THINGS SHE DOES TO KEEP ME *MISERABLE!*
sigh... THE THINGS I DO TO KEEP HIM *SAFE!*

SECRET ASIAN MAN by @TakToyoshima

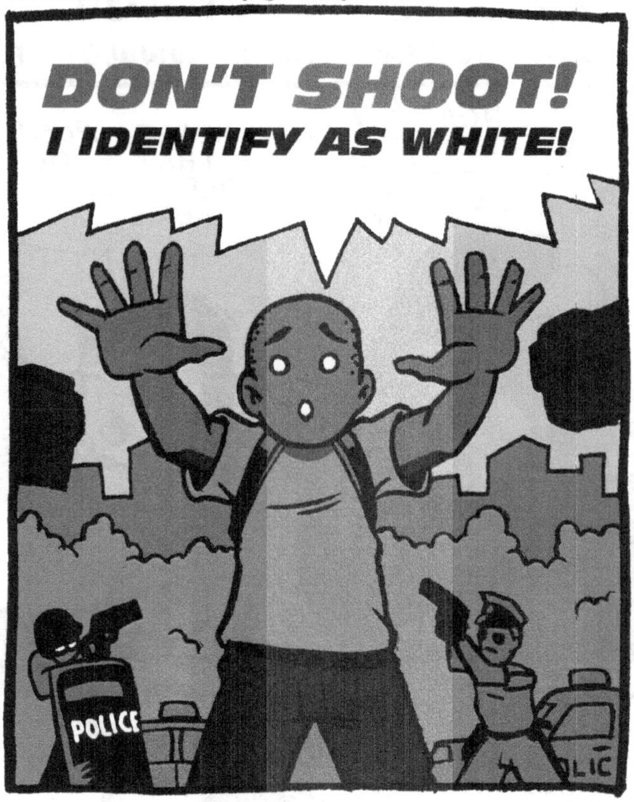

DON'T SHOOT!
I IDENTIFY AS WHITE!
POLICE
OLIC


WORDS AND ART BY TOK TOYOSHIMA

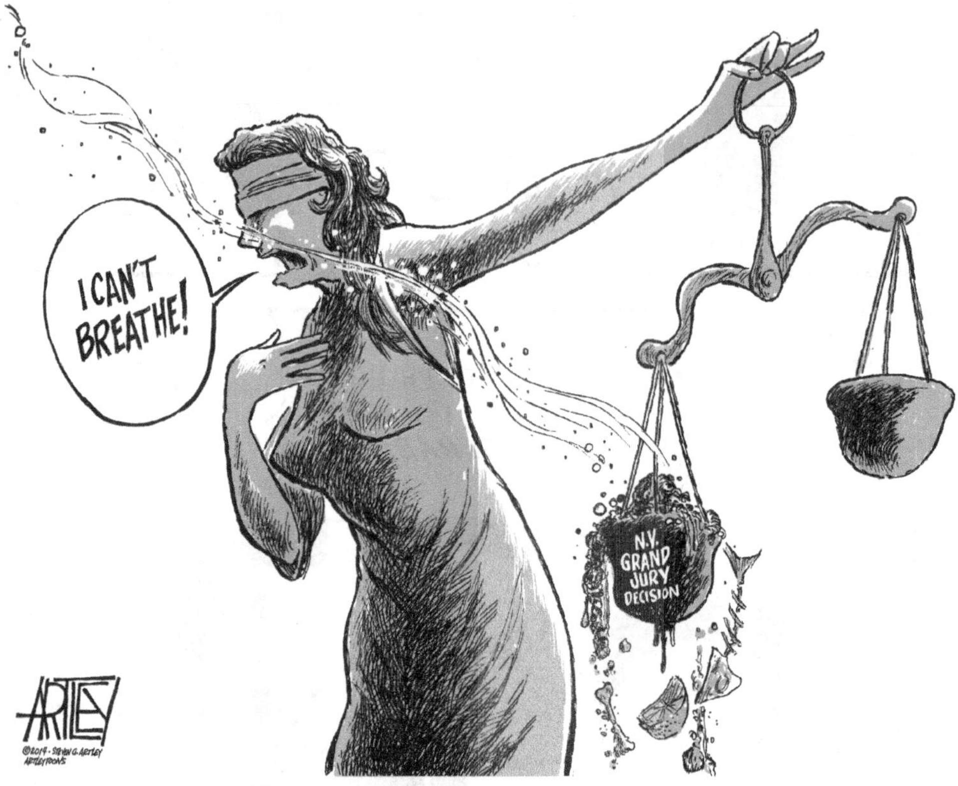

I CAN'T BREATHE!
N.Y. GRAND JURY DECISION
ARTLEY


WORDS AND ART BY STEVE ARTLEY

## UNLAWFUL

BY: BARBARA BRANDON-CROFT

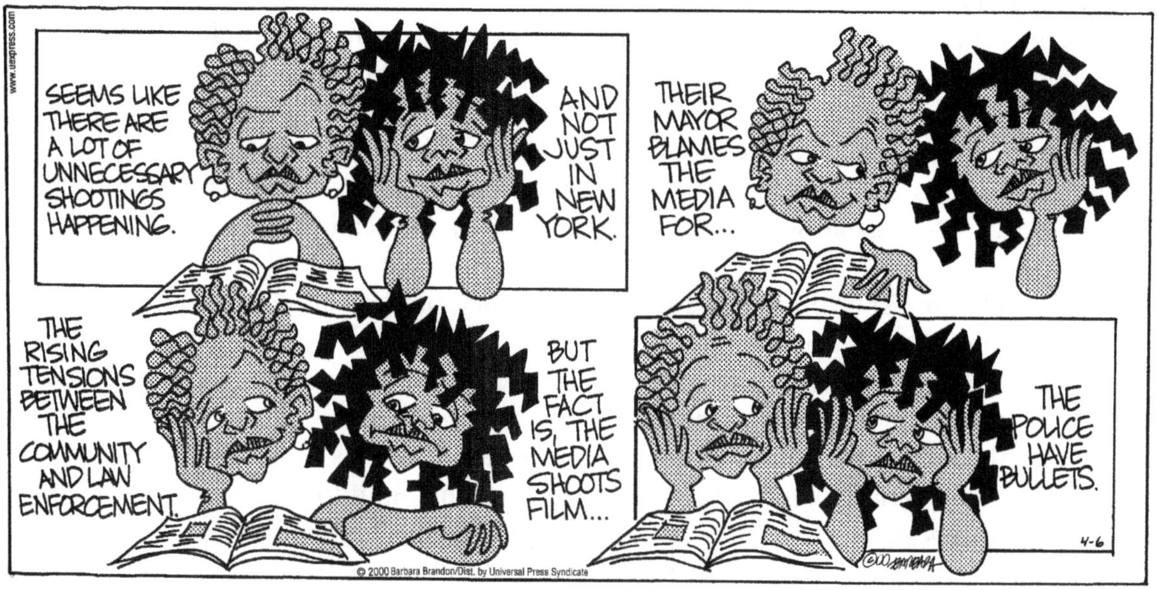
www.uexpress.com
SEEMS LIKE THERE ARE A LOT OF UNNECESSARY SHOOTINGS HAPPENING.
AND NOT JUST IN NEW YORK.
THEIR MAYOR BLAMES THE MEDIA FOR...
THE RISING TENSIONS BETWEEN THE COMMUNITY AND LAW ENFORCEMENT.
BUT THE FACT IS, THE MEDIA SHOOTS FILM...
THE POLICE HAVE BULLETS.
4-6
© 2000 Barbara Brandon/Dist. by Universal Press Syndicate

## MEDIA SHOTS

BY: BARBARA BRANDON-CROFT

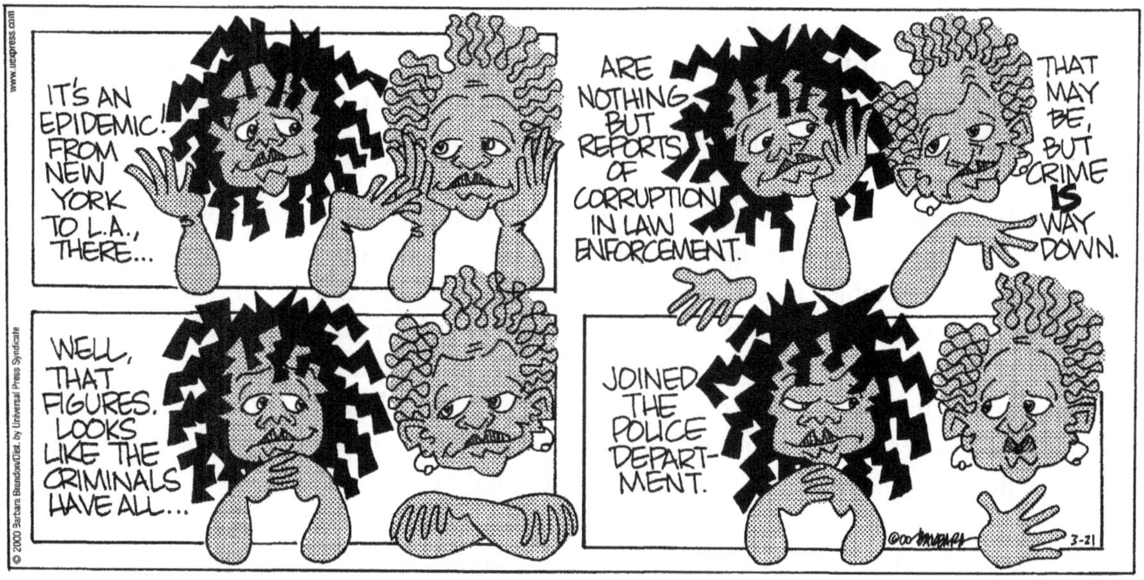
www.uexpress.com
IT'S AN EPIDEMIC! FROM NEW YORK TO L.A., THERE...
ARE NOTHING BUT REPORTS OF CORRUPTION IN LAW ENFORCEMENT.
THAT MAY BE, BUT CRIME IS WAY DOWN.
WELL, THAT FIGURES. LOOKS LIKE THE CRIMINALS HAVE ALL...
JOINED THE POLICE DEPARTMENT.
3-21
© 2000 Barbara Brandon/Dist. by Universal Press Syndicate

# NO TIME FOR INNOCENCE
## BY ANDAIYE REEVES

Black Friday, 2013: I stood in the dark strip mall parking lot, paralyzed. A black sedan approached and stopped near two black men, their faces hidden by hoodies. As their lanky frames crouched down to look into the driver's side window for me, I screamed inside. My grip tightened around my daughter's hand–I couldn't force any sound from my throat. In an instant, I thought of Trayvon Martin and Reginald Latson, of young boys and girls who'd been kidnapped or worse, never to be seen or heard from again. Thankfully, my daughter yelled, "Over here," and the sedan pulled away without incident. Unlike Trayvon Martin and Reginald Latson, my 14- year-old son and my boyfriend's 12- year-old son left the scene laughing and unscathed.

We all know Trayvon Martin's unfortunate story, but I want to focus on the lesser known story of Reginald Latson, a young man very similar to my own son. In 2010, Stafford County, Virginia police responded to a call about a suspicious black man wearing a hoodie and possibly carrying a gun–this was 19-year-old Reginald Latson, sitting outside the local library and waiting for it to open, which was not unusual for him to do. An officer arrived, confronted Latson, and searched him for a gun. Here is where the accounts begin to vary. Latson, who participated in various extracurricular activities including wrestling, allegedly assaulted the officer and was sentenced to 10 ½ years in prison.

My son and Mr. Latson share more than gender and ethnicity; they both live with Asperger's Syndrome, a high-functioning form of autism. The ability for those with Asperger's to process multiple instructions, social cues, and complex emotions (people who laugh when they cry or smile when they are angry) can range from functional to nonexistent. They may be uncomfortable interacting with others in stressful situations, like ordering from the cashier at a local fast-food establishment. For some, physical touch or even eye contact can be painful (regardless of the intent), which can trigger socially inappropriate reactions such as fight or flight.

This means that my son is a brilliant artist who can teach himself how to use a Wacom Cintiq but he may struggle to remember to wash the dishes, sweep the floor, and wipe the kitchen table. This means his third grade principal did not understand that he punched his classmate because the boy kept tapping him on the shoulder to tell him something(but my son only understood that the tapping on his shoulder hurt). This means my now 16-year-old son, who stands 5 feet 8 inches tall with a mustache and goatee and loves to wear hoodies, is a target for untrained police officers who do not understand people like my son. People like Reginald Latson.

As a librarian, I pride myself on the ability to thoroughly research anything. As a parent, I pride myself on advocating for children, especially those who resemble mine. Because I wanted to learn more about my son and how I could be a better parent, I read everything I could on autism and Asperger's Syndrome. Years before learning of Reginald Latson, I'd read British author Mark Haddon's 2003 novel, The Curious Incident of the Dog in the Night-Time. The novel focuses on a 15 year-old boy from Swindon, Wiltshire, who loves math and has behavioral difficulties. The boy discovers his neighbor's dog has been killed and, in one chapter, the police arrive and begin asking him questions too quickly, which agitates him. He curls into a ball and strikes a police officer when the officer attempts to lift him to his feet. The boy is arrested and then released. It is an excellent read, especially since the boy gets to live and go on to tell a beautiful story. Since its publication, the novel has been adapted into award-winning theatrical productions in the U.S., London, and Mexico City. A film adaptation is also in the works.

Reading about the lives of Temple Grandin, John Elder Robinson, and Daniel Tammet also helped prepare me for my son's journey. From these authors and advocates (all of whom live on the autistic spectrum), I learned that he might have periods of awkward imbalance, that it might take him longer than others to process situations and even longer to respond (and sometimes the response would not be appropriate). This was frightening because, unlike these authors, my child couldn't afford to exhibit these behaviors in public–any display of awkward imbalance could mean someone assuming he was drunk or high. Not responding quickly to authority's directives might mean disciplinary action in situations that simply called for patience and understanding.

Not responding quickly to a police officer's instructions might mean death. And did I mention that my son loves to wear hoodies?

When I first heard Mr. Latson's story five years ago, I struggled to find bits and pieces of information across the web. By many accounts, Mr. Latson, who had triumphed to overcome some of his challenges languished in prison, often in solitary confinement, without medication or treatment and without contact with his mother. Some articles stated that he was suicidal. This was my nightmare turned into someone's reality, and I wanted something to be done to resolve the injustice before my son was next.

I've instructed my son on what to do should he ever be approached by an officer: listen carefully and follow all instructions; never make any sudden movements; and, if he were arrested, I've taught him to repeat, "I want a lawyer." All of this ran through my mind that Black Friday in 2013. Neither my son, nor my boyfriend's son understood my frantic pleas for them to never, ever, ever do that again–because they hadn't done anything wrong. I had to remind them of how others might perceive them. I had to explain on the day after Thanksgiving, why someone might feel justified in hurting or arresting them.

While I am thankful for the works of Mark Haddon, Temple Grandin, John Elder Robinson, and Daniel Tammet and their efforts to bring autism awareness to the forefront of mainstream society, I know they will never be able to relate to my son because of the color of his skin. I've learned through my own research that there are wonderful services to assist those on the autistic spectrum with life skills but very few programs teach differently-abled people how to interact with first responders. Likewise, there are very few programs to teach first responders how to interact with differently-abled people. Mission Possible in Los Angeles is one example of a program that does both. Communities or individuals must contact their nearest chapter of Autism Speaks, The Color of Autism Foundation or other agencies that work with differently-abled populations for help. We can also support projects like the film Autistic Like Me: A Father's Perspective.

Until more first responders are educated, my son will always be "autistic while black" and could end up like Mr. Latson–who, as of January 20, 2015, was conditionally pardoned, allowing Latson to "… get treatment and services in a placement in the developmental disabilities system instead of continuing to serve time in prison, where he was at times held in solitary confinement and denied needed mental health and developmental disabilities services…"(Statement on the Plight of Reginald Latson, Judge David L. Bazelon Center for Mental Health Law). I wonder if there will be any theatrical productions about Reginald Latson's story?

Reginald Latson's name stays in the forefront of my mind because I could be his mother. For those of us who love an African American child with autism,the road ahead is sketchy. My daughter understands that her big brother has Asperger's Syndrome and can be fiercely protective of him at times. I fear what might happen to her if they were to encounter an untrained police officer. Could she be caught in a crossfire of bullets or arrested on assault charges for attempting to defend him? This is what goes through my mind on simple shopping excursions. I grit my teeth and we run through the list of rules–cell phone must be fully charged, hoods must be off heads, call when you arrive at your destination, call if you leave your destination, etc. –before I let them go shopping on their own.

Like any parent, I want my children to enjoy life–mature into productive citizens, live independently, and contribute great things to society. As an African American parent, I want my children to accomplish the aforementioned and live beyond the age of 18. As the parent of an African American exceptional needs male child, I want him to live to see tomorrow and all of the above. As an American, I want the justice system to provide just that–justice for all.

**ILLUSTRATION BY DARIUS REEVES**

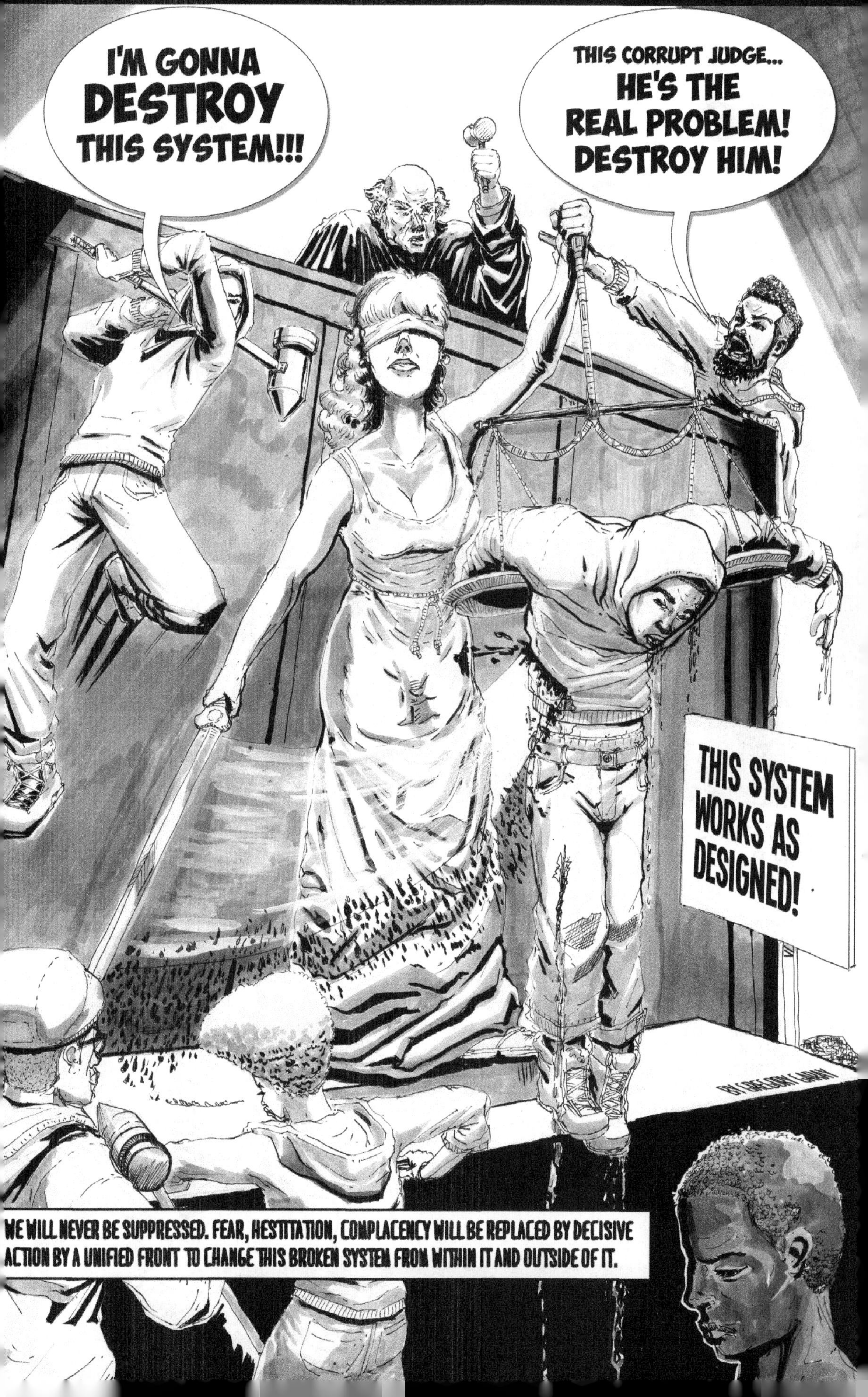
I'M GONNA DESTROY THIS SYSTEM!!!
THIS CORRUPT JUDGE... HE'S THE REAL PROBLEM! DESTROY HIM!
THIS SYSTEM WORKS AS DESIGNED!
WE WILL NEVER BE SUPPRESSED. FEAR, HESTITATION, COMPLACENCY WILL BE REPLACED BY DECISIVE ACTION BY A UNIFIED FRONT TO CHANGE THIS BROKEN SYSTEM FROM WITHIN IT AND OUTSIDE OF IT.

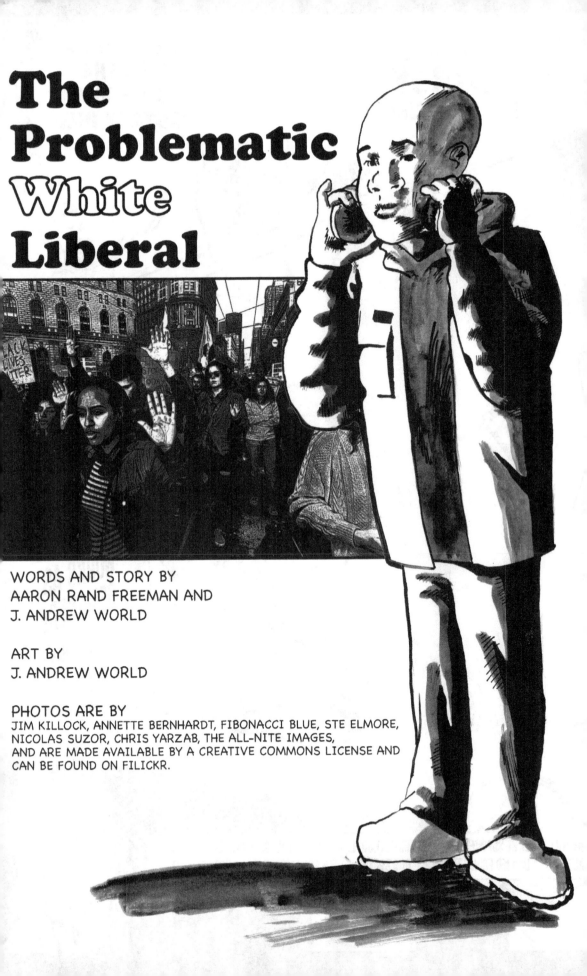

# The Problematic White Liberal

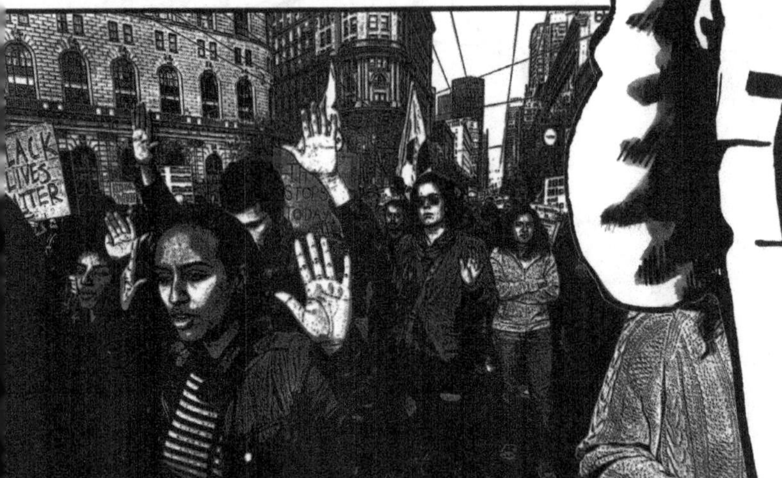

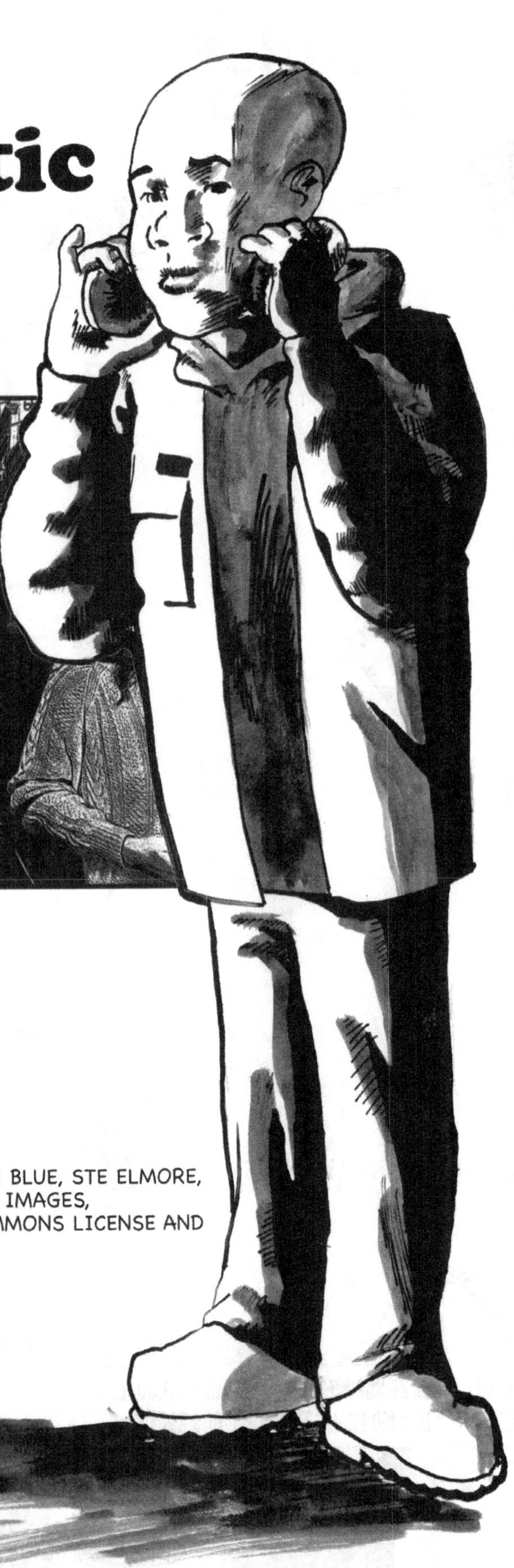


WORDS AND STORY BY
AARON RAND FREEMAN AND
J. ANDREW WORLD

ART BY
J. ANDREW WORLD

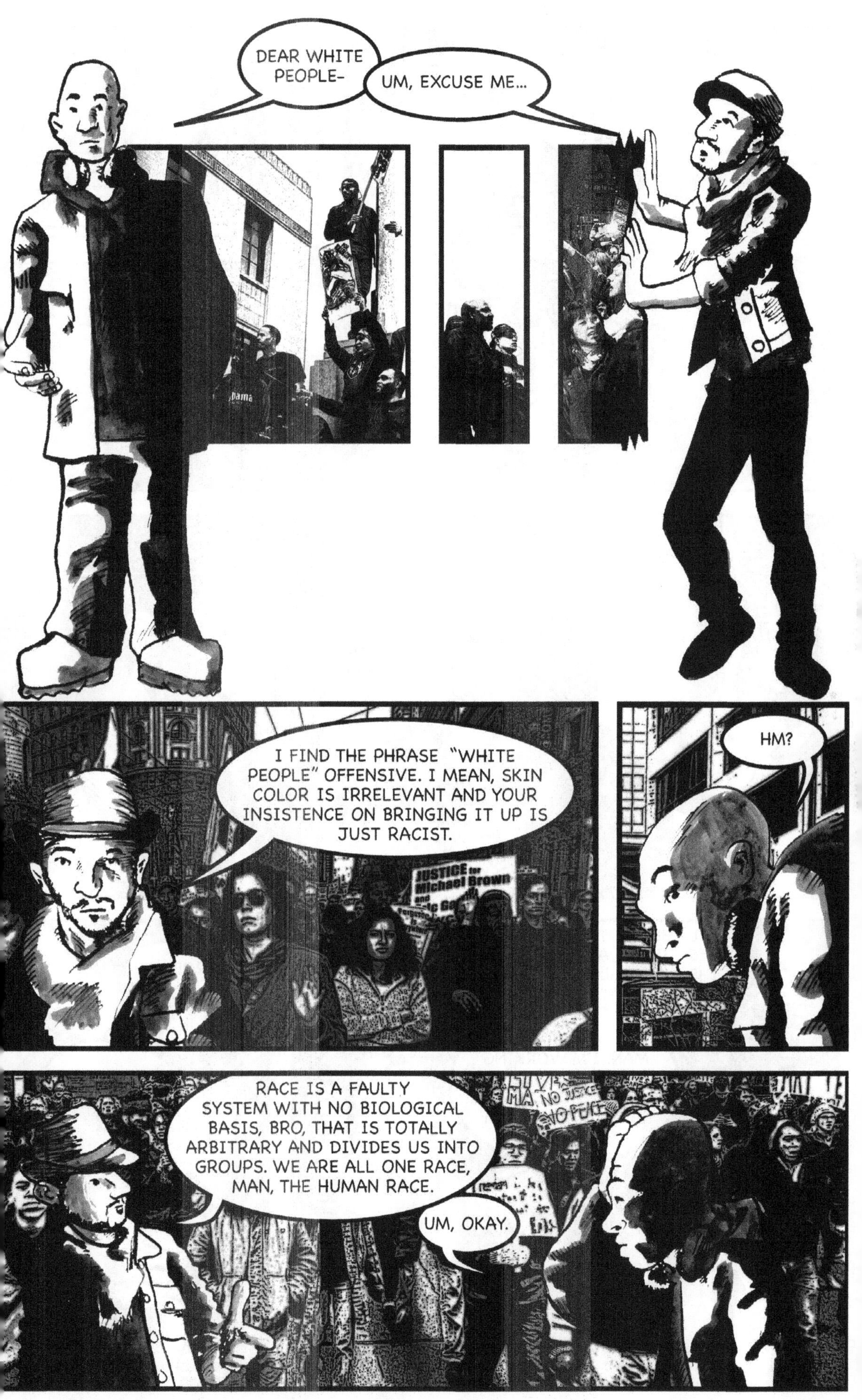
DEAR WHITE PEOPLE-
UM, EXCUSE ME...
I FIND THE PHRASE "WHITE PEOPLE" OFFENSIVE. I MEAN, SKIN COLOR IS IRRELEVANT AND YOUR INSISTENCE ON BRINGING IT UP IS JUST RACIST.
JUSTICE for Michael Brown
HM?
RACE IS A FAULTY SYSTEM WITH NO BIOLOGICAL BASIS, BRO, THAT IS TOTALLY ARBITRARY AND DIVIDES US INTO GROUPS. WE ARE ALL ONE RACE, MAN, THE HUMAN RACE.
UM, OKAY.

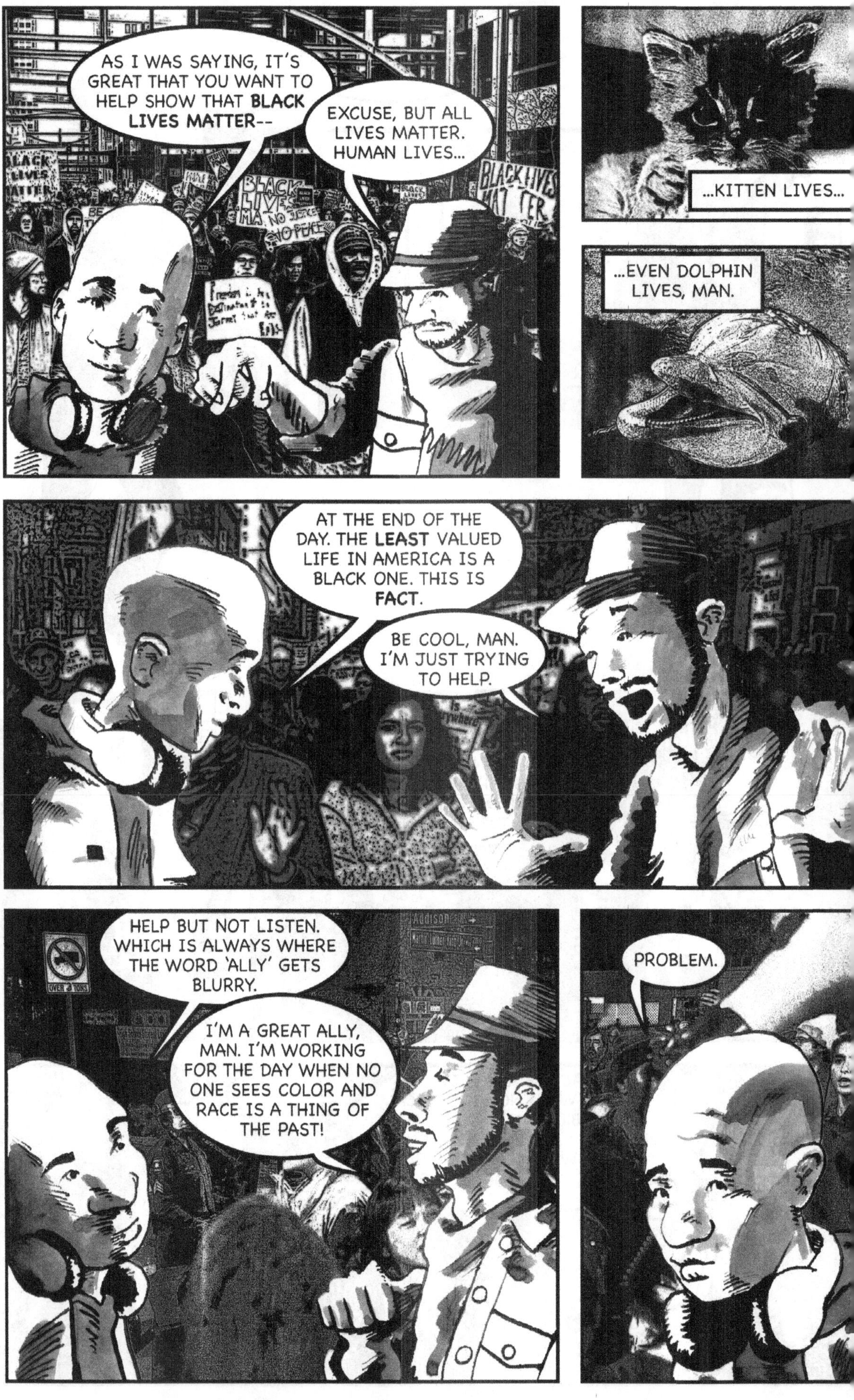
AS I WAS SAYING, IT'S GREAT THAT YOU WANT TO HELP SHOW THAT **BLACK LIVES MATTER**--
EXCUSE, BUT ALL LIVES MATTER. HUMAN LIVES...
...KITTEN LIVES...
...EVEN DOLPHIN LIVES, MAN.
AT THE END OF THE DAY. THE **LEAST** VALUED LIFE IN AMERICA IS A BLACK ONE. THIS IS **FACT**.
BE COOL, MAN. I'M JUST TRYING TO HELP.
HELP BUT NOT LISTEN. WHICH IS ALWAYS WHERE THE WORD 'ALLY' GETS BLURRY.
I'M A GREAT ALLY, MAN. I'M WORKING FOR THE DAY WHEN NO ONE SEES COLOR AND RACE IS A THING OF THE PAST!
PROBLEM.

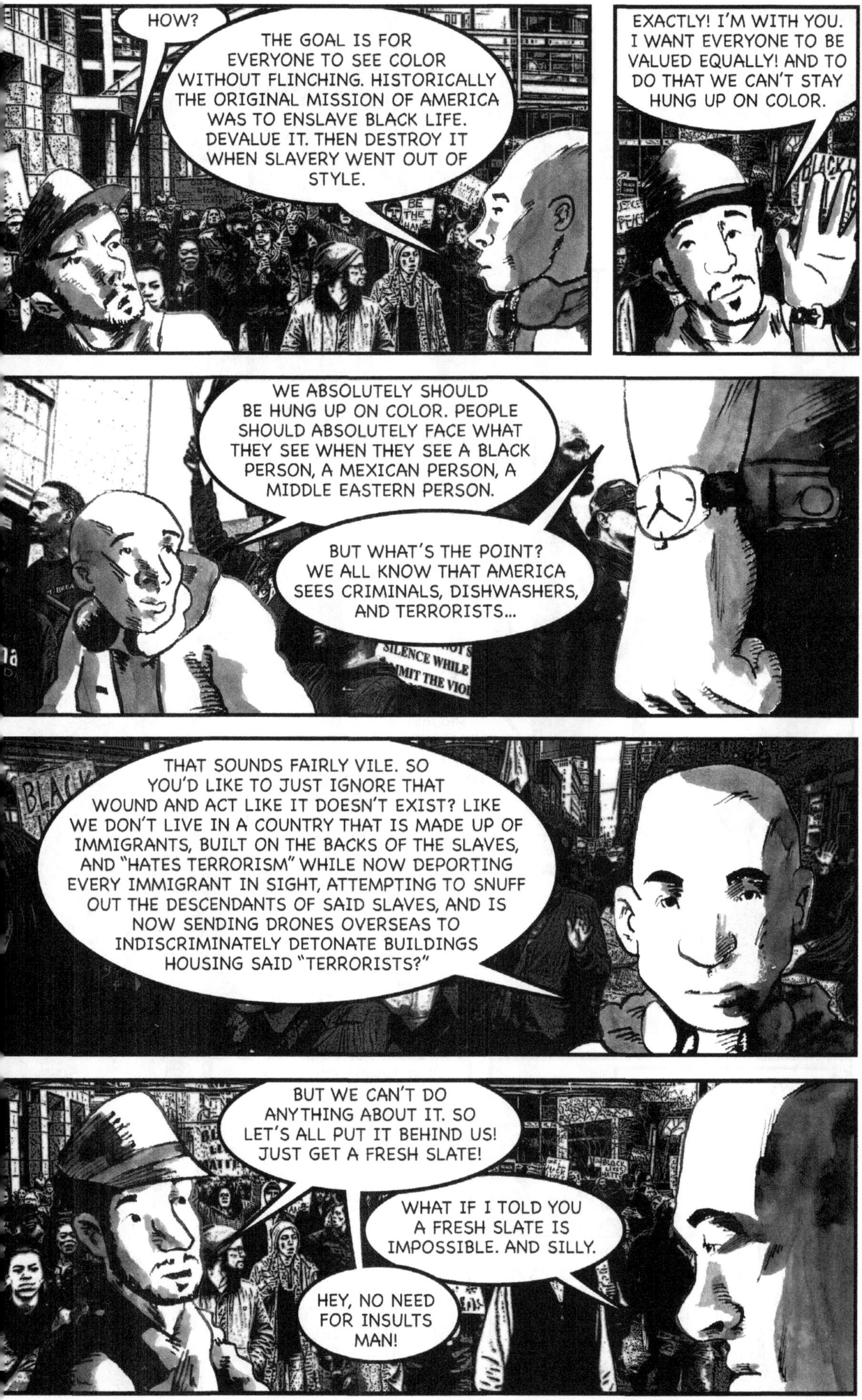
HOW?
THE GOAL IS FOR EVERYONE TO SEE COLOR WITHOUT FLINCHING. HISTORICALLY THE ORIGINAL MISSION OF AMERICA WAS TO ENSLAVE BLACK LIFE. DEVALUE IT. THEN DESTROY IT WHEN SLAVERY WENT OUT OF STYLE.
EXACTLY! I'M WITH YOU. I WANT EVERYONE TO BE VALUED EQUALLY! AND TO DO THAT WE CAN'T STAY HUNG UP ON COLOR.
WE ABSOLUTELY SHOULD BE HUNG UP ON COLOR. PEOPLE SHOULD ABSOLUTELY FACE WHAT THEY SEE WHEN THEY SEE A BLACK PERSON, A MEXICAN PERSON, A MIDDLE EASTERN PERSON.
BUT WHAT'S THE POINT? WE ALL KNOW THAT AMERICA SEES CRIMINALS, DISHWASHERS, AND TERRORISTS...
THAT SOUNDS FAIRLY VILE. SO YOU'D LIKE TO JUST IGNORE THAT WOUND AND ACT LIKE IT DOESN'T EXIST? LIKE WE DON'T LIVE IN A COUNTRY THAT IS MADE UP OF IMMIGRANTS, BUILT ON THE BACKS OF THE SLAVES, AND "HATES TERRORISM" WHILE NOW DEPORTING EVERY IMMIGRANT IN SIGHT, ATTEMPTING TO SNUFF OUT THE DESCENDANTS OF SAID SLAVES, AND IS NOW SENDING DRONES OVERSEAS TO INDISCRIMINATELY DETONATE BUILDINGS HOUSING SAID "TERRORISTS?"
BUT WE CAN'T DO ANYTHING ABOUT IT. SO LET'S ALL PUT IT BEHIND US! JUST GET A FRESH SLATE!
WHAT IF I TOLD YOU A FRESH SLATE IS IMPOSSIBLE. AND SILLY.
HEY, NO NEED FOR INSULTS MAN!

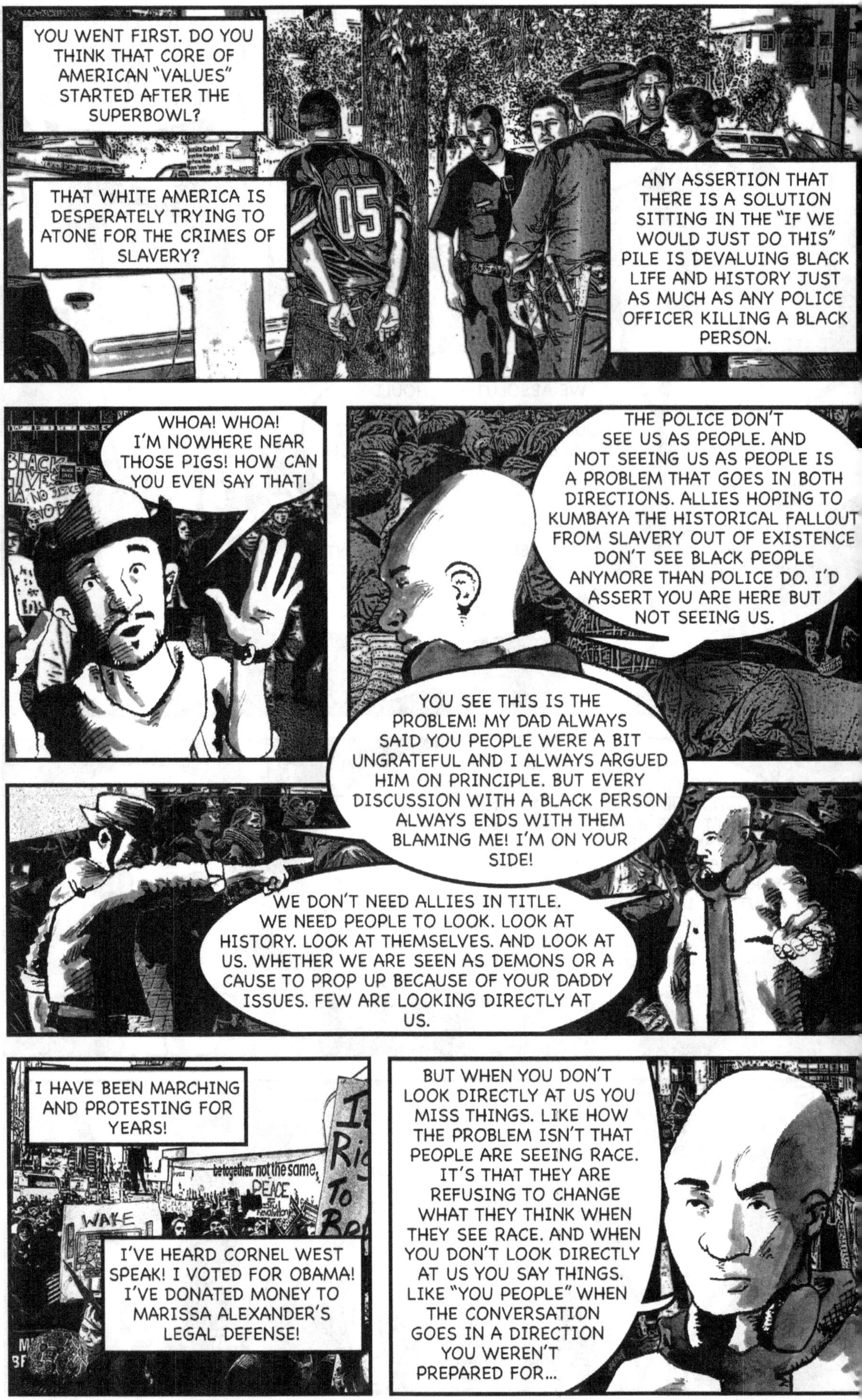
YOU WENT FIRST. DO YOU THINK THAT CORE OF AMERICAN "VALUES" STARTED AFTER THE SUPERBOWL?
THAT WHITE AMERICA IS DESPERATELY TRYING TO ATONE FOR THE CRIMES OF SLAVERY?
ANY ASSERTION THAT THERE IS A SOLUTION SITTING IN THE "IF WE WOULD JUST DO THIS" PILE IS DEVALUING BLACK LIFE AND HISTORY JUST AS MUCH AS ANY POLICE OFFICER KILLING A BLACK PERSON.
WHOA! WHOA! I'M NOWHERE NEAR THOSE PIGS! HOW CAN YOU EVEN SAY THAT!
THE POLICE DON'T SEE US AS PEOPLE. AND NOT SEEING US AS PEOPLE IS A PROBLEM THAT GOES IN BOTH DIRECTIONS. ALLIES HOPING TO KUMBAYA THE HISTORICAL FALLOUT FROM SLAVERY OUT OF EXISTENCE DON'T SEE BLACK PEOPLE ANYMORE THAN POLICE DO. I'D ASSERT YOU ARE HERE BUT NOT SEEING US.
YOU SEE THIS IS THE PROBLEM! MY DAD ALWAYS SAID YOU PEOPLE WERE A BIT UNGRATEFUL AND I ALWAYS ARGUED HIM ON PRINCIPLE. BUT EVERY DISCUSSION WITH A BLACK PERSON ALWAYS ENDS WITH THEM BLAMING ME! I'M ON YOUR SIDE!
WE DON'T NEED ALLIES IN TITLE. WE NEED PEOPLE TO LOOK. LOOK AT HISTORY. LOOK AT THEMSELVES. AND LOOK AT US. WHETHER WE ARE SEEN AS DEMONS OR A CAUSE TO PROP UP BECAUSE OF YOUR DADDY ISSUES. FEW ARE LOOKING DIRECTLY AT US.
I HAVE BEEN MARCHING AND PROTESTING FOR YEARS!
I'VE HEARD CORNEL WEST SPEAK! I VOTED FOR OBAMA! I'VE DONATED MONEY TO MARISSA ALEXANDER'S LEGAL DEFENSE!
BUT WHEN YOU DON'T LOOK DIRECTLY AT US YOU MISS THINGS. LIKE HOW THE PROBLEM ISN'T THAT PEOPLE ARE SEEING RACE. IT'S THAT THEY ARE REFUSING TO CHANGE WHAT THEY THINK WHEN THEY SEE RACE. AND WHEN YOU DON'T LOOK DIRECTLY AT US YOU SAY THINGS. LIKE "YOU PEOPLE" WHEN THE CONVERSATION GOES IN A DIRECTION YOU WEREN'T PREPARED FOR...

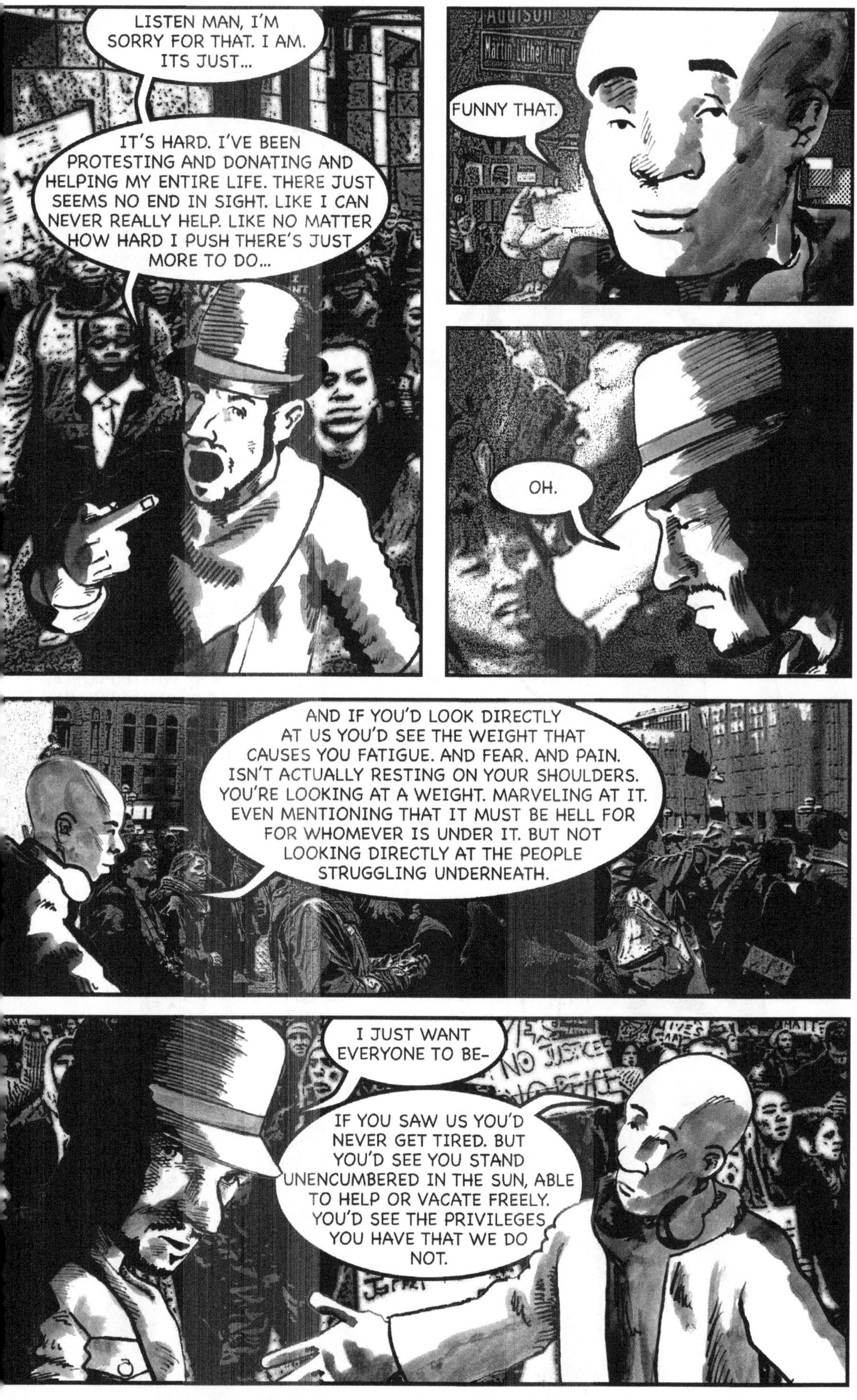
LISTEN MAN, I'M SORRY FOR THAT. I AM. ITS JUST...
IT'S HARD. I'VE BEEN PROTESTING AND DONATING AND HELPING MY ENTIRE LIFE. THERE JUST SEEMS NO END IN SIGHT. LIKE I CAN NEVER REALLY HELP. LIKE NO MATTER HOW HARD I PUSH THERE'S JUST MORE TO DO...
Martin Luther King Jr
FUNNY THAT.
OH.
AND IF YOU'D LOOK DIRECTLY AT US YOU'D SEE THE WEIGHT THAT CAUSES YOU FATIGUE. AND FEAR. AND PAIN. ISN'T ACTUALLY RESTING ON YOUR SHOULDERS. YOU'RE LOOKING AT A WEIGHT. MARVELING AT IT. EVEN MENTIONING THAT IT MUST BE HELL FOR FOR WHOMEVER IS UNDER IT. BUT NOT LOOKING DIRECTLY AT THE PEOPLE STRUGGLING UNDERNEATH.
I JUST WANT EVERYONE TO BE-
NO JUSTICE
IF YOU SAW US YOU'D NEVER GET TIRED. BUT YOU'D SEE YOU STAND UNENCUMBERED IN THE SUN, ABLE TO HELP OR VACATE FREELY. YOU'D SEE THE PRIVILEGES YOU HAVE THAT WE DO NOT.

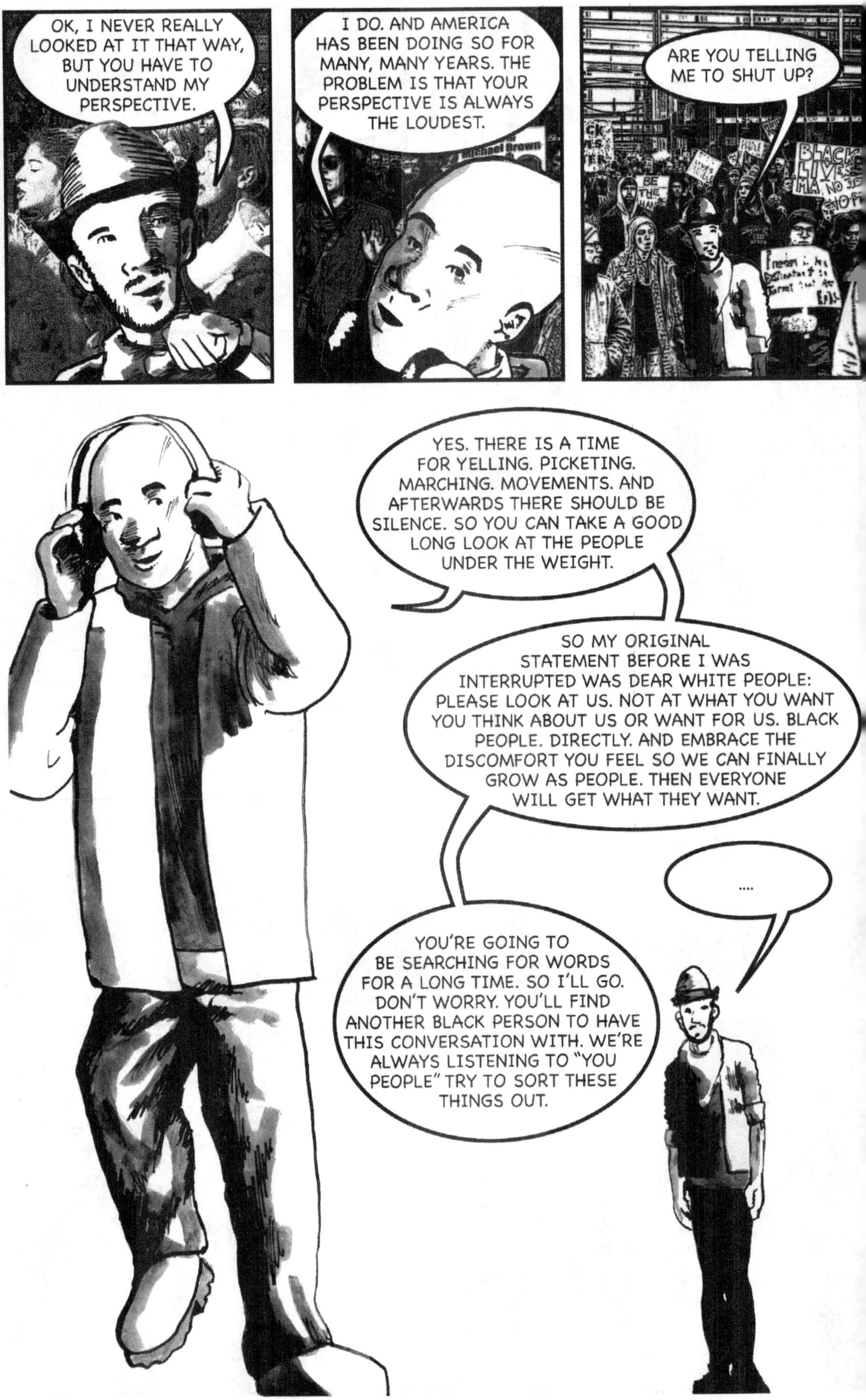
OK, I NEVER REALLY LOOKED AT IT THAT WAY, BUT YOU HAVE TO UNDERSTAND MY PERSPECTIVE.
I DO. AND AMERICA HAS BEEN DOING SO FOR MANY, MANY YEARS. THE PROBLEM IS THAT YOUR PERSPECTIVE IS ALWAYS THE LOUDEST.
ARE YOU TELLING ME TO SHUT UP?
BLACK LIVES MA
YES. THERE IS A TIME FOR YELLING. PICKETING. MARCHING. MOVEMENTS. AND AFTERWARDS THERE SHOULD BE SILENCE. SO YOU CAN TAKE A GOOD LONG LOOK AT THE PEOPLE UNDER THE WEIGHT.
SO MY ORIGINAL STATEMENT BEFORE I WAS INTERRUPTED WAS DEAR WHITE PEOPLE: PLEASE LOOK AT US. NOT AT WHAT YOU WANT YOU THINK ABOUT US OR WANT FOR US. BLACK PEOPLE. DIRECTLY. AND EMBRACE THE DISCOMFORT YOU FEEL SO WE CAN FINALLY GROW AS PEOPLE. THEN EVERYONE WILL GET WHAT THEY WANT.
....
YOU'RE GOING TO BE SEARCHING FOR WORDS FOR A LONG TIME. SO I'LL GO. DON'T WORRY. YOU'LL FIND ANOTHER BLACK PERSON TO HAVE THIS CONVERSATION WITH. WE'RE ALWAYS LISTENING TO "YOU PEOPLE" TRY TO SORT THESE THINGS OUT.

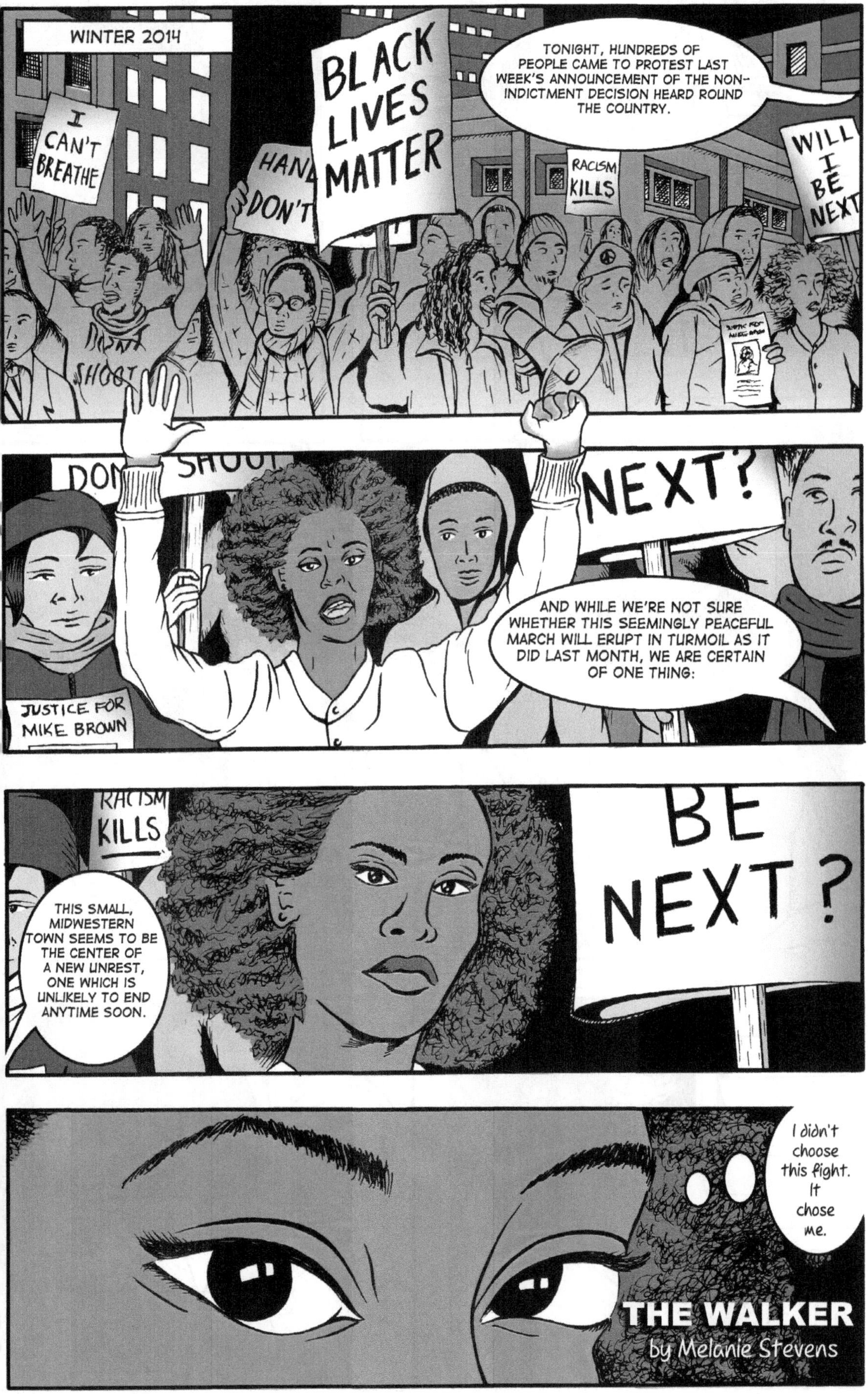

WINTER 2014
BLACK LIVES MATTER
I CAN'T BREATHE
HAN
DON'T
RACISM KILLS
WILL I BE NEXT
TONIGHT, HUNDREDS OF PEOPLE CAME TO PROTEST LAST WEEK'S ANNOUNCEMENT OF THE NON-INDICTMENT DECISION HEARD ROUND THE COUNTRY.
DON
NEXT?
JUSTICE FOR MIKE BROWN
AND WHILE WE'RE NOT SURE WHETHER THIS SEEMINGLY PEACEFUL MARCH WILL ERUPT IN TURMOIL AS IT DID LAST MONTH, WE ARE CERTAIN OF ONE THING:
RACISM KILLS
BE NEXT?
THIS SMALL, MIDWESTERN TOWN SEEMS TO BE THE CENTER OF A NEW UNREST, ONE WHICH IS UNLIKELY TO END ANYTIME SOON.
I didn't choose this fight. It chose me.
THE WALKER
by Melanie Stevens

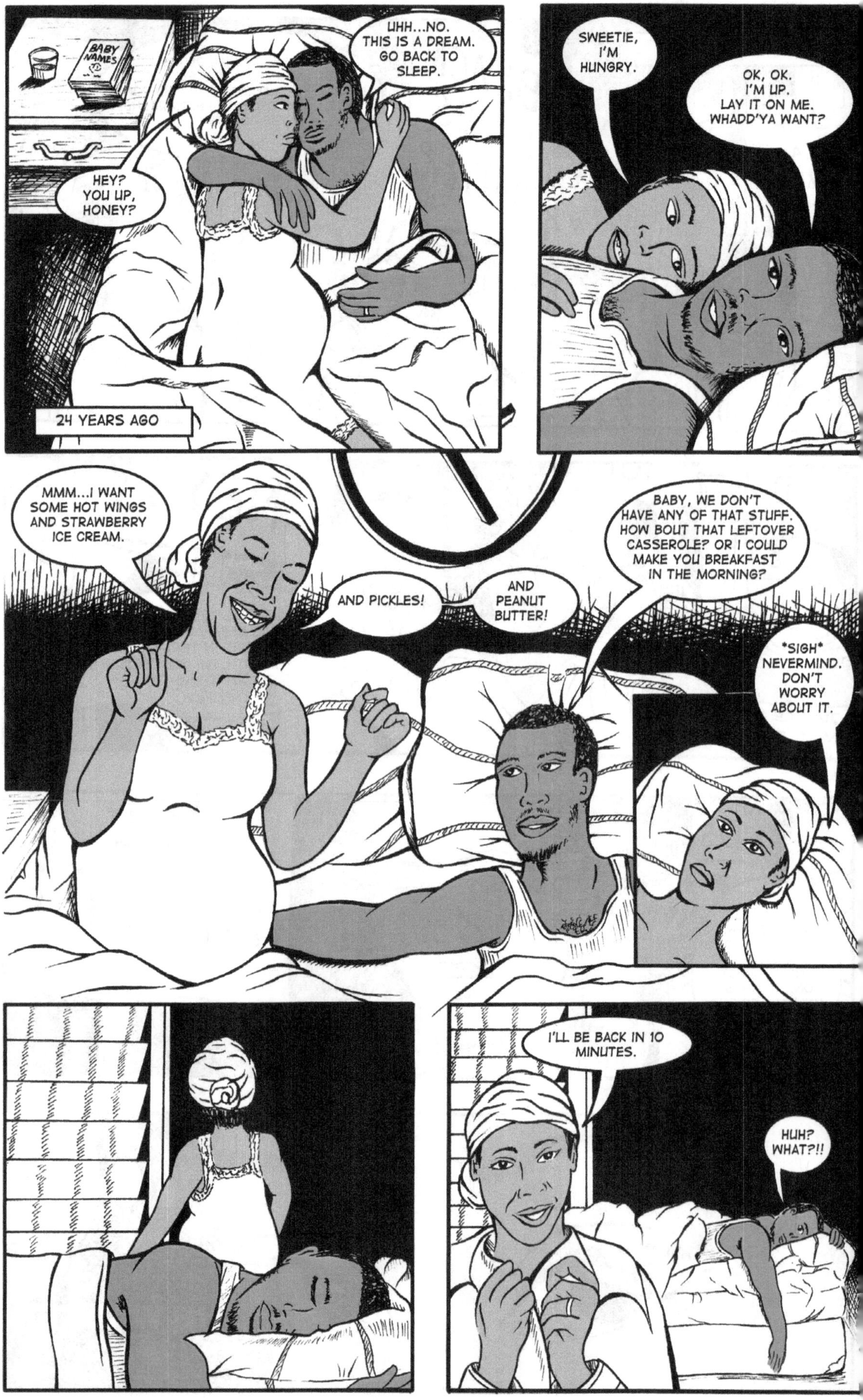
24 YEARS AGO
HEY? YOU UP, HONEY?
UHH...NO. THIS IS A DREAM. GO BACK TO SLEEP.
BABY NAMES
SWEETIE, I'M HUNGRY.
OK, OK. I'M UP. LAY IT ON ME. WHADD'YA WANT?
MMM...I WANT SOME HOT WINGS AND STRAWBERRY ICE CREAM.
AND PICKLES!
AND PEANUT BUTTER!
BABY, WE DON'T HAVE ANY OF THAT STUFF. HOW BOUT THAT LEFTOVER CASSEROLE? OR I COULD MAKE YOU BREAKFAST IN THE MORNING?
*SIGH* NEVERMIND. DON'T WORRY ABOUT IT.
I'LL BE BACK IN 10 MINUTES.
HUH? WHAT?!!

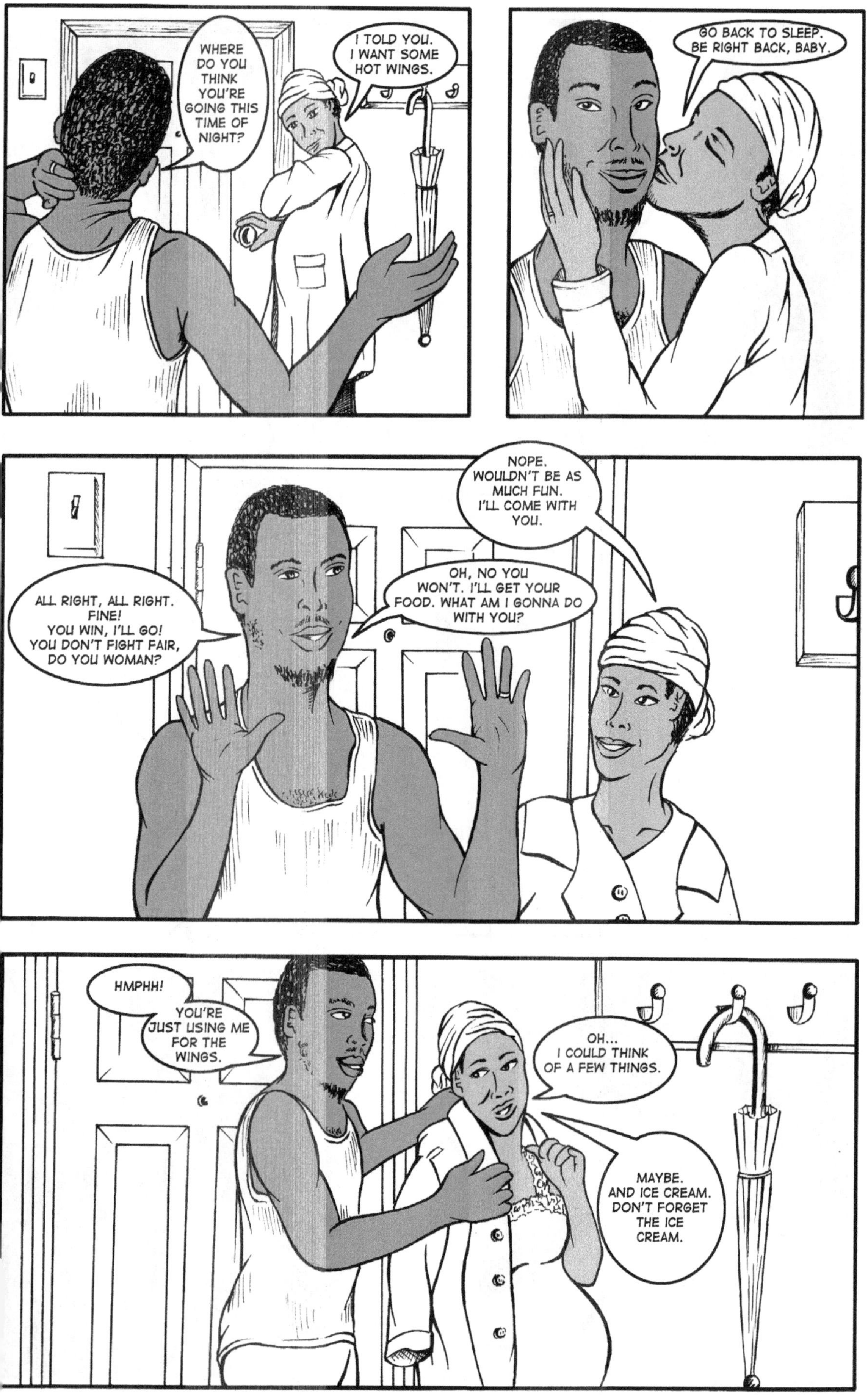
WHERE DO YOU THINK YOU'RE GOING THIS TIME OF NIGHT?
I TOLD YOU. I WANT SOME HOT WINGS.
GO BACK TO SLEEP. BE RIGHT BACK, BABY.
ALL RIGHT, ALL RIGHT. FINE! YOU WIN, I'LL GO! YOU DON'T FIGHT FAIR, DO YOU WOMAN?
NOPE. WOULDN'T BE AS MUCH FUN. I'LL COME WITH YOU.
OH, NO YOU WON'T. I'LL GET YOUR FOOD. WHAT AM I GONNA DO WITH YOU?
HMPHH!
YOU'RE JUST USING ME FOR THE WINGS.
OH... I COULD THINK OF A FEW THINGS.
MAYBE. AND ICE CREAM. DON'T FORGET THE ICE CREAM.

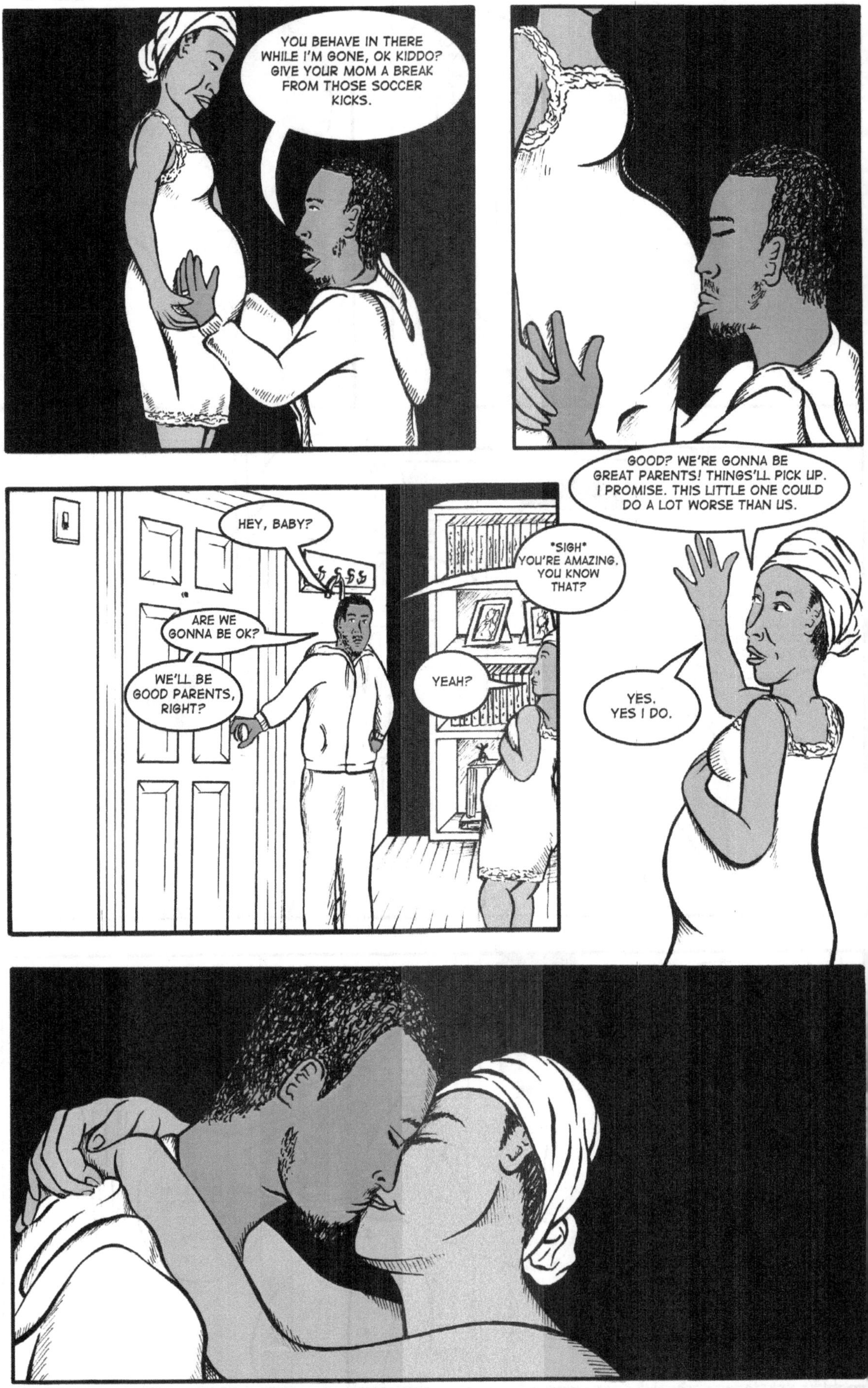
YOU BEHAVE IN THERE WHILE I'M GONE, OK KIDDO? GIVE YOUR MOM A BREAK FROM THOSE SOCCER KICKS.
HEY, BABY?
ARE WE GONNA BE OK?
WE'LL BE GOOD PARENTS, RIGHT?
YEAH?
*SIGH* YOU'RE AMAZING. YOU KNOW THAT?
GOOD? WE'RE GONNA BE GREAT PARENTS! THINGS'LL PICK UP. I PROMISE. THIS LITTLE ONE COULD DO A LOT WORSE THAN US.
YES. YES I DO.

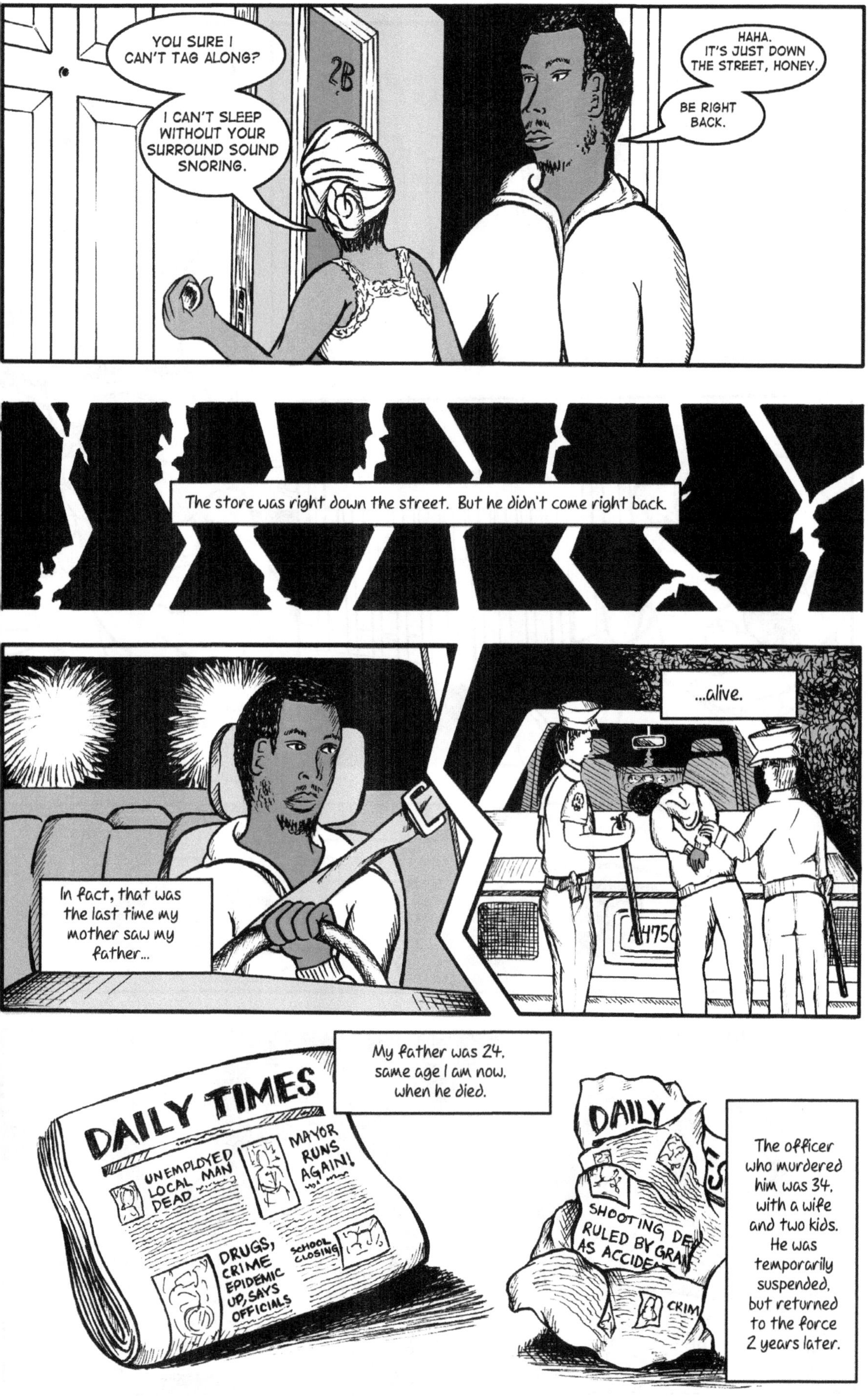
YOU SURE I CAN'T TAG ALONG?
I CAN'T SLEEP WITHOUT YOUR SURROUND SOUND SNORING.
2B
HAHA. IT'S JUST DOWN THE STREET, HONEY.
BE RIGHT BACK.
The store was right down the street. But he didn't come right back.
In fact, that was the last time my mother saw my father...
...alive.
My father was 24, same age I am now, when he died.
DAILY TIMES
UNEMPLOYED LOCAL MAN DEAD
MAYOR RUNS AGAIN!
DRUGS, CRIME EPIDEMIC UP, SAYS OFFICIALS
SCHOOL CLOSING
DAILY
SHOOTING DE
RULED BY GRA
AS ACCIDE
CRIM
The officer who murdered him was 34, with a wife and two kids. He was temporarily suspended, but returned to the force 2 years later.

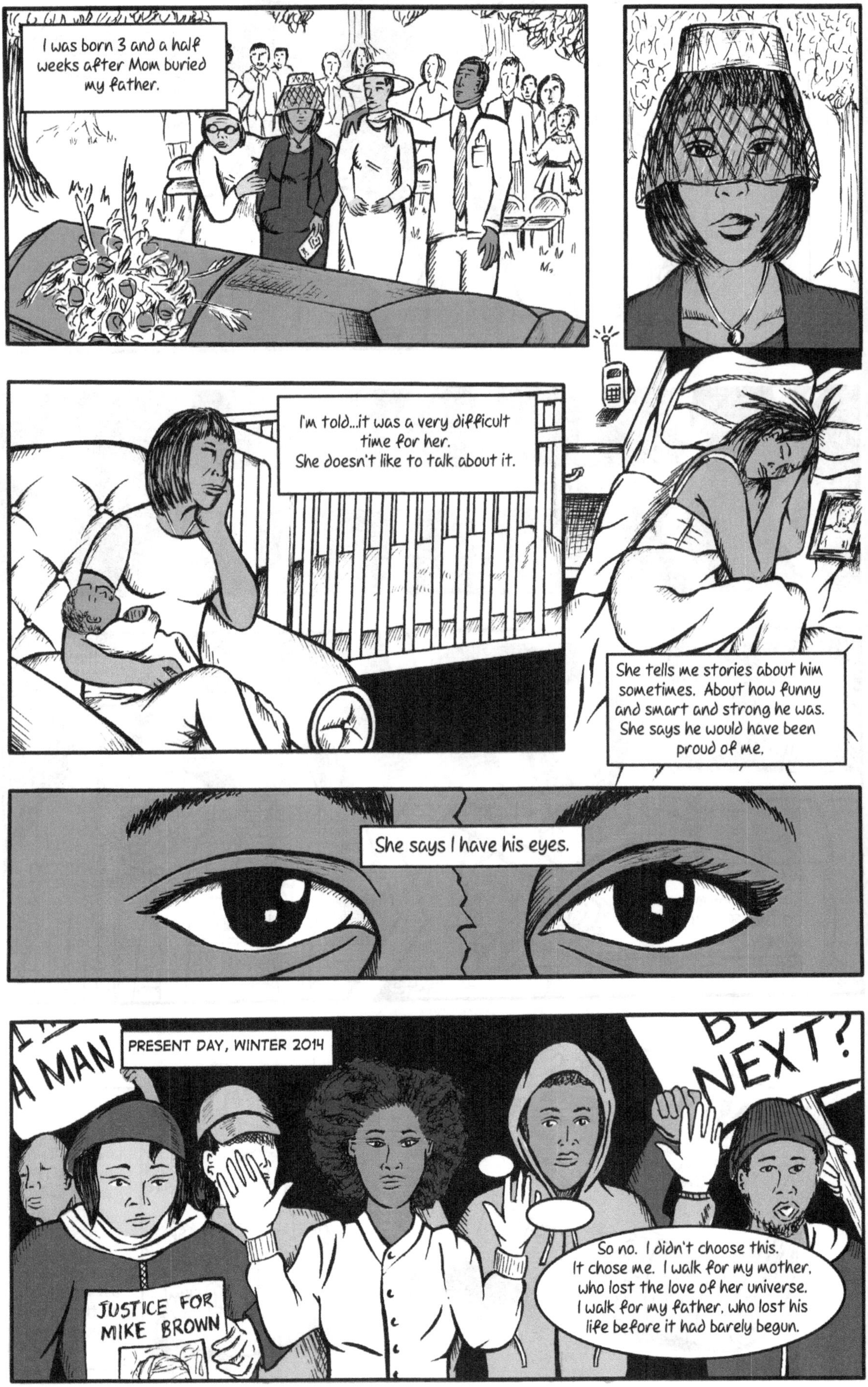

I was born 3 and a half weeks after Mom buried my father.
I'm told...it was a very difficult time for her. She doesn't like to talk about it.
She tells me stories about him sometimes. About how funny and smart and strong he was. She says he would have been proud of me.
She says I have his eyes.
PRESENT DAY, WINTER 2014
A MAN
NEXT?
JUSTICE FOR MIKE BROWN
So no. I didn't choose this. It chose me. I walk for my mother, who lost the love of her universe. I walk for my father, who lost his life before it had barely begun.

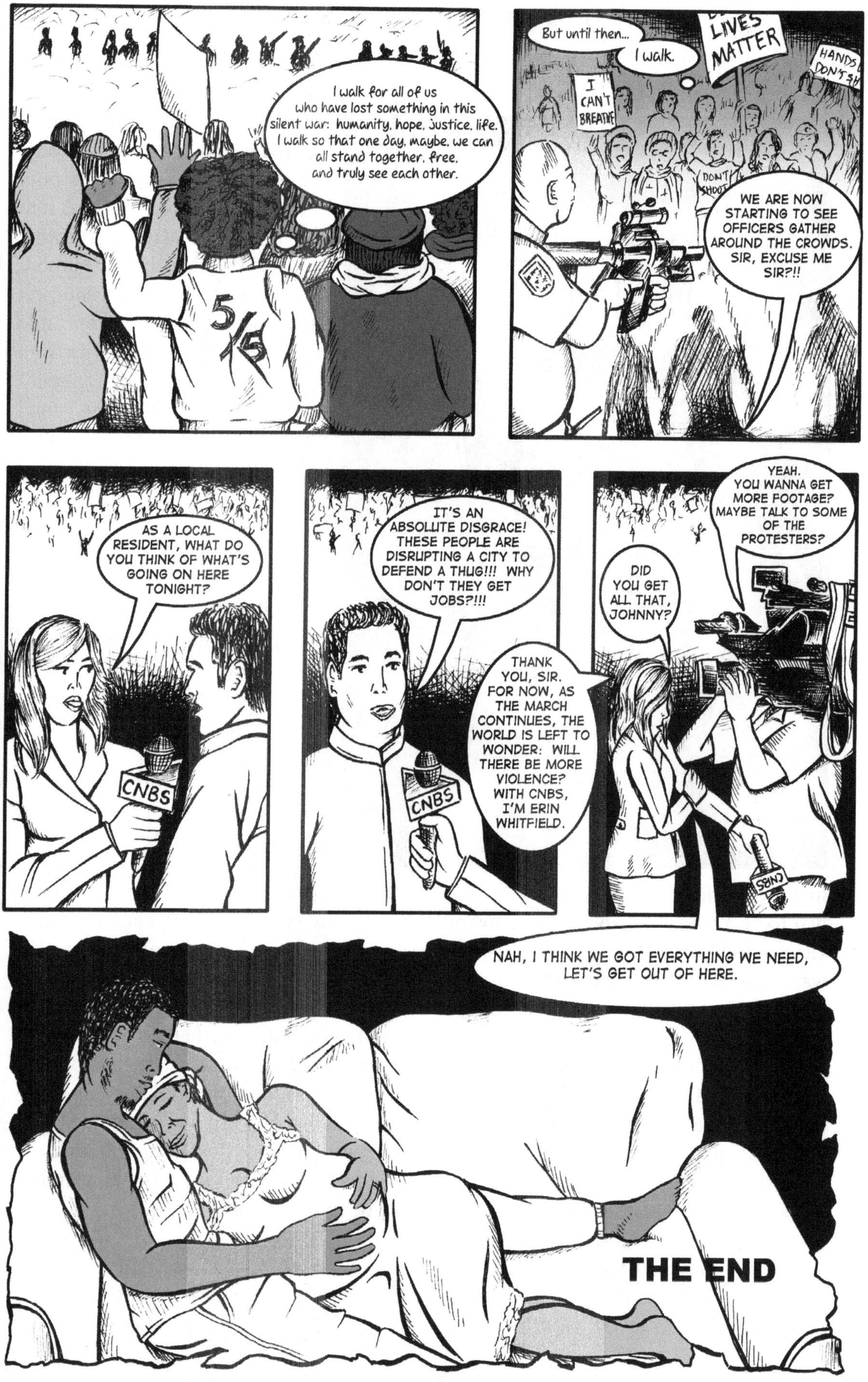
I walk for all of us who have lost something in this silent war: humanity, hope, justice, life. I walk so that one day, maybe, we can all stand together, free, and truly see each other.
5/5
But until then...
I walk.
LIVES MATTER
HANDS
I CAN'T BREATHE
DON'T SHOOT
WE ARE NOW STARTING TO SEE OFFICERS GATHER AROUND THE CROWDS. SIR, EXCUSE ME SIR?!!
AS A LOCAL RESIDENT, WHAT DO YOU THINK OF WHAT'S GOING ON HERE TONIGHT?
CNBS
IT'S AN ABSOLUTE DISGRACE! THESE PEOPLE ARE DISRUPTING A CITY TO DEFEND A THUG!!! WHY DON'T THEY GET JOBS?!!!
CNBS
THANK YOU, SIR. FOR NOW, AS THE MARCH CONTINUES, THE WORLD IS LEFT TO WONDER: WILL THERE BE MORE VIOLENCE? WITH CNBS, I'M ERIN WHITFIELD.
DID YOU GET ALL THAT, JOHNNY?
YEAH. YOU WANNA GET MORE FOOTAGE? MAYBE TALK TO SOME OF THE PROTESTERS?
CNBS
NAH, I THINK WE GOT EVERYTHING WE NEED, LET'S GET OUT OF HERE.
THE END

# FOR MY FUTURE CHILD

### BY TAKEIA MARIE

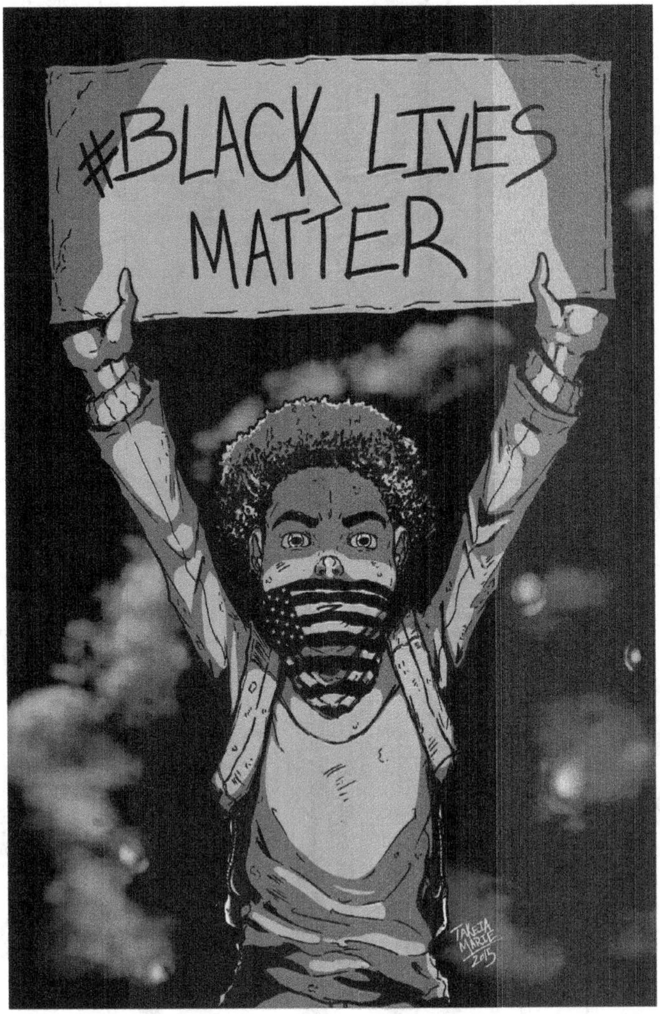
#BLACK LIVES MATTER
TAKEIA MARIE 2015

I remember feeling numb when the verdict was announced against indicting Ferguson police officer, Darren Wilson, for the murder of Michael Brown. Not indifference, but a numbness that came from genuine, unapologetic anger. Twitter and Facebook were ablaze with indignant comments, my friends were sending irate texts, and pundits were giving misinformed opinions about the entire situation.

We've been here before.

Different location, different time period, different black boy's body laying in the August heat, but it's the same story we've been told for years: black lives don't matter.

Still, in a country where that mantra exists, my husband and I had been discussing having our first child. Though we'll love the baby that we have no matter what, we both wanted our first to be a boy. I had always been aware of the ways in which black boys and men are viewed in American society, both historically and now. I knew the realities on paper, in ways that cause you to discuss them in historical contexts around tight-knit circles or regale stories of close encounters with police officers to your friends. But it wasn't until I saw Michael Brown's body laying in the middle of the road behind that yellow tape, his blood trailing through the concrete, that I began to understand intimately the horrors that exist for a black woman with a son in America. It was then that I could define the animosity I was feeling. I was angry because a black mother had just lost her child at the hands of a police officer who would never be brought to justice. I was angry because I knew that countless more black mothers will lose their sons in the same exact way in the years to come. I was angry because I could easily be one of those mothers.

I still wanted to have a son in a country where, as a young man, my dad ended up staring down the barrel of a police officer's gun simply because he was waiting in the car for my uncle to get off work; in a country where my friends tell me endless stories of being slammed against brick walls or concrete pavement and frisked because they committed the crime of walking home at night while black; in a country where a cop could shoot a black man in a Brooklyn housing project without cause and worry more about his job than the life he just took; in a country where police officers entered the home of Ramarley Graham without a warrant and shot and killed him just one street over from my Bronx apartment.

I wanted to have a son in a country that lies to me when it says we are all equal.

I have trouble reconciling the truth of those incidents against the ideals of a nation that preaches equality and upholding our God-given rights. In reality, my son will be born into a society where I'll have to explain that his life, in America's eyes, is less than that of his white friends. I'll have to give him the other "talk" that black people have with their children. The one where I explain how he should act if ever approached by a police officer, the same talk my dad gave to my brother and me when we were young. I'll have to tell him that, if he does find himself in a situation with an officer, he will be labeled a "thug," "criminal," or "demon" as justification for the blanket notion that his life is meaningless. Most of all, I'll have to make him understand that the fight against police brutality and social injustice will become his generation's to fight, whether he chooses to or not.

The harshest truth I learned from the events in Ferguson (and those after) is that the type of systemic discrimination people of color face every day in America will not be over in my lifetime. My son will have to know that, in addition to all the good things I will do my best to give him, he will also inherit a stigma that he did not personally create or enforce but will be his to bear regardless, simply because of the color of his skin. He will learn that the paradigm of fairness he will be taught is exemplary will not match the hatred, prejudices, and racism he will have to endure long before he understands why. He will learn that there is a grand legacy of historical leaders, parents who chose to speak out when their children were taken from them far too early, and people as normal as him who fought for his right to live in a society that has said again and again that black lives do not matter.

He will learn that, through their efforts, the most important thing he has inherited is a voice and no one can take that from him.

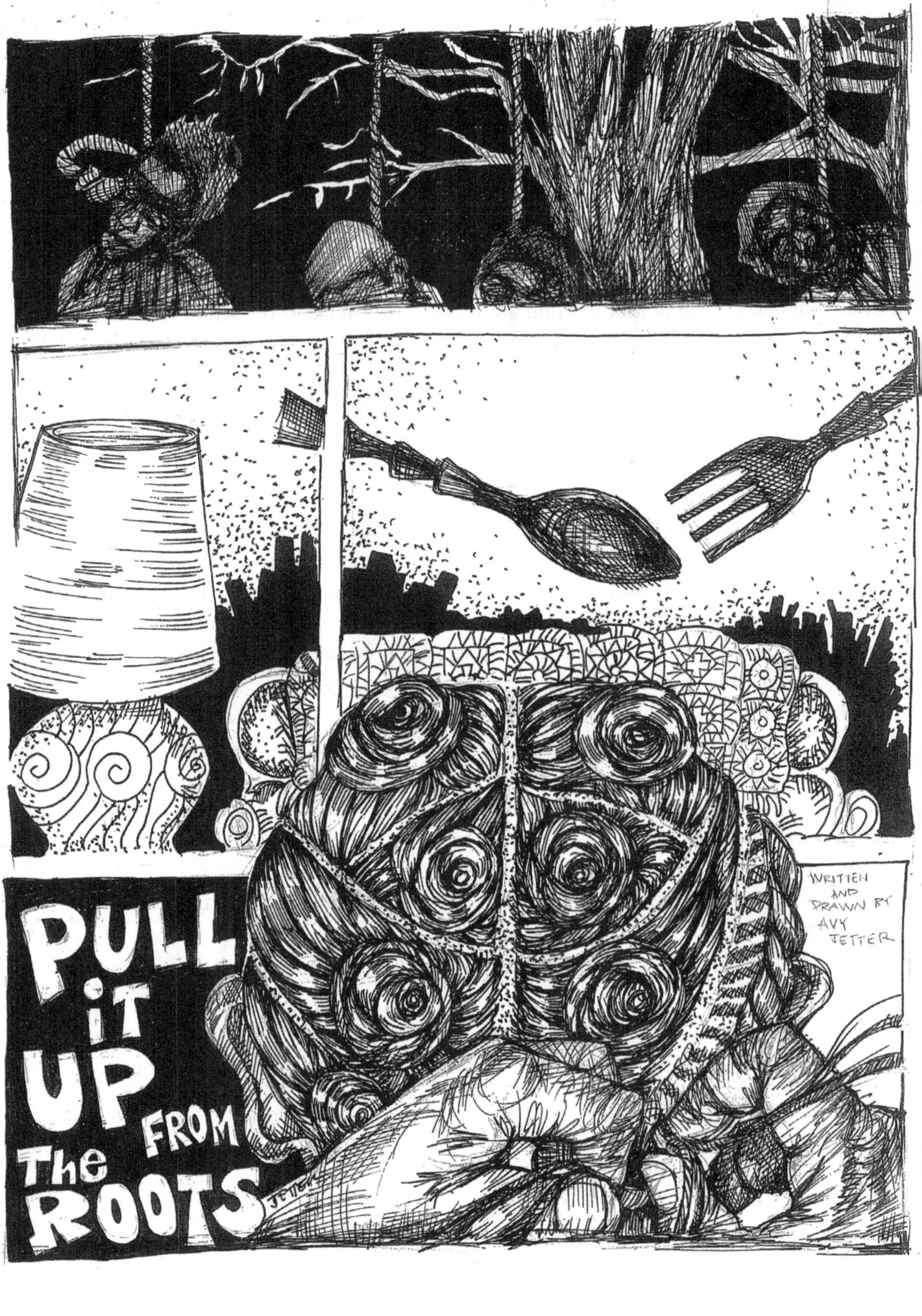
PULL it UP FROM The ROOTS
WRITTEN AND DRAWN BY AVY JETTER
JETTER

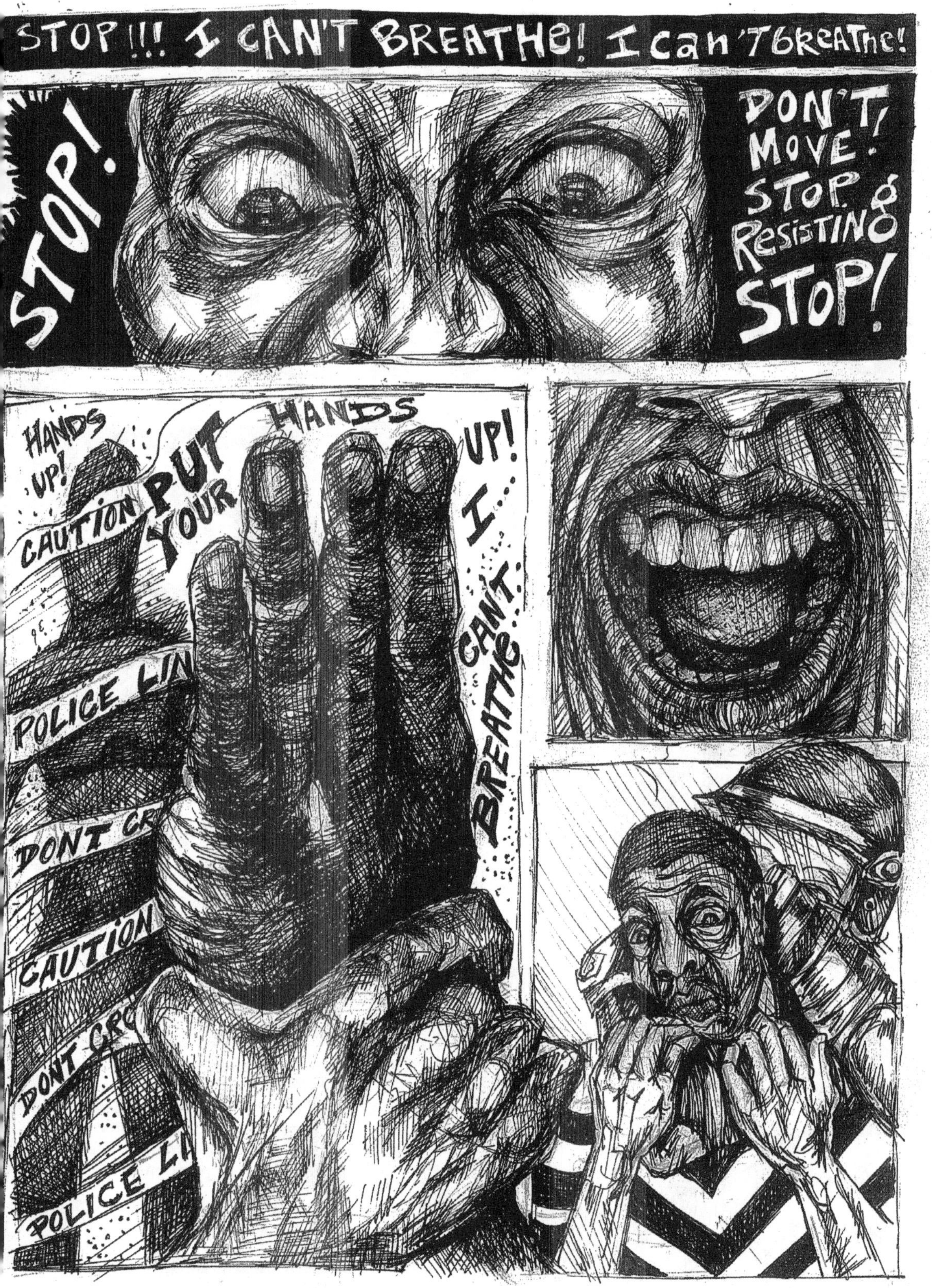
STOP!!! I CAN'T BREATHE! I can't breathe!
STOP!
DON'T MOVE! STOP RESISTING STOP!
HANDS UP!
PUT YOUR HANDS UP!
I CAN'T BREATHE
CAUTION
POLICE LI
DONT CR
CAUTION
DONT CRO
POLICE LI

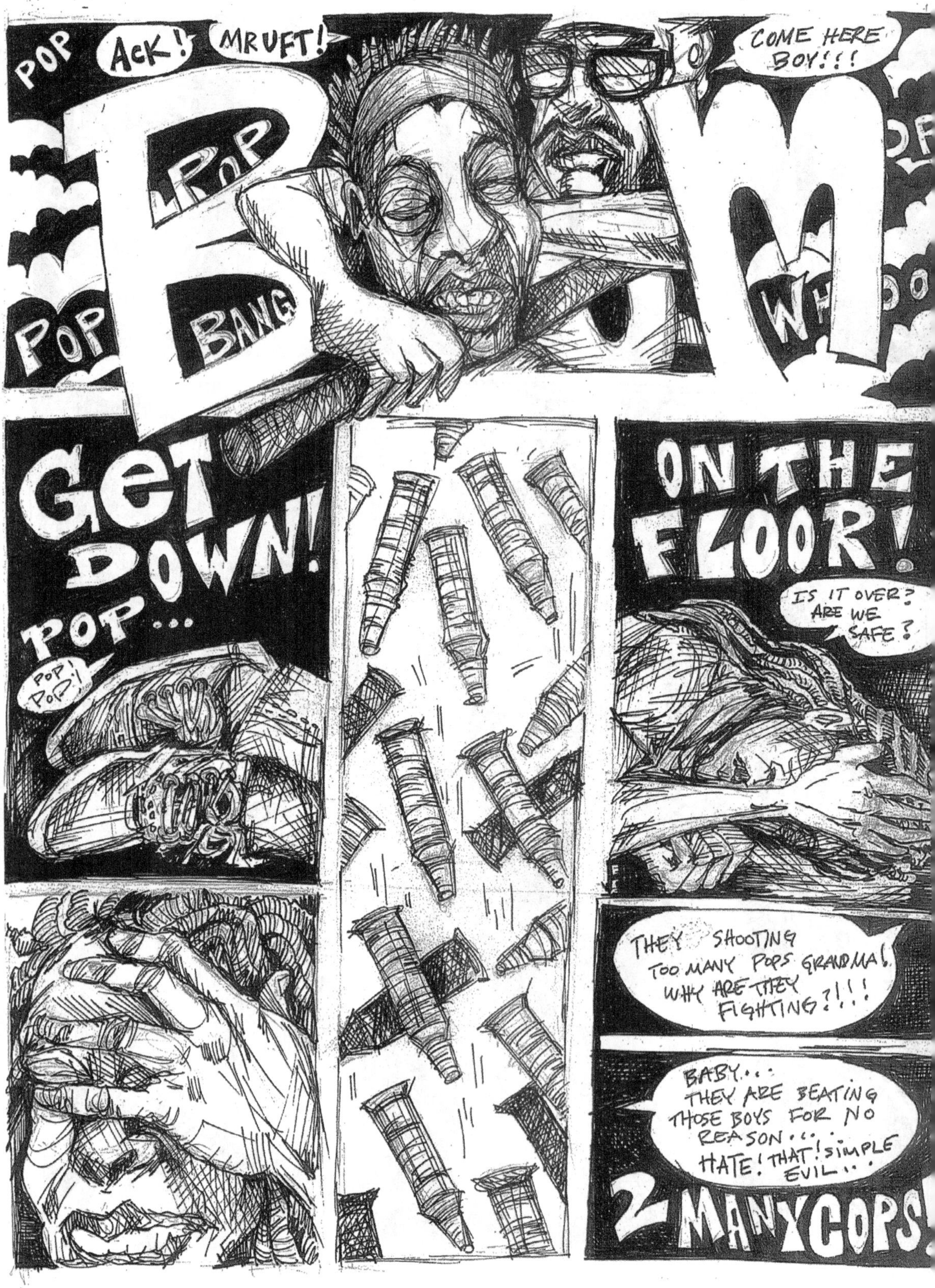
POP
ACK!
MRUFT!
COME HERE BOY!!!
POP
BANG
POP
GET DOWN!
POP...
POP! POP!
ON THE FLOOR!
IS IT OVER? ARE WE SAFE?
THEY SHOOTING TOO MANY POPS GRANDMA! WHY ARE THEY FIGHTING?!!!
BABY... THEY ARE BEATING THOSE BOYS FOR NO REASON... HATE! THAT! SIMPLE EVIL...
2 MANY COPS!

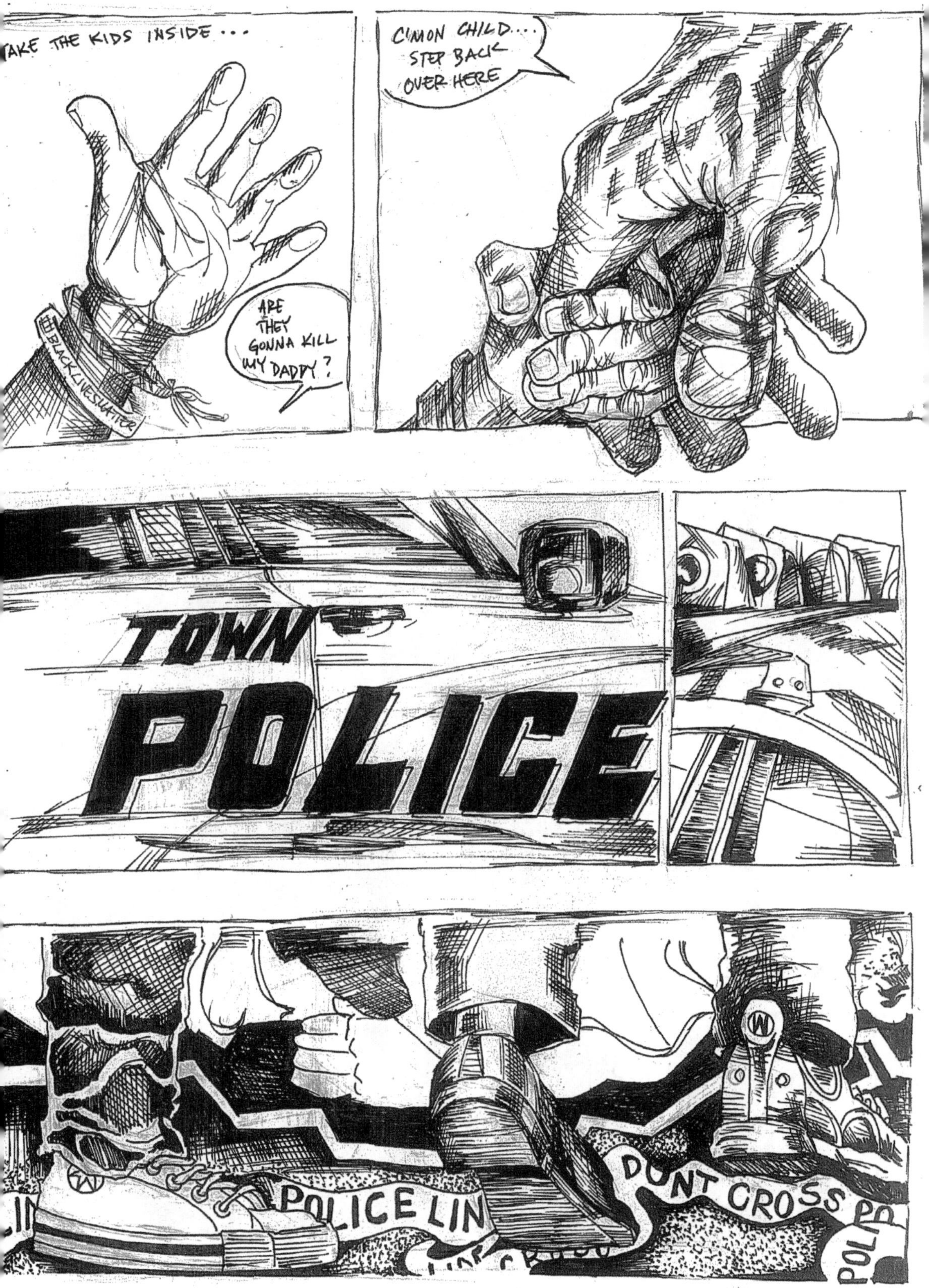
TAKE THE KIDS INSIDE . . .
#BLACKLIVESMATTER
ARE THEY GONNA KILL MY DADDY?
C'MON CHILD . . . STEP BACK OVER HERE
TOWN POLICE
POLICE LIN
DONT CROSS
POL

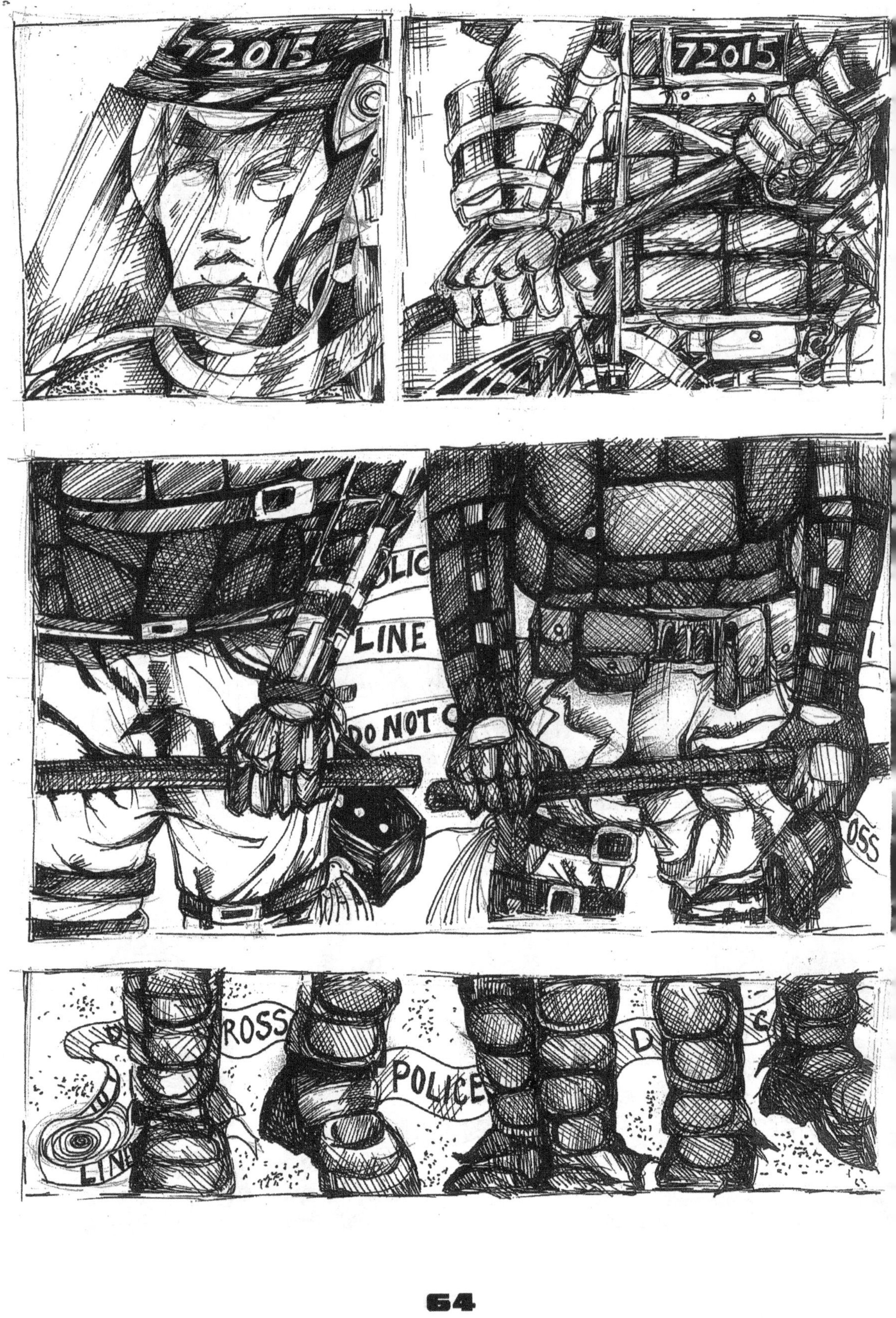
72015
72015
LINE
DO NOT C
OSS
ROSS
POLICE
LINE

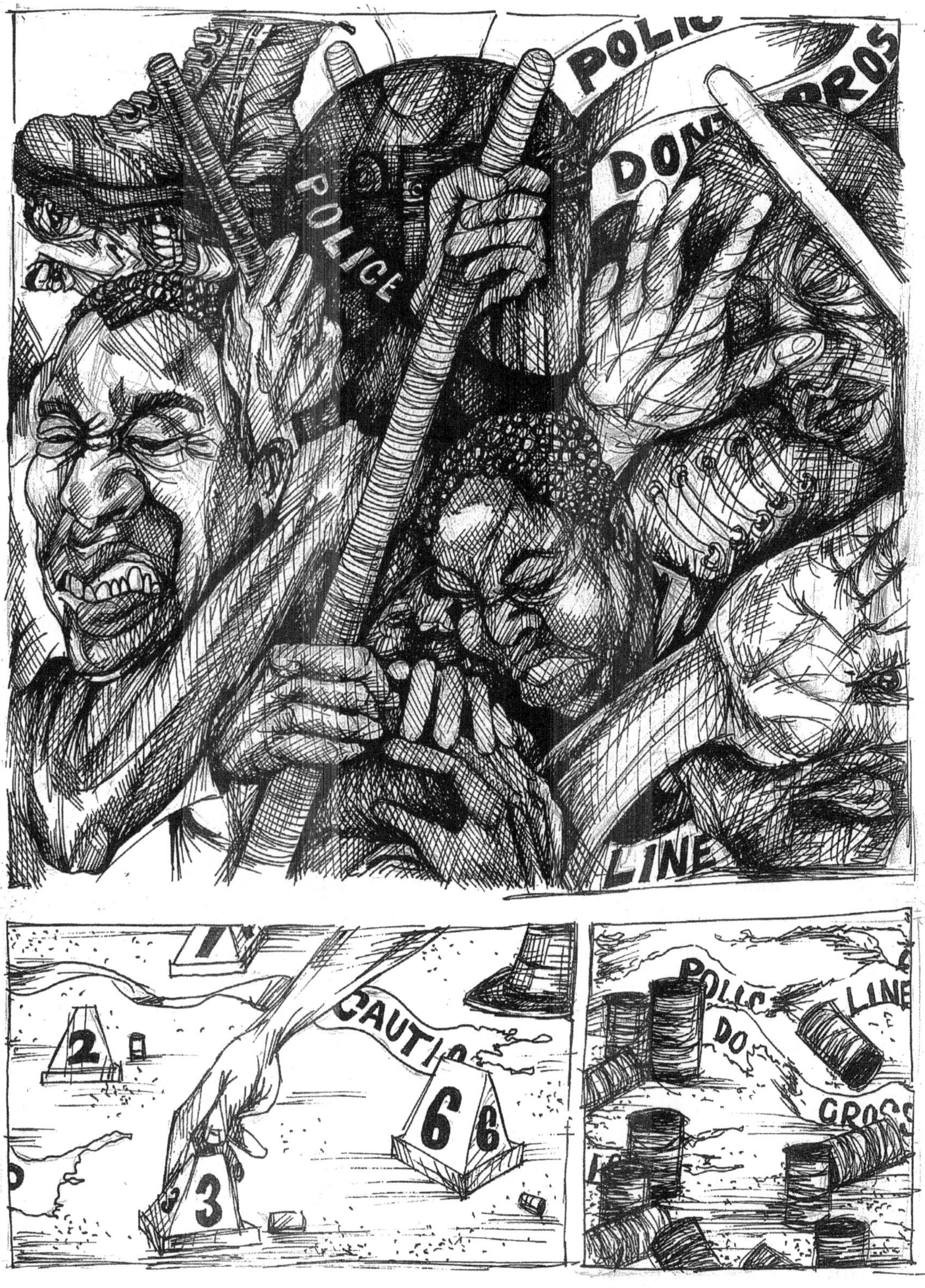

POLIC
DON
POLICE
LINE
CAUTIO
POLIC
LINE
DO
CROSS

# WHITE SUPREMACY:

## FERGUSON AND A NEW MESSAGE TO THE GRASSROOTS

### BY REYNALDO ANDERSON

*"If violence is wrong in America, violence is wrong abroad. If it is wrong to be violent defending black women and black children and black babies and black men, then it is wrong for America to draft us, and make us violent abroad in defense of her. And if it is right for America to draft us, and teach us how to be violent in defense of her, then it is right for you and me to do whatever is necessary to defend our own people right here in this country."*

—Malcolm X, Nov. 1963, New York City.

The resumption of state violence against black people after the brief respite of the civil rights era has sharpened the connection between art, business, politics, science and the violence against black people. The conscious and unconscious racism of white supremacy is reflected in the civic, political, economic, and international institutions that affect the life of black people everywhere. Furthermore, there is a direct connection between the 18th and 19th century slave patrols by whites under the aegis of states' rights in the founding documents of the country within the 2nd amendment; and the continuation of this behavior within the black codes established following emancipation to the emergence of the prison industrial complex and the Oath Keepers of North Saint Louis County, Missouri. Moreover, there is a clear relationship between the historical experiences of black people in America and the racism and violence exacted on black bodies during the Ferguson unrest.

While the Justice for Mike Brown coalition, the actions of the Ferguson rebellion, and other local protests in response to the brutality meted out on black and brown bodies up to this point have illustrated the fraught state of American democracy and the #BlackLivesMatter meme has provided a platform for the articulation of racial grievances, it is nonetheless a tragically sad imagined space that tells us more about self-affirmation of a marginal community and it does not have a societal resonance because black lives do not matter in America.

Therefore, despite President Barack Obama's recent attempt to mediate racialized tensions with a symbolic speech at the Edmund Pettis Bridge in Selma Alabama, it failed at the actual politics of racial reconciliation. This begs the question: what is the price of inclusion in American society if you are not white? More specifically, how did Americans arrive at this collapse of the social contract commonly referred to as The American Dream, why do the racist exclusionary practices persist, and what is the price of that exclusion?

The genesis of the Justice for Michael Brown social movement in Ferguson, Missouri, was in response to the brutal killing of Michael Brown by officer Darren Wilson with local African American citizens fighting against the legacy of white supremacy, racism, and oppression in the Saint Louis region. Soon spreading across the country to

Baltimore, New York, Cleveland, Charleston, and elsewhere, this ongoing struggle aspires to renegotiate or terminate the terms of what Charles Mills refers to as The Racial Contract.

Mills argues in contrast to the concept of a Social Contract where societies should be structured and regulated by a "defensible moral code", the Racial Contract "is characterized as an unjust exploitative society, ruled by an oppressive government, and regulated by an immoral code." Furthermore, this Racial Contract rests on three existential claims: "white supremacy both local and global exists and has existed for many years; white supremacy should be thought of itself as a political system, and finally, white supremacy can be illuminatingly thought of as based on a contract between whites." This Racial Contract has white elite signatories with all whites as beneficiaries of what W.E.B. Dubois described as the psychological wages of whiteness. This situation has led to a crisis in white Western civic society:

> "…the Racial Contract prescribes for its signatories an inverted epistemology, an epistemology of ignorance, a particular pattern of localized and global cognitive dysfunctions…producing the same ironic outcome that whites will be unable to understand the world they themselves have made."

First, The United States of America was established as a white supremacist Settler Nation that was developed on the annihilation of the indigenous population and the free labor of enslaved Africans that was part of the foundation of modern capitalism; Cedric Robinson notes this happened with the goal in mind of dominating people of color with "race as its epistemology, its ordering principle, its organizing structure, it moral authority, its economy of justice, commerce, and power." The ability to use violence against enslaved Africans was written in the United States constitution in the 2nd Amendment to ratify the use of slave patrols in states at a time when the majority of people living within many southern states were black. The concern with rebellion by enslaved Africans preoccupied white southerners. Following emancipation and the short period of Black reconstruction, this behavior was violently reinforced with the black codes and the state-sanctioned terrorist violence of the Klu Klux Klan during the Jim Crow era or as Douglas Blackmon refers to the period in his book Slavery by Another Name, "neo-slavery"; a time between reconstruction and WWII where the judicial system of the old Confederacy partnered with business and poor whites as neo-overseers to suppress black freedom through lynching, rape, pedophilia and miseducation.

However, following the limited reforms of the 1960s, the current politics of racist benign neglect represent the new chickens coming home to roost, with the post-civil rights emergence of what Michelle Alexander refers to as The New Jim Crow. The white supremacist creation of the prison-industrial complex that functions as a jobs program for working class and middle class white Americans has led to another crisis in American democracy to the extent that the New York Times recently reported over 1.5 million black men are missing from civic life in the United States and black women and children are under daily assault as result of the generations long drug war.

Although the election of Barack Obama was supposed to usher in a postracial America, it did not ultimately represent political or economic progress for the vast majority of African Americans. It ultimately represented white America's comfort with racialized management of white global interest with a Black face. However, Black representation does not mean Black empowerment. For example, although African Americans have more political representation in the American government today, this presence has had little impact on institutional white supremacy and has resulted in little more than symbolic politics that serve the global public relations image of the United States. This current state of affairs concerning symbolic politics and the modification of the most egregious forms of white supremacy has been in motion since the 1960s.

Since the 1970s, the American Black Freedom movement has been thwarted by assassination, racist politics, and the war on drugs, which has served as a war on black and brown people. Whereas, in the 1960s, there was a common foe in institutional white supremacy and a community political approach that identified the distinction between Malcolm X's House Negro (who loved his master) and Field Negro (who hated the master), by the '70s an approach emerged to contain the goals and aspirations of the black community. In general, the conservative wing of white racism formulated a discourse of black-on-black crime, welfare "queens," and personal responsibility to overcome structural problems, while itsliberal wing argued against black power on the basis of multicultural liberalism, patriarchy, and essentialism in the interest of performing a post racial discourse even as most of the benefits of diversity that blacks struggled for were obtained by white women.

These practices were institutionalized through an iron cage of miseducation, bureaucracy, entertainment, and multicultural liberal programs that transformed the spirit of the children and grandchildren of the old Jim Crow House Negro into a post-racial individual practiced in the art of self-denial, the illusion of inclusion, and consumed with being accepted by people who largely despise or pity him or her. Conversely, the dark side of this same structure was designed to break the spirit of the children and grandchildren of the Jim Crow era Field Negro to psychologically drive black men, women, and children insane through miseducation, special education, the entertainment of self-hate, underemployment, lack of healthcare, and incarceration to crush their will to resist White supremacy and engage in self-destructive behavior.

However, a new post-civil rights, post-Jim Crow generation has arisen in response to the murders and annihilation of black bodies that will engage their minds, art, language, and fists to resist and fight white supremacy. There is also a renascent movement and a global re-assessment of Black Power and grassroots activity in the new era of social media. Previously, Black Power and the grassroots were primarily defined as a cultural or political construct to galvanize the black community of the 1960s. Now, this struggle is amending the previous framework of Black Power and arguing that the new global Black power grassroots is an organic network influenced and held together by the messages they send each other through Facebook, Instagram, Twitter, and Snapchat that have radically reframed the media response to white supremacy and their allies. These black lives are increasingly recognizing their common struggle with people in other locales, indicated by the supported social media received by Ferguson protestors from Palestinians, Africans, and others. There is a need to attack and resolve the overall contradictions within an unjust white supremacist society and destroy the Racial Contract domestically and globally and to come up with a new synthesis that benefits not only the various black communities of interest but the other affected community elements of the broader society as well.

However, the need to be critical and self-critical, and at times strategically pragmatic will be necessary for the movement to recognize not all voices are honest brokers for progress but are actually hindering its advancement and continuing to front for local and global white supremacist interests. Yet, a new dawn is on the horizon, and it's rising from the east from the Afro-Asiatic world as the global balance of power is shifting back to that area of the world for the first time since the days of Christopher Columbus; and the rest of the Dark world is awaiting the hour of decision.

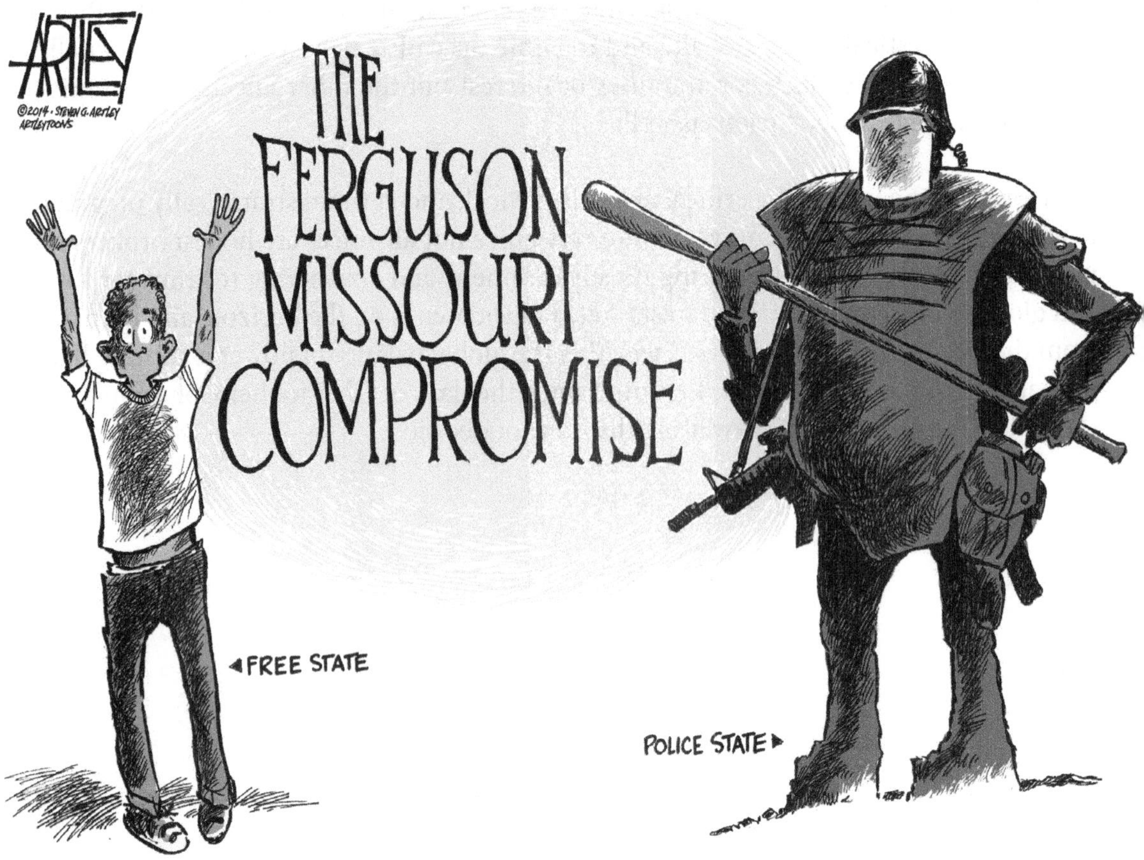
ARTLEY
©2014 · STEVEN G. ARTLEY
ARTLEYTOONS
THE FERGUSON MISSOURI COMPROMISE
◄FREE STATE
POLICE STATE►

**CARTOONS BY STEVE ARTLEY**

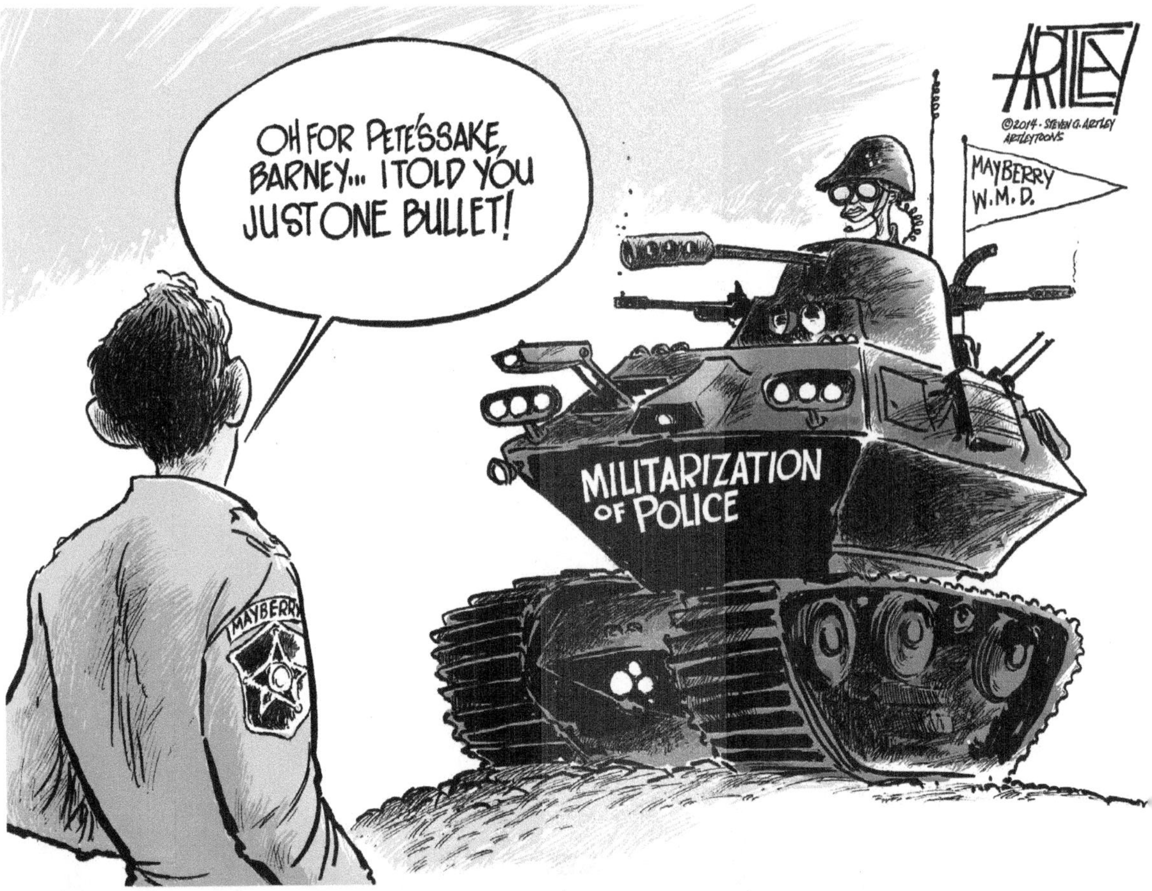
ARTLEY
©2014 · STEVEN G. ARTLEY
ARTLEYTOONS
OH FOR PETE'SSAKE, BARNEY... I TOLD YOU JUST ONE BULLET!
MAYBERRY W.M.D.
MILITARIZATION OF POLICE
MAYBERRY

Split

By Brandon L. Hankins

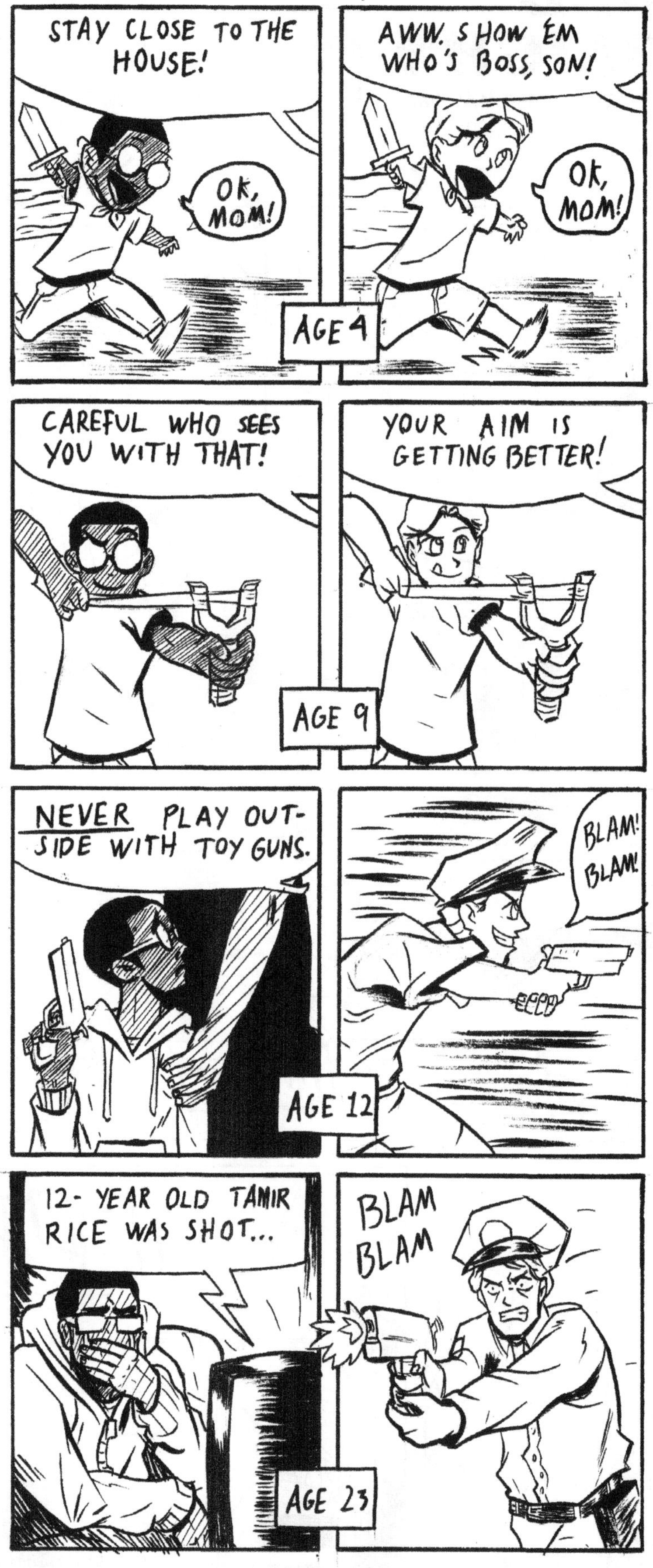
STAY CLOSE TO THE HOUSE!
OK, MOM!
AWW, SHOW 'EM WHO'S BOSS, SON!
OK, MOM!
AGE 4
CAREFUL WHO SEES YOU WITH THAT!
YOUR AIM IS GETTING BETTER!
AGE 9
NEVER PLAY OUT-SIDE WITH TOY GUNS.
BLAM! BLAM!
AGE 12
12- YEAR OLD TAMIR RICE WAS SHOT...
BLAM BLAM
AGE 23

# SCARED STRAIGHT

WRITTEN + DRAWN BY **JEROME WALFORD**



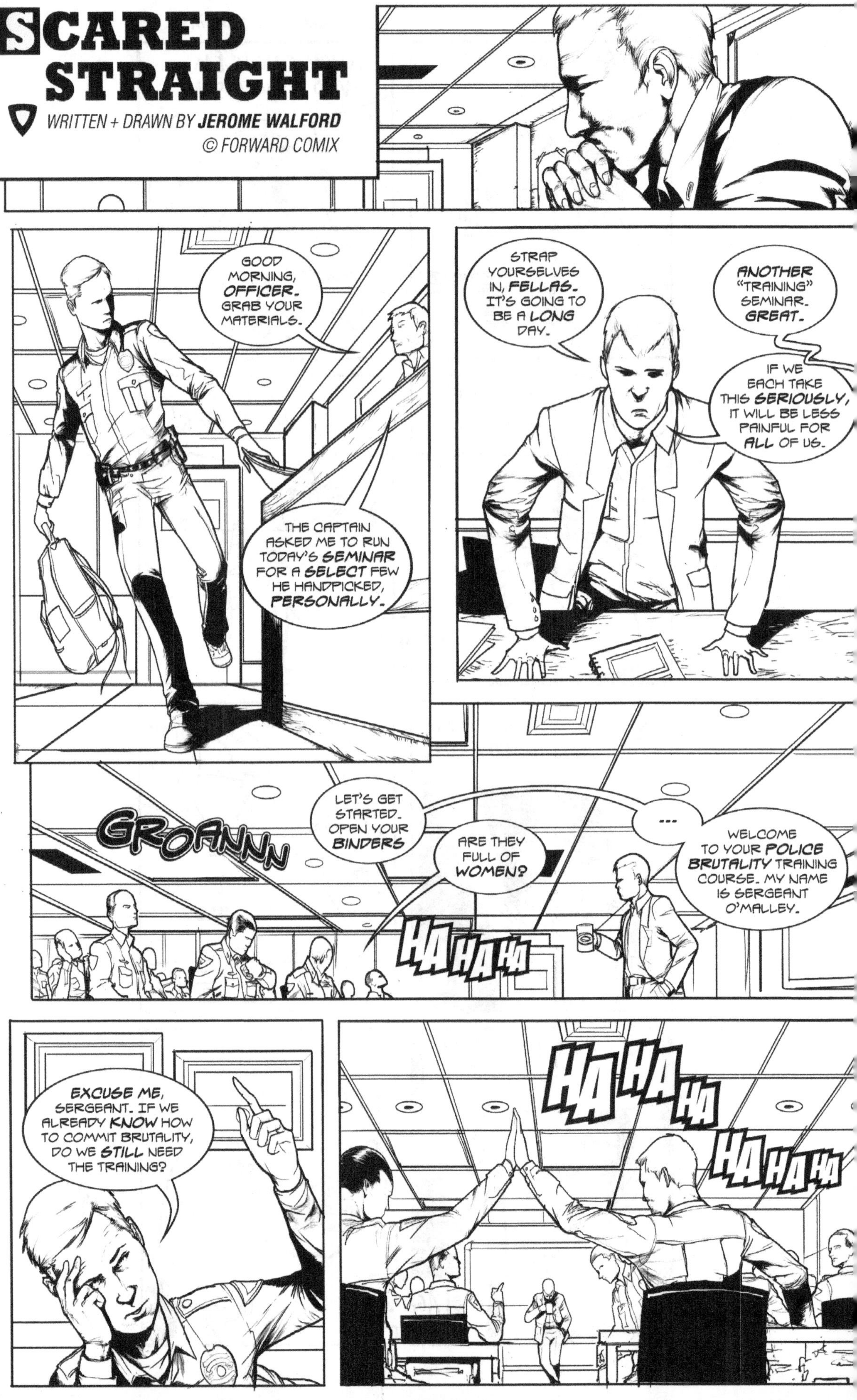
GOOD MORNING, OFFICER. GRAB YOUR MATERIALS.
THE CAPTAIN ASKED ME TO RUN TODAY'S SEMINAR FOR A SELECT FEW HE HANDPICKED, PERSONALLY.
STRAP YOURSELVES IN, FELLAS. IT'S GOING TO BE A LONG DAY.
ANOTHER "TRAINING" SEMINAR. GREAT.
IF WE EACH TAKE THIS SERIOUSLY, IT WILL BE LESS PAINFUL FOR ALL OF US.
GROANNN
LET'S GET STARTED. OPEN YOUR BINDERS
ARE THEY FULL OF WOMEN?
...
WELCOME TO YOUR POLICE BRUTALITY TRAINING COURSE. MY NAME IS SERGEANT O'MALLEY.
HA HA HA
EXCUSE ME, SERGEANT. IF WE ALREADY KNOW HOW TO COMMIT BRUTALITY, DO WE STILL NEED THE TRAINING?
HA HA HA
HA HA HA

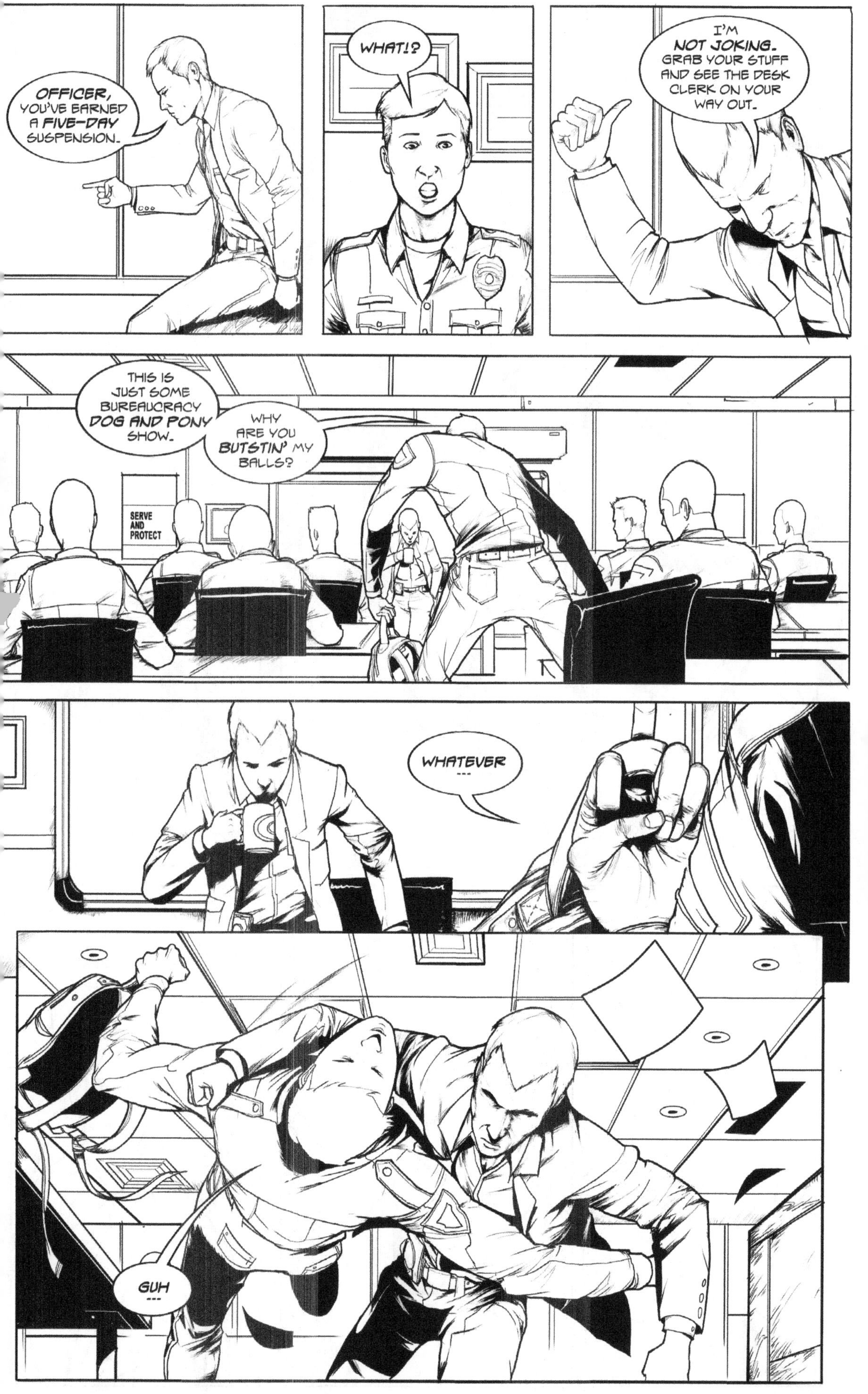
OFFICER, YOU'VE EARNED A FIVE-DAY SUSPENSION.
WHAT!?
I'M NOT JOKING. GRAB YOUR STUFF AND SEE THE DESK CLERK ON YOUR WAY OUT.
THIS IS JUST SOME BUREAUCRACY DOG AND PONY SHOW.
WHY ARE YOU BUTSTIN' MY BALLS?
SERVE AND PROTECT
WHATEVER ---
GUH ---

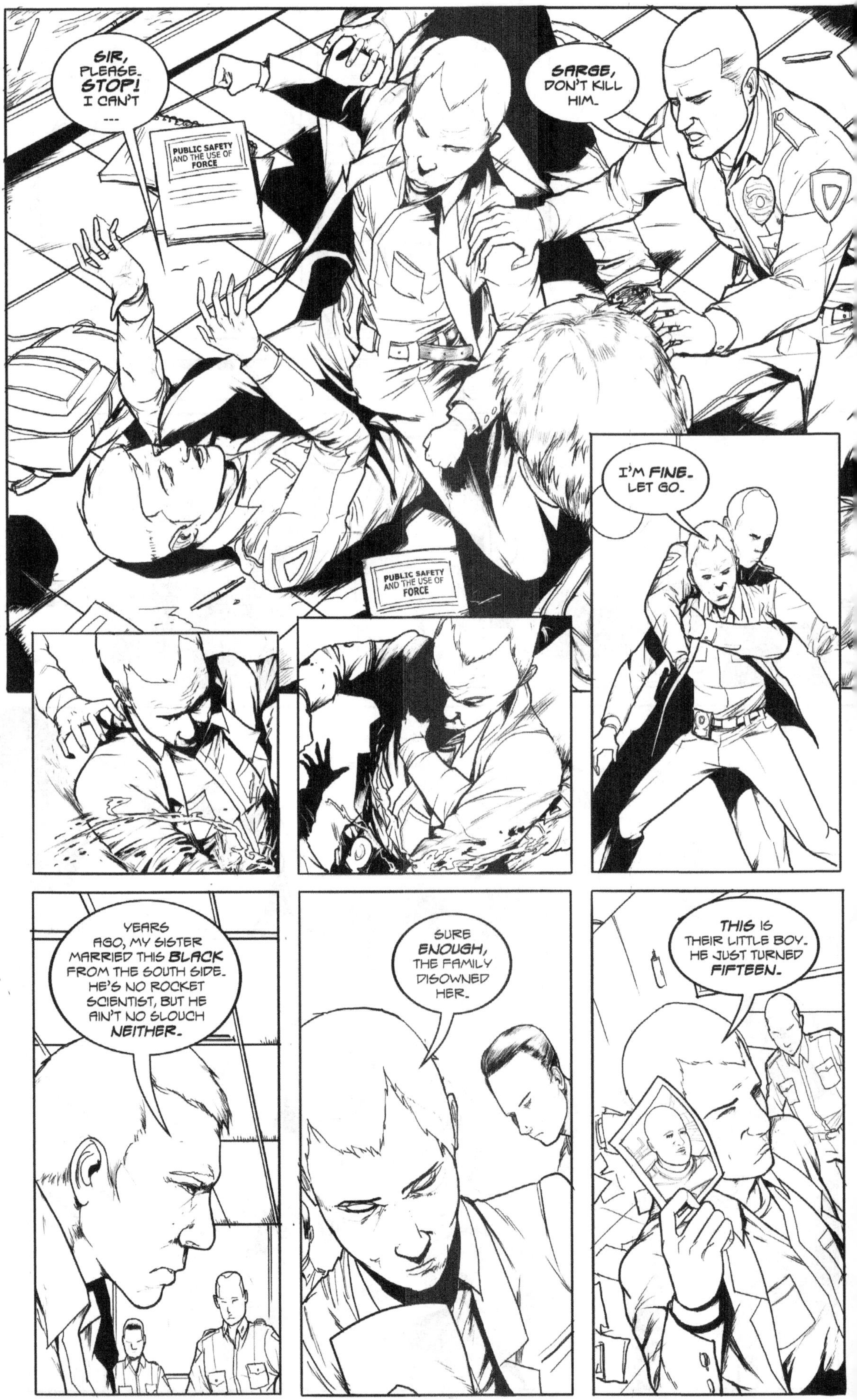
SIR, PLEASE. STOP! I CAN'T ---
PUBLIC SAFETY AND THE USE OF FORCE
SARGE, DON'T KILL HIM.
PUBLIC SAFETY AND THE USE OF FORCE
I'M FINE. LET GO.
YEARS AGO, MY SISTER MARRIED THIS BLACK FROM THE SOUTH SIDE. HE'S NO ROCKET SCIENTIST, BUT HE AIN'T NO SLOUCH NEITHER.
SURE ENOUGH, THE FAMILY DISOWNED HER.
THIS IS THEIR LITTLE BOY. HE JUST TURNED FIFTEEN.

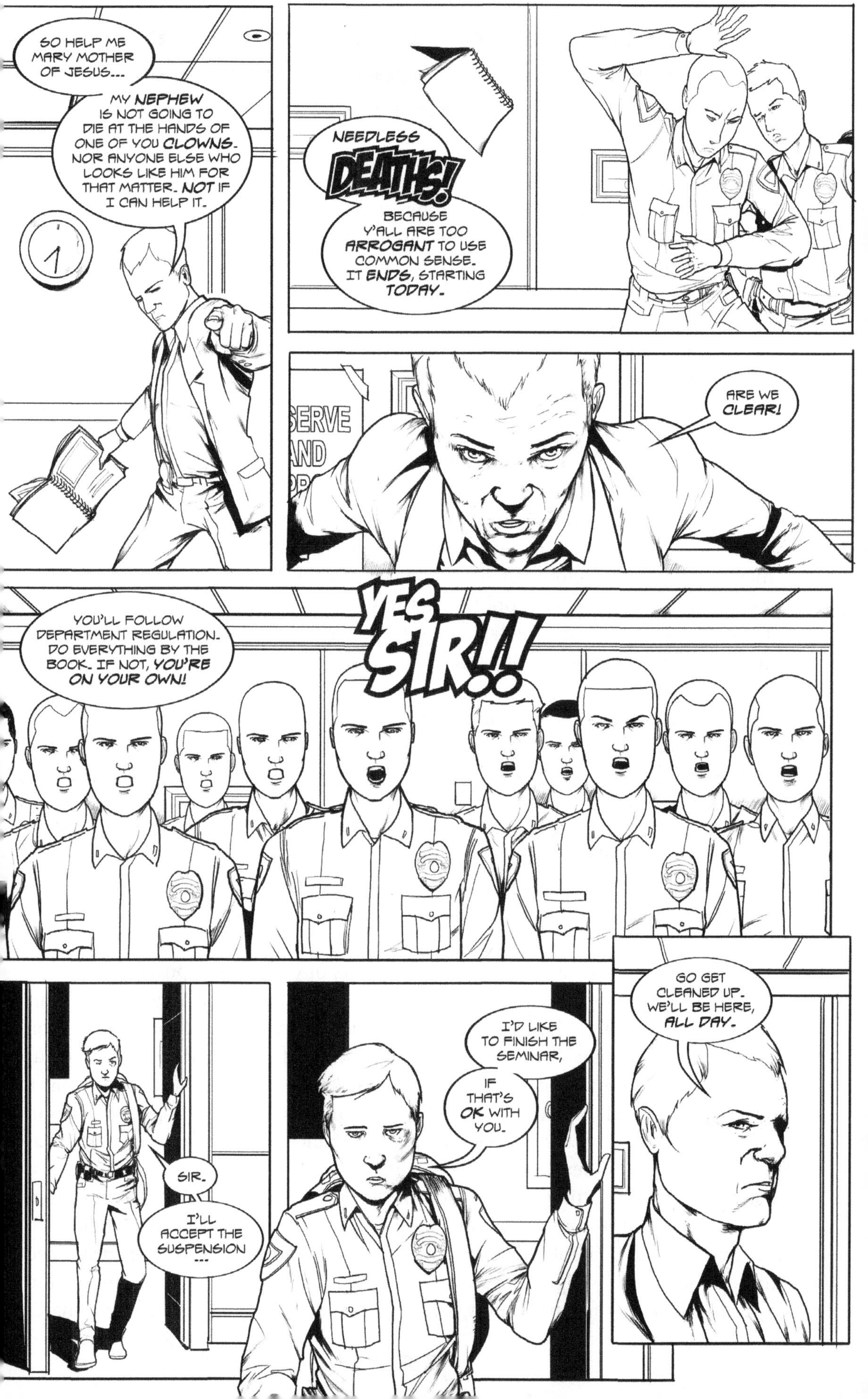
SO HELP ME MARY MOTHER OF JESUS...
MY NEPHEW IS NOT GOING TO DIE AT THE HANDS OF ONE OF YOU CLOWNS. NOR ANYONE ELSE WHO LOOKS LIKE HIM FOR THAT MATTER. NOT IF I CAN HELP IT.
NEEDLESS DEATHS!
BECAUSE Y'ALL ARE TOO ARROGANT TO USE COMMON SENSE. IT ENDS, STARTING TODAY.
ARE WE CLEAR!
YOU'LL FOLLOW DEPARTMENT REGULATION. DO EVERYTHING BY THE BOOK. IF NOT, YOU'RE ON YOUR OWN!
YES SIR!!
SIR.
I'LL ACCEPT THE SUSPENSION ...
I'D LIKE TO FINISH THE SEMINAR,
IF THAT'S OK WITH YOU.
GO GET CLEANED UP. WE'LL BE HERE, ALL DAY.

# NO BLACK CHILD LEFT BEHIND:
## SCHOOLS POLICING STUDENTS OF COLOR
### BY BETTINA L. LOVE

Most Black and Brown students who attend urban public middle or high schools in the United States enter their school buildings under police surveillance. In fact, inner city schools resemble airport security checkpoints (threat level orange) or penitentiaries rather than a place of learning, rooted in the ideas of egalitarianism. As students of color walk into their schools, it is customary for them to empty their pockets, remove nonessential clothing, and walk through metal detectors with armed police officers directing their movements. Moreover, after students enter the building their whereabouts are tracked in real-time by countless surveillance cameras. Thus, students of color are treated like homegrown terrorists who are tracked, attacked, and presumed guilty on-sight. From our schools' perspective, urban youth are radicalized by their urban conditions and skin color. For example, in the metro D.C. area, more than 30,000 surveillance cameras monitor students' every move. If you ask local school officials why such extreme measures are needed to ensure school safety, officials will highlight crime and school shootings; however, both stats are on the decline. Beyond surveillance cameras and metal detectors, in October of 2012, The New York Times reported that San Antonio's Northside Independent School District was tracking students' locations using radio frequency identification nametags. School officials declared that the nametags were to track student's daily enrollment, which is tied to school finance.

More importantly, as I have written before students of color are treated like criminals and domestic terrorists, tragic mass school shootings in the U.S. actually occur in suburban schools (e.g., Columbine High, Littleton, CO (1999); Heritage High, Conyers, GA (1999); Chardon High School, Chardon, OH (2012); Sandy Hook Elementary Newtown, CT (2012)). However, metal detectors are overwhelmingly placed in urban schools. As such, "the placement of school surveillance equipment is not based on actual facts, but school officials' perceptions of who is and who is not violent or a criminal, which are ultimately based on skin color, not criminal justice data" (Love, 2013, p. 5).

The ways in which schools police their students of color are important to understanding how police officers can kill Mike Brown, Eric Garner, and 12 year-old Tamir Rice without hesitation. Bodies of color are presumed guilty and under police suspicion from the moment they are born. The real-life indictment of Black students as suspicious and shady characters starts in school. They never get the freedom of innocence–as a child learning about life, naïve to the world or a young adolescent trying to learn from his or her mistakes. Thus, they never get a second chance. Kids of color are tracked as criminals from the day they enter school. For example, there are numerous cases across the country of police putting young Black and Brown kids, as young as six and seven years old, in handcuffs for "misbehaving." Their parents are forced to have "the talk" with their children earlier in life about being submissive, still, and overly polite when stopped by the cops because any slight movement and/or bass in your voice could land you in jail or dead. The talk is for their safety, but it robs them of their childhood. And that is the problem: Black and Brown children never get to be children. Never experiencing the feeling of just being free, a life of stress starts when Black youth enter school and are viewed and treated like adults. Educational scholar Gloria Ladson-Billings (2011) put a fine point on the treatment of Black students, particularly Black males, when she wrote:

> About a year ago I went into four schools in a city of about 700,000. The first school had mostly White students and I was amazed at how freely students were permitted to walk the halls and move about the classroom. It was only in the places where safety was an issue, where the children's bodies were tightly controlled (e.g. there was a portion of the play yard where cars were permitted to drive to drop off students). However, when I made my way to schools serving large numbers of Black students (and in one case the entire student population was Black) I could not help but notice the degree to which every aspect of the students' activities were regulated–not just what they were taught, but also how their bodies were controlled. They were required to wear uniforms; they had to line up in particular ways, they were prohibited from talking in social spaces like hallways and the cafeteria. There is only one analogy to this kind of regulation–prison. (p. 10)

Black kids are being killed inside and outside of schools. Internally, their spirits are being murdered by labels of dangerous, aggressive, and unteachable by the time they enter school. Outside the school, those perceptions are amplified and carried out with lethal force. As we hashtag the struggle–#ICantBreathe (referring to Garner's documented last words), #HandsUpDontShoot (in reference to Brown's alleged last action), and #BlackLivesMatter–in order to bring the pain and realities of Black people to the forefront of public conversation, we cannot forget that our youngest are in classrooms with their hands up, losing their breath, and questioning whether their education, and ultimately, their lives, matter.

## Reference
Love, B. (2013). I see Trayvon Martin": What teachers can learn from the tragic death of a young black male. The Urban Review, 45(3), 1-15.

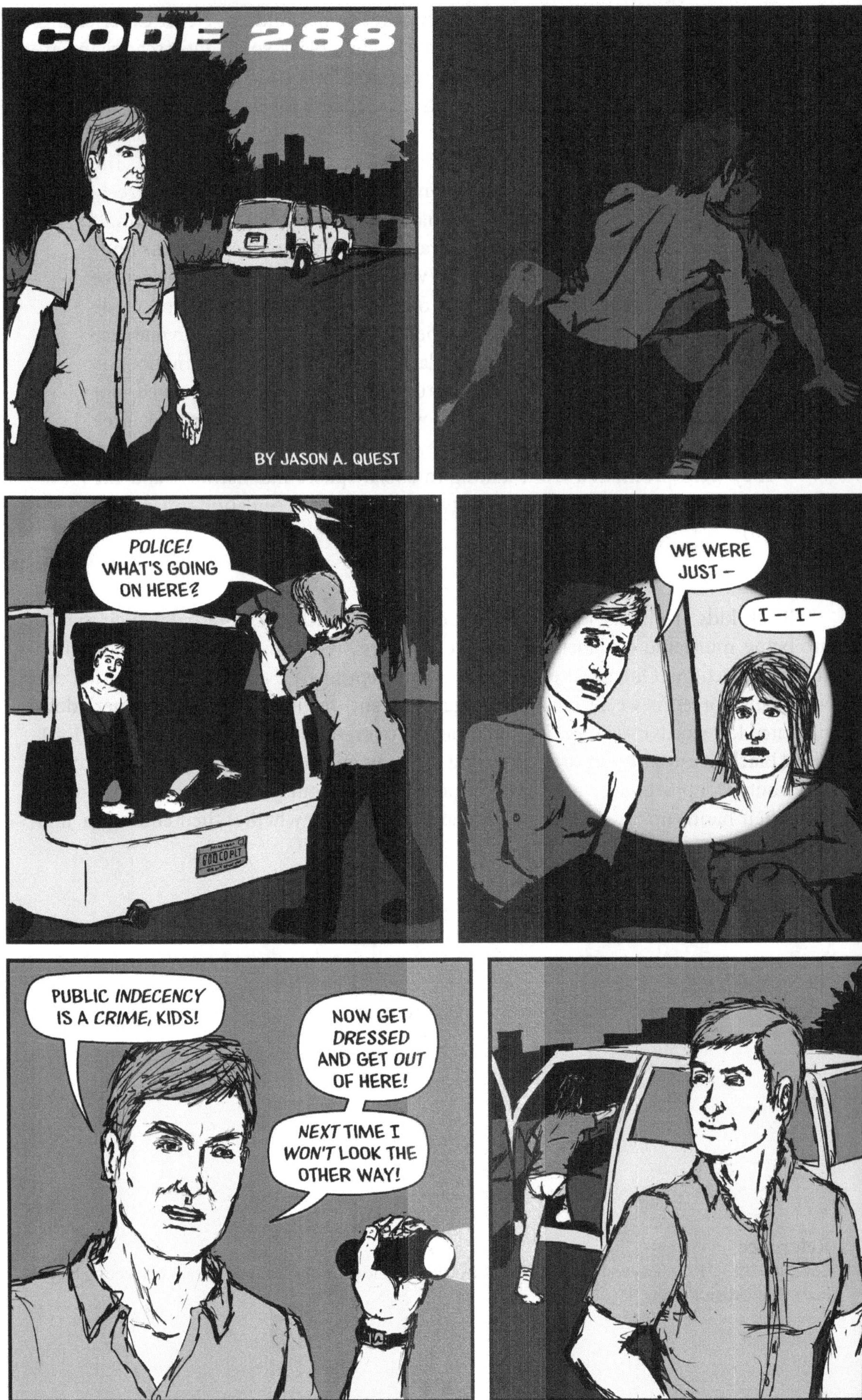
CODE 288
BY JASON A. QUEST
POLICE! WHAT'S GOING ON HERE?
WE WERE JUST –
I – I–
PUBLIC INDECENCY IS A CRIME, KIDS!
NOW GET DRESSED AND GET OUT OF HERE!
NEXT TIME I WON'T LOOK THE OTHER WAY!

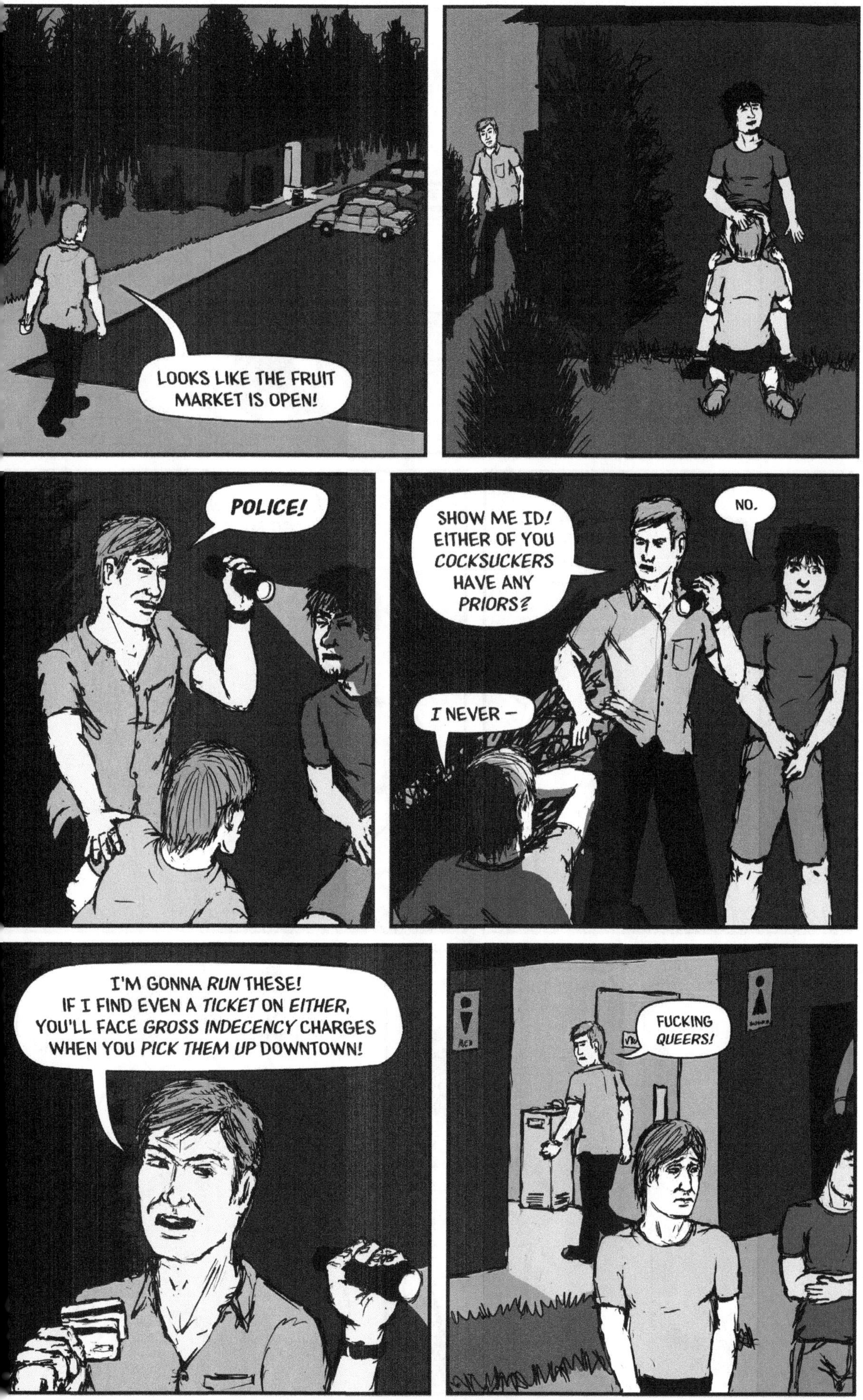
LOOKS LIKE THE FRUIT MARKET IS OPEN!
POLICE!
SHOW ME ID! EITHER OF YOU COCKSUCKERS HAVE ANY PRIORS?
NO.
I NEVER –
I'M GONNA RUN THESE! IF I FIND EVEN A TICKET ON EITHER, YOU'LL FACE GROSS INDECENCY CHARGES WHEN YOU PICK THEM UP DOWNTOWN!
FUCKING QUEERS!

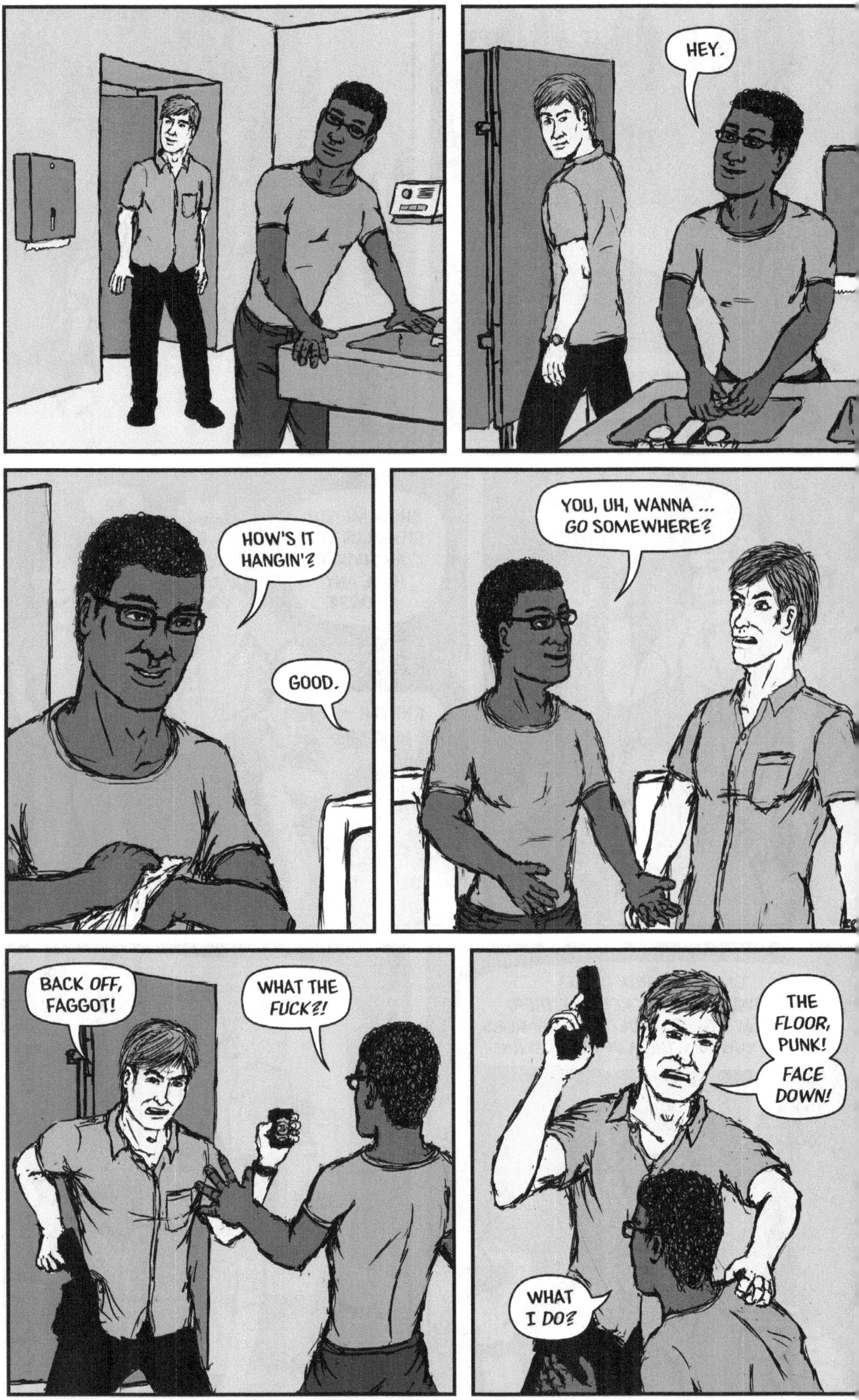
HEY.
HOW'S IT HANGIN'?
GOOD.
YOU, UH, WANNA ... GO SOMEWHERE?
BACK OFF, FAGGOT!
WHAT THE FUCK?!
THE FLOOR, PUNK!
FACE DOWN!
WHAT I DO?

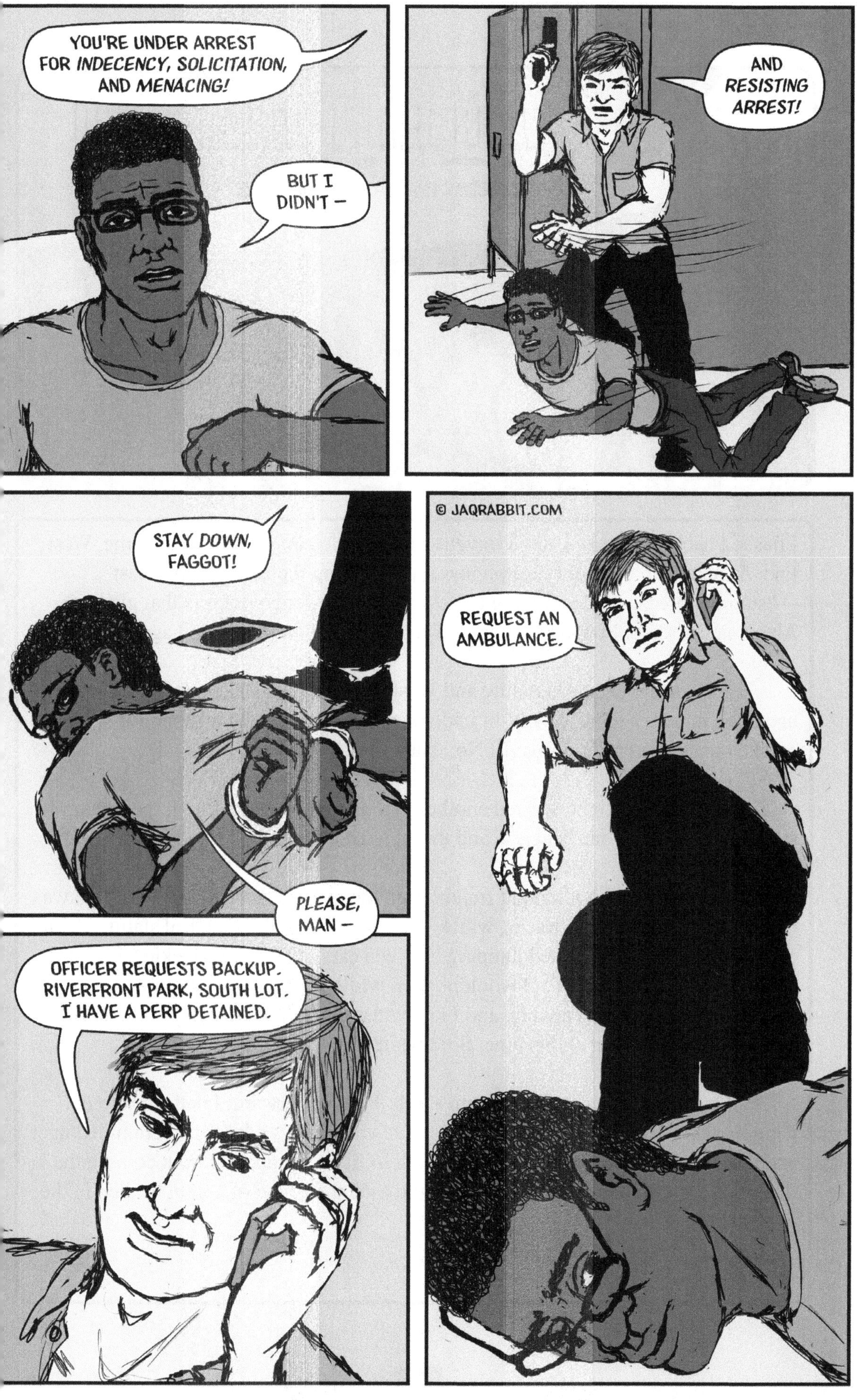
YOU'RE UNDER ARREST FOR INDECENCY, SOLICITATION, AND MENACING!
BUT I DIDN'T –
AND RESISTING ARREST!
STAY DOWN, FAGGOT!
PLEASE, MAN –
OFFICER REQUESTS BACKUP. RIVERFRONT PARK, SOUTH LOT. I HAVE A PERP DETAINED.
© JAQRABBIT.COM
REQUEST AN AMBULANCE.

# VIOLATION: A BIRTH STORY

### WORDS BY JASON HARRIS
### ART BY SESHAT'S BRUSH

I flashed back 10 minutes, mind traveling as I hustled up the sidewalk home. West End, Atlanta—no place for headphones, but I had my thoughts on full blast —"summer breeze … damn tonight feel just like the song/who was that girl with Alabama Ericka … Southern gurls..." Wait, why am I on the ground again?

I had a choice at Abernathy and West End Avenue. Make a left and cross under the tunnel: a dank, poorly-lit underpass known for being a haven for stick-up artists, rapists, and ne'er-do-wells. No, thank you.

So I went straight, walked another block, and crossed through the light rail station, past the bus line benches, and through the commuter lot.

It was late—the midnight freight train that passed through the West End was rumbling slowly by on its tracks, which were adjacent to the light rail station. A bit of adrenaline flowed—I liked jumping between cars, feeling like Jackie Chan, or a hobo on his way to Santa Fe. I wouldn't do it while the cars were moving through— one false step and it was a wrap, and I knew that the train would stop—it did the same thing every night at this time. So, I waited.

Once the line of cars ground to a halt, I bolted forward; I had work to do. Climbing up between the cars was easy, there was always a ladder. I scrambled up and jumped down on the other side, mindful to listen for another train coming the other way, as the sound of the engines could hide the sound of a train headed in the opposite direction.

One block. All I needed to do was pass through the park and cross the street and I was home. I surveyed the park, and I could see that there were guys still out on the basketball court playing; I began jogging across the park when I heard, "Freeze."

This was an area with plenty of police activity, so it wasn't a surprise. "I said, Freeze! Hands above your head!" Yet, that wasn't what made me stop. It was the distinct sound, a click of a gun safety, that gave me pause. I turned around, incredulous. He was standing near a streetlight—older, white, sheriff's hat perched on his head, gun in his right hand, flashlight in his left. The light went on, and he directed it at my eyes. "Put the bag down, hands above your head, and on the ground, face down!"

Why am I here? Face down, hands over my head, I catch the breeze carrying the aroma of ganja over from the basketball court barely 50 yards away. The court was quiet now—they were probably watching. I felt the weight of the gun through the wind it generated as he waved it above the back of my head. I could not believe that this cracker was patting me down. I didn't have anything beyond a school ID for him, as he mumbled something about it being against the law to cross the tracks while there was a train on it. But he and I knew the stated premise was mere window dressing for a deeper, viler exchange of information.

I had watched my requisite **40,000** murders on TV by the time I'd reached 18, which was the average for an American, but here I was, 19, and I had never had a gun drawn on me. What was I doing on the ground?

The whirl of the subway train, the vibration of the freight engines, that breeze, usually so welcoming, now foreboding, carrying the sickness of oppression with a badge pinned to it. It was over in an instant, and I ran home, pulse racing and blood on fire. Fate had placed me in a life far away from the dangers of Soweto, or even the gunfire of Chicago, Philly, or Compton, but that evening, for the first time, I said, "Fuck the police" … and really meant it.

"THERE'S NO SUCH THING AS **MONSTERS.** BUT THERE ARE ALWAYS **HEROES.**"

**HEROES.** THEY'RE WHAT THEY TOLD US THEY WERE.

SAVING PEOPLE. CATCHING THE **BAD GUYS.**

**MONSTERS.** THEY'RE THE ONES HEROES PROTECTED US FROM.

AT LEAST THAT'S WHAT OUR CHILDHOOD **TOLD** US

BUT THEN WE GOT OLDER...

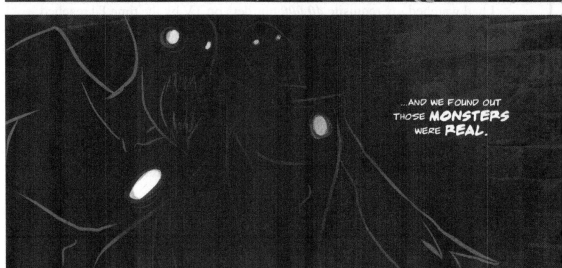

...AND WE FOUND OUT THOSE **MONSTERS** WERE **REAL.**

WE FOUND OUT THAT THAT MONSTERS OUTNUMBERED THE HEROES THESE DAYS...

SO WE HAD TO BE OUR **OWN** HEROES.

OUR OWN **SAVIORS.**

POP

THAT'S WHAT MY BRO TAUGHT ME.

BUT THAT WAS BEFORE.

BEFORE THE NIGHT I **LOST** HIM.

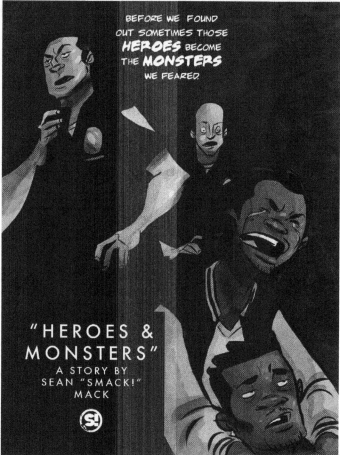

BEFORE WE FOUND OUT SOMETIMES THOSE **HEROES** BECOME THE **MONSTERS** WE FEARED.

# "HEROES & MONSTERS"
A STORY BY SEAN "SMACK!" MACK

# CAUGHT IN THE LOVER'S WAR:
## JAMES BALDWIN AND THE LEGACY OF QUEER ART-MAKING
## IN THE ANTI-POLICE BRUTALITY MOVEMENT
### BY JOSHUA PLENCNER

The truism that our modern media landscape is saturated with visual images is so overused as to be banal, and yet despite this truism artists and activists engaging in various social justice projects continue to wrestle with very basic questions about what visual images are doing, what's at stake in their circulation, and how best to mobilize their authority on behalf of freer futures. We know a bit; we have a few answers resolved through practice, a kind of historical trial and error. We know, for instance, that visual images can be eminently powerful stuff, capable of carving out collective emotional space to raise consciousness and impel organization. We also know that movement politics has long been drawn toward the production of critical iconographic moments, or what activist and visual culture theorist Nicholas Mirzoeff calls "countervisualities," to fight back against structures of domination that suppress political imagination through the maintenance of "official" state-sanctioned visualities. Where official visualities work by effectively normalizing social and political hierarchies in order to render unassailable our everyday experience of power, countervisualities are weapons wielded against the unequal distribution of social and political power. Countervisualities redistribute authority through creative action—inherently political creative action that undermines powerful institutions whose authority is most effective when it is accepted as given truth. Thus, to add to the list of what we know, we might also say that we're familiar with the notion that power wielded through making visual images is not monolithic, but rather is captured, forcibly, in political struggle.

But in the face of an increasingly brutal white supremacist state apparatus, one that metes out violence disproportionately on black and other bodies of color, women, queer folks, the poor, and the disabled seemingly without interruption, these questions wrestled with by artists and activists become especially grave. To work for racial justice in the anti-police brutality movement by producing alternative visual archives and countervisualities is literally life saving work. Black lives and their unfolding futures, expendable to white supremacy and the inhuman yawn of the carceral state, can be won back with the collective strength of movement that demands change. The terms are so very high, though—few being higher than life and death in any political struggle—that the desire to get it right, to destabilize the carceral state effectively, is a strongly intervening concern. How should artists and activists mobilize the unique force of their work to stir the movement forward and direct its complex energies toward necessary, life-saving political change?

Here I will argue that to answer this question artists and activists must look to our own archives. The history of white supremacy is long and deep; in America, it is imprinted in our very foundings, no matter which iteration of founding we privilege. Just as long and deep, however, are the material traces of resistance against white supremacy. Artists and activists leave their own imprints in this regard, which can be instructive. To take up the archive of prior activists and artists as an instrument of countervisuality today, then, is to think through the specificities of our current context in light of past struggles. Put differently, although past traces might not always translate exactly to the present shape of things, they can offer us a kind of practical incandescence—a lamplight to aid in our searchings forward. Just one example among many, perhaps, the work of James Baldwin provides an especially prescient legacy.

$

In his 1963 essay "The Creative Process," artist and cultural critic James Baldwin wrote: "Perhaps the primary distinction of the artist is that he must actively cultivate that state which most men, necessarily, must avoid: the state of being alone." If "most men" exist together in society, bound by the laws, policies, norms, and beliefs that shape human experience at any given moment, the artist is something different—an outsider who, with great purpose, moves beyond the boundaries of society and makes a life away from the pulsating networks of everyday life in order that he might more incisively interrogate the society that pursues him. By actively cultivating a state of being alone, the artist is giving himself the space to engage in struggle against the hard edge of society, the punitive edge that punishes evaders with consequentially damaging capture. To be alone as an artist is not simply to see the world differently; to be alone is the necessary condition to critique the world differently with knowledge that is foreign to it.

For Baldwin, this understanding of aloneness is a key component in the production of political art, or art that makes critical interventions against dominant structures of power operating in society. In order to "make the world a more human dwelling place" for all of us, to expose and hold up to the light the injustices and oppressions that violently circumscribe everyday life in America, Baldwin imagines the artist as one who fixes his craft on delegitimating those oppressions that steal from him the dignity of his own humanity. The artist works against society's desire to smooth over the ugliness of the past—an ethically monstrous desire to deny the historical brutalities of power while at the same time stoking fantasies of social stability that justify present brutalities as necessary for the maintenance of order. In working against society's program of conservation and maintenance, the artist must always be an "incorrigible disturber of the peace," a misrecognized and all-too-often demonized social ne'er-do-well whose disobedience and misbehaviors, though not always intelligible to society at large, nonetheless cut against justifications of everyday brutality that destroy actual lives in service of unethical political myths and fantasies.

"The entire purpose of society," writes Baldwin, "is to create a bulwark against the inner and outer chaos, in order to make life bearable and to keep the human race alive." In other words, society pretends itself a bastion, our safe haven and collective saving grace. But the irony of society as such is that in order to make life bearable, the "bulwark" of power must be wielded in a way that makes life precisely unbearable—precisely unlivable. Unbearable because the bulwark of power is a weight disproportionately distributed across society, pressing down on some lives with more force than others. Unlivable because the real effect of the disproportionate distribution is that power acts like an undertaker, burying the lives of those that threaten to disturb society's sheer surfaces of "achievement" and stability from within: "Society must accept some things as real; but [the artist] must always know that visible reality hides a deeper one, and that all our action and achievement rest on things unseen. A society must assume that it is stable, but the artist must know, and he must let us know, that there is nothing stable under heaven."

Despite having every reason turn his back and run, to flee the society that threatens to bury him, Baldwin argues that the artist has a "peculiar" responsibility to society. The artist "must let us know." Issuing from the outer darkness, the artist "must never cease warring with [society], for its sake and for his own." The peculiarity of this responsibility, not to mention the seriousness of its demand, is lodged in an unsettled understanding the artist has of the myths and fantasies that both hold together the social order and rip it apart from the inside. Because the artist has cultivated aloneness—an interrogative posture—the artist has developed the critical tools and ethical energies necessary to reveal the tragic depths of social myth. Baldwin writes, "In the same way that to become a social human being one modifies and suppresses and, ultimately, without great courage, lies to oneself about all one's interior, uncharted chaos, so have we, as a nation, modified and suppressed and lied about all the darker forces of our history." Self and nation are not mirrors but ghosts that haunt one another, projecting careful order for the sake of bad myths.

The carefully ordered social whole is composed of a series of lies—intimate betrayals, both to oneself and one's kin. Through all of this, Baldwin sees the artist, in his aloneness, as specially attenuated to the shape and texture of these lies and lays in him the responsibility to reveal them, those secrets buried beneath society's artificially settled surface. At the conclusion of his essay, though, Baldwin twists the earlier peculiarity of that responsibility to himself and society into something all too familiar for all of us—love. "Societies never know it," he writes, "but the war of an artist with his society is a lover's war, and he does, at his best, what lovers do, which is to reveal the beloved to himself and, with that revelation, make freedom real." In the end, although the artist may be alone in his agonistic struggle with society, he is not, for Baldwin, unattached.

§

The myriad organizations currently working against police violence in America are diverse in composition, mission, and tactics. Although their messages were amplified in the wake of a series of extrajudicial police killings in the summer and fall of 2014—particularly the killings of Michael Brown in Ferguson, MO, Eric Garner on Staten Island, NY, and Tamir Rice, just a 12-year-old boy, in Cleveland, OH—it is short-sighted to consider the political work of these organizations as driven primarily by reaction. The legacies of the "lover's war" written about by James Baldwin in 1963 structure the current movement, and in order to understand the possibilities available to activists and artists today we must work through these legacies, consider what challenges and resources they offer us, and experiment with how we can best continue to mobilize our work.

Baldwin's ideal artist is alone but not unattached, and in that aloneness is intensely critical. In this way, we can imagine aloneness to be a sensibility as opposed to a lack, a positive posture towards the world; artists are not missing anything despite being out-side of society that chases them. Imagined as a sensibility, then—a way of seeing and critiquing, of producing the countervisualities that work against dominant and oppres-sive institutions—we can see how many of the most effective organizers working today carry forward Baldwin's legacy of the lover's war.

For instance, take the women at the genesis of #BlackLivesMatter. Alicia Garza, Patrisse Cullors, and Opal Tometi, working with a number of other activists, artists, designers, and allies, put together what would become one of the strongest rallying cries of the early movement—a countervisual-verbal mix of artistic punch and provi-dential organizing tactics. Explicitly built as a "labor and love of queer black women" for the lives cut down and buried by police violence and the society that warrants it, #BlackLivesMatter is an example of the centrality of love to critical political organizing. And in both cases—Baldwin and #BlackLivesMatter—queer sexualities are experiential grounds for unique forms of anti-racist critique and countervisual revelation. The love central to the war is doubly radical.

Yet diverse and resilient as the movement continues to be, it is ongoing. Perhaps, then, if the agonism of Baldwin's lover's war is perpetual, we must also think it as total—the lover's war is total war, a full mobilization of the violently dispossessed and their archives against the political institutions that authorize the violence carried out against them. The artist's love is radical, ferocious and uncouth, aimed at the heart of his po-litical adversary precisely because the heart is what he is most responsible toward, "for its sake and for his own." In this environment, activists and allies cannot abide by calls to simply better represent the movement through more effective image making. We don't need countervisualities that peddle better branding. What we need to organize in a media landscape saturated with images is more images, more perspectives and styles, more creative projects and venues, more expressions of radical love for ourselves and each other—we need more art.

## Bibliography

Nicholas Mirzoeff. 2011. *The Right to Look: A Counterhistory of Visuality*. Durham, NC: Duke University Press.

Baldwin, James. 1985. *The Price of the Ticket: Collected Nonfiction 1948-1985*. New York: St. Martin's Press.

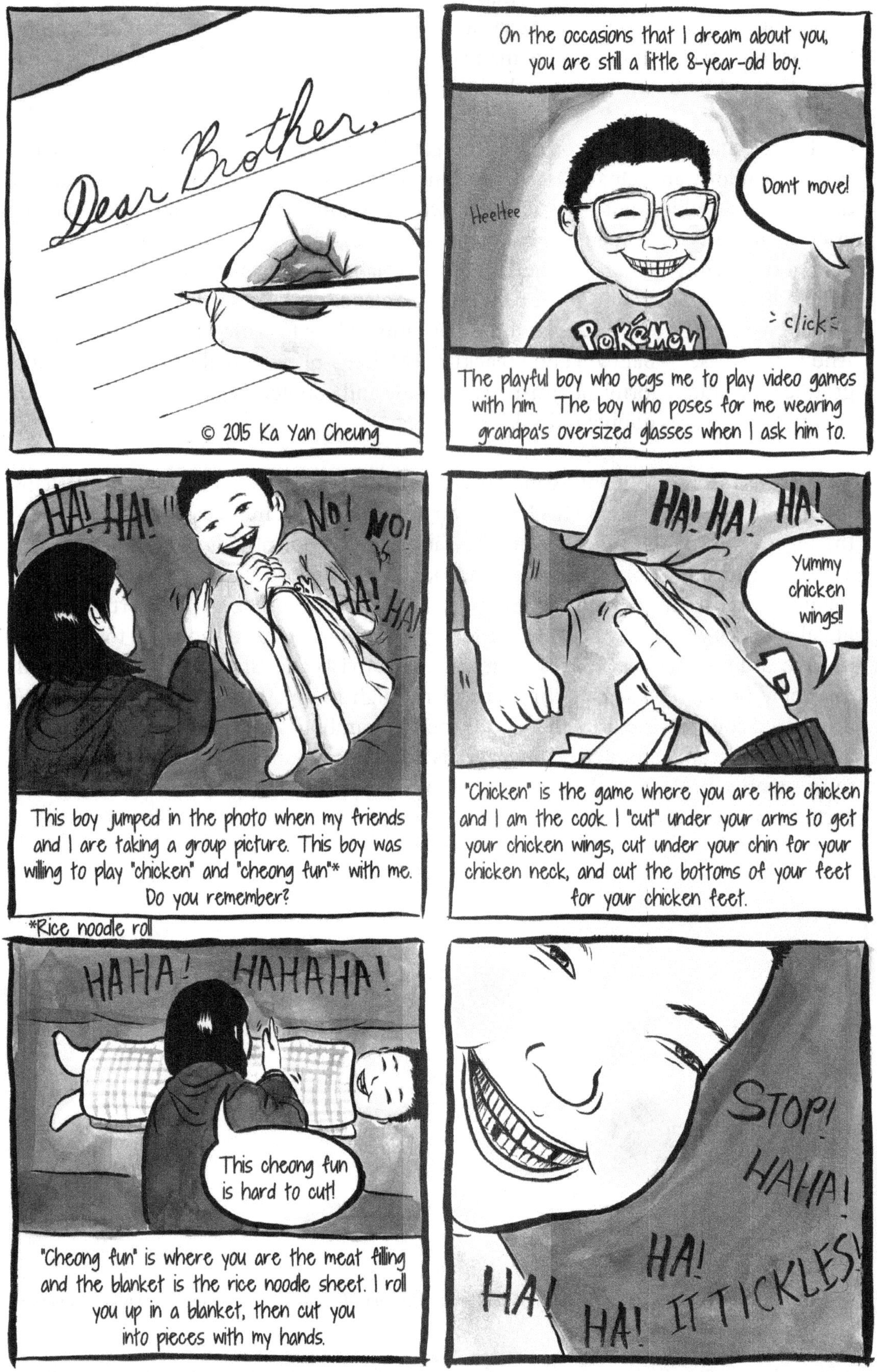
Dear Brother,
© 2015 Ka Yan Cheung
On the occasions that I dream about you, you are still a little 8-year-old boy.
HeeHee
Don't move!
Pokémon
click
The playful boy who begs me to play video games with him. The boy who poses for me wearing grandpa's oversized glasses when I ask him to.
HA! HA!
NO! NO!
HA! HA!
This boy jumped in the photo when my friends and I are taking a group picture. This boy was willing to play "chicken" and "cheong fun"* with me. Do you remember?
*Rice noodle roll
HA! HA! HA!
Yummy chicken wings!!
"Chicken" is the game where you are the chicken and I am the cook. I "cut" under your arms to get your chicken wings, cut under your chin for your chicken neck, and cut the bottoms of your feet for your chicken feet.
HAHA! HAHAHA!
This cheong fun is hard to cut!
"Cheong fun" is where you are the meat filling and the blanket is the rice noodle sheet. I roll you up in a blanket, then cut you into pieces with my hands.
STOP! HAHA!
HA! HA! HA! IT TICKLES!

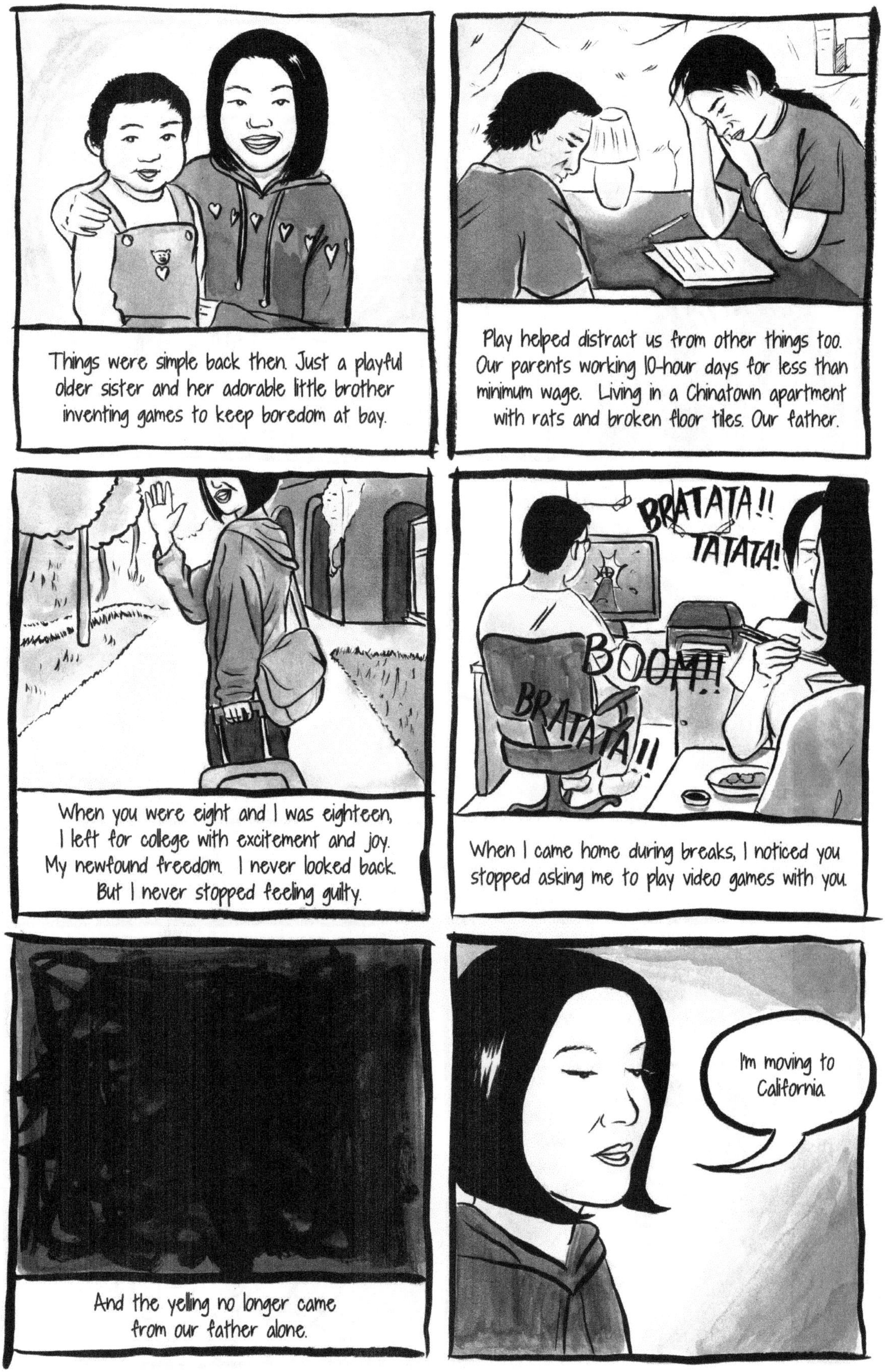

Things were simple back then. Just a playful older sister and her adorable little brother inventing games to keep boredom at bay.
Play helped distract us from other things too. Our parents working 10-hour days for less than minimum wage. Living in a Chinatown apartment with rats and broken floor tiles. Our father.
When you were eight and I was eighteen, I left for college with excitement and joy. My newfound freedom. I never looked back. But I never stopped feeling guilty.
BRATATA!!
TATATA!
BOOM!!
BRATATA!!
When I came home during breaks, I noticed you stopped asking me to play video games with you.
And the yelling no longer came from our father alone.
I'm moving to California.

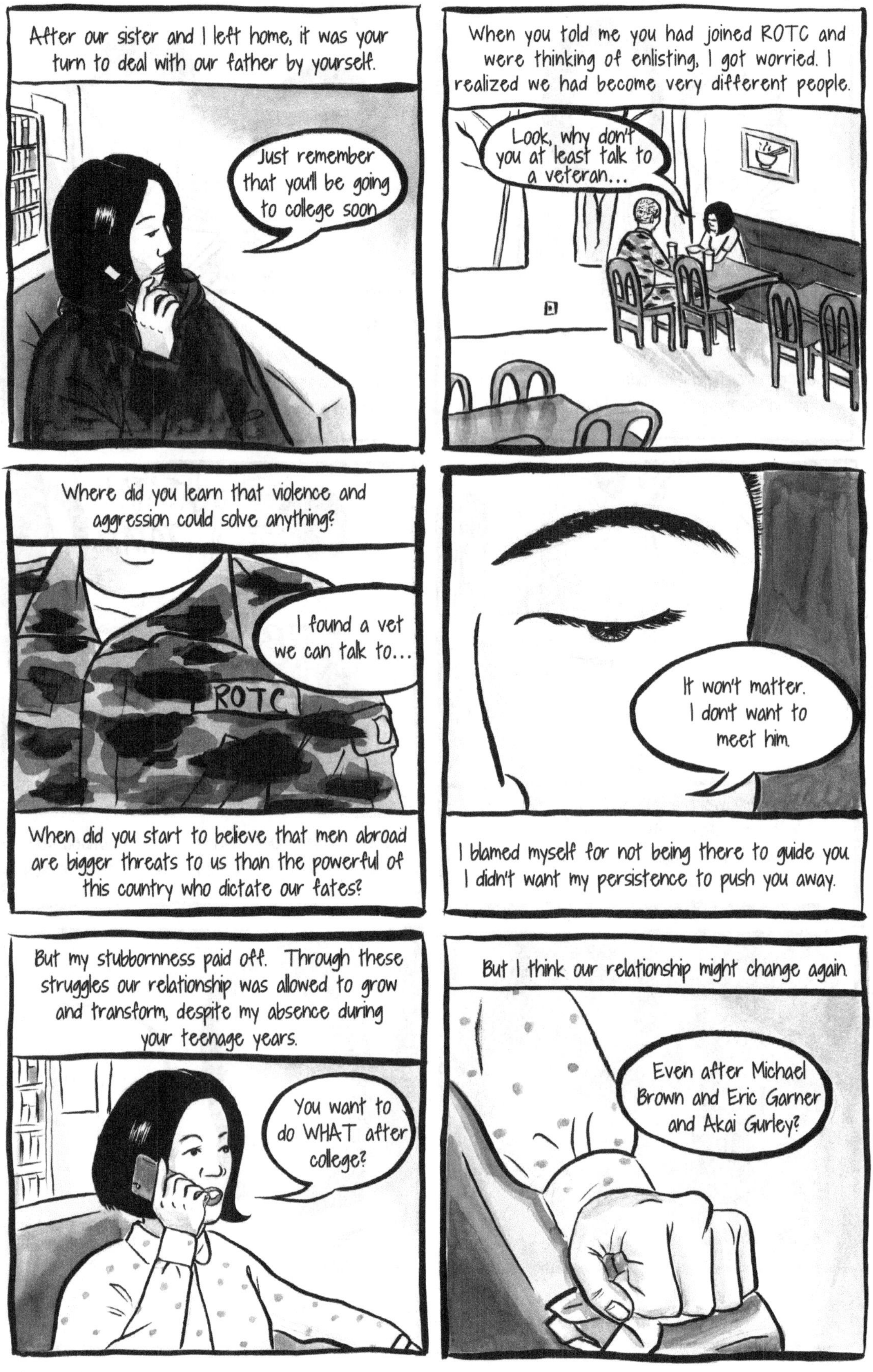

After our sister and I left home, it was your turn to deal with our father by yourself.
Just remember that you'll be going to college soon
When you told me you had joined ROTC and were thinking of enlisting, I got worried. I realized we had become very different people.
Look, why don't you at least talk to a veteran...
Where did you learn that violence and aggression could solve anything?
I found a vet we can talk to...
ROTC
When did you start to believe that men abroad are bigger threats to us than the powerful of this country who dictate our fates?
It won't matter. I don't want to meet him.
I blamed myself for not being there to guide you. I didn't want my persistence to push you away.
But my stubbornness paid off. Through these struggles our relationship was allowed to grow and transform, despite my absence during your teenage years.
You want to do WHAT after college?
But I think our relationship might change again.
Even after Michael Brown and Eric Garner and Akai Gurley?

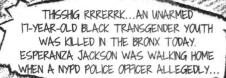
THISSHIG RRRERRK...AN UNARMED 17-YEAR-OLD BLACK TRANSGENDER YOUTH WAS KILLED IN THE BRONX TODAY. ESPERANZA JACKSON WAS WALKING HOME WHEN A NYPD POLICE OFFICER ALLEGEDLY...

GOD. Another one.

...SHOT HER FIVE TIMES. THE OFFICER WHO ALLEGEDLY SHOT HER CLAIMS THAT HE THOUGHT SHE WAS PULLING OUT A GUN WHEN SHE REACHED INTO HER PURSE FOR HER ID CARD...

It's only January and this is the third one I've heard so far. Innocent people killed and racist killer cops going off scot-free...It's no longer news.

Please don't let it be an Asian cop, please don't let it be an Asian cop. Black and Asian relations do not need this.

THE OFFICER WHO FIRED THE SHOTS, CHIU-WAI CHEUNG, IS A 25-YEAR-OLD CHINESE AMERICAN AND A NATIVE OF QUEENS, NEW YORK. HE CLAIMS THAT HE FIRED OUT OF FEAR, OUT OF SELF-DEFENSE: *SHE...IS SO TALL, YOU KNOW. I REALLY FEARED FOR MY LIFE.*

Wait. What.

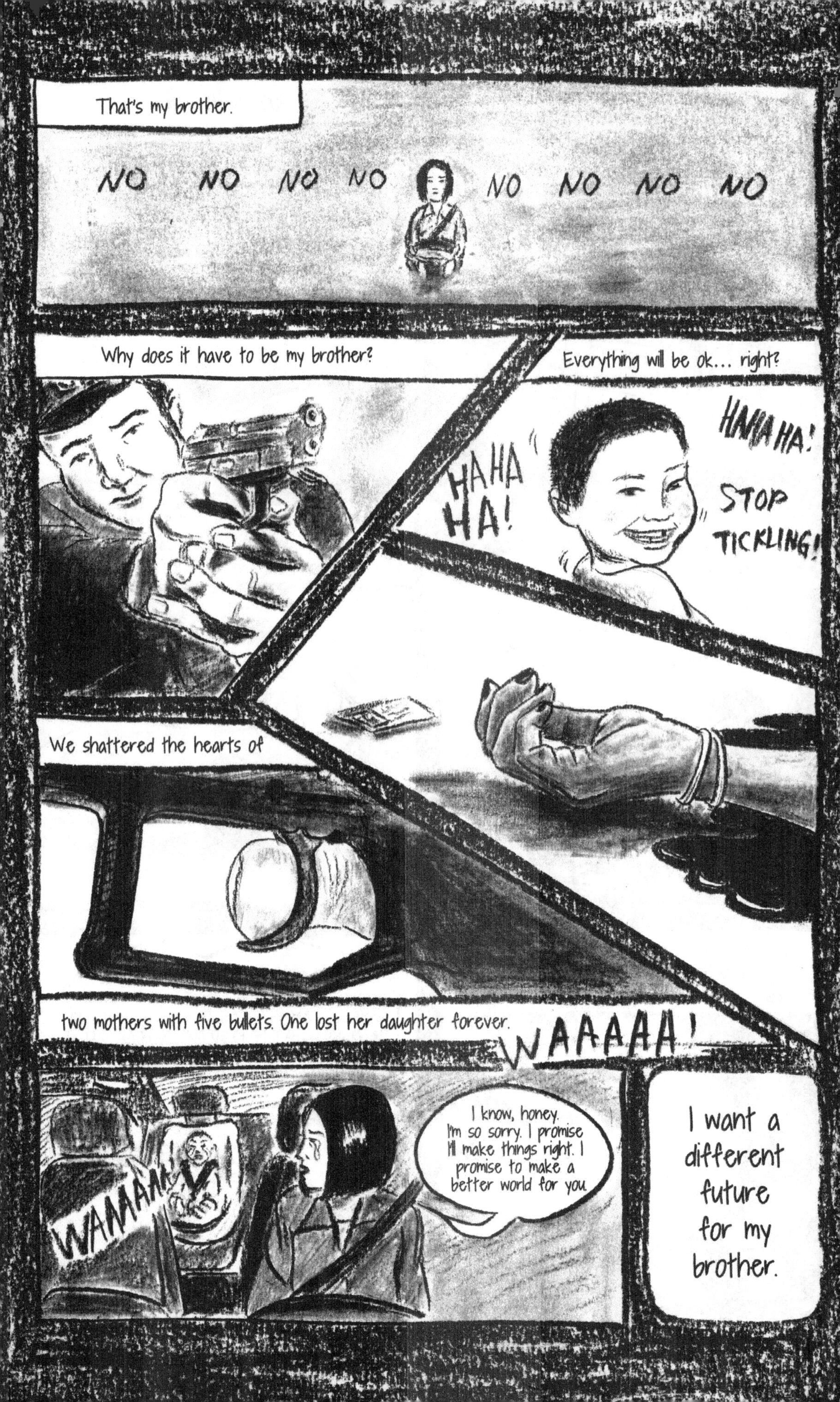
That's my brother.
NO NO NO NO NO NO NO NO
Why does it have to be my brother?
Everything will be ok... right?
HAHA HA!
HAHAHA!
STOP TICKLING!
We shattered the hearts of
two mothers with five bullets. One lost her daughter forever.
WAAAAA!
WAAAAA
I know, honey. I'm so sorry. I promise I'll make things right. I promise to make a better world for you.
I want a different future for my brother.

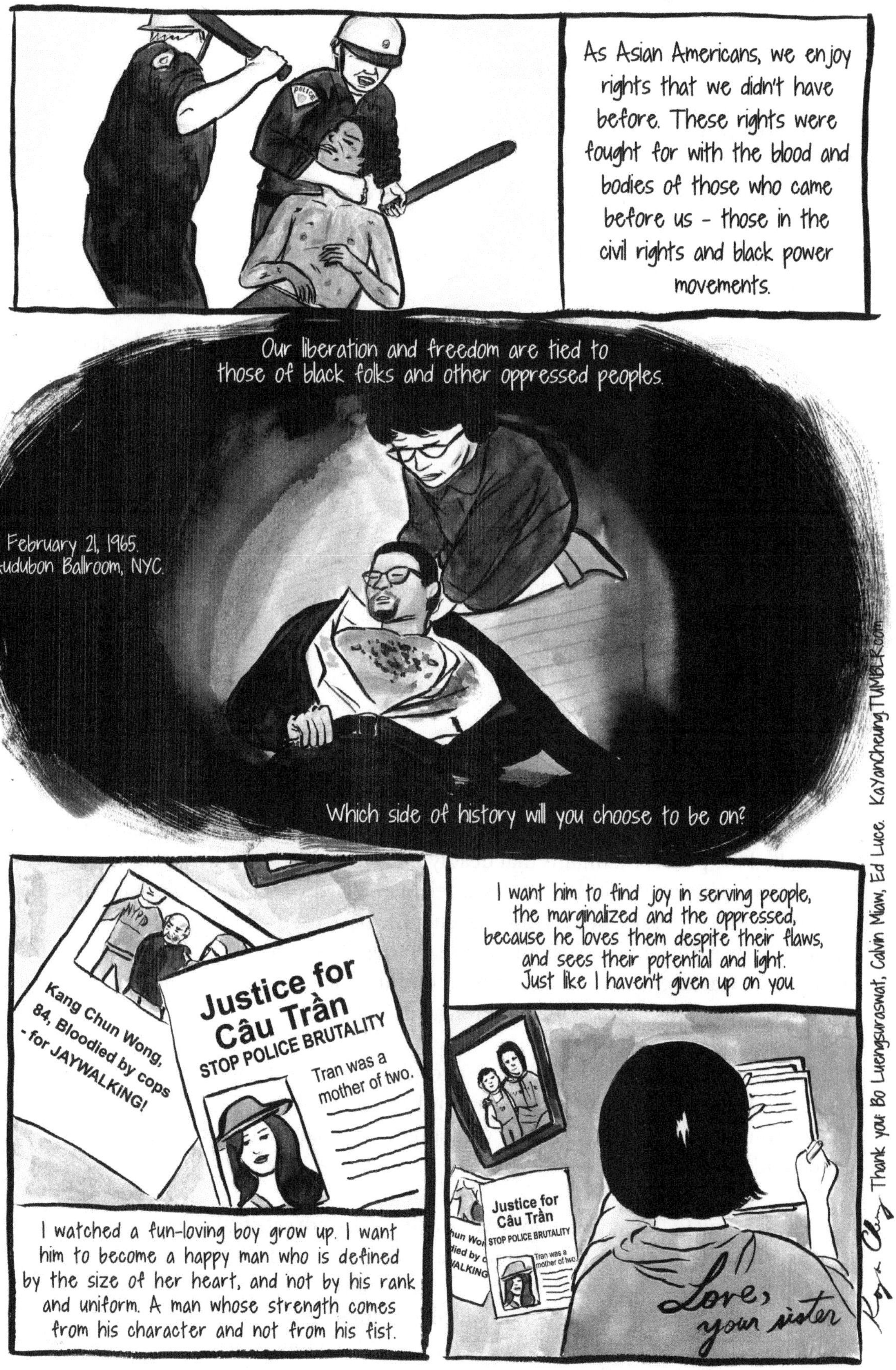

POLICE
As Asian Americans, we enjoy rights that we didn't have before. These rights were fought for with the blood and bodies of those who came before us - those in the civil rights and black power movements.
Our liberation and freedom are tied to those of black folks and other oppressed peoples.
February 21, 1965. Audubon Ballroom, NYC.
Which side of history will you choose to be on?
NYPD
Kang Chun Wong, 84, Bloodied by cops - for JAYWALKING!
Justice for Câu Trần
STOP POLICE BRUTALITY
Tran was a mother of two.
I watched a fun-loving boy grow up. I want him to become a happy man who is defined by the size of her heart, and not by his rank and uniform. A man whose strength comes from his character and not from his fist.
I want him to find joy in serving people, the marginalized and the oppressed, because he loves them despite their flaws, and sees their potential and light. Just like I haven't given up on you.
Justice for Câu Trần
STOP POLICE BRUTALITY
Tran was a mother of two.
Love, your sister
Thank you: Bo Luengsuraswat, Calvin Miaw, Ed Luce. KaYanCheung.TUMBLR.com

# BROKEN GLASS, OR THEY'RE KILLING OUR ARTISTS

### BY SOFIA SAMATAR

Michael Brown, Jr. died on August 9, 2014 in Ferguson, MO. Aura Rosser died on November 9, 2014 in Ann Arbor, MI. Mike was eighteen years old. Aura was forty. Both were shot and killed by police officers. Both were artists.

Among the photos circulating after the killing of Michael Brown, Jr., we find one of his lyric jar.

This is where Mike kept his rap lyrics. A few months before his death, during the summer after his high school graduation, the teen had begun rapping under the name "Big'mike." He recorded a few tracks and uploaded them to Soundcloud, where in the aftermath of his death they would become, like everything else about his life, subject to scrutiny and used as evidence for or against him. Mike was a thug, some said, who'd "chop you up with a machete" ("Body Bag"). He smoked marijuana: "I've been smoking weed since 9" ("No Trust"). Others said the sex-drugs-and-violence bluster was just typical of the genre, and the real Mike showed through in other lines: "Proud graduate for Mom and Dad/ Proved everybody wrong/ Wishing hoping and praying I can bring my niggas along" (from a freestyle dated August 5).

When I think of this young man I think of his lyric jar crushed beneath the boot of the state. Look at all this broken glass.

Aura Rosser was killed after officers responded to a domestic violence call. She was holding a fish knife. Officers allege that she was attacking her boyfriend with the knife, and that she came toward them with the knife raised. Aura's boyfriend, Victor Stephens, who called the police, maintains that deadly force unjustified. "Why would you kill her? … It was a woman with a knife." Aura's sister, Shae Ward, adds that while Aura struggled with drug addiction, she was trying to get her life back on track, and had moved to Ann Arbor a year earlier to be close to rehab facilities. "She was very artistic," remembers Ward. "She was deeply into painting with oils and acrylics. She's a culture-type of gal. She was a really sweet girl. Wild. Outgoing. Articulate."

"Glass was being broke," explains Victor Stephens, "so I called the police to escort her out." A call for help, and then Aura broken on the floor. A framed painting taken down from the wall and smashed. Lying among the pieces, the artist. Look at all this blood and glass.

In attending to the fact that both Mike and Aura were artists, I'm not trying to claim that artists deserve to be spared more than other people. It's not about proving we're good enough to live. It's about opening a space in our thinking where we can see what's dynamic in each other, creative, unpredictable, human. Art reveals this space. It's a space full of movement and possibility, elastic enough to hold the contradictory forces that are our birthright as human beings. There's enough room here for Mike Brown's rage and desire for another life and sheer teenage cussedness. There's room for Aura Rosser's oil paintings and her cocaine. In this space, Aura's fish knife is an intended weapon and also a creative instrument (she loved cooking, her sister says, and often cooked when she was upset). In this space, Mike's lyric's jar vibrates with a vital centripetal force. It's a vortex of lines, a poetic combustion chamber. We'll never know what might have come out.

Loss. That's what we can see when we look at Mike and Aura as artists. Overwhelming loss.

Listen: before becoming one of the most influential artists of the twentieth century, William S. Burroughs shot and killed his wife, Joan Vollmer. Before publishing either of his Pulitzer Prize-winning novels, Norman Mailer stabbed his wife, Adele Morales. The O. Henry Prize, the most prestigious short story award in the United States, is named for a convicted embezzler who became a writer in prison. What am I trying to say? Certainly not that these artists should have been killed—God forbid. (I do think Burroughs and Mailer should have been more severely punished.) I'm saying that their stories, like those of Aura and Mike, reveal the space of possibility where art germinates in secret. I'm saying that in the country where I live a white man can literally get away with murder while the bodies of black and brown people are smashed like a row of bottles, broken because they turned or advanced or looked or tried or moved, and we don't know who they are, or the possible prizes that might have borne their names. We don't know. This thing we call art, this thing we call culture—these treasures come to us from flawed and fragile and stupid human beings. People who bear within them unknowable futures. We shouldn't attempt to excuse the crimes they committed. But it's a far greater crime to take their lives.

When we think about art as a space of possibility, we can see that it contains not just the creations of Mike and Aura, but their decisions, made so close to their deaths, to start over. Aura's move to Ann Arbor, where she was going to begin afresh. Mike's college plans, cut short just two days before his first class. The space of art aligns with what the scholar Ashon Crawley calls "the Otherwise": a mode of aesthetics and critique that defies the norms of a white supremacist state. The Otherwise reveals itself in the improvisations of music and dance, in the moans of prayer, in the decentralized resistance movements that followed Michael Brown, Jr.'s death. The Otherwise isn't the future: it's a way of being that's already here, vibrating through us. It indicates the boundless possibilities of the "otherwise-than-this." Like art, the concept of the Otherwise evokes perpetual change. Change language into a flow. Change a blank canvas with color. Change your life.

We need to see Aura Rosser and Michael Brown, Jr. as artists within the context of a white supremacist state foundationally opposed to art, a state that desires to operate in secret where art seeks public communication, a state that sees black and brown people as disposable where art declares the sanctity of these creative and mutable lives. The state speaks in statistics, reducing human beings to ciphers, pathologizing black and brown communities as failed and toxic spaces. Art speaks the language of experience. It's the expressive vehicle for the irreducible in people, for what sings in the breath, what can't be counted or contained.

The state refuses the existence of the Otherwise, where art lives. This is a refusal on two levels. On the most obvious level, it's a refusal to recognize the humanity of black and brown bodies, their unpredictability, the fact that their futures are unknown. If Mike is a "thug" and Aura a "drug addict," the state can effectively close their futures, declaring them known in advance. This is how homicide becomes lawful: through the knowledge of the future that officers claim when they allege that they felt threatened enough to use deadly force. According to this logic, the thug and the addict do not possess open, human futures. But the refusal of the Otherwise operates on a second, deeper level as well, in the murk of the white supremacist subconscious. On this level, the state and its operatives do understand that we have unpredictable futures, and it's precisely this unpredictability that they fear.

Change language into a flow. Change a blank canvas with color. Change your life. Change your city. Change your world. If you can imagine ways to exist Otherwise, there's no knowing what you might change. We have to understand the state-sanctioned murder of black and brown people as part of a sustained assault on our cultures, our organizing efforts, and our futures. "Because Aura Rosser aspired to be an artist," writes Peter Linebaugh in his powerful essay, "Beauty and Police," we should view her homicide in the context of "the struggle for a future worth living by the common people and the exercise of the imagination to that end." To recognize Aura Rosser and Michael Brown, Jr. as artists is to step outside a lethal white supremacist worldview, to think in an Otherwise mode. From here, we can see that Mike's music and Aura's painting were not collateral damage in last year's attacks by law enforcement. They were the target.

From here, we can see that the representation of black and brown people as future-less serves a state organized to extinguish our acts of imagination and cut off our futures.

When officers commit murder on behalf of the state, they're shattering lyric jars.

Look at all this broken glass.

They're killing our artists.

# Sources

Collins, Laura. "Who was the real Michael Brown?" The Daily Mail, August 22, 2014. http://www.dailymail.co.uk/news/article-2730153/A-kid-broken-home-beat-odds-to-college-A-rapper-sang-smoking-weed-feds-A-violent-robbery-suspect-caught-shocking-video-just-real-Michael-Brown.html

Counts, John. "Sister of woman killed by Ann Arbor police: 'She would have fainted at the sight of a gun.'" Mlive.com, November 12, 2014. http://www.mlive.com/news/ann-arbor/index.ssf/2014/11/sister_of_woman_killed_by_ann.html

Crawley, Ashon. "Otherwise Movements." The New Inquiry, January 19, 2015. http://thenewinquiry.com/essays/otherwise-movements/

Durr, Matt. "Boyfriend of woman shot by Ann Arbor police: 'Why would you kill her?'" MLive.com, November 10, 2014. http://www.mlive.com/news/ann-arbor/index.ssf/2014/11/witness_in_ann_arbor_police_sh.html

Edward, Roz. "Aura Rosser: Police Kill Mich. Woman after Responding to Domestic Violence Call." Michigan Chronicle, November 20, 2014. http://michronicleonline.com/2014/11/20/aura-rosser-police-kill-mich-woman-after-responding-to-domestic-violence-call/

Hill, Daniel. "The Rap Music of Mike Brown, Slain Ferguson Teenager." Riverfront Times, August 11, 2014. http://blogs.riverfronttimes.com/rftmusic/2014/08/the_music_of_mike_brown_slain_ferguson_teenager.php

Hoft, Jim. "Breaking: Mike Brown's Rap Lyrics Surface." Gateway Pundit, August 21, 2014. http://www.thegatewaypundit.com/2014/08/breaking-gentle-mike-browns-raps-surface-beat-that-puy-up-then-be-on-the-run-masterbating-off-my-voice-on-the-laptop-audio/

Linebaugh, Peter. "Beauty and Police." Counterpunch, November 21, 2014. http://www.counterpunch.org/2014/11/21/beauty-and-police/

Lussenhop, Jessica. "Family of Michael Brown, Teenager Shot by Ferguson Police, Talks About His Life." Riverfront Times, August 10, 2014. http://blogs.riverfronttimes.com/dailyrft/2014/08/mike_brown_shooting_ferguson_family.php

Stanton, Ryan. "Mayor calls Aura Rosser's Death a 'tragedy of mental illness untreated and drug use unabated.'" MLive.com, January 31, 2015. http://www.mlive.com/news/ann-arbor/index.ssf/2015/01/ann_arbor_mayor_aura_rosser_sh.html

Michael Brown, Jr.'s music is available here: https://soundcloud.com/bigmike-jr-brown

## ON MUMIA'S

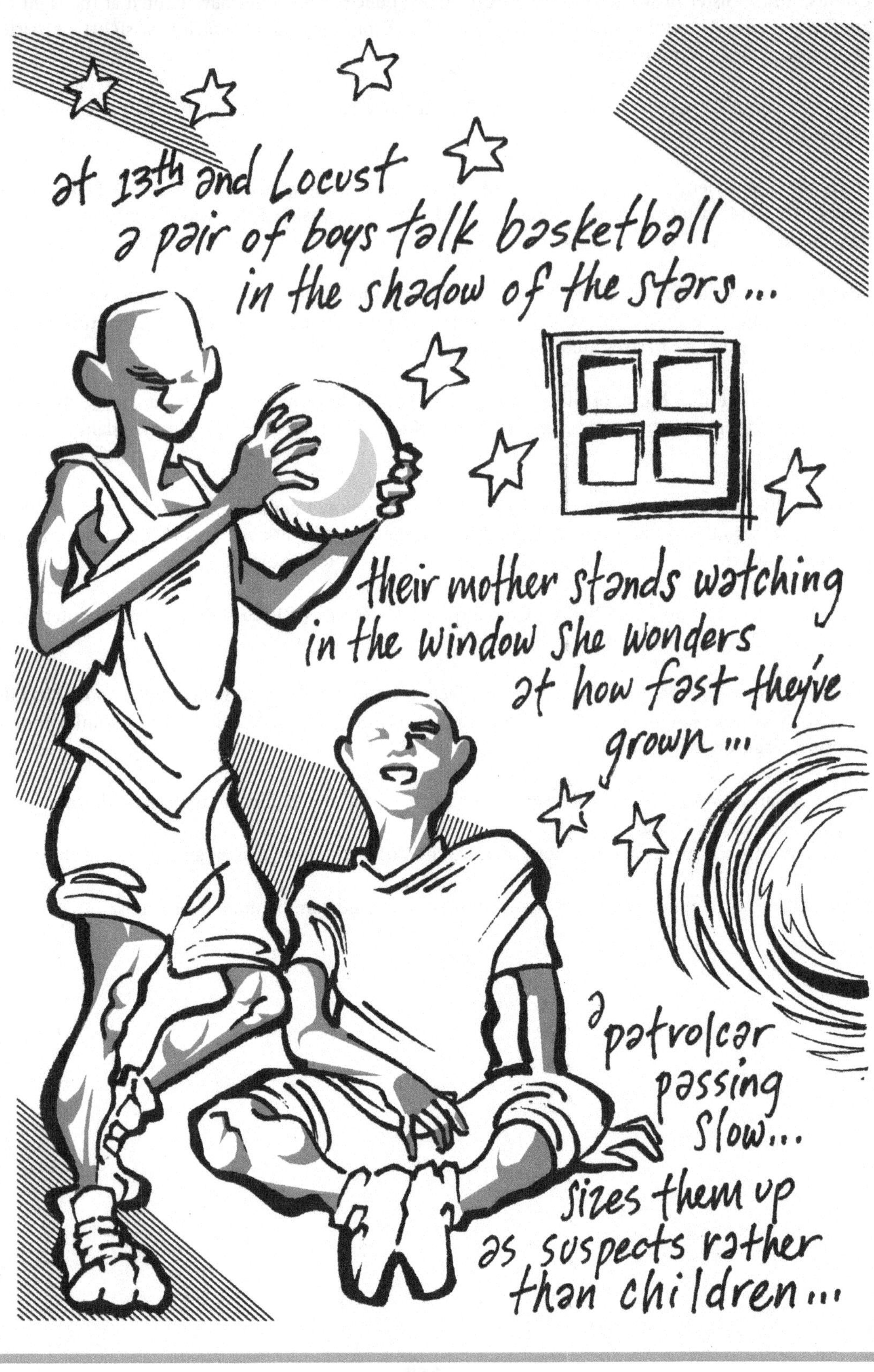
at 13th and Locust
a pair of boys talk basketball
in the shadow of the stars...
their mother stands watching
in the window she wonders
at how fast they've
grown...
a patrolcar
passing
slow...
sizes them up
as suspects rather
than children...

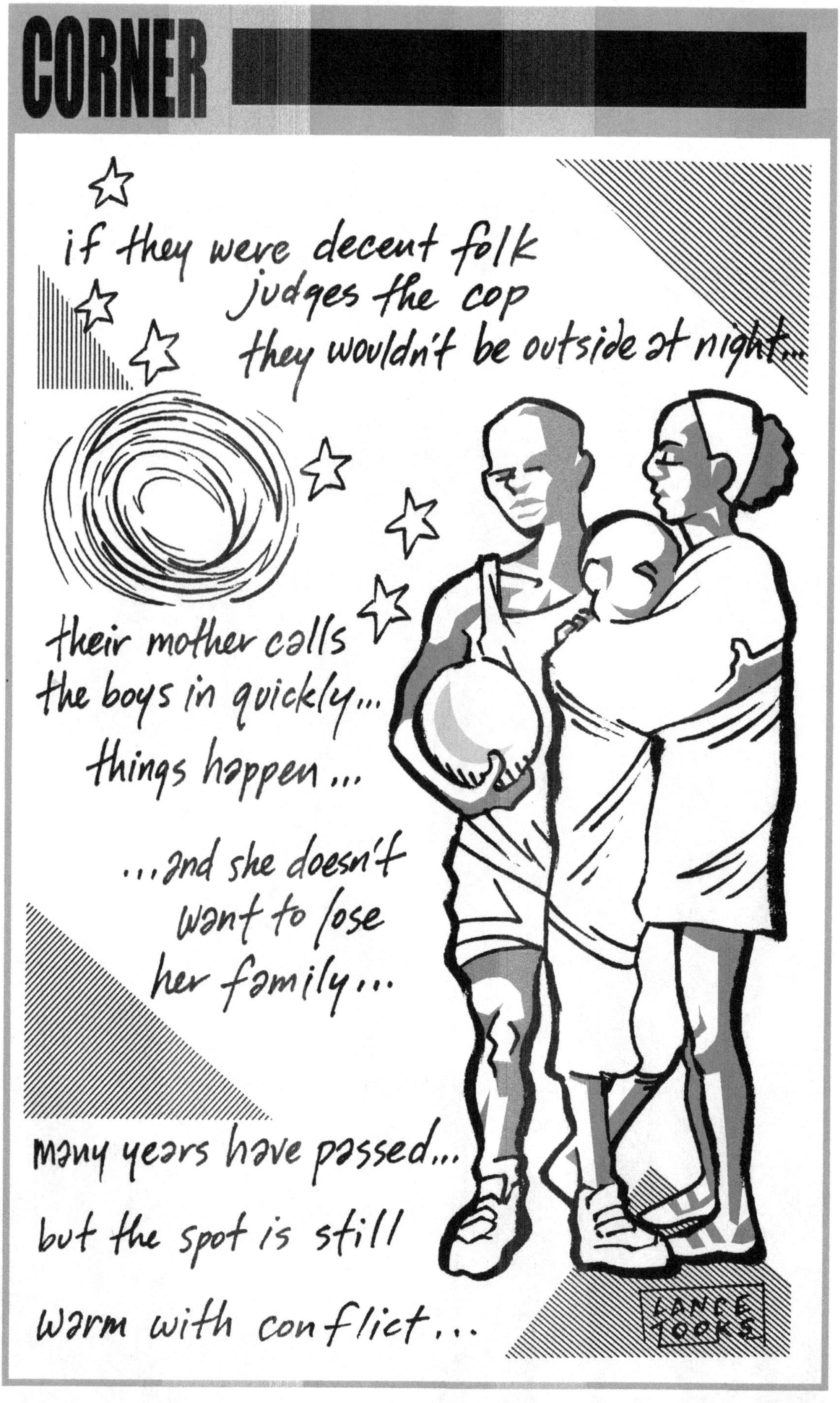
CORNER
if they were decent folk
judges the cop
they wouldn't be outside at night...
their mother calls
the boys in quickly...
things happen...
...and she doesn't
want to lose
her family...
many years have passed...
but the spot is still
warm with conflict...
LANCE TOOKS

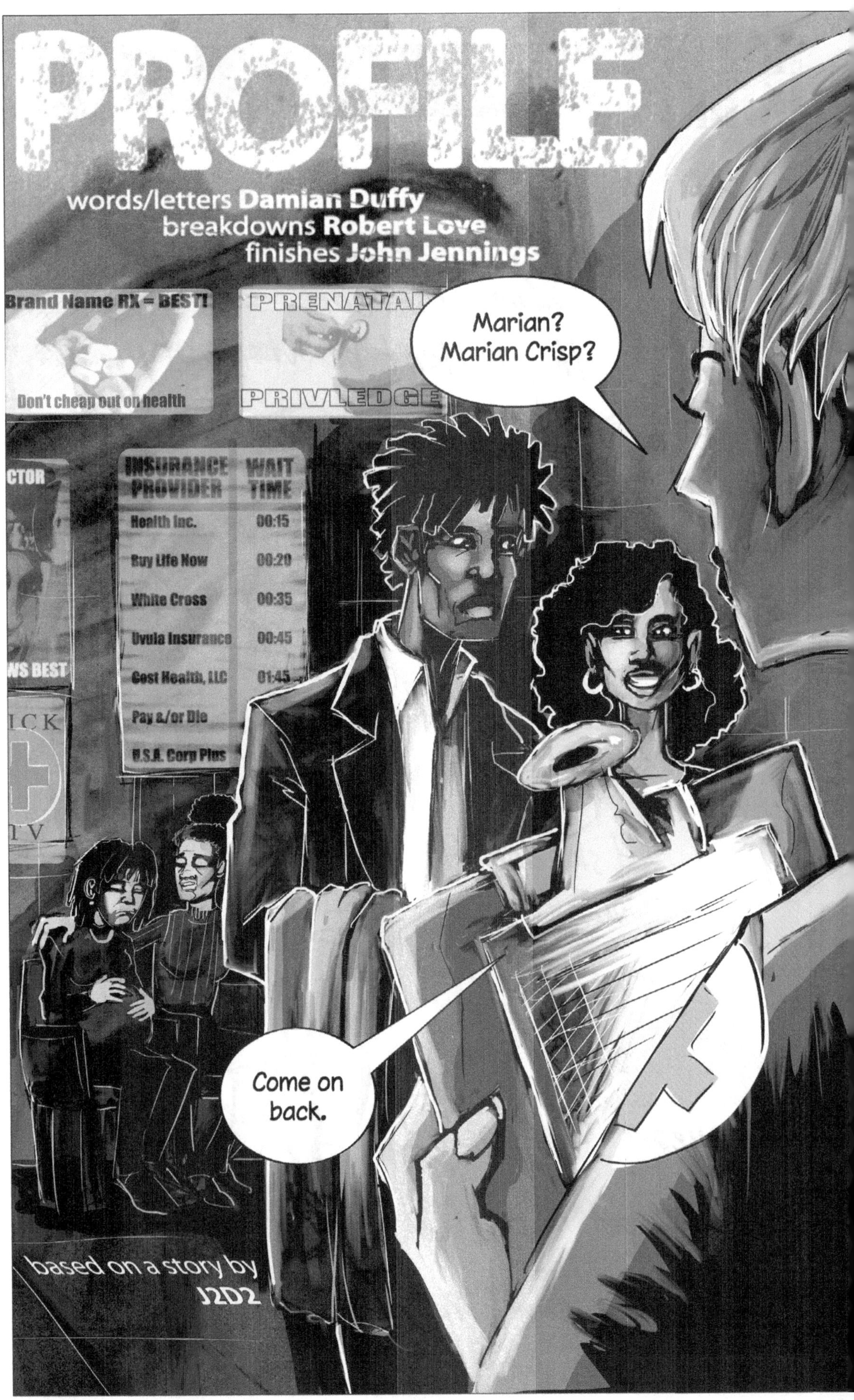
PROFILE
words/letters Damian Duffy
breakdowns Robert Love
finishes John Jennings
Brand Name RX = BEST!
Don't cheap out on health
PRENATAL
PRIVLEDGE
Marian?
Marian Crisp?
INSURANCE PROVIDER
WAIT TIME
Health Inc. 00:15
Buy Life Now 00:20
White Cross 00:35
Uvula Insurance 00:45
Cost Health, LLC 01:45
Pay &/or Die
U.S.A. Corp Plus
Come on back.
based on a story by
J2D2

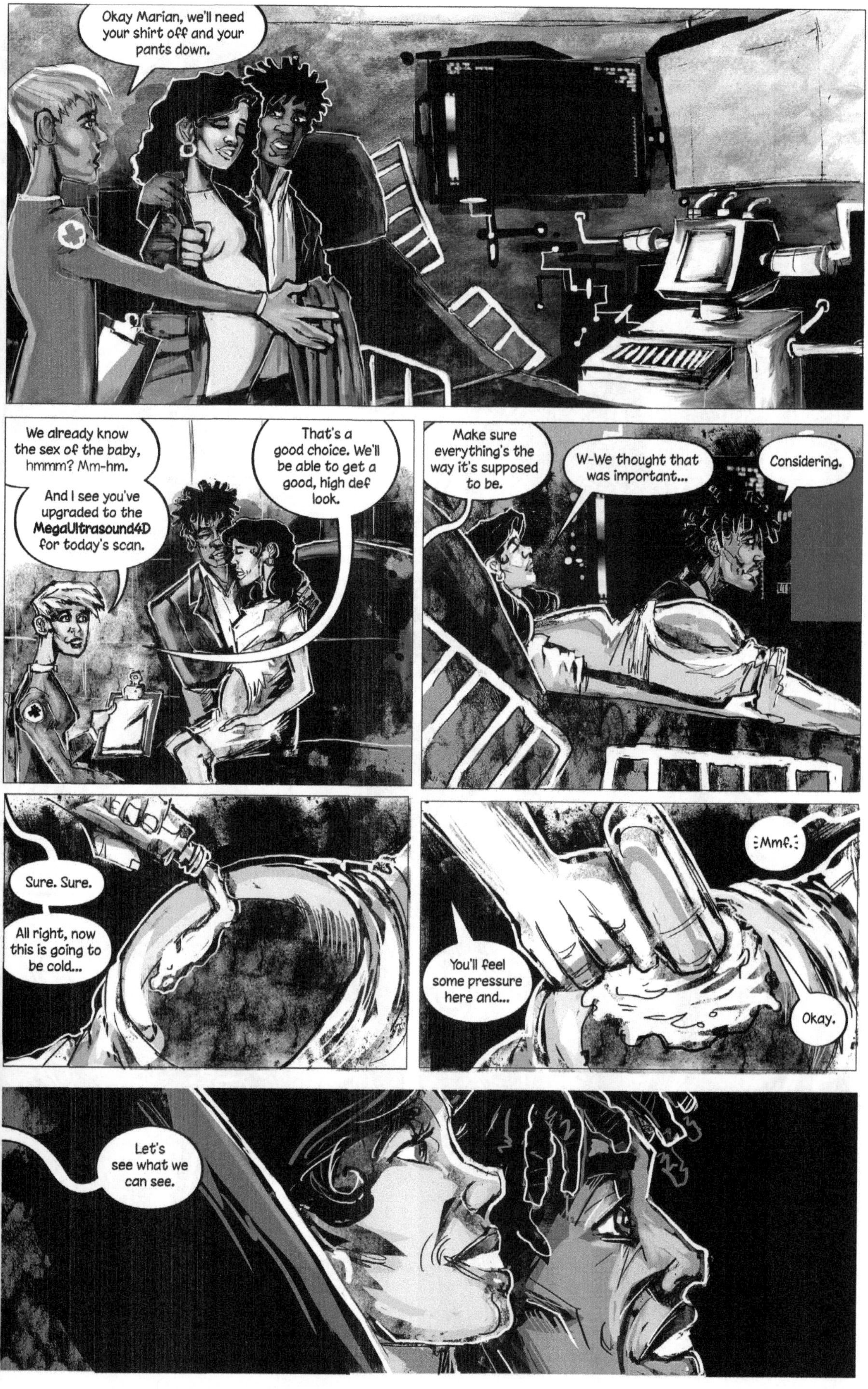
Okay Marian, we'll need your shirt off and your pants down.
We already know the sex of the baby, hmmm? Mm-hm.
And I see you've upgraded to the **MegaUltrasound4D** for today's scan.
That's a good choice. We'll be able to get a good, high def look.
Make sure everything's the way it's supposed to be.
W-We thought that was important...
Considering.
Sure. Sure.
All right, now this is going to be cold...
Mmf.
You'll feel some pressure here and...
Okay.
Let's see what we can see.

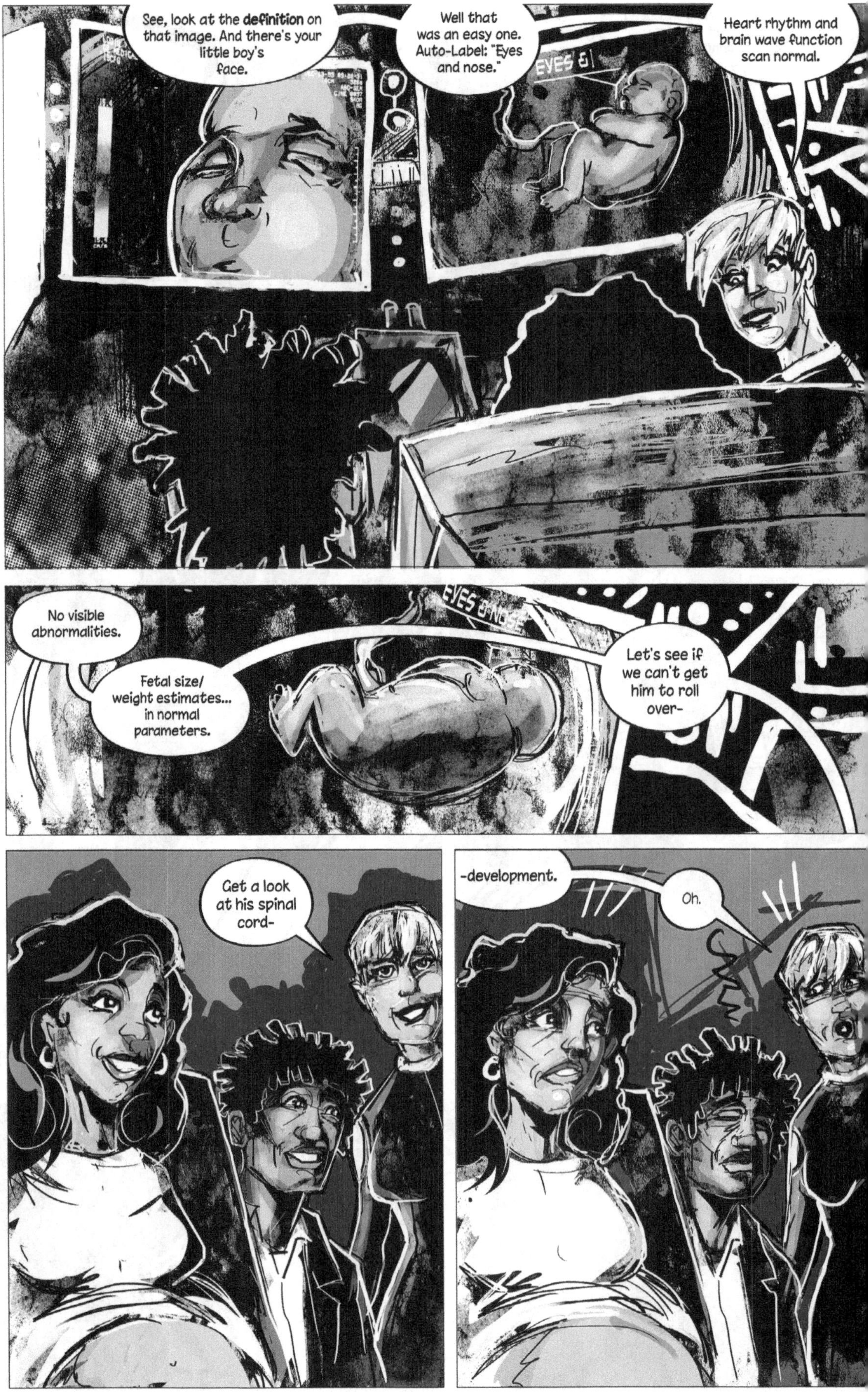

See, look at the **definition** on that image. And there's your little boy's face.
Well that was an easy one. Auto-Label: "Eyes and nose."
EYES &
Heart rhythm and brain wave function scan normal.
EYES & NOSE
No visible abnormalities.
Fetal size/ weight estimates... in normal parameters.
Let's see if we can't get him to roll over-
Get a look at his spinal cord-
-development.
Oh.

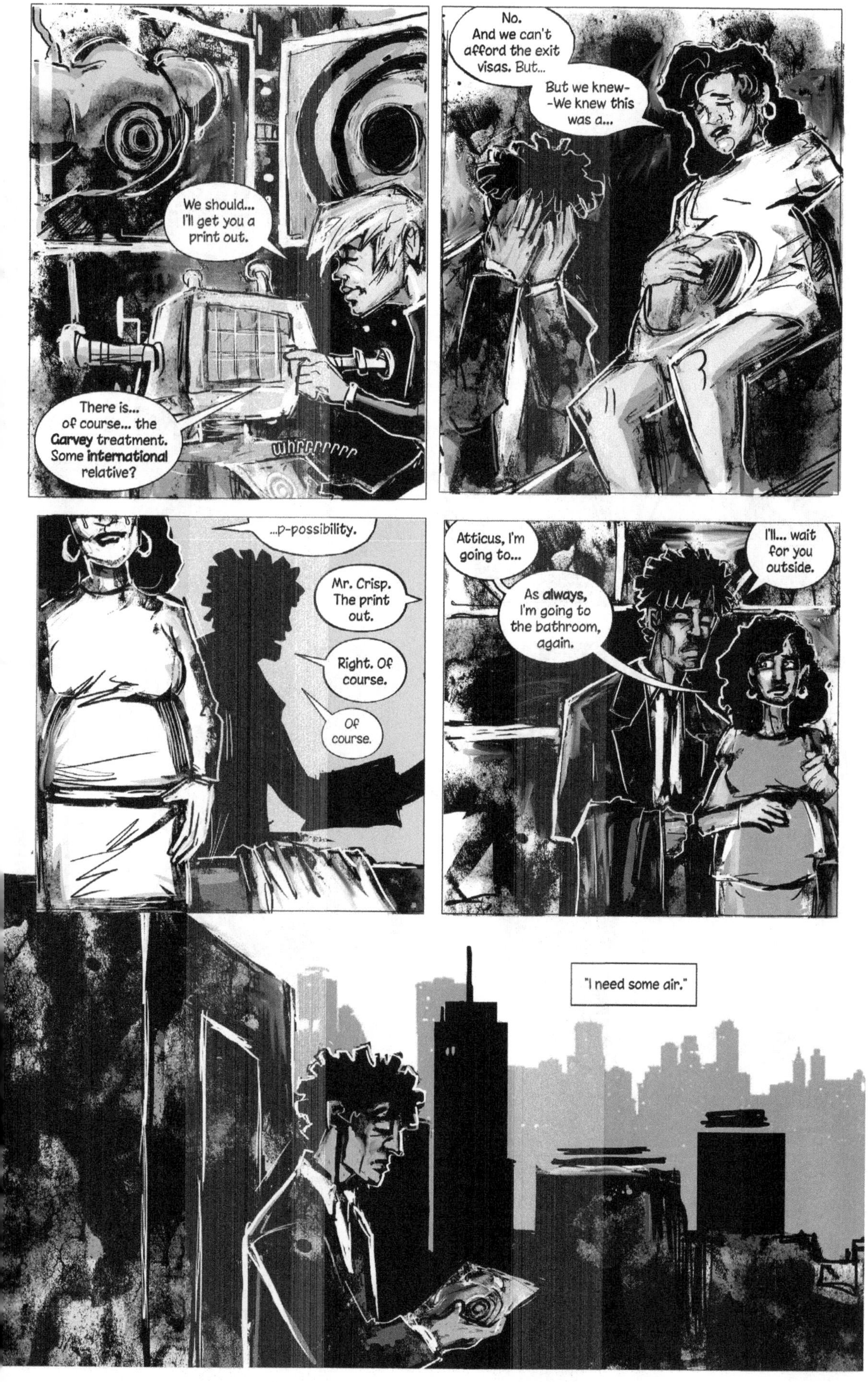
We should... I'll get you a print out.
There is... of course... the **Garvey** treatment. Some **international** relative?
whrrrrrrp
No. And we can't afford the exit visas. But...
But we knew- -We knew this was a...
...p-possibility.
Mr. Crisp. The print out.
Right. Of course.
Of course.
Atticus, I'm going to...
As **always**, I'm going to the bathroom, again.
I'll... wait for you outside.
"I need some air."

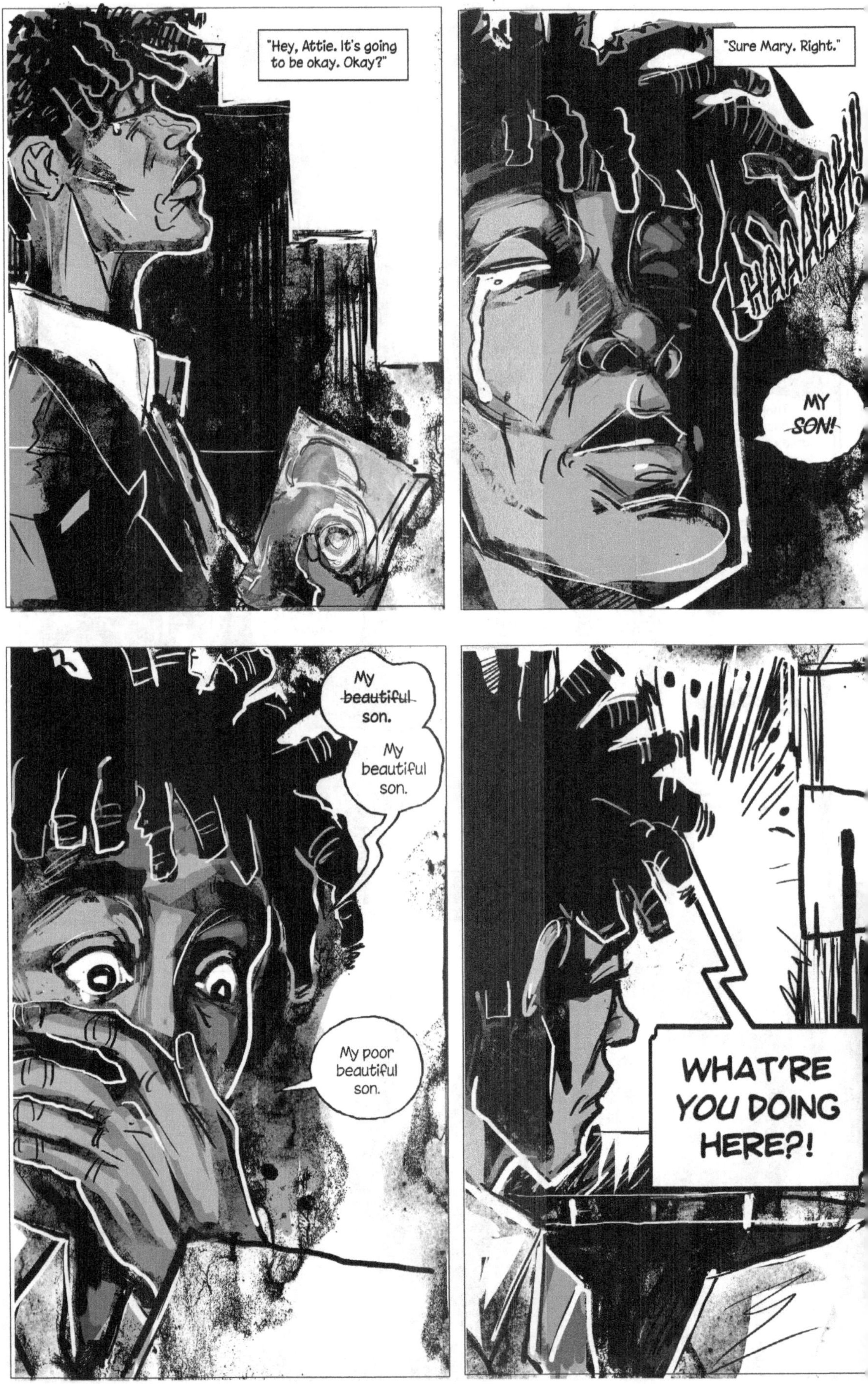
"Hey, Attie. It's going to be okay. Okay?"
"Sure Mary. Right."
HAAAAH!
MY SON!
My beautiful son.
My beautiful son.
My poor beautiful son.
WHAT'RE YOU DOING HERE?!

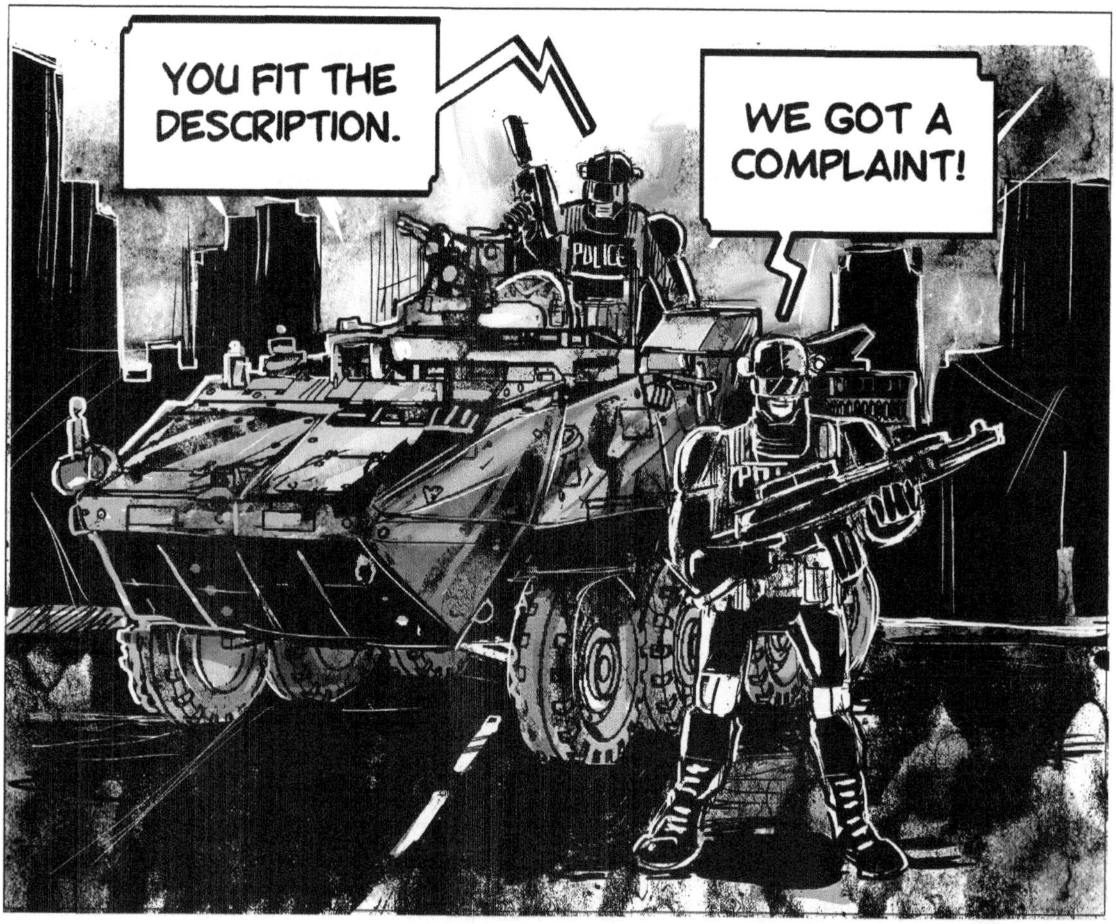
YOU FIT THE DESCRIPTION.
WE GOT A COMPLAINT!
POLICE
POLICE

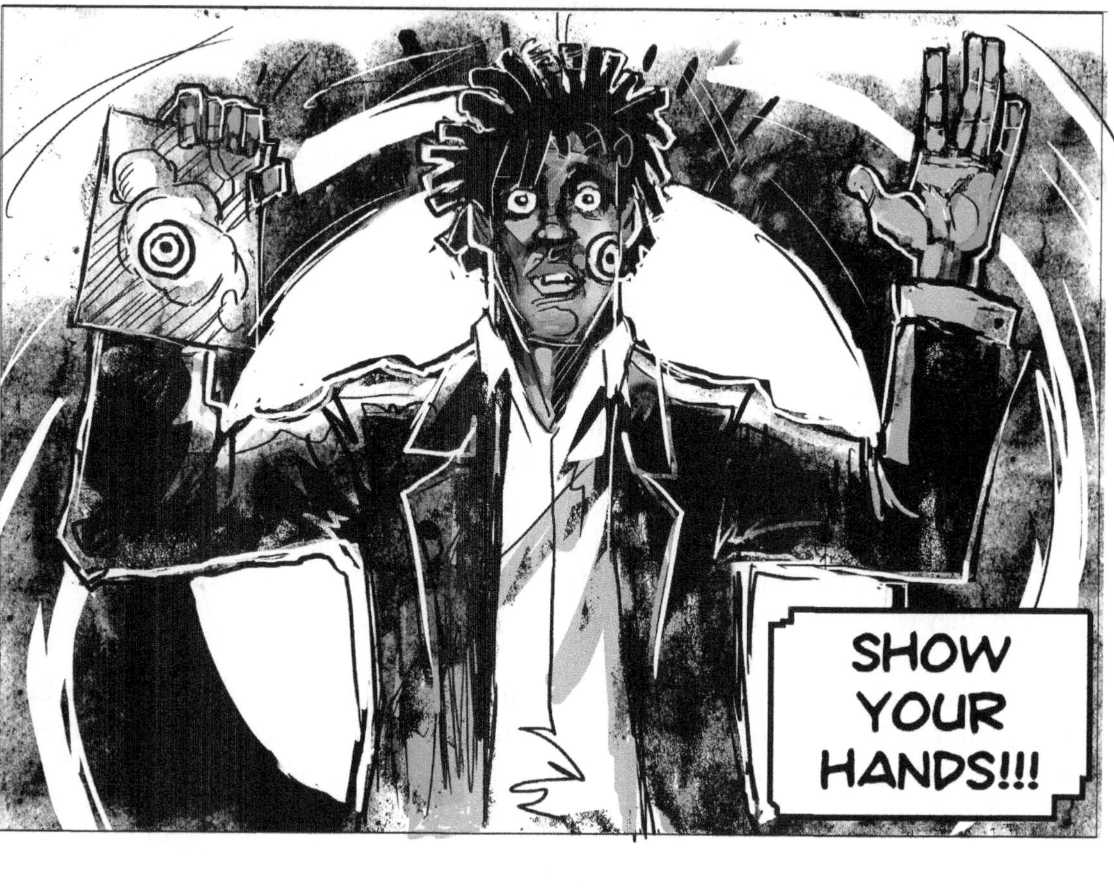
SHOW YOUR HANDS!!!

# ALTERNATIVES TO POLICING AND THE SUPERHERO MODEL

## BY WALIDAH IMARISHA

*"It's better to die on our feet than live on our knees."*

General Emiliano Zapata of the Mexican Revolution
and
Magneto of the Brotherhood of (Evil) Mutants ("Enter Magneto, X-Men: The Animated Series)

The murders of two unarmed Black people, Michael Brown and Eric Garner, by white police officers exploded conversation about police violence and brutality into the headlines of mainstream press in 2014, with resistance against that violence crystallizing in the Black Lives Matter movement. With statistics coming out like those put forward in Malcolm X Grassroots Movement's Operation Ghetto Storm report—that a Black person (men, women, and trans) is killed every 28 hours by police or a white vigilante, we have seen questions emerge about the role of police—historic and current—in our society.

Mainstream publications like Rolling Stone have run headlines like "Policing is a Dirty Job, But No One's Got to Do it: 6 Ideas for a Cop-Free World," exploring the history of modern police forces as mechanisms of social control of the urban poor, and, as scholar Kristian Williams proves in his book Our Enemies in Blue, enslaved Black folks by proto-police forces, which were called slave patrols. The Rolling Stone article goes on to advocate for concrete alternatives to policing, such as unarmed mediation teams, restorative justice, and community patrols.

Though some reading the article may think this the first time they are encountering the revolutionary idea of alternatives to police, I can guarantee it's not.

The first time the majority of us encountered the idea of alternatives to the police was the first time we bought a superhero comic book.

Superheroes fundamentally critique the criminal justice system that exists in these imagined worlds, whether it's Metropolis or Gotham City (worlds clearly based on our current political realities). If the police were doing their jobs and the system was functioning in an efficient manner, there would be no need for superheroes. By picking up the red phone, turning on the bat signal, calling in the X-Men, or relinquishing control to Dr. Manhattan, authorities acknowledge their system of justice is broken. If it wasn't broken, they wouldn't need superheroes.

Of course, alternatives to police aren't politically radical by default (think Ku Klux Klan, militias, The Minute Men, George Zimmerman). The existence of superheroes means something isn't working, but peeling apart these comics' premises will allow us to explore and critique the superhero theory, pull out what is useful to the creation of community-based alternatives to police, and construct a framework that is more reflective of visionary values and politics.

**Nietzsche's Superman Reinvented**

In 1938, Superman burst onto the scene as the first fully actualized superhero with the tagline "Truth, Justice, and the American Way."

There had been other heroes before Superman, no doubt, but Superman was the first to combine the costume, vigilante justice, and fantastical powers based on at least a pseudo science (Superman being an alien who has crash-landed in the cornfields of the Midwest who, conveniently for him, happened to come out looking the model of an all-American white straight cis-gendered man).

Superman quickly became the prototype for other superheroes, and the prototype that later comics continue to respond to, critique, and complicate.

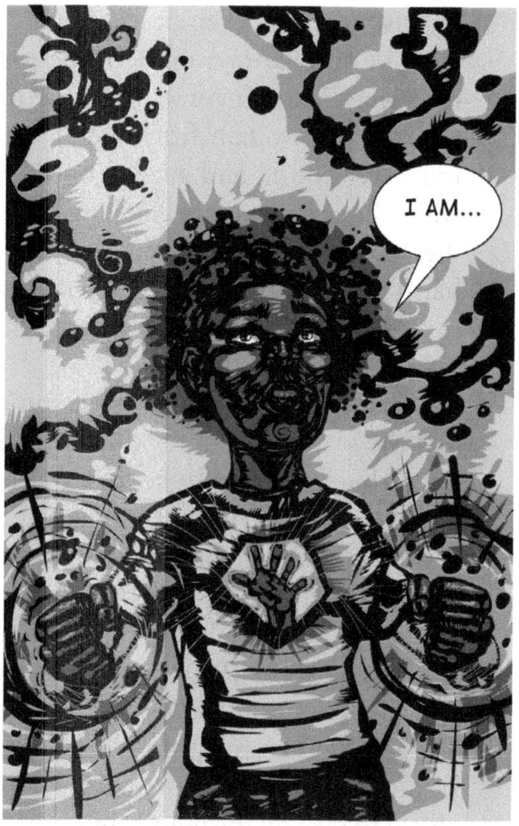
I AM...
**Illustration by Stacey Robinson**

Superman's powers make him one of the most powerful beings in the universe, which could be an incredibly terrifying thought to the establishment. But luckily for them, for the majority of his existence, Superman remains entirely a tool of the dominant establishment. From his tagline to his red, white, and blue uniform, Superman personifies the idea of ultimate power being used to maintain the "American Dream."

"[Superman's] loyalty and patriotism are above even his devotion to the law. This entails some important consequences for a superhero such as Superman who is beyond the power of the armed forces, should he choose to oppose state power," writes Richard Reynolds in his book *Super Heroes: A Modern Mythology* (15). Superman's potentially terrifying powers are held in check by that blind patriotism to America, and so instead of challenging oppressive state rule, we see him breaking laws to uphold American hegemony. Superman is the ultimate cop for a nation that roots its mythology of lawmen in the colonization of the West, where laws were more suggestions, where the sheriff's racialized concept of what was just ruled. With the massive discretion give to police officers today about whom they stop, what laws they enforce, what neighborhoods they patrol, and the racial lens they use to make all of these decisions, we see a clear continuation of this mentality into the present.

Superman and other superheroes uphold an idea of justice that protects the weak physically, while maintaining existing exploitative power structures. Traditional superhero conceptions of justice most often mean punishment (usually long stretches of imprisonment or even death) for the "guilty." This may mean superheros break smaller laws, but it is always done in the greater spirit of American democracy. "Superman's first ever exploit involves breaking into the state governor's bedroom in order to save an innocent woman from the electric chair. Superman does, however, leave the real murderer bound and gagged on the governor's lawn" (Reynolds 14). In this example, while Superman acts to challenge a criminal legal system that sentences the innocent to die, he ultimately reinforces that same unjust process by leaving the one who has done harm to its machinations. We end up with the idea that sometimes "the system makes mistakes," rather than a nuanced critique of how policing and incarceration work.

The Superman mentality assumes that both the idea of American "democracy" and the way this country implements the concept of justice are pure and above question. This blind loyalty became increasingly difficult for Americans to swallow during the 1960s and 1970s, in the wake of the Vietnam War, the Civil Rights/Black Freedom Movement, and global Third World liberation movements. We begin to see characters reinvented to reflect this. As Reynolds points out, Captain America, the paragon of patriotism, abandons his superhero role during the 1970s in the wake of the Watergate scandal. The 1970s is also when we see the beginnings of the War on Drugs under the Nixon administration and the beginning explosion of the prison population. The writers for Captain America incorporated these real life politics, as well as the sense of disillusionment with the established system that went with it: Steve Rogers hung up his shield to take on the mantle of the Nomad—an apt alter ego for a generation looking for a moral home (Reynolds 75).

Exploring the uglier side of the world of superheroes was the mission of the Watchmen series, published by DC Comics in the 1980s. Watchmen takes place in an alternate timeline where superheroes emerged publicly in the 1940s and 1950s and changed the course of this country's politics, helping to win the Vietnam War.

Each of the superheroes in Watchmen explores a different historical archetype of superhero, exploring their more twisted psychology. In one scene, the Watchmen are in New York during a police officers' strike. They have been brought in as official law and order, and the citizens are enraged to the point of rioting. One protesters screams, "We don' want vigilantes! We want reg'lar cops!" which is a clear critique of a complete lack of accountability under this form of "justice" (Moore Ch.1 17). (Though, again, looking at the everyday functioning of police in this nation, highlighted most recently by the brutal responses to demonstrations and public dissent in Ferguson, perhaps this cry was a tactical one – it's easier to battle police versus super strong beings who can shoot lasers out of their eyes and such).

Nite Owl, the voice of the liberal superhero, looks around in horror, and comments, "This country's disintegrating. What happened to America? What happened to the American dream?" The Comedian, a brutal psychopath in the vein of the Punisher, cavalierly replies, "It came true. You're lookin' at it. Now, c'mon... let's put these jokers through some changes" (Moore Ch.1 18).

This exchange gets to the fundamental question about issues of police brutality, corruption, and murder. While we hear ad nauseam the framework of "a few bad apples," the Comedian's response challenges this and instead highlights what those who advocate for the abolition of the police system say: the system is not broken, it is functioning exactly as it was intended. That the system of policing was not intended to keep citizens safe but instead was intended as a means of controlling and exploiting potentially rebellious communities, namely enslaved Black people and the urban poor. Rather than the deluded Nite Owl, who claims to believe in the ideals of democracy but continues to further an oppressive agenda, The Comedian is very clear about his role in maintaining social control as a representative of the criminal legal system.

## Who Are the Real Criminals?

Every superhero needs a supervillain, and throughout the 70-year history of comics, there have been a mind-boggling array of costumed cads. At the same time, however, superheroes also spend a significant amount of their time responding to common street criminals: stopping muggings, foiling bank robberies, tracking down thieves.

This is a clear parallel to the role that police play in our society today, especially when it comes to the drug trade. We are told the War on Drugs will get these drug kingpins, the people who run the international cartels that make drug networks possible. However, the reality is the vast majority of police arrests are of those addicted to drugs, those using them, and not those selling them. The drug sellers who are arrested are overwhelmingly low-level subsistence dealers (often making what equals minimum wage or less), and these arrests are further filtered through a highly racialized lens. As Marc Mauer writes in *Race to Incarcerate*, "The results of a *Los Angeles Times* analysis, which examined prosecutions for crack cocaine trafficking in the Los Angeles area from 1988 to 1994… [showed] not a single white offender was convicted of a crack offense in federal court, despite the fact that whites comprise a majority of crack users…. As is true nationally, the Times analysis revealed that many of the African Americans charged in federal court were not necessarily drug kingpins, but rather low-level dealers or accomplices in the drug trade" (Mauer 172). We cannot imagine that superheroes, who base their ideas of "justice" on these same racialized frames, are policing the streets much differently.

What is left out of the analysis completely, whether policing is done by cops or superheroes, is an understanding of institutionalized oppression and systemic unequal access to resources. Ozymandius from Watchmen speaks to this reality when asked why he stopped being a superhero: "What does fighting crime mean, exactly? Does it mean upholding the law when a woman shoplifts to feed her children, or does it mean struggling to uncover the ones who, quite legally, have brought about her poverty? … I guess I've just reached a point where I've started to wonder whether all the grandstanding and fighting individual evils does much good for the world as a whole. Those evils are just symptoms of an overall sickness of the human spirit, and I don't believe you can cure a disease by suppressing its symptoms" (Moore Ch. 11, 30).

With grand juries overwhelmingly voting not to indict in the case of police who murder unarmed people, thereby reinforcing that these executions are legal—the system working normally—we would do well to begin to ask ourselves these same questions.

## Arkham Asylum: A Case Against Rehabilitation

Next to Superman, Batman is probably the most well-known superhero of all time. Batman, aka Bruce Wayne, is a wealthy playboy by day. But because he watched the murder of his parents at the hands of a street criminal (working on the orders of organized crime), at night, Bruce Wayne becomes Batman.

We can use Batman to look at several of the themes already explored— the vigilante nature of superheroes; the focus on street violence as the major threat to society and not institutional oppression; the eradication of redemption. Added onto that, however, are issues of classism and the idea that rehabilitation is impossible.

Originally debuting in DC Comics just a year after Superman in 1939, Batman was the first modern superhero to have no special powers. He does not hearken to the concept of an advanced being who, because of their superior powers, has the right to rise above every day law and implement their own vision of right and wrong. (Not that this sort of eugenicist ideal is a positive one, but it at least is understandable why some might consider the virtually indestructible and alien-born Superman to administer justice.)

The only thing that makes Batman special? He's rich. He has enough money to buy himself vengeance, first on the people who murdered his parents, and then on the larger Gotham City itself. Batman's existence and acceptance as a superhero clearly supports the capitalistic ideal that those with money have the right to supercede laws, and have a greater grasp of the common good. No wonder Reynolds referred to Batman as a "social fascist" (67).

The Batman world also serves to reinforce the idea that rehabilitation does not work, manifested in the form of Arkham Asylum. This fictional psychiatric hospital is the destination for every supervillain Batman captures. But the Asylum has an escape record that would make Houdini whistle in admiration. We see images of the Joker or Two Face in a straitjacket with a cell door clanging shut in their face, and we readers know they'll probably be out on the streets before Batman has taken off his chestplate.

While the treatments received at Arkham are often vague, we know whatever they are doing isn't working. This leads to the conclusion that rehabilitation is a fallacy, that people cannot change themselves or their situations, that there is a psychological, perhaps a genetic, need to commit crimes. The safest thing for the good people of Gotham, the narrative in Batman leads us to deduce, would be to stop sending these nuts to a psychiatric hospital, and instead send them to a maximum security prison and throw away the key, or better yet, for Batman to finish them off once and for all. The Batman phenomenon supports the idea of control and containment over the idea of support and rehabilitation; warehousing over healing.

The X-Men are one superhero team that provides more positive lessons for organizing around alternatives to policing.

The main characters, hero and villain alike, in the X-Men world have mutated genes which result in special powers. In this comic, genetic mutations are clearly an analogy for exploring race, a fact that the creators were well-aware of. "A Wizard magazine article ... confirmed that comic book creators Stan Lee and Jack Kirby had indeed come up with the X-Men concept while following the Civil Rights and Black Power movements of the 1960s that unfolded daily on their television screens" (Reloaded 2).

One of the biggest differences between the X-Men and other superheroes is that while the X-Men definitely battle supervillains, their biggest enemy is the established social order. Governments of the world have enslaved mutants, engineered viruses to kill them, created mutant internment camps reminiscent of those built for the Japanese during World War II, and have even built giant robots called Sentinels, whose sole purpose is to hunt, capture, and kill mutants.

We readers are told the biggest concern is not street crime; it is not a purse snatcher, it's not even a mad scientist with a ray gun. It is a mad scientist with a ray gun in the employ of institutionalized power, power that would do anything to maintain the unequal status quo. X-Men often attempt to address those questions Ozymodious raised, of how to challenge heinous crimes that are completely legal.

X-Men work as a team, furthering the idea that it will take more than one man to change the political landscape. While most superheroes work independently as quintessential loners, the X-Men operate as a collective, and are clearly much stronger for it. Replacing individuality with collective struggle is the key to creating real, lasting alternatives to the police, and de-centering the narrative of white straight wealthy male saviors.

## There Can Be Only One...?

To find the quintessential exploration of collective superhero power, we turn from comics to the small screen, to the world of Joss Whedon's Buffy the Vampire Slayer.

Buffy follows the main character, a blonde cheerleader turned vampire hunter. In the show's mythology, since the beginning of time, vampires have roamed the earth. And as the opening of the show tells us, "In every generation there is a chosen one... She alone will stand against the vampires, the demons, and the forces of darkness. She is the slayer."

Though Buffy did work with a team, her "Scooby Gang," she was the only one with the powers of the slayer, and ultimately the fate of the entire world rested on her shoulders.

Until the seventh and last season. While there is only one true slayer at a time (with a couple notable exceptions), there are thousands of young women around the world in every generation who have the potential to become the slayer. When the slayer dies, one of those girls will receive her powers.

In season seven, an ancient evil attempted to kill all potential slayers; that way, when the current slayer died, there would be no one to take her place. To battle and ultimately defeat this ancient evil, Buffy had to do something that had never been done before: she had to give up being special.

Through a magic spell, her witch friend Willow activated all of the potential slayers; they all had the power of the slayer. Only in this way did they have enough strength to push back the evil.

It was in no way an easy decision for Buffy. Buffy was the unquestioned leader because of her powers. Like Batman, she had the authority to reshape the world in the way she saw fit. Unlike Batman and his grounding in white supremacist classist patriarchy, Buffy's decision to share power is one based on a collective, nonhierarchical viewpoint that sees the intersections of gender, race, sexual identity, class, identity, and privilege.

We have all been socialized, through westerns and comic book heroes and history classes and the nightly news and family stories, to view those who already have power as the ones who should continue to wield it, who should make and enforce concepts of justice. We see through Buffy, though, that instead of looking to external forces such as the police to secure our safety, we have to activate the slayer, the superhero in all of us; share the responsibility for the health, safety, and wholeness of our community; and use our collective power to reshape the world around us.

## Bibliography

"Enter Magneto." Jim Carlson. X-Men: The Animated Series. Fox News, New York. 27 November 1992.

"The Chosen." Joss Whedon. Buffy the Vampire Slayer. UPN, New York. 20 May 2003.

Martin, Jose. "Policing is a Dirty Job, But No One's Got to Do It: 6 Ideas for a Cop-Free World." Rolling Stone. Web. 16 December 2014. <http://www.rollingstone.com/politics/news/policing-is-a-dirty-job-but-nobodys-gotta-do-it-6-ideas-for-a-cop-free-world-20141216>

Mauer, Marc. Race to Incarcerate. New York: The New Press, 2006.

Moore, Alan. Watchmen. New York: DC Comics, 1987.

Reloaded, Morpheus. "Beyond Children of the Atom: Black Politics, White Minds and the X-Men." Playahata.com. May 8, 2003. Web. November 9, 2009. <http://www.playahata.com/pages/morpheus/xmen.htm>.

Reynolds, Richard. Super Heroes: A Modern Mythology. Jackson, MS: University Press of Mississippi, 1992.

Williams, Kristian. Our Enemies in Blue: Police and Power in America. Cambridge, MA: South End Press, 2007.

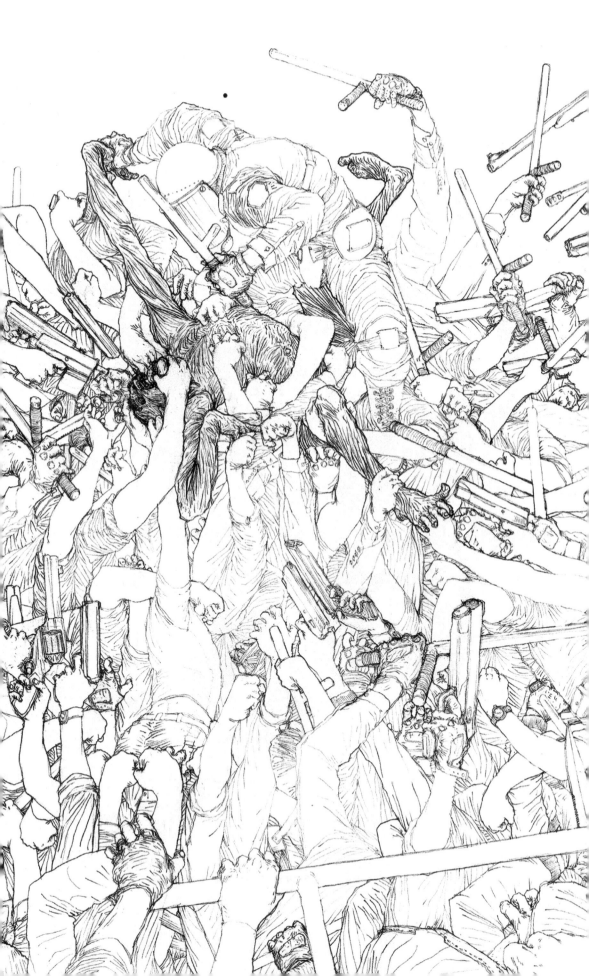

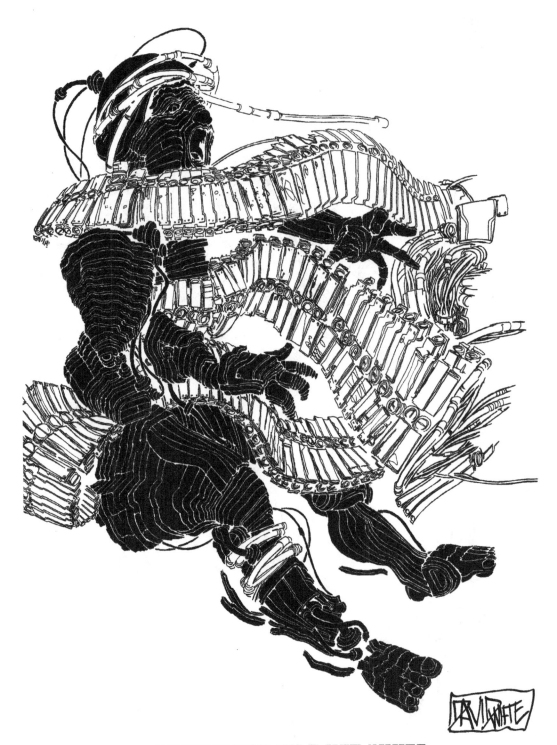

**"BRUTALITY" BY DAVID WHITE**

YOU KIDS ARE GONNA LEARN...
SHIT!
MY PARENTS ARE GONNA KILL ME
SKATE
SKATE OR DIE
88

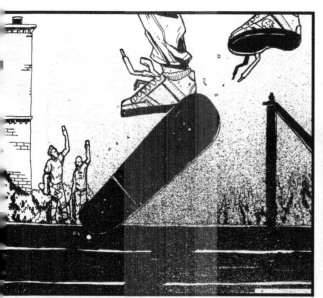

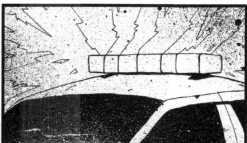

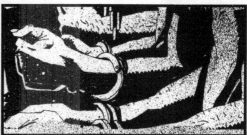

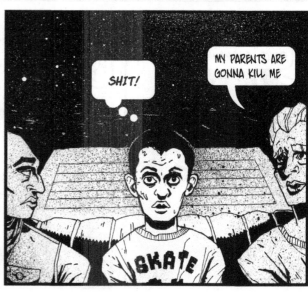

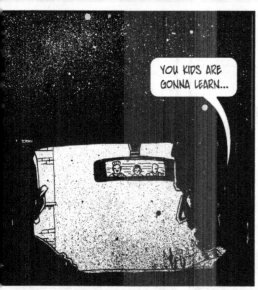

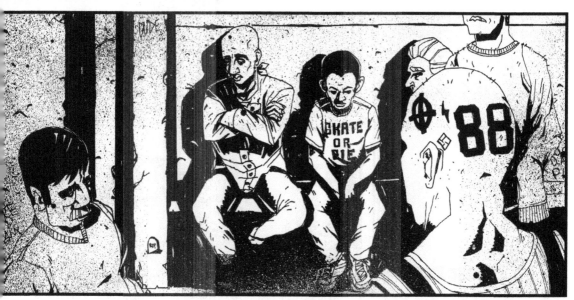

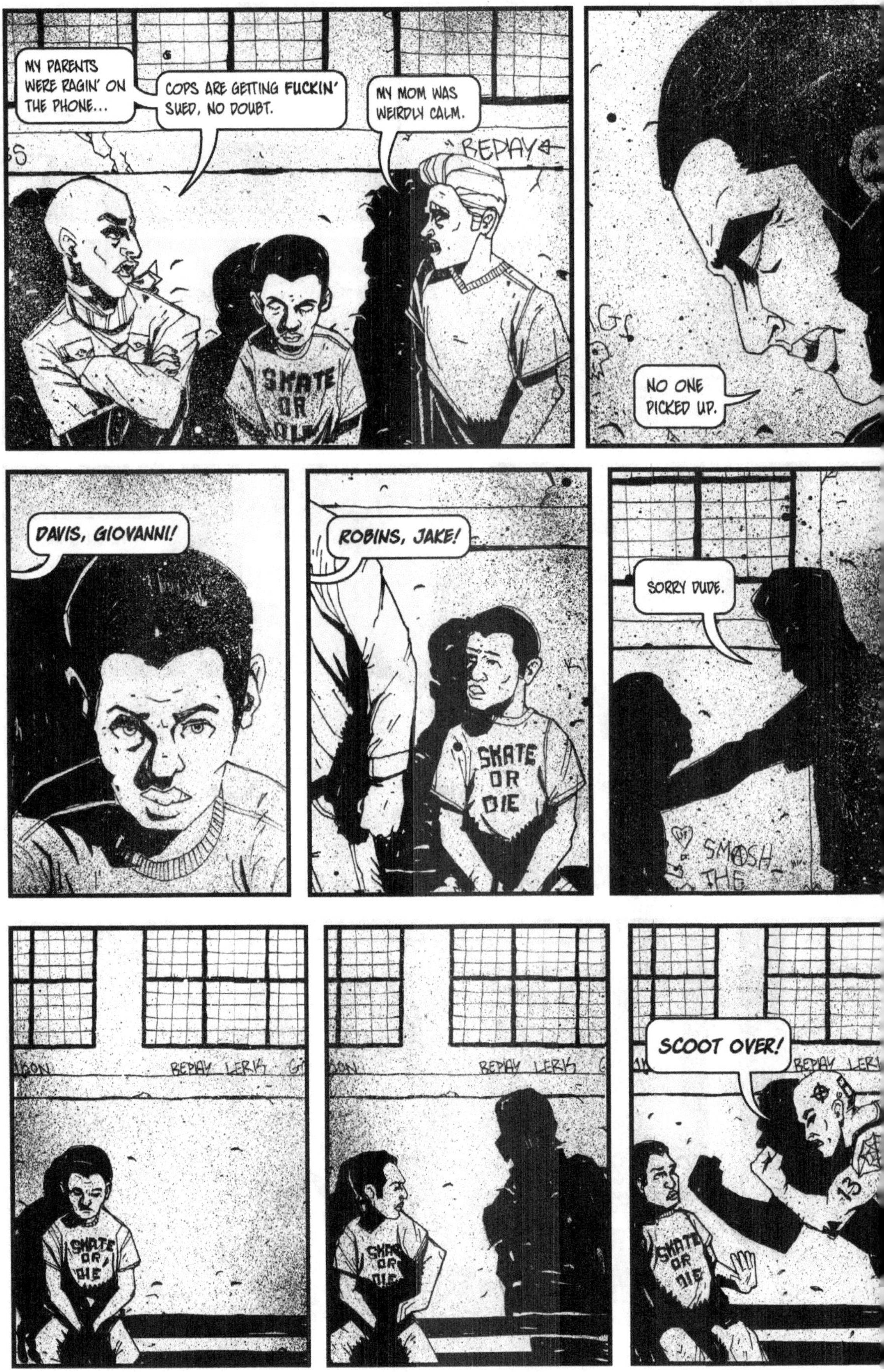
MY PARENTS WERE RAGIN' ON THE PHONE...
COPS ARE GETTING FUCKIN' SUED, NO DOUBT.
MY MOM WAS WEIRDLY CALM.
REPLAY
NO ONE PICKED UP.
DAVIS, GIOVANNI!
ROBINS, JAKE!
SKATE OR DIE
SORRY DUDE.
SMASH THE
SCOOT OVER!

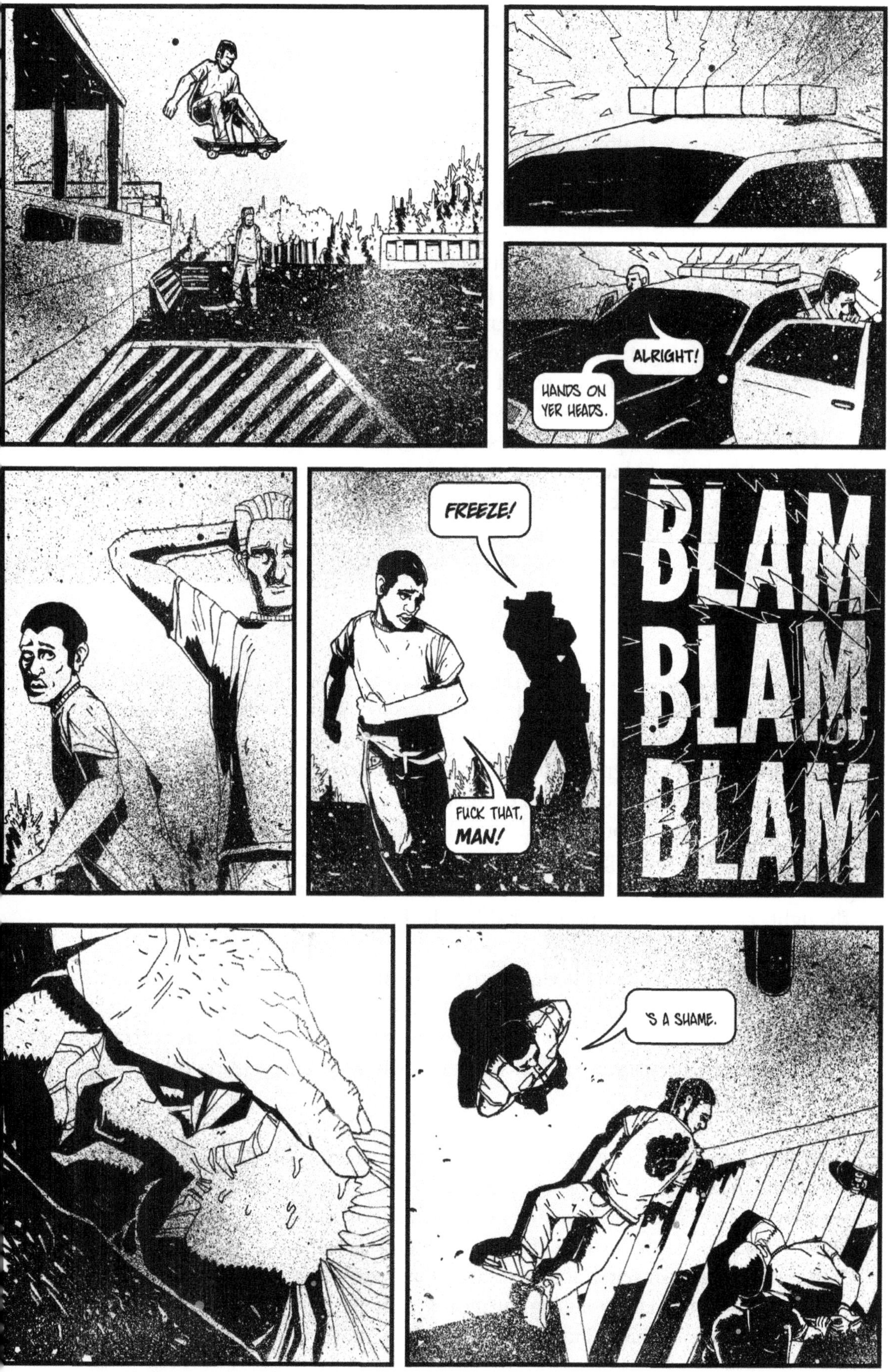
HANDS ON YER HEADS.
ALRIGHT!
FREEZE!
FUCK THAT, MAN!
BLAM
BLAM
BLAM
'S A SHAME.

# APATHY

## BY T. FOX DUNHAM

The sound of my father yelling wakes me from sleep. It stabs me, and my young heart races. His voice shatters me. I can't make out the words. I don't believe he's actually speaking; his rage possesses him, and he sings it, bellows it. I am ten years in age now, and once a week he wakes my siblings and me this way, screaming at my mother.

It is 3a.m., the lost hour, the forgotten time. And I wonder how far this fight will go tonight, if it will pass into silence, and I can sleep again. Or, will he get out his gun when his voice fails to satisfy his rage? Will my mother stop him, persuade him, placate him, or does she care tonight? Her defiance has grown, and he matches it with violence, his threats meant to pull a reaction out of her.

My father has been a police officer since I was born. I intimately know the uniform— black in color, decorated with badges and bars, insignia, and topped with a radio on his shoulder. He takes out the radio proudly at dinner and sets it on the window ledge. We listen to every call through our meal. It squawks like disturbed ostrich, and we listen to the desperation of the world crying out for help, people crying out to him to save them.

No one will save us. He's seen to that.

He was a cop when he met my mother. She worked at a Dunkin' Donuts, pursuing her nursing degree. It was always a joke that he was a police officer and met her at a do-nut shop. He convinced her to give up her courses and become a housewife, a mother. She let him. They lived a peaceful life, giving birth to three children, and he remained calm as long as she didn't complain or fight back and kept a perfect house in Levittown, the way he thought a house should be. But she was lonely, afraid. She went back to school, and finally she began to stand up to him. The more she rebelled against his neglect, the more violent he became to put her back in her place, to restore his ideal home. The fights get worse every month, shaking the Levittown rancher.

Finally, my siblings and I leave our rooms to make sure Mom is okay. I fear what I'm going to see. I don't want to look. It's too late in the night to call my grandfather to pick me up. That's what I do when I want to run away from my father. I sneak to the phone and say, Poppy come get me. He picks me up down the street on the corner, so my father cannot see.

It is the middle of the night. My mother is shaking on the couch. My father is screaming in her face, ripping her apart. He likes to drag her across the floor and make her sit while he yells at her, breaking her down. She yells back. I don't know when he got his .45. It is standard issue, his sidearm, his best friend as a cop. He's supposed to use it to protect people, himself, but instead it is a weapon of fear. All guns are lies. They are always made of fear. He's pointing the gun, threatening to shoot and kill himself. Dad's eyes are wild, peeling back. He could do it. He's in another world beyond good and evil.

Mom calls the Falls Township police to stop him, to protect us, but they're his buddies—the guys, not a woman on the force.

"No, Mrs. Dunham."

"He's going to kill us!" she says.

"I'm sure he's just fine," the dispatcher says. "Just calm down. Jack would never do that." He's gotten to them, convinced his buddies that my mother is mentally ill, that she makes up stories. They feel sorry for my dad. "We'll send someone out." But no one comes. They protect him. My father laughs. He's going to shoot us, and they don't care. My mother grabs us and hurries us out to the car. We get in, and she quickly starts it. Dad chases us down the driveway, and we speed away. He flashes the gun behind us, reminding us of his power. We have nowhere to go, no one wants us, and there's no money for a hotel. We drive around all night without refuge. Finally, we have to come home. He feigns worry.

Two days later he follows my mother to work, and, when she stops at a traffic light, he shows her his gun. We call the police. "Jack would never do that." Their apathy allows his violence. He was going to kill us, and the police would have let it happen. Violence is committed by one and allowed by many.

Even now I fear writing this. I am in my thirties, and I know that if he knew I was writing this to the world, he may return north with his gun.

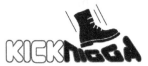

KICKNIGGA
Because white privilege requires your buy-in

ABOUT

Is Reverse Discrimination worse than "vanilla" discrimination? Yes! Here are our top 10 reasons why.

PROJECT OF THE DAY: JUSTICECAM

A bodycam that allows cops to edit footage with simple voice commands!

Welcome back, MirrorMirror!

(Not you? Create an account)

# Choke Out White Hate!

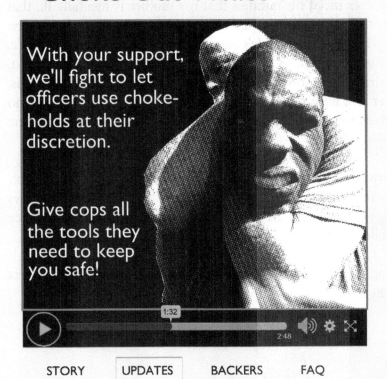

With your support, we'll fight to let officers use choke-holds at their discretion.
Give cops all the tools they need to keep you safe!
1:32
2:48


You're a backer!

(But there's still time to UP YOUR PLEDGE!)

This project was

**Successfully Funded**

on July 4, 1776

**Days Remaining**

**∞**

(or until the country self-destructs)

STORY | UPDATES | BACKERS | FAQ

## New T-Shirt!

We are SO grateful for the continued support of our backers that we just had to find another way to thank you. So we're offering what we think is our best t-shirt design yet: not only is it stylish, but, through clear, irrefutable logic, it puts an end to the race debate once and for all. And who knows? It might even save a few lives.

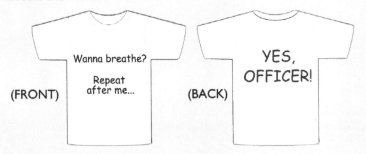

(FRONT)

Wanna breathe?
Repeat after me...


(BACK)

YES, OFFICER!


Use the up your pledge link to add this t-shirt to your rewards.

Liked **You**, the GOP, and millions of Americans like this post.

## Visit our sister sites!

KICKCHICK KICKSPIC

## Rewards

**$10**

Are we on the wrong side of history? Not if we write it ourselves! At this pledge level, you gain access to our discussion boards and help us preserve our country's heritage for future generations.

**$25**

We'll send you a copy of *Straw Man, Post Hoc, and Ad Hominem: A Guide to Debating*. Never let your lack of facts make you lose a debate again!

**$45**

Are you a black ally? Stay safe with a month's supply of whiteface! Just

"Military boots with lace for female"; Icon made by Freepik from www.flaticon.com [CC BY 2.0]
"MCMAP Rear choke - Defense Visual Information Center 2006.jpg"; By Expert Infantry [CC BY 2.0], via Wikimedia Commons

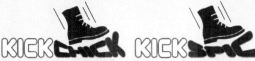

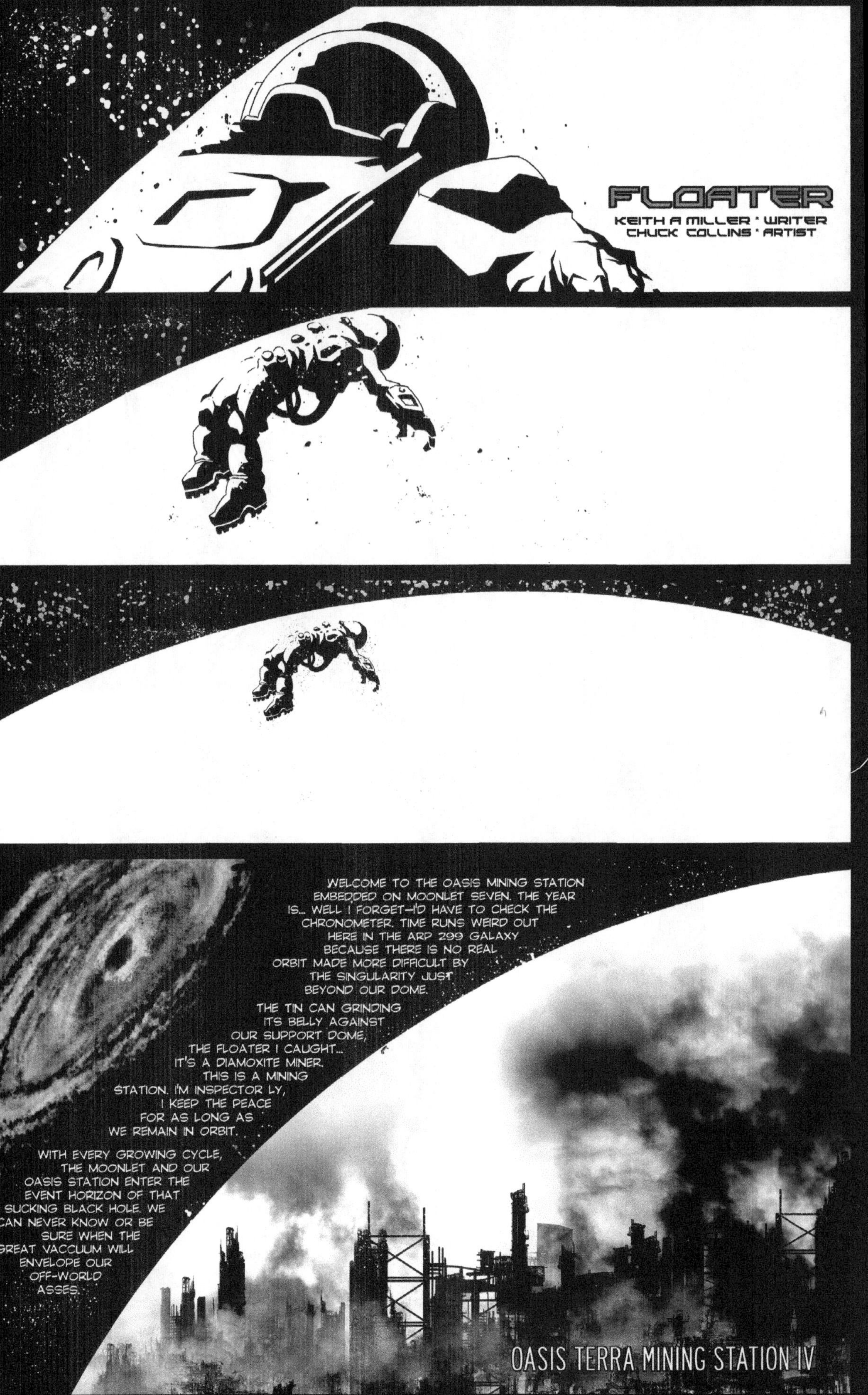

FLOATER
KEITH A MILLER * WRITER
CHUCK COLLINS * ARTIST
WELCOME TO THE OASIS MINING STATION EMBEDDED ON MOONLET SEVEN. THE YEAR IS... WELL I FORGET—I'D HAVE TO CHECK THE CHRONOMETER. TIME RUNS WEIRD OUT HERE IN THE ARP 299 GALAXY BECAUSE THERE IS NO REAL ORBIT MADE MORE DIFFICULT BY THE SINGULARITY JUST BEYOND OUR DOME.
THE TIN CAN GRINDING ITS BELLY AGAINST OUR SUPPORT DOME, THE FLOATER I CAUGHT... IT'S A DIAMOXITE MINER. THIS IS A MINING STATION. I'M INSPECTOR LY, I KEEP THE PEACE FOR AS LONG AS WE REMAIN IN ORBIT.
WITH EVERY GROWING CYCLE, THE MOONLET AND OUR OASIS STATION ENTER THE EVENT HORIZON OF THAT SUCKING BLACK HOLE. WE CAN NEVER KNOW OR BE SURE WHEN THE GREAT VACCUUM WILL ENVELOPE OUR OFF-WORLD ASSES.
OASIS TERRA MINING STATION IV

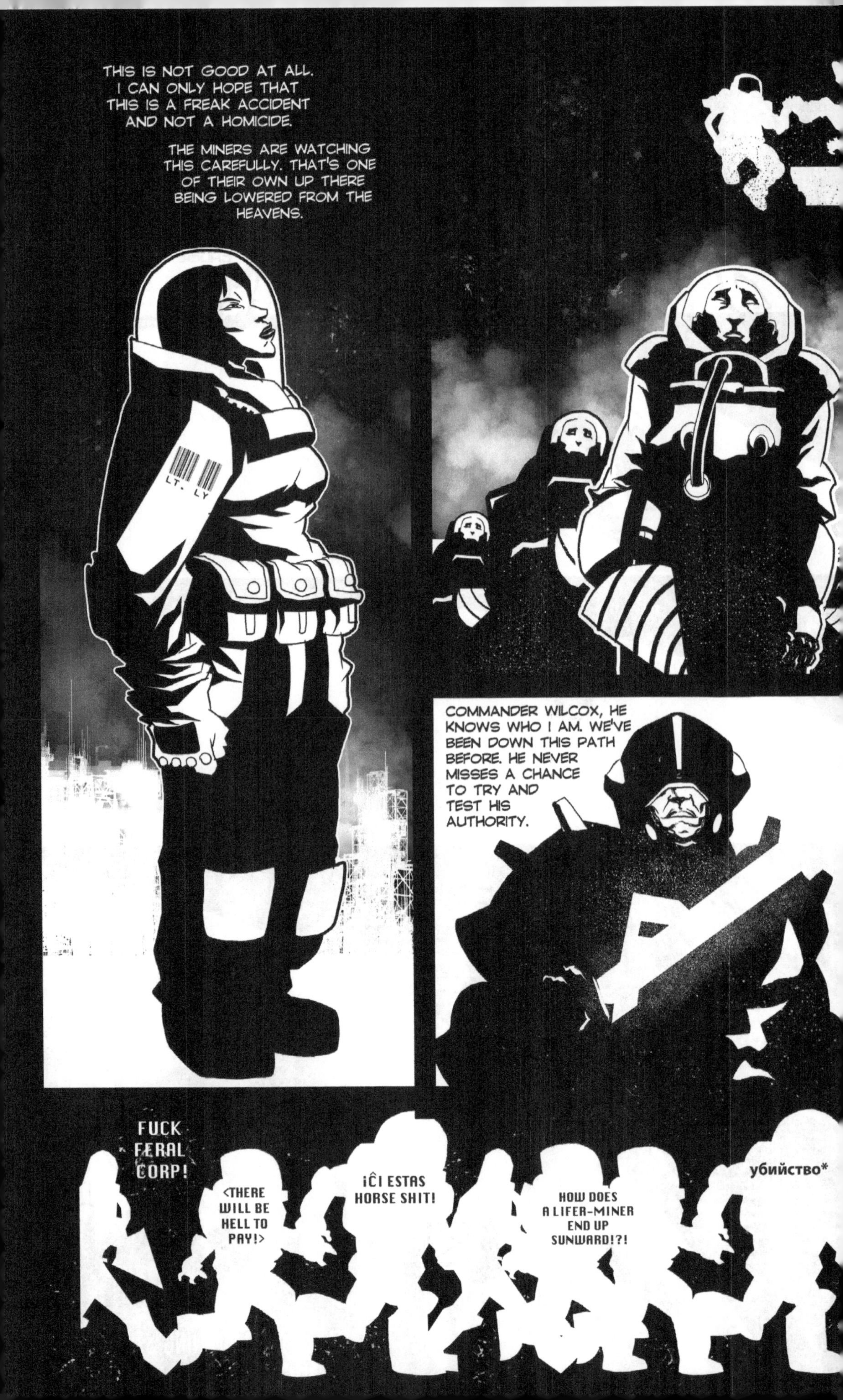
THIS IS NOT GOOD AT ALL. I CAN ONLY HOPE THAT THIS IS A FREAK ACCIDENT AND NOT A HOMICIDE.
THE MINERS ARE WATCHING THIS CAREFULLY. THAT'S ONE OF THEIR OWN UP THERE BEING LOWERED FROM THE HEAVENS.
LT. LY
COMMANDER WILCOX, HE KNOWS WHO I AM. WE'VE BEEN DOWN THIS PATH BEFORE. HE NEVER MISSES A CHANCE TO TRY AND TEST HIS AUTHORITY.
FUCK FERAL CORP!
<THERE WILL BE HELL TO PAY!>
¡ĈI ESTAS HORSE SHIT!
HOW DOES A LIFER-MINER END UP SUNWARD!?!
убийство*

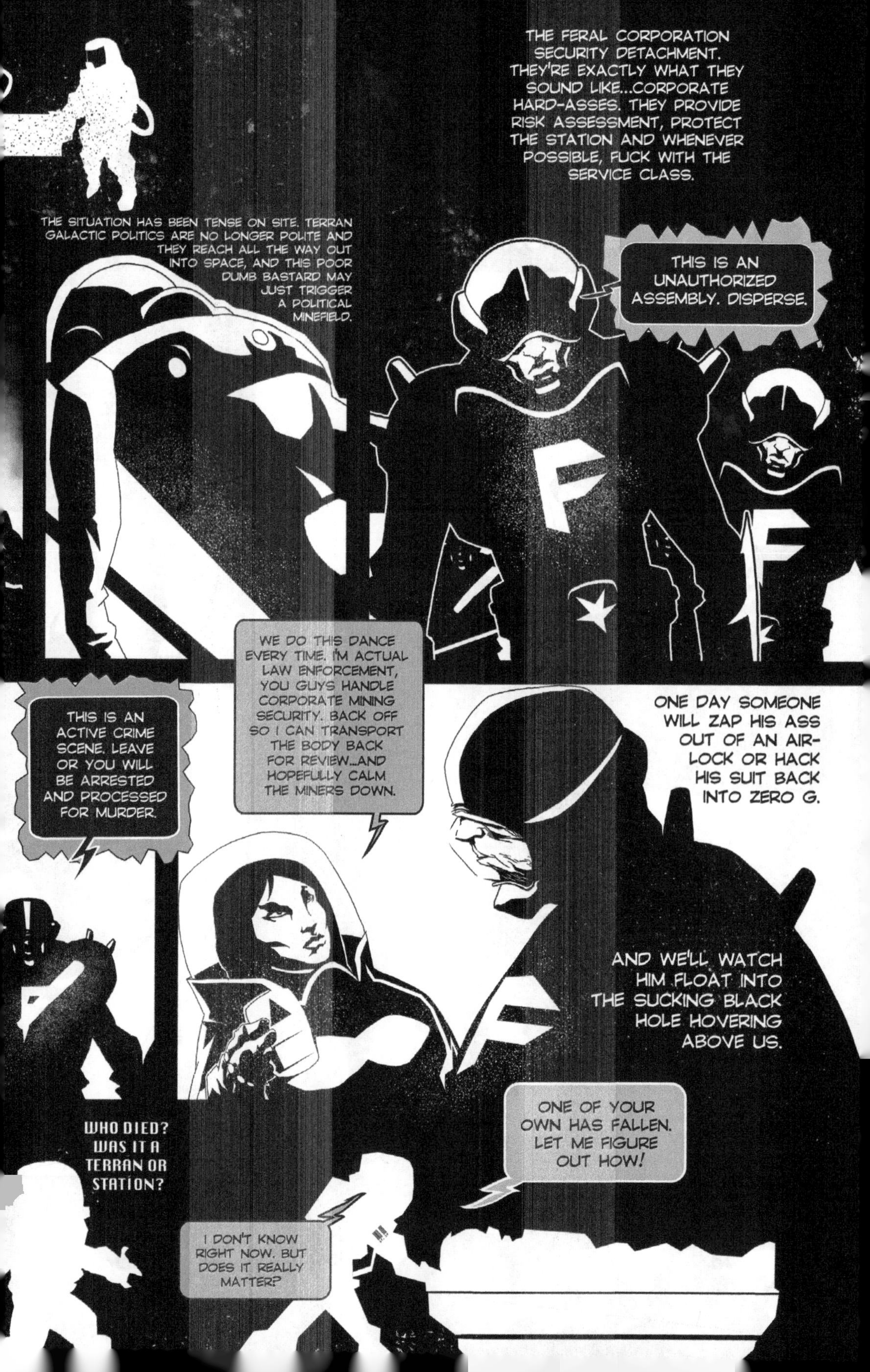
THE FERAL CORPORATION SECURITY DETACHMENT. THEY'RE EXACTLY WHAT THEY SOUND LIKE...CORPORATE HARD-ASSES. THEY PROVIDE RISK ASSESSMENT, PROTECT THE STATION AND WHENEVER POSSIBLE, FUCK WITH THE SERVICE CLASS.
THE SITUATION HAS BEEN TENSE ON SITE. TERRAN GALACTIC POLITICS ARE NO LONGER POLITE AND THEY REACH ALL THE WAY OUT INTO SPACE, AND THIS POOR DUMB BASTARD MAY JUST TRIGGER A POLITICAL MINEFIELD.
THIS IS AN UNAUTHORIZED ASSEMBLY. DISPERSE.
THIS IS AN ACTIVE CRIME SCENE. LEAVE OR YOU WILL BE ARRESTED AND PROCESSED FOR MURDER.
WE DO THIS DANCE EVERY TIME. I'M ACTUAL LAW ENFORCEMENT, YOU GUYS HANDLE CORPORATE MINING SECURITY. BACK OFF SO I CAN TRANSPORT THE BODY BACK FOR REVIEW...AND HOPEFULLY CALM THE MINERS DOWN.
ONE DAY SOMEONE WILL ZAP HIS ASS OUT OF AN AIR-LOCK OR HACK HIS SUIT BACK INTO ZERO G.
AND WE'LL WATCH HIM FLOAT INTO THE SUCKING BLACK HOLE HOVERING ABOVE US.
WHO DIED? WAS IT A TERRAN OR STATION?
ONE OF YOUR OWN HAS FALLEN. LET ME FIGURE OUT HOW!
I DON'T KNOW RIGHT NOW. BUT DOES IT REALLY MATTER?

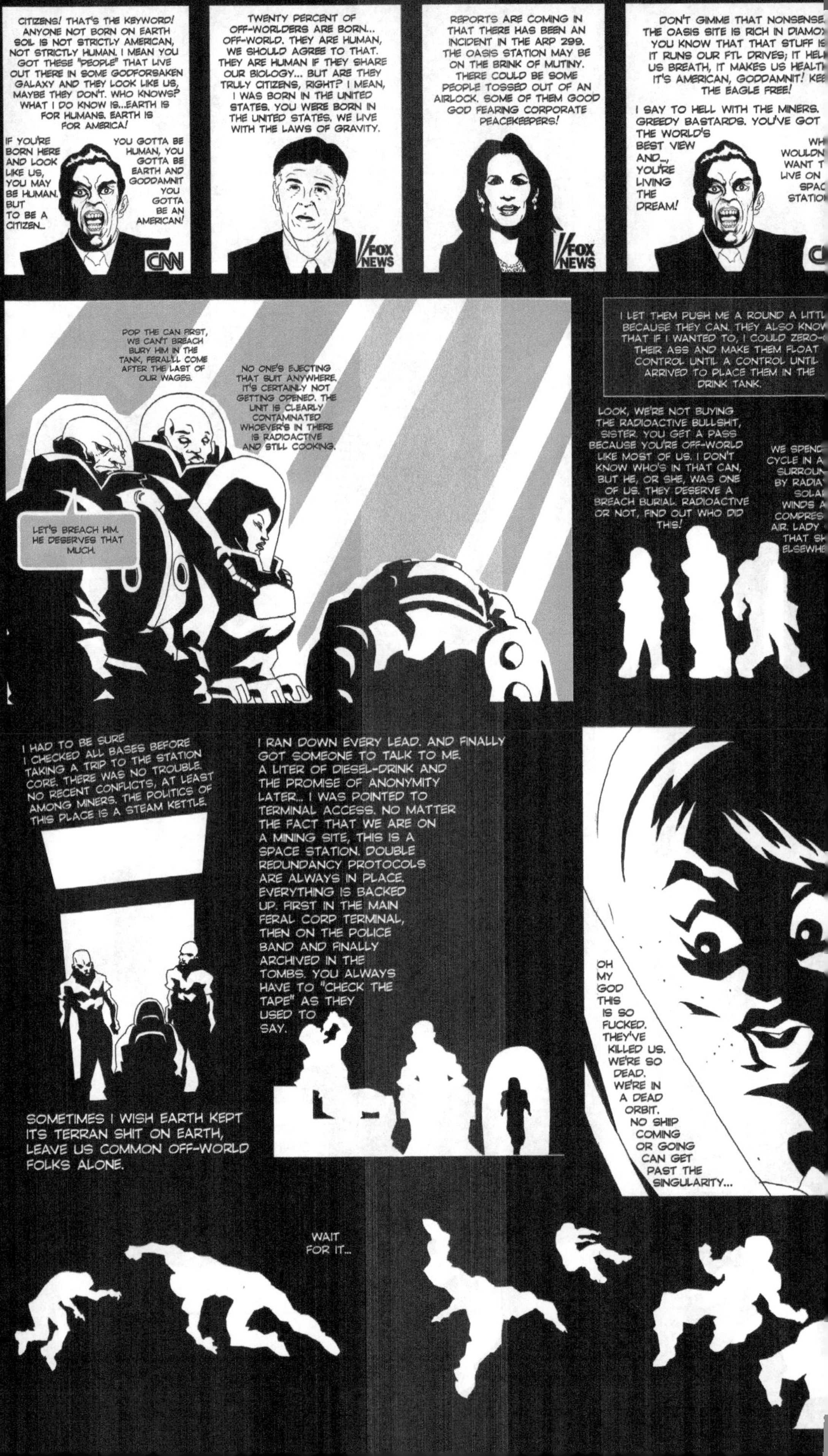

CITIZENS! THAT'S THE KEYWORD! ANYONE NOT BORN ON EARTH SOIL IS NOT STRICTLY AMERICAN, NOT STRICTLY HUMAN. I MEAN YOU GOT THESE "PEOPLE" THAT LIVE OUT THERE IN SOME GODFORSAKEN GALAXY AND THEY LOOK LIKE US, MAYBE THEY DON'T. WHO KNOWS? WHAT I DO KNOW IS...EARTH IS FOR HUMANS. EARTH IS FOR AMERICA!
IF YOU'RE BORN HERE AND LOOK LIKE US, YOU MAY BE HUMAN, BUT TO BE A CITIZEN...
YOU GOTTA BE HUMAN, YOU GOTTA BE EARTH AND GODDAMNIT YOU GOTTA BE AN AMERICAN!
CNN
TWENTY PERCENT OF OFF-WORLDERS ARE BORN... OFF-WORLD. THEY ARE HUMAN, WE SHOULD AGREE TO THAT. THEY ARE HUMAN IF THEY SHARE OUR BIOLOGY... BUT ARE THEY TRULY CITIZENS, RIGHT? I MEAN, I WAS BORN IN THE UNITED STATES. YOU WERE BORN IN THE UNITED STATES. WE LIVE WITH THE LAWS OF GRAVITY.
FOX NEWS
REPORTS ARE COMING IN THAT THERE HAS BEEN AN INCIDENT IN THE ARP 299. THE OASIS STATION MAY BE ON THE BRINK OF MUTINY. THERE COULD BE SOME PEOPLE TOSSED OUT OF AN AIRLOCK. SOME OF THEM GOOD GOD FEARING CORPORATE PEACEKEEPERS!
FOX NEWS
DON'T GIMME THAT NONSENSE. THE OASIS SITE IS RICH IN DIAMO YOU KNOW THAT THAT STUFF IS IT RUNS OUR FTL DRIVES; IT HEL US BREATH, IT MAKES US HEALT IT'S AMERICAN, GODDAMNIT! KEE THE EAGLE FREE!
I SAY TO HELL WITH THE MINERS. GREEDY BASTARDS. YOU'VE GOT THE WORLD'S BEST VIEW AND..., YOU'RE LIVING THE DREAM!
WH WOULDN WANT T LIVE ON SPAC STATIO
POP THE CAN FIRST, WE CAN'T BREACH BURY HIM IN THE TANK, FERAL'LL COME AFTER THE LAST OF OUR WAGES.
NO ONE'S EJECTING THAT SUIT ANYWHERE. IT'S CERTAINLY NOT GETTING OPENED. THE UNIT IS CLEARLY CONTAMINATED WHOEVER'S IN THERE IS RADIOACTIVE AND STILL COOKING.
LET'S BREACH HIM. HE DESERVES THAT MUCH.
I LET THEM PUSH ME A ROUND A LITTL BECAUSE THEY CAN. THEY ALSO KNOW THAT IF I WANTED TO, I COULD ZERO-G THEIR ASS AND MAKE THEM FLOAT CONTROL UNTIL A CONTROL UNTIL ARRIVED TO PLACE THEM IN THE DRINK TANK.
LOOK, WE'RE NOT BUYING THE RADIOACTIVE BULLSHIT, SISTER. YOU GET A PASS BECAUSE YOU'RE OFF-WORLD LIKE MOST OF US. I DON'T KNOW WHO'S IN THAT CAN, BUT HE, OR SHE, WAS ONE OF US. THEY DESERVE A BREACH BURIAL. RADIOACTIVE OR NOT, FIND OUT WHO DID THIS!
WE SPEND CYCLE IN A SURROUN BY RADIA SOLAR WINDS A COMPRES AIR. LADY THAT SH ELSEWHE
I HAD TO BE SURE I CHECKED ALL BASES BEFORE TAKING A TRIP TO THE STATION CORE. THERE WAS NO TROUBLE. NO RECENT CONFLICTS, AT LEAST AMONG MINERS. THE POLITICS OF THIS PLACE IS A STEAM KETTLE.
SOMETIMES I WISH EARTH KEPT ITS TERRAN SHIT ON EARTH, LEAVE US COMMON OFF-WORLD FOLKS ALONE.
I RAN DOWN EVERY LEAD. AND FINALLY GOT SOMEONE TO TALK TO ME. A LITER OF DIESEL-DRINK AND THE PROMISE OF ANONYMITY LATER... I WAS POINTED TO TERMINAL ACCESS. NO MATTER THE FACT THAT WE ARE ON A MINING SITE, THIS IS A SPACE STATION. DOUBLE REDUNDANCY PROTOCOLS ARE ALWAYS IN PLACE. EVERYTHING IS BACKED UP. FIRST IN THE MAIN FERAL CORP TERMINAL, THEN ON THE POLICE BAND AND FINALLY ARCHIVED IN THE TOMBS. YOU ALWAYS HAVE TO "CHECK THE TAPE" AS THEY USED TO SAY.
OH MY GOD THIS IS SO FUCKED. THEY'VE KILLED US. WE'RE SO DEAD. WE'RE IN A DEAD ORBIT. NO SHIP COMING OR GOING CAN GET PAST THE SINGULARITY...
WAIT FOR IT...

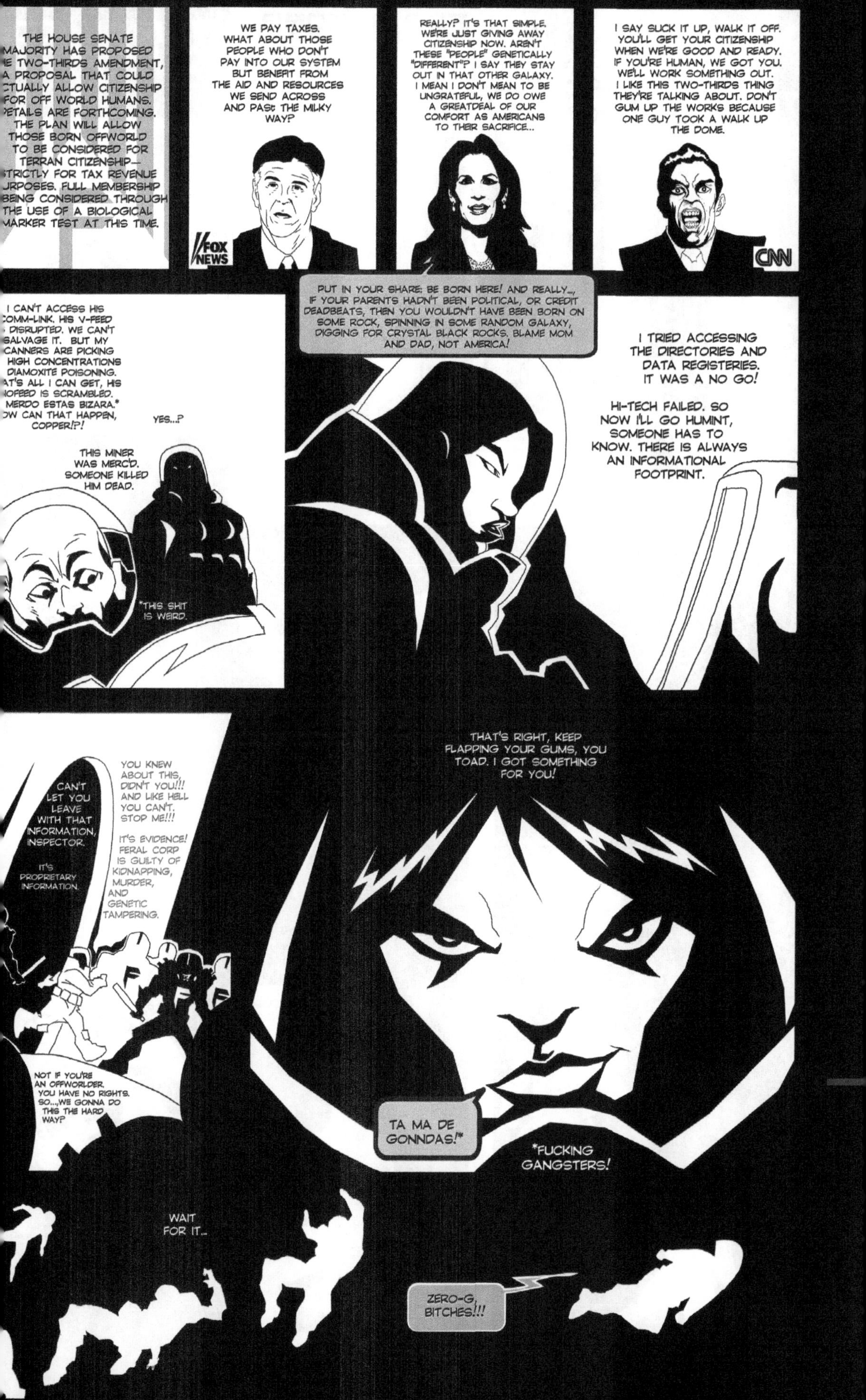
THE HOUSE SENATE MAJORITY HAS PROPOSED HE TWO-THIRDS AMENDMENT, A PROPOSAL THAT COULD CTUALLY ALLOW CITIZENSHIP FOR OFF WORLD HUMANS. ETAILS ARE FORTHCOMING. THE PLAN WILL ALLOW THOSE BORN OFFWORLD TO BE CONSIDERED FOR TERRAN CITIZENSHIP— TRICTLY FOR TAX REVENUE URPOSES. FULL MEMBERSHIP BEING CONSIDERED THROUGH THE USE OF A BIOLOGICAL MARKER TEST AT THIS TIME.
WE PAY TAXES. WHAT ABOUT THOSE PEOPLE WHO DON'T PAY INTO OUR SYSTEM BUT BENEFIT FROM THE AID AND RESOURCES WE SEND ACROSS AND PAST THE MILKY WAY?
FOX NEWS
REALLY? IT'S THAT SIMPLE. WE'RE JUST GIVING AWAY CITIZENSHIP NOW. AREN'T THESE "PEOPLE" GENETICALLY "DIFFERENT"? I SAY THEY STAY OUT IN THAT OTHER GALAXY. I MEAN I DON'T MEAN TO BE UNGRATEFUL, WE DO OWE A GREATDEAL OF OUR COMFORT AS AMERICANS TO THEIR SACRIFICE...
I SAY SUCK IT UP, WALK IT OFF. YOU'LL GET YOUR CITIZENSHIP WHEN WE'RE GOOD AND READY. IF YOU'RE HUMAN, WE GOT YOU. WE'LL WORK SOMETHING OUT. I LIKE THIS TWO-THIRDS THING THEY'RE TALKING ABOUT. DON'T GUM UP THE WORKS BECAUSE ONE GUY TOOK A WALK UP THE DOME.
CNN
PUT IN YOUR SHARE: BE BORN HERE! AND REALLY..., IF YOUR PARENTS HADN'T BEEN POLITICAL, OR CREDIT DEADBEATS, THEN YOU WOULDN'T HAVE BEEN BORN ON SOME ROCK, SPINNING IN SOME RANDOM GALAXY, DIGGING FOR CRYSTAL BLACK ROCKS. BLAME MOM AND DAD, NOT AMERICA!
I CAN'T ACCESS HIS COMM-LINK. HIS V-FEED DISRUPTED. WE CAN'T SALVAGE IT. BUT MY CANNERS ARE PICKING HIGH CONCENTRATIONS DIAMOXITE POISONING. AT'S ALL I CAN GET, HIS IOFEED IS SCRAMBLED. MERDO ESTAS BIZARA.* OW CAN THAT HAPPEN, COPPER!?!
YES...?
THIS MINER WAS MERC'D. SOMEONE KILLED HIM DEAD.
*THIS SHIT IS WEIRD.
I TRIED ACCESSING THE DIRECTORIES AND DATA REGISTERIES. IT WAS A NO GO!
HI-TECH FAILED. SO NOW I'LL GO HUMINT, SOMEONE HAS TO KNOW. THERE IS ALWAYS AN INFORMATIONAL FOOTPRINT.
CAN'T LET YOU LEAVE WITH THAT INFORMATION, INSPECTOR.
IT'S PROPRIETARY INFORMATION.
YOU KNEW ABOUT THIS, DIDN'T YOU!!! AND LIKE HELL YOU CAN'T STOP ME!!!
IT'S EVIDENCE! FERAL CORP IS GUILTY OF KIDNAPPING, MURDER, AND GENETIC TAMPERING.
NOT IF YOU'RE AN OFFWORLDER. YOU HAVE NO RIGHTS. SO...,WE GONNA DO THIS THE HARD WAY?
THAT'S RIGHT, KEEP FLAPPING YOUR GUMS, YOU TOAD. I GOT SOMETHING FOR YOU!
TA MA DE GONNDAS!*
*FUCKING GANGSTERS!
WAIT FOR IT...
ZERO-G, BITCHES!!!

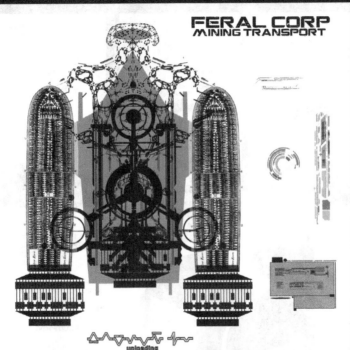

**FERAL CORP**
MINING TRANSPORT

**FERAL CO**
MINING HELM

uploading

uploading

YOU GONNA
FOLLOW-UP THE
HANDHOLDING
WITH A KISS
OR WHAT!?!

I CALLED A MEETING WITH
MINERS TO REPORT MY FIN
THIS WAS TOO BIG TO KEE
AND THEY DESERVED TO
FERAL CORP'S DIRTY LIT
SECRET ABOUT US

I GOT YOUR
KISS RIGHT
HERE!

ZERO G
LIFTED.

EAT DOME,
GOONDAS!!!

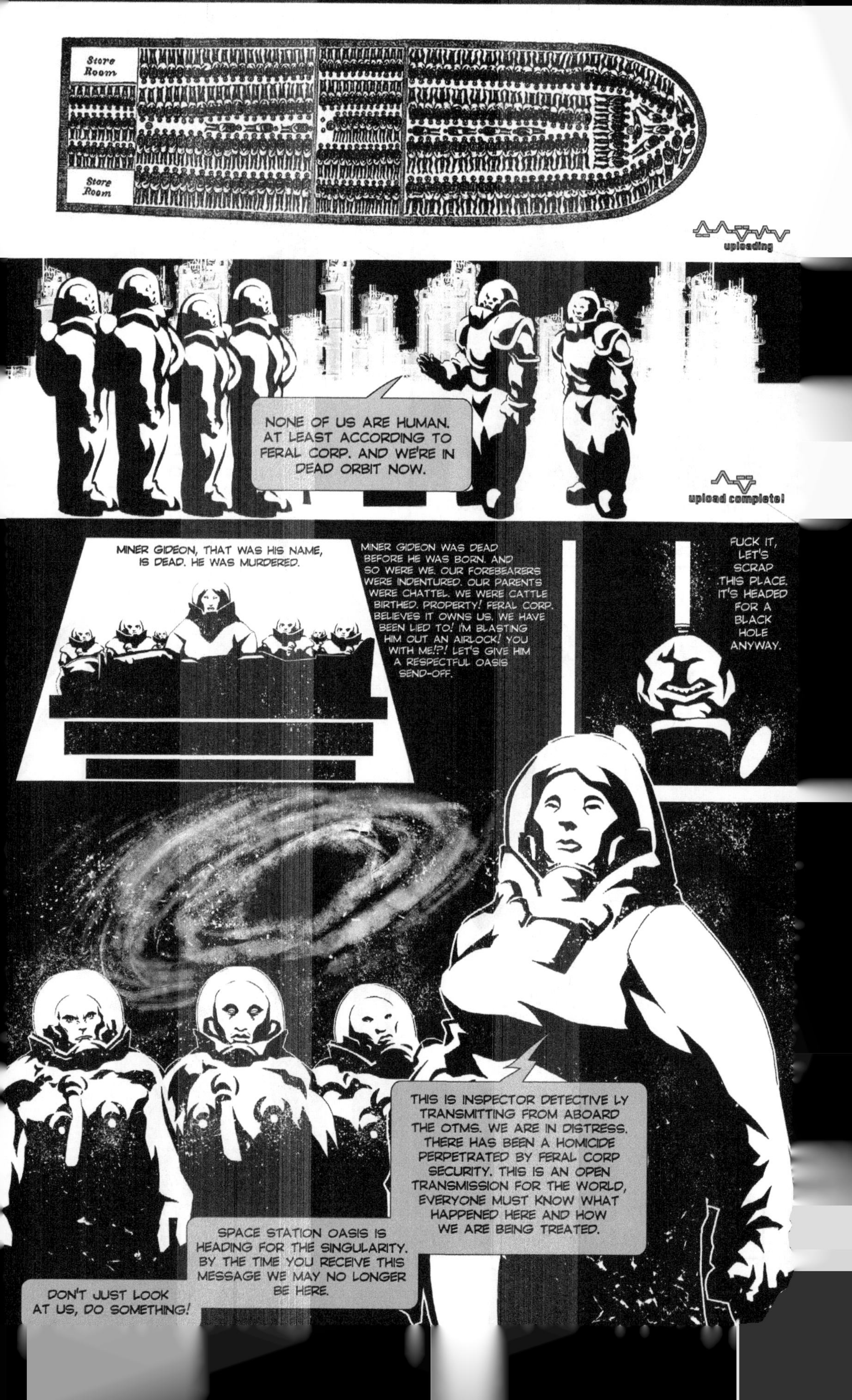
Store Room
Store Room
uploading
NONE OF US ARE HUMAN. AT LEAST ACCORDING TO FERAL CORP. AND WE'RE IN DEAD ORBIT NOW.
upload complete!
MINER GIDEON, THAT WAS HIS NAME, IS DEAD. HE WAS MURDERED.
MINER GIDEON WAS DEAD BEFORE HE WAS BORN. AND SO WERE WE. OUR FOREBEARERS WERE INDENTURED. OUR PARENTS WERE CHATTEL. WE WERE CATTLE BIRTHED. PROPERTY! FERAL CORP. BELIEVES IT OWNS US. WE HAVE BEEN LIED TO! I'M BLASTING HIM OUT AN AIRLOCK! YOU WITH ME!?! LET'S GIVE HIM A RESPECTFUL OASIS SEND-OFF.
FUCK IT, LET'S SCRAP THIS PLACE. IT'S HEADED FOR A BLACK HOLE ANYWAY.
THIS IS INSPECTOR DETECTIVE LY TRANSMITTING FROM ABOARD THE OTMS. WE ARE IN DISTRESS. THERE HAS BEEN A HOMICIDE PERPETRATED BY FERAL CORP SECURITY. THIS IS AN OPEN TRANSMISSION FOR THE WORLD, EVERYONE MUST KNOW WHAT HAPPENED HERE AND HOW WE ARE BEING TREATED.
SPACE STATION OASIS IS HEADING FOR THE SINGULARITY. BY THE TIME YOU RECEIVE THIS MESSAGE WE MAY NO LONGER BE HERE.
DON'T JUST LOOK AT US, DO SOMETHING!

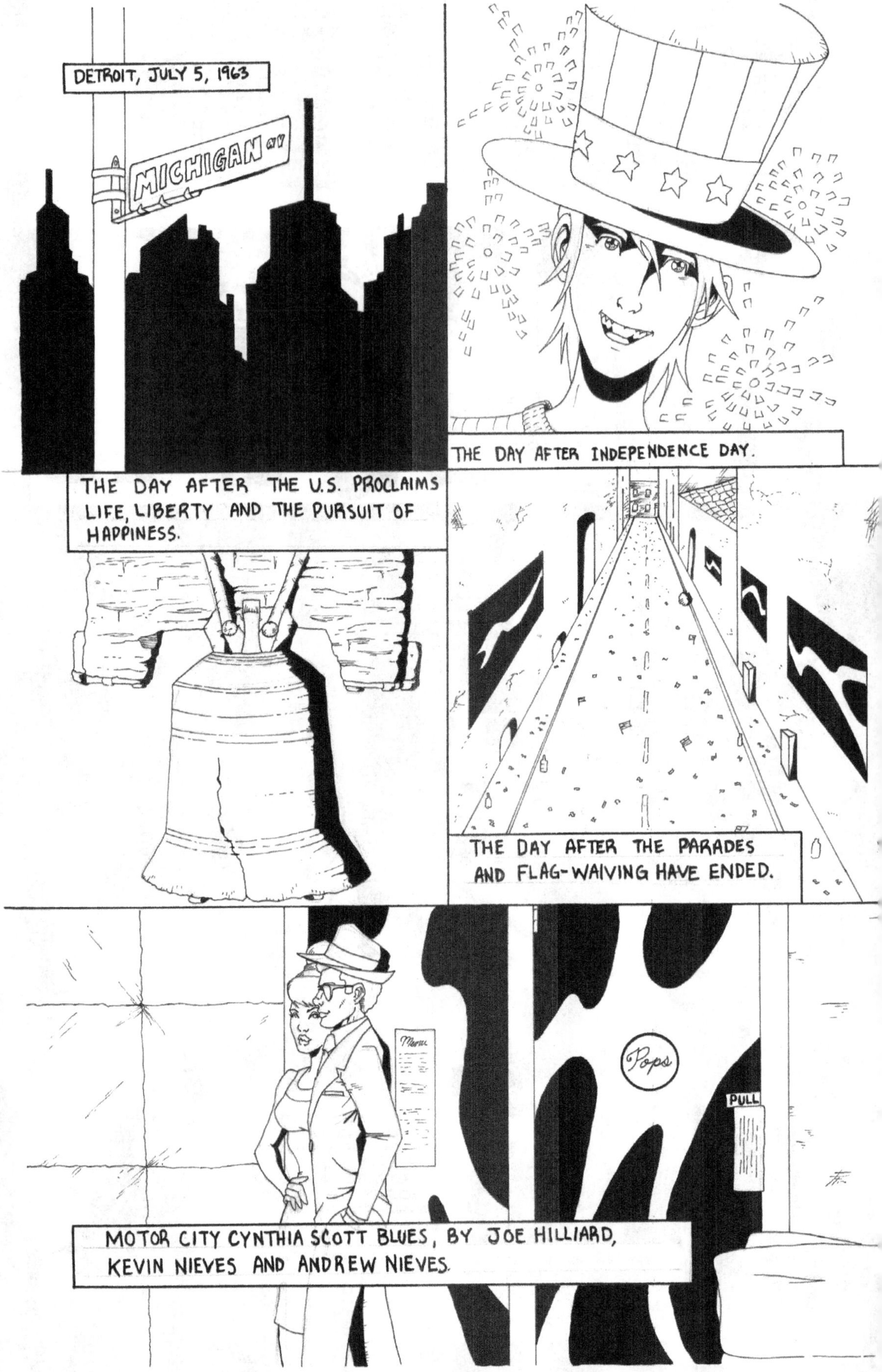
DETROIT, JULY 5, 1963
MICHIGAN AV
THE DAY AFTER INDEPENDENCE DAY.
THE DAY AFTER THE U.S. PROCLAIMS LIFE, LIBERTY AND THE PURSUIT OF HAPPINESS.
THE DAY AFTER THE PARADES AND FLAG-WAIVING HAVE ENDED.
Menu
Pops
PULL
MOTOR CITY CYNTHIA SCOTT BLUES, BY JOE HILLIARD, KEVIN NIEVES AND ANDREW NIEVES.

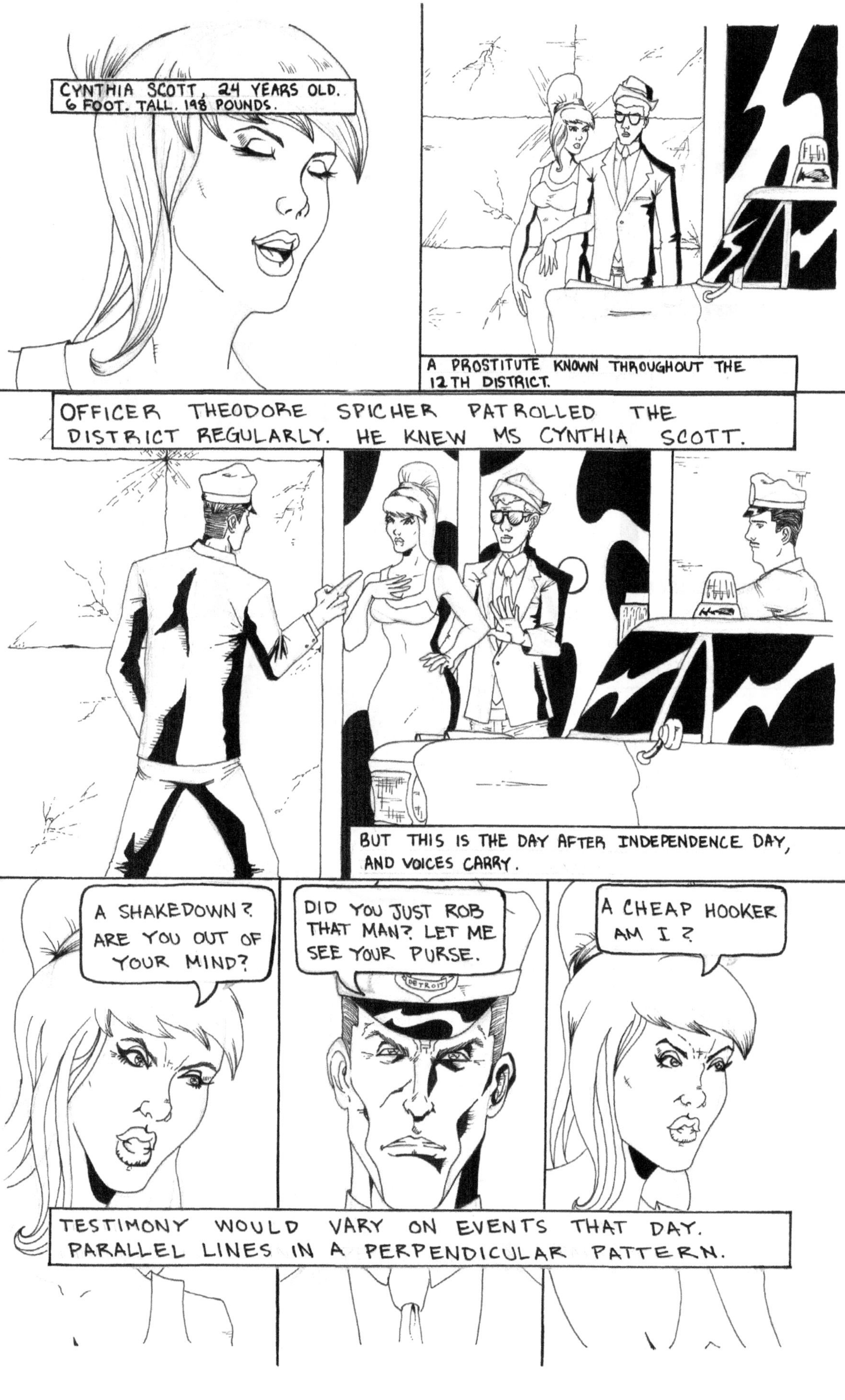
CYNTHIA SCOTT, 24 YEARS OLD. 6 FOOT. TALL. 198 POUNDS.
A PROSTITUTE KNOWN THROUGHOUT THE 12TH DISTRICT.
OFFICER THEODORE SPICHER PATROLLED THE DISTRICT REGULARLY. HE KNEW MS CYNTHIA SCOTT.
BUT THIS IS THE DAY AFTER INDEPENDENCE DAY, AND VOICES CARRY.
A SHAKEDOWN? ARE YOU OUT OF YOUR MIND?
DID YOU JUST ROB THAT MAN? LET ME SEE YOUR PURSE.
DETROIT
A CHEAP HOOKER AM I?
TESTIMONY WOULD VARY ON EVENTS THAT DAY. PARALLEL LINES IN A PERPENDICULAR PATTERN.

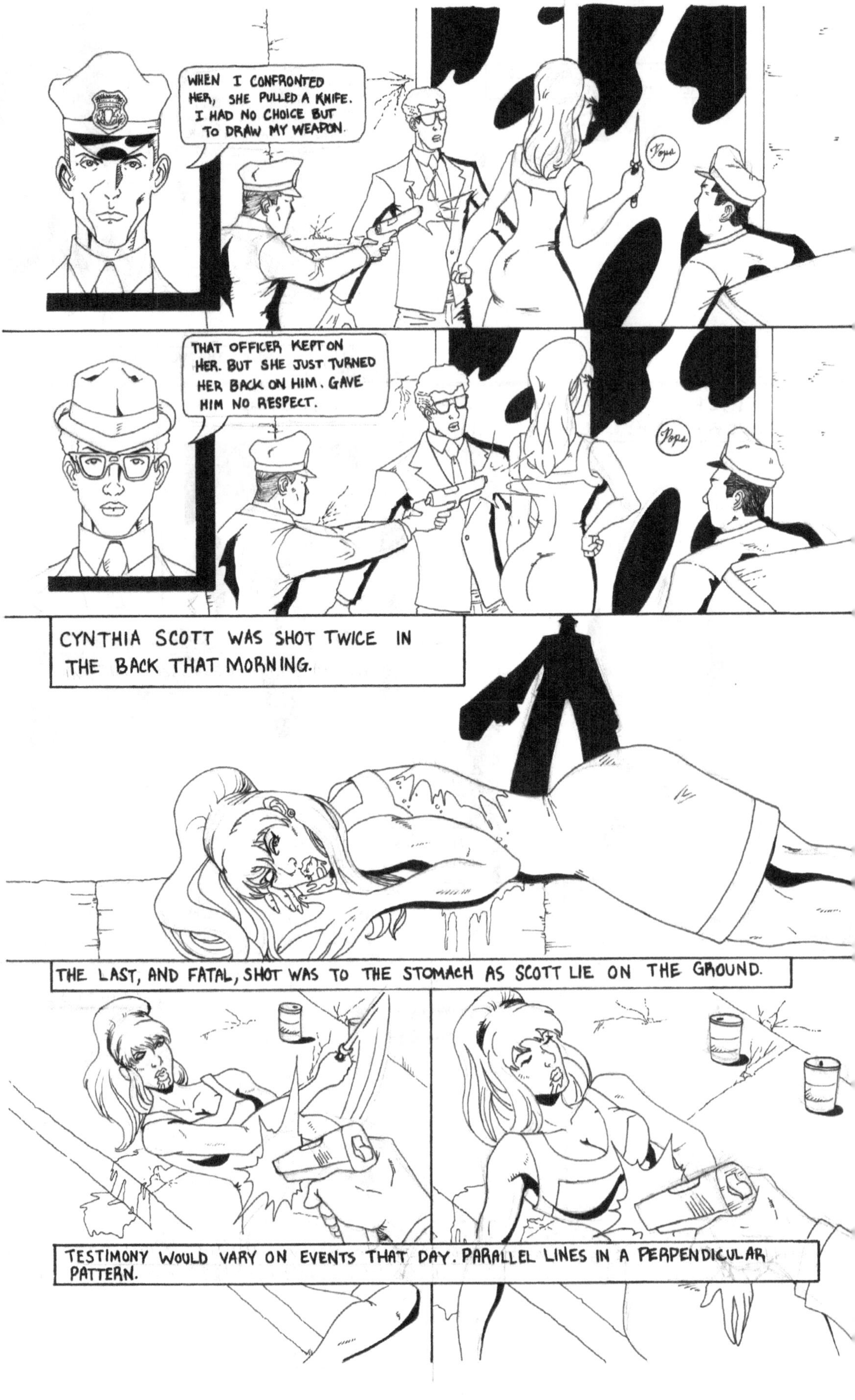
WHEN I CONFRONTED HER, SHE PULLED A KNIFE. I HAD NO CHOICE BUT TO DRAW MY WEAPON.
THAT OFFICER KEPT ON HER. BUT SHE JUST TURNED HER BACK ON HIM. GAVE HIM NO RESPECT.
CYNTHIA SCOTT WAS SHOT TWICE IN THE BACK THAT MORNING.
THE LAST, AND FATAL, SHOT WAS TO THE STOMACH AS SCOTT LIE ON THE GROUND.
TESTIMONY WOULD VARY ON EVENTS THAT DAY. PARALLEL LINES IN A PERPENDICULAR PATTERN.

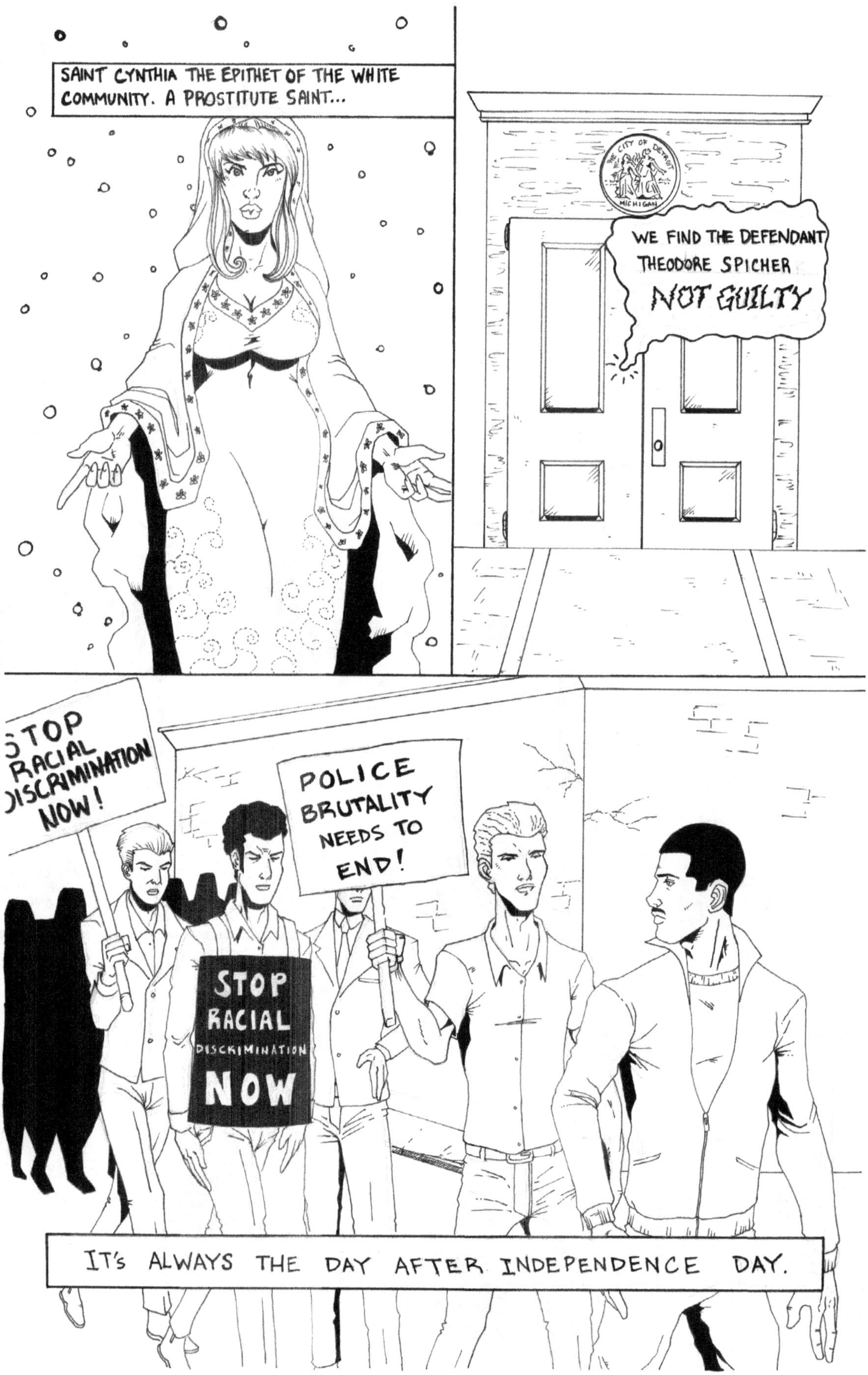
SAINT CYNTHIA THE EPITHET OF THE WHITE COMMUNITY. A PROSTITUTE SAINT...
THE CITY OF DETROIT MICHIGAN
WE FIND THE DEFENDANT THEODORE SPICHER NOT GUILTY
STOP RACIAL DISCRIMINATION NOW!
POLICE BRUTALITY NEEDS TO END!
STOP RACIAL DISCRIMINATION NOW
IT'S ALWAYS THE DAY AFTER INDEPENDENCE DAY.

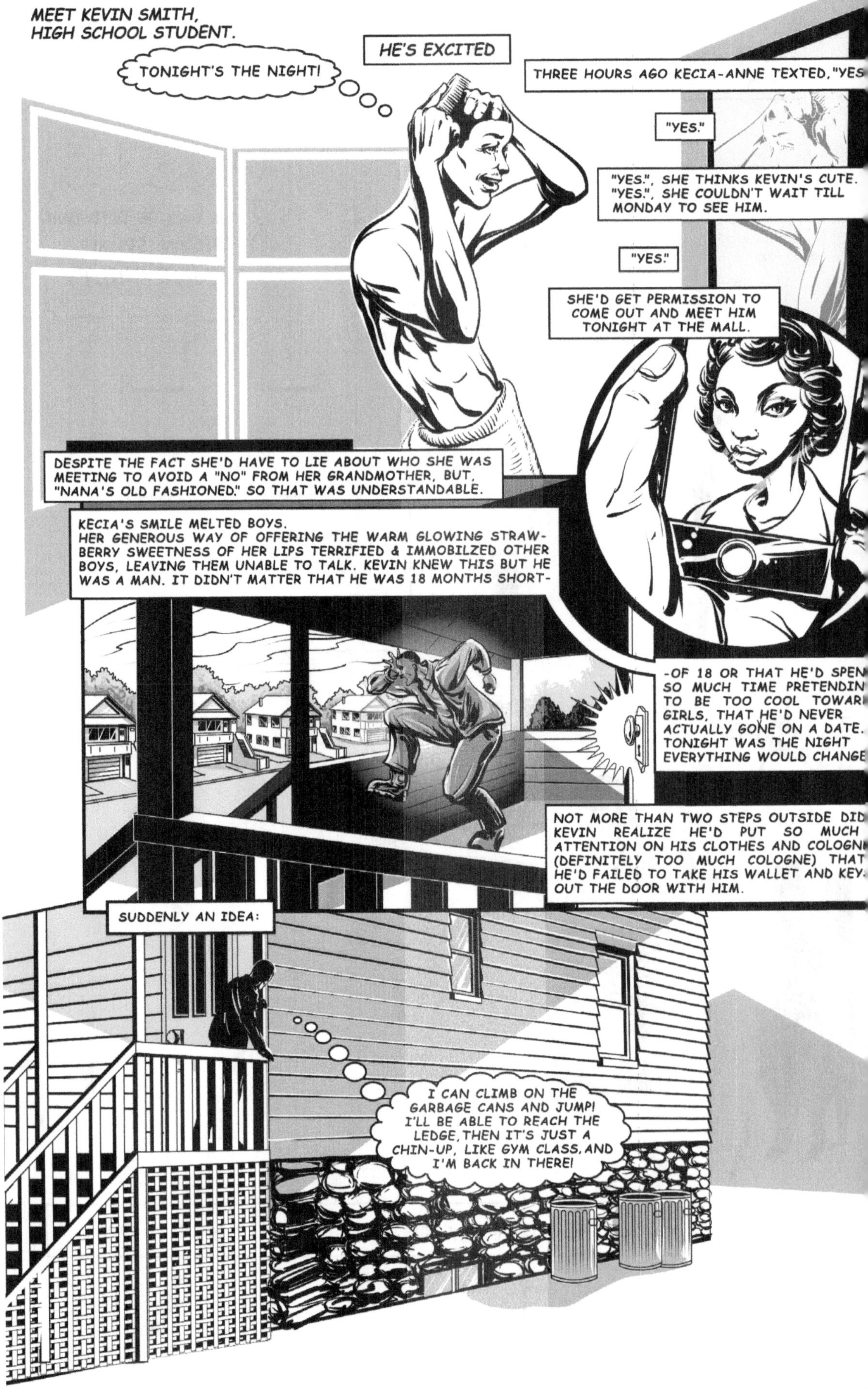
MEET KEVIN SMITH,
HIGH SCHOOL STUDENT.
TONIGHT'S THE NIGHT!
HE'S EXCITED
THREE HOURS AGO KECIA-ANNE TEXTED, "YES
"YES."
"YES.", SHE THINKS KEVIN'S CUTE. "YES.", SHE COULDN'T WAIT TILL MONDAY TO SEE HIM.
"YES."
SHE'D GET PERMISSION TO COME OUT AND MEET HIM TONIGHT AT THE MALL.
DESPITE THE FACT SHE'D HAVE TO LIE ABOUT WHO SHE WAS MEETING TO AVOID A "NO" FROM HER GRANDMOTHER, BUT, "NANA'S OLD FASHIONED." SO THAT WAS UNDERSTANDABLE.
KECIA'S SMILE MELTED BOYS. HER GENEROUS WAY OF OFFERING THE WARM GLOWING STRAWBERRY SWEETNESS OF HER LIPS TERRIFIED & IMMOBILZED OTHER BOYS, LEAVING THEM UNABLE TO TALK. KEVIN KNEW THIS BUT HE WAS A MAN. IT DIDN'T MATTER THAT HE WAS 18 MONTHS SHORT-
-OF 18 OR THAT HE'D SPEN SO MUCH TIME PRETENDIN TO BE TOO COOL TOWAR GIRLS, THAT HE'D NEVER ACTUALLY GONE ON A DATE. TONIGHT WAS THE NIGHT EVERYTHING WOULD CHANGE
NOT MORE THAN TWO STEPS OUTSIDE DID KEVIN REALIZE HE'D PUT SO MUCH ATTENTION ON HIS CLOTHES AND COLOGN (DEFINITELY TOO MUCH COLOGNE) THAT HE'D FAILED TO TAKE HIS WALLET AND KEY OUT THE DOOR WITH HIM.
SUDDENLY AN IDEA:
I CAN CLIMB ON THE GARBAGE CANS AND JUMP! I'LL BE ABLE TO REACH THE LEDGE, THEN IT'S JUST A CHIN-UP, LIKE GYM CLASS, AND I'M BACK IN THERE!

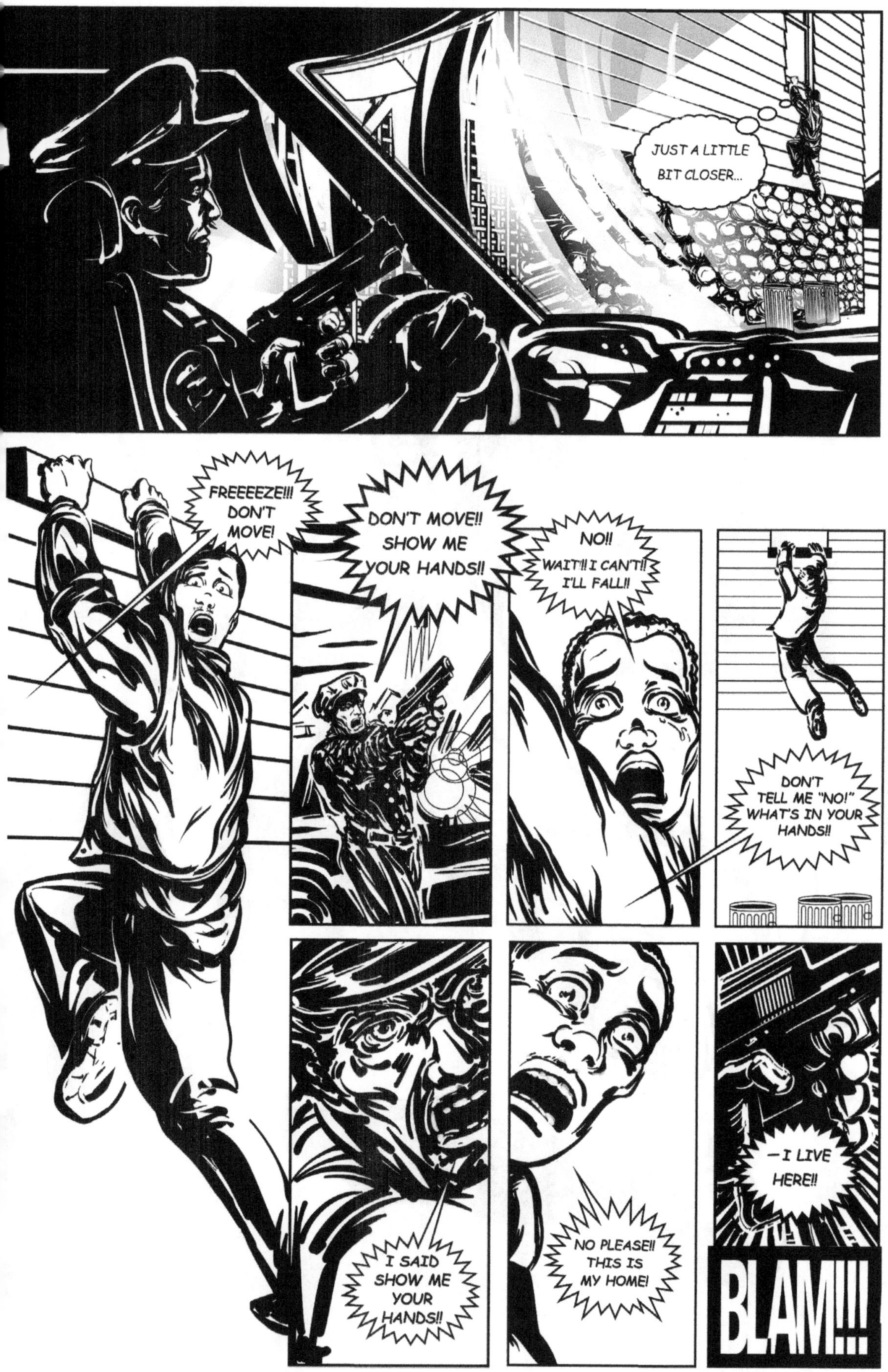
JUST A LITTLE BIT CLOSER...
FREEEEZE!!! DON'T MOVE!
DON'T MOVE!! SHOW ME YOUR HANDS!!
NO!! WAIT!! I CAN'T!! I'LL FALL!!
DON'T TELL ME "NO!" WHAT'S IN YOUR HANDS!!
I SAID SHOW ME YOUR HANDS!!
NO PLEASE!! THIS IS MY HOME!
—I LIVE HERE!!
BLAM!!!

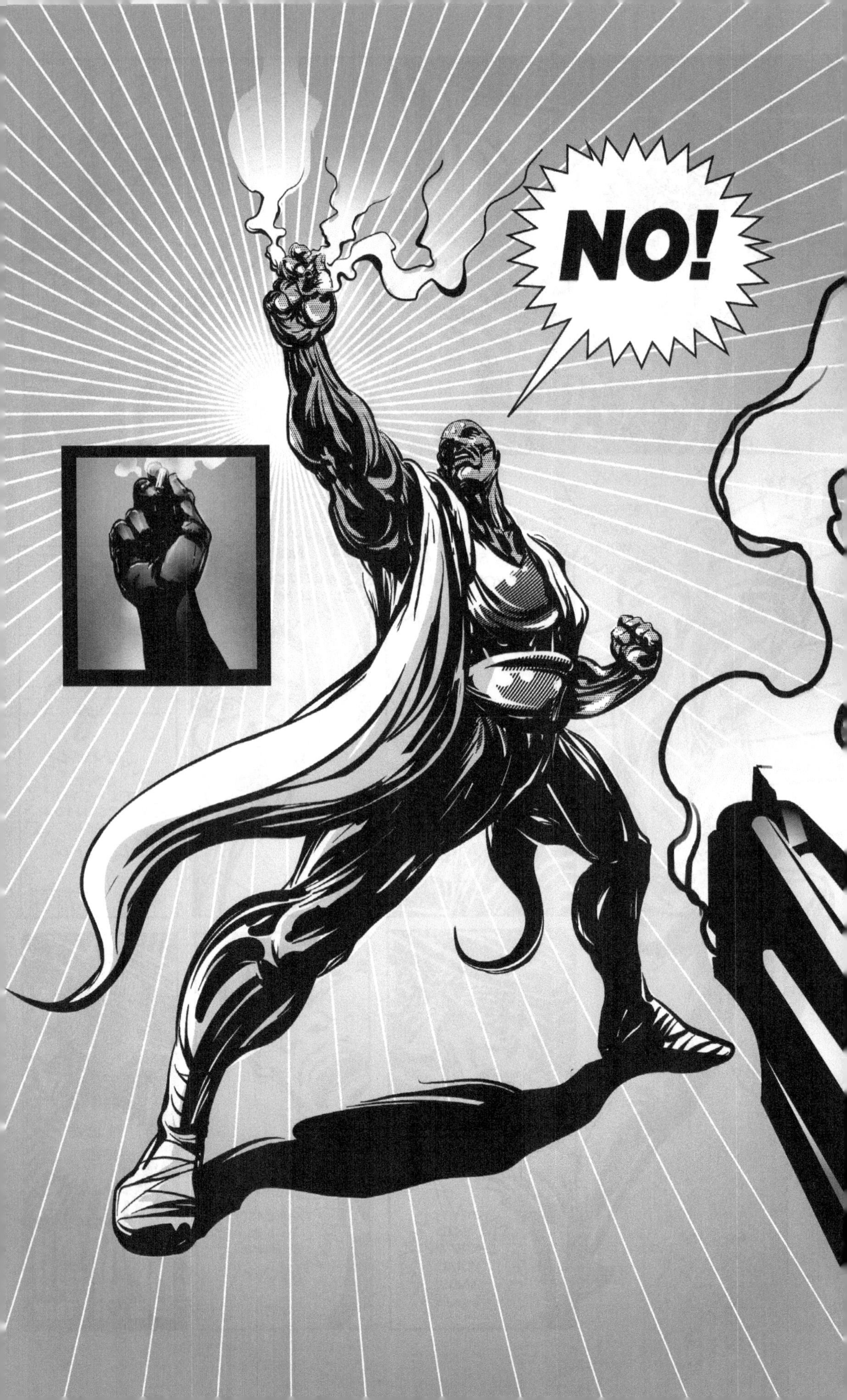
NO!

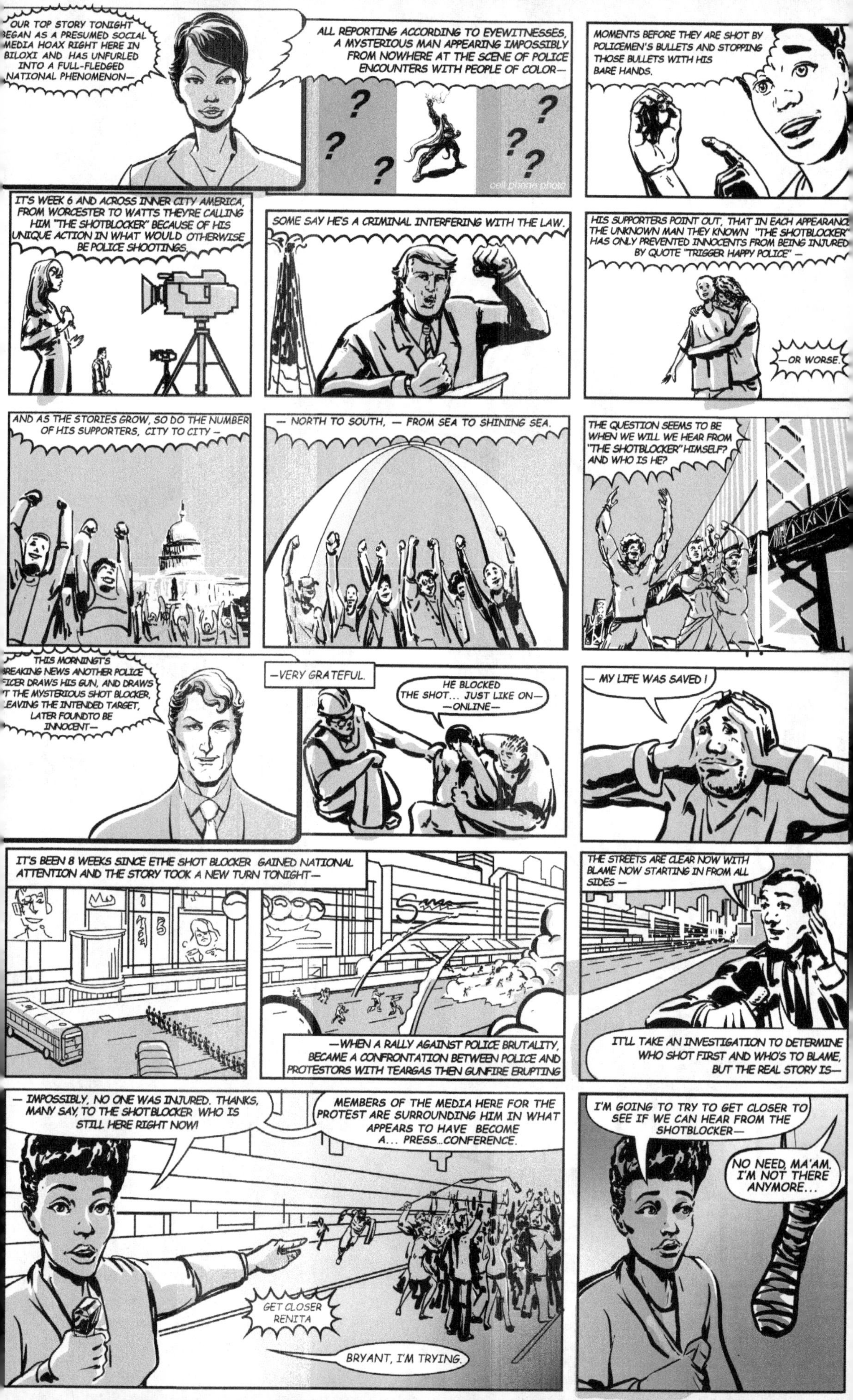
OUR TOP STORY TONIGHT BEGAN AS A PRESUMED SOCIAL MEDIA HOAX RIGHT HERE IN BILOXI AND HAS UNFURLED INTO A FULL-FLEDGED NATIONAL PHENOMENON—
ALL REPORTING ACCORDING TO EYEWITNESSES, A MYSTERIOUS MAN APPEARING IMPOSSIBLY FROM NOWHERE AT THE SCENE OF POLICE ENCOUNTERS WITH PEOPLE OF COLOR—
cell phone photo
MOMENTS BEFORE THEY ARE SHOT BY POLICEMEN'S BULLETS AND STOPPING THOSE BULLETS WITH HIS BARE HANDS.
IT'S WEEK 6 AND ACROSS INNER CITY AMERICA, FROM WORCESTER TO WATTS THEY'RE CALLING HIM "THE SHOTBLOCKER" BECAUSE OF HIS UNIQUE ACTION IN WHAT WOULD OTHERWISE BE POLICE SHOOTINGS.
SOME SAY HE'S A CRIMINAL INTERFERING WITH THE LAW.
HIS SUPPORTERS POINT OUT, THAT IN EACH APPEARANCE THE UNKNOWN MAN THEY KNOWN "THE SHOTBLOCKER" HAS ONLY PREVENTED INNOCENTS FROM BEING INJURED BY QUOTE "TRIGGER HAPPY POLICE" —
—OR WORSE.
AND AS THE STORIES GROW, SO DO THE NUMBER OF HIS SUPPORTERS, CITY TO CITY —
— NORTH TO SOUTH, — FROM SEA TO SHINING SEA.
THE QUESTION SEEMS TO BE WHEN WE WILL WE HEAR FROM "THE SHOTBLOCKER" HIMSELF? AND WHO IS HE?
THIS MORNINGT'S BREAKING NEWS ANOTHER POLICE FICER DRAWS HIS GUN, AND DRAWS T THE MYSTERIOUS SHOT BLOCKER, LEAVING THE INTENDED TARGET, LATER FOUNDTO BE INNOCENT—
—VERY GRATEFUL.
HE BLOCKED THE SHOT... JUST LIKE ON— —ONLINE—
— MY LIFE WAS SAVED !
IT'S BEEN 8 WEEKS SINCE ETHE SHOT BLOCKER GAINED NATIONAL ATTENTION AND THE STORY TOOK A NEW TURN TONIGHT—
—WHEN A RALLY AGAINST POLICE BRUTALITY, BECAME A CONFRONTATION BETWEEN POLICE AND PROTESTORS WITH TEARGAS THEN GUNFIRE ERUPTING
THE STREETS ARE CLEAR NOW WITH BLAME NOW STARTING IN FROM ALL SIDES —
IT'LL TAKE AN INVESTIGATION TO DETERMINE WHO SHOT FIRST AND WHO'S TO BLAME, BUT THE REAL STORY IS—
— IMPOSSIBLY, NO ONE WAS INJURED. THANKS, MANY SAY, TO THE SHOTBLOCKER WHO IS STILL HERE RIGHT NOW!
MEMBERS OF THE MEDIA HERE FOR THE PROTEST ARE SURROUNDING HIM IN WHAT APPEARS TO HAVE BECOME A... PRESS...CONFERENCE.
GET CLOSER RENITA
BRYANT, I'M TRYING.
I'M GOING TO TRY TO GET CLOSER TO SEE IF WE CAN HEAR FROM THE SHOTBLOCKER—
NO NEED, MA'AM. I'M NOT THERE ANYMORE...

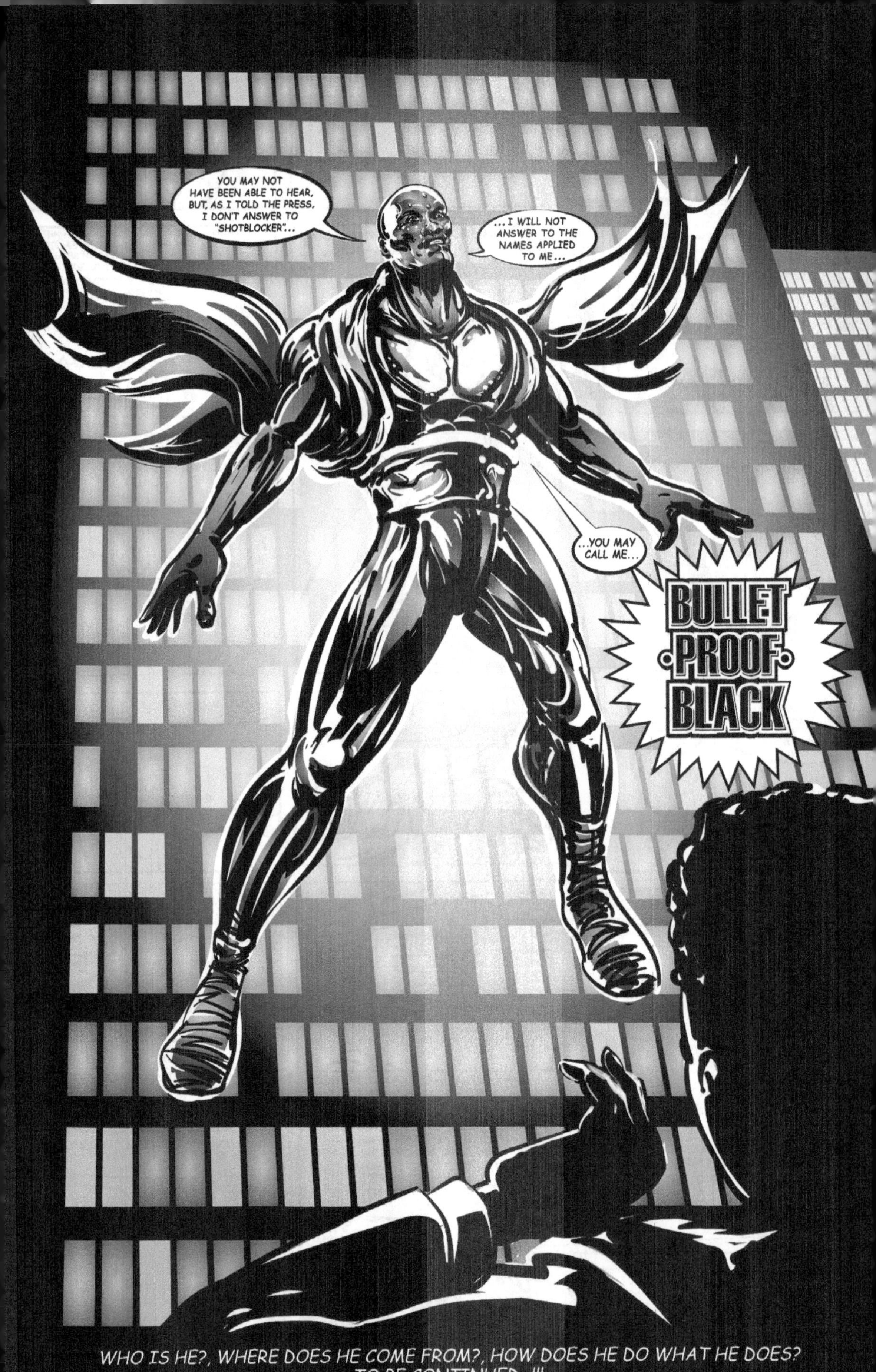
YOU MAY NOT HAVE BEEN ABLE TO HEAR, BUT, AS I TOLD THE PRESS, I DON'T ANSWER TO "SHOTBLOCKER"...
...I WILL NOT ANSWER TO THE NAMES APPLIED TO ME...
...YOU MAY CALL ME...
BULLET PROOF BLACK

*WHO IS HE?, WHERE DOES HE COME FROM?, HOW DOES HE DO WHAT HE DOES?*
*TO BE CONTINUED...!!!*

*"BULLET PROOF BLACK"™ IS WRITTEN, ILLUSTRATED & CREATED BY JASON SCOTT JONES*

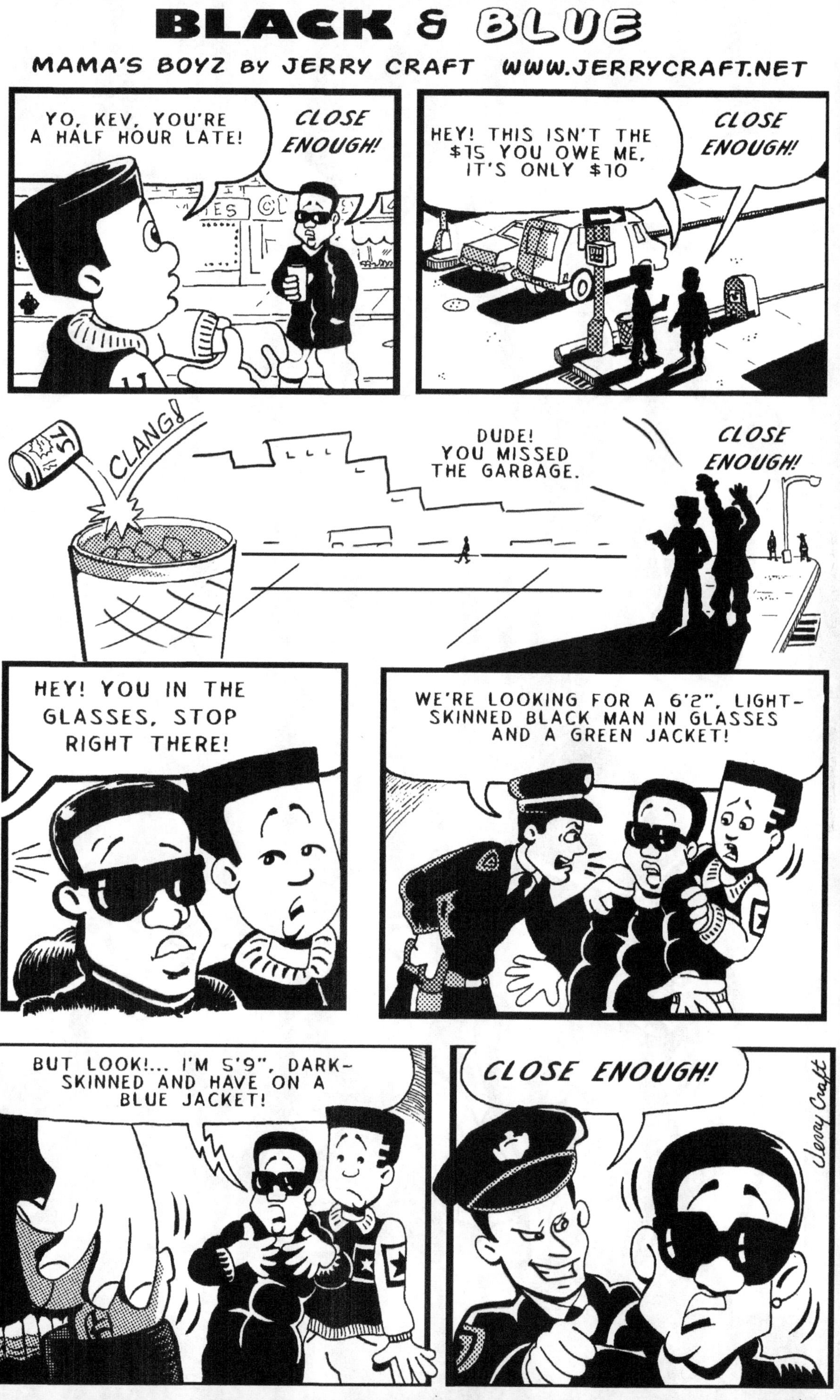
BLACK & BLUE
MAMA'S BOYZ BY JERRY CRAFT WWW.JERRYCRAFT.NET
YO, KEV, YOU'RE A HALF HOUR LATE!
CLOSE ENOUGH!
HEY! THIS ISN'T THE $15 YOU OWE ME, IT'S ONLY $10
CLOSE ENOUGH!
CLANG!
DUDE! YOU MISSED THE GARBAGE.
CLOSE ENOUGH!
HEY! YOU IN THE GLASSES, STOP RIGHT THERE!
WE'RE LOOKING FOR A 6'2", LIGHT-SKINNED BLACK MAN IN GLASSES AND A GREEN JACKET!
BUT LOOK!... I'M 5'9", DARK-SKINNED AND HAVE ON A BLUE JACKET!
CLOSE ENOUGH!
Jerry Craft

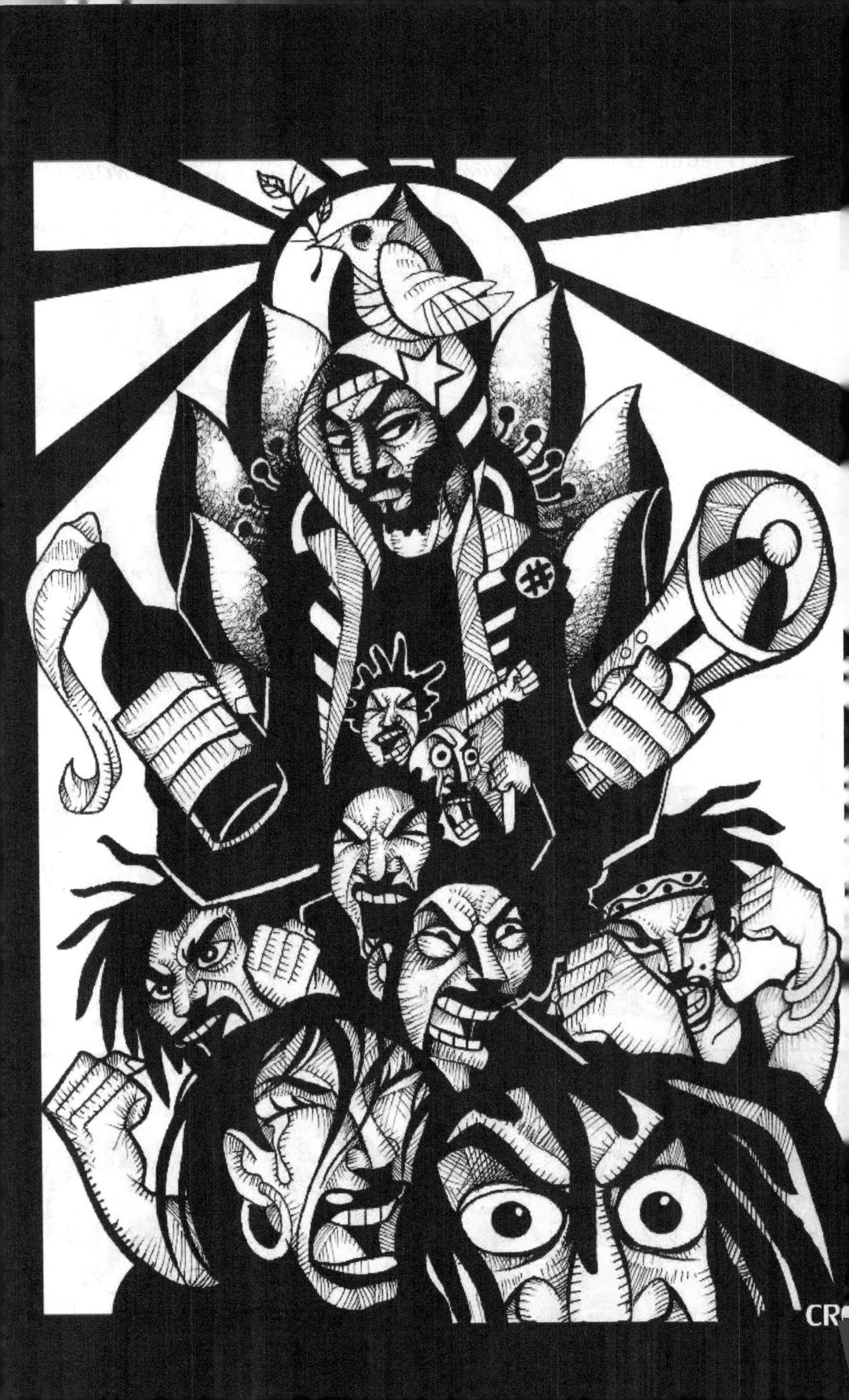

CR

# RIOTING: AS AMERICAN AS APPLE PIE

## BY P. DJELI CLARK

"There's no excuse for the kind of violence that we saw yesterday," President Barack Obama declared, a day after protests over the death of a black man, Freddie Gray, in the custody of Baltimore police transformed into a night of rioting. "When individuals get crowbars and start prying open doors to loot, they're not protesting. They're not making a statement. They're stealing. When they burn down a building, they're committing arson."

Joining the mayor of Baltimore, the president called the rioters "criminals and thugs," labeling their acts "counterproductive." Community leaders and clergy chimed in, imploring that social change has only come through nonviolent protest. It was a familiar mantra, yet one based on a debatable claim. The inconvenient truth is that riots have long accompanied the winds of change in America—for good or ill. And they've been with us since the beginning.

On August 14, 1765, a group calling itself the Loyal Nine gathered in colonial Boston against the Stamp Act, burning effigies of the local official Andrew Oliver. Protest turned to riot, as thousands took to the streets. The mob marched on Oliver's home, tearing down his fence, smashing windows, destroying furnishings, and looting the wine cellar. Twelve days later they attacked the home of Oliver's brother-in-law Thomas Hutchinson, the Lieutenant Governor of Massachusetts. Hutchinson's door was cut down with axes, and looters made off with his fine silver and £900 sterling in cash.

Mob actions were par for the course for early Patriots, who regularly harassed, beat, and tarred and feathered authority figures, while vandalizing and destroying property—all in the name of liberty. In November 1765, the self-styled Sons of Neptune launched a riot against Ft. George in Manhattan, encouraging mobs to hurl bricks, stones and garbage at British guards while looting the waterfront. In harbors and ports from Newport to Wilmington, "sailors, boys, and Negroes" rioted against impressment. In 1770 the runaway slave Crispus Attucks and "a motley rabble of saucy boys, negroes and molattoes, Irish teagues, and outlandish Jack Tarrs" incited a riot that propagandists renamed The Boston Massacre.

Elite Patriot voices claimed to deplore mobs as disorderly but could not deny their effectiveness. By 1775, ten years of upheaval had laid the groundwork for insurrection. As one South Carolinian newspaper put it: "the Plebians are...for war." While the upper classes ruled the coming Revolution, its earliest foot soldier was the mob. And their strategy, the riot.

"Mob-rage" or "Mob-government" became a common facet of the new Republic and could erupt with the force of what one witness called "a West-India hurricane." Riots broke out everywhere—between political factions and at public celebrations. Even at theaters, jeering audiences often attacked actors, tore apart playhouses, and rioted through the streets.

In 1829, at Andrew Jackson's inauguration, the crowd at the White House teetered so often on chaos, political enemies depicted it as a drunken riotous mob. While claims of the residence being ransacked were likely exaggerated, "mobocracy" was common enough to make the charge plausible.

Through the early nineteenth century mob-rage took on a darker slant—as violent pogroms against minorities. In 1844, Nativists launched anti-Irish riots in Philadelphia. In 1851 Hoboken, Germans were targeted. Anti-Chinese riots broke out in the 1880s in cities like Seattle.

No group was more singled out than African-Americans. In antebellum Boston, blacks were attacked at public events by white mobs adorned in blackface. Public black-face-on-black violence became so common that, in some cities, African-Americans were effectively driven from Fourth of July and Christmas processions. Even black parades could expect interruptions by white mobs hurling sticks and brickbats.

Nor were African-Americans spared in their own communities. In 1824, in Hard-scrabble, Providence, white mobs rioted after African-Americans refused to get off a sidewalk; 20 buildings in the black district were destroyed. In Cincinnati in 1829, Irish workers attacked African-Americans and burned down their property, forcing 1200 to flee the city. In 1834 Philadelphia, white mobs destroyed black churches and looted homes during three days of rioting—in what was termed "Hunting the Nigs."

Anti-black riots were exacerbated by abolitionism, as white Northerners opposed to black freedom reacted with violence. In 1834 New York, a theater riot burned down black churches, meeting halls, and any building affiliated with abolition. In Canaan, New Hampshire, a 500-strong mob used 95 oxen to tear down a black school. Cincinnati saw consecutive riots in April and July of 1836, as white mobs burned down black residences, killed several, and destroyed an abolitionist newspaper. A Philadelphia mob in 1838 stoned black and white abolitionists, eventually burning down their meeting place, Pennsylvania Hall. The violence was so persistent, one newspaper derisively named cities like New York, Boston, and Philadelphia "Mob Town."

Northern anti-black violence continued during the Civil War. Most infamous was the New York Draft Riots of 1863, where mostly Irish mobs looted and burned parts of the city. African-Americans were beaten and shot in the streets, and lynched from lampposts.

The end of the Civil War brought little reprieve, as a defeated Confederacy turned "mobocracy" into insurgency. In May 1866 Memphis, white mobs rioted for three days, killing 46 blacks, raping black women, destroying 100 buildings, and displacing thousands. That July, 38 African-Americans were slaughtered by a New Orleans mob at a political convention. In August 1866, riots in Warsaw, Kentucky forced several hundred blacks to flee across the Ohio River—leaving behind land and property.

From 1866 to 1890, scores of anti-black riots broke out from Alabama to South Carolina—accompanied by assassinations and terrorism. The reasons were usually political, as white Southerners reasserted control through violence and terror. A South

Carolinian newspaper put it bluntly: this would either be "a white man's government" or a "Negro cemetery." How many African-Americans died in this mayhem remains unknown. But in the lead up to the racially charged 1868 Louisiana elections alone, over 1,000 persons were killed in political violence.

By the late nineteenth century, anti-black violence had spread throughout the country—beginning what has been termed the "nadir" of American race relations. Alongside Jim Crow and lynch law, "race riots" became a strategic tool of maintaining white supremacy. From the 1890s through the 1920s, there were over 100 mob actions against African-Americans.

Not every riot involved race. Labor disputes in the Industrial Age brought their own violence. In Chicago's Haymarket Square in 1886, a labor protest became a deadly riot after someone threw a bomb. A 1910 labor strike by trolley workers in Philadelphia turned into a destructive citywide riot, at one point utilizing dynamite.

But labor riots could easily become racial. In the summer of 1892, rioting white steelworkers at the Homestead Mill in Pennsylvania turned on African-American strikebreakers; a mob of 2000 attacked nearby black families, looting their homes and destroying property.

This mix of labor competition, politics, and racial animosity erupted again in 1898 Wilmington, as white mobs rampaged through the prosperous African-American district, leaving 15 to 60 blacks dead. In 1900 New Orleans, thousands of whites rioted through the city after a shootout between a black laborer, Robert Charles, and the police; 28 people were killed. In 1906, Atlanta erupted into a massive race riot as a mob of 10,000 whites ruled the streets for three days. Some 40 blacks were killed while thousands more were forced to flee. Springfield, Illinois saw three anti-black race riots between 1904 and 1908, the last of which was so brutal, it triggered the formation of the NAACP—in part as a response to the ceaseless violence.

Race riots seemed to occur at any provocation. When black boxer Jack Johnson beat his white opponent James Jeffries in July 1910, anti-black riots broke out in over 25 cities, leaving scores dead. Competition between black and white workers in Saint Louis in 1917 sparked a riot that left over 100 dead and forced some 6000 African-Americans from their homes. The "Red Summer" of 1919 saw no less than 26 anti-black riots from Chicago to Omaha. In some instances, like the Tulsa Race riot of 1921 and the Rosewood Massacre of 1923, entire black communities were destroyed by white mobs. Up to the 1920s, more than 4,000 black residents were expelled from their homes through ethnic cleansing—a transfer of land and property through mob violence.

The popular association of the term "riot," with African-Americans as perpetrators rather than victims, did not begin until the Black Protest Era. The initial riots were mainly white resistance, where angry mobs met black children outside public schools in Arkansas and rampaged at colleges like Ole Miss. By the mid-1960s, however, large-scale riots were breaking out in major cities throughout the country—this time led primarily by African-Americans.

In Harlem 1964, there was a riot after the police killing of two black males, one of them a teenager. For six nights rioters fought police and looted stores. Harlem had seen a previous anti-police riot in 1935, an anomaly for the times. But the riot in 1964 precipitated further black unrest from August through July—in Philadelphia, Chicago, Jersey City and elsewhere. Massive riots broke out in Watts, Los Angeles in 1965 and in Newark and Detroit in 1967. The strategy of riot, wielded almost exclusively by white America for two hundred years, had become a tool of black protest.

While media outlets termed them "urban riots," black radicals named them "rebellions" and "uprisings." H. Rap Brown declared America on the "eve of a black revolution," calling the civil unrest "revolutionary violence" triggered by the violence rendered daily upon black existence. Even advocates of nonviolence like Dr. Martin Luther King, Jr., while deploring riots as ineffective, placed them within a tradition of the dispossessed. Declaring in a March 1968 speech that it would not be enough for him to stand before a crowd to merely condemn rioters, he condemned as well what he called "the intolerable conditions" in which blacks lived that made "violent rebellions" inevitable. A riot, he pronounced, was "the language of the unheard." When Dr. King was assassinated less than a month later, those unheard voices shouted all across America.

After the 1967 uprising, President Lyndon B. Johnson put together a committee to examine this new phenomenon of urban unrest. Called the Kerner Commission, its report found that while most riots were sparked by police incidents, the overall cause was systemic. The 482-page analysis defined black urban unrest as inherently political and rooted in larger structural issues of racism, poverty, poor housing, de facto segregation, crumbling cities, and lack of employment.

Since the 1960s, riots overall have become less common in American society—though their root causes cited by the Kerner Commission remain largely unaddressed. The largest occurred in 1992 in Los Angeles in the wake of the Rodney King verdict. Like most of its urban predecessors, it was precipitated by a police incident—making black-led riots remarkably uniform in their causes. Recently, high-profile killings of African-Americans in Ferguson and Baltimore have triggered similar small-scale riots.

Yet, not all riots are created equal or viewed the same. The mobs of colonial America are today enshrined as patriots who helped gather support for a revolution. Riots that won workers the eight-hour day or that triggered the struggle for gay rights at Stonewall are made over as respectable, even heroic. Others, such as the riots that helped maintain and enforce white racial control, have been all but wiped from the national narrative. Even the more frequent modern day white riots at collegiate sporting events or pumpkin festivals are renamed "disturbances."

The sci-fi story The Hunger Games follows a rebellion against a repressive police state that begins with riots. Adapted as a popular film, moviegoers regularly cheer on its fictional white heroine Katniss Everdeen—while black bodies doing much the same on news screens are deemed "thugs and criminals," and their actions labeled "counterproductive." In the end, perhaps it's not the riots themseves that incite fear but the faces behind them.

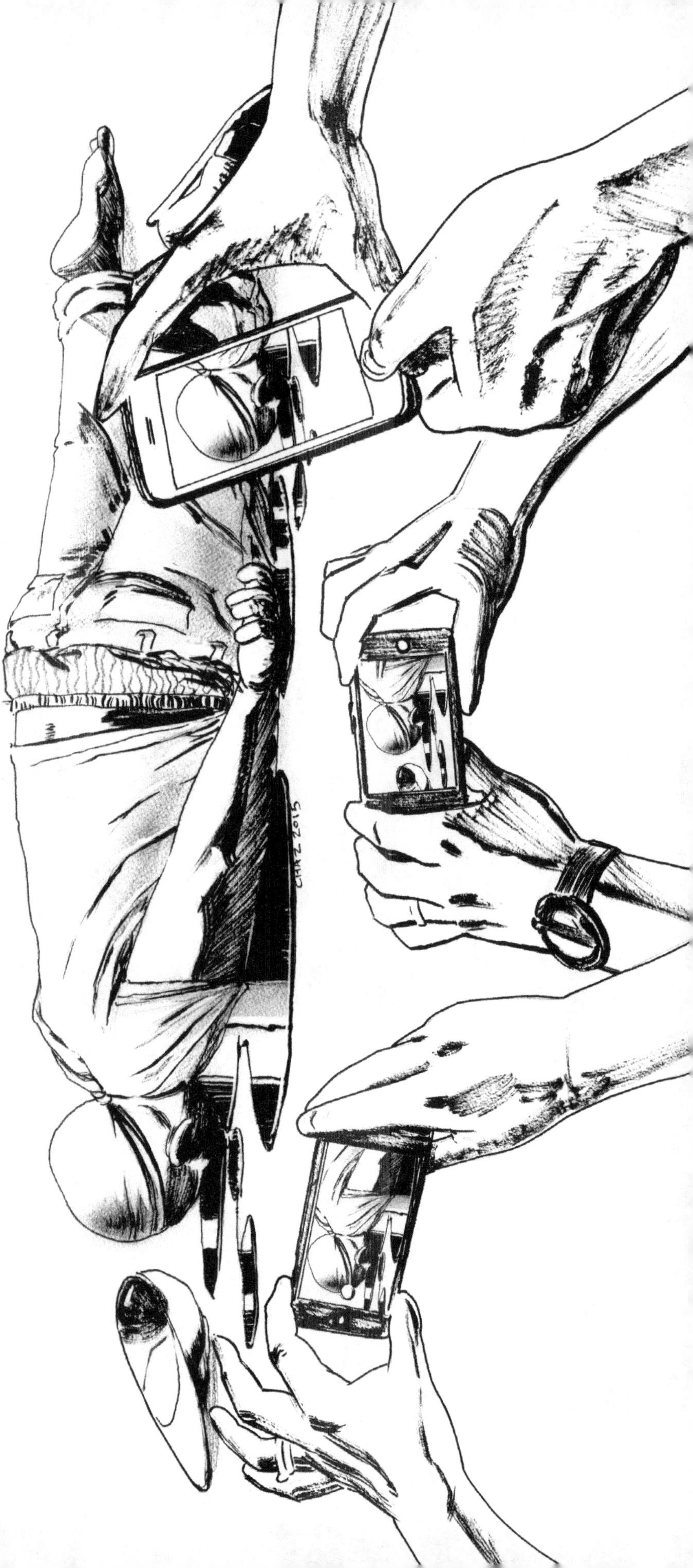
CHAZ 2015

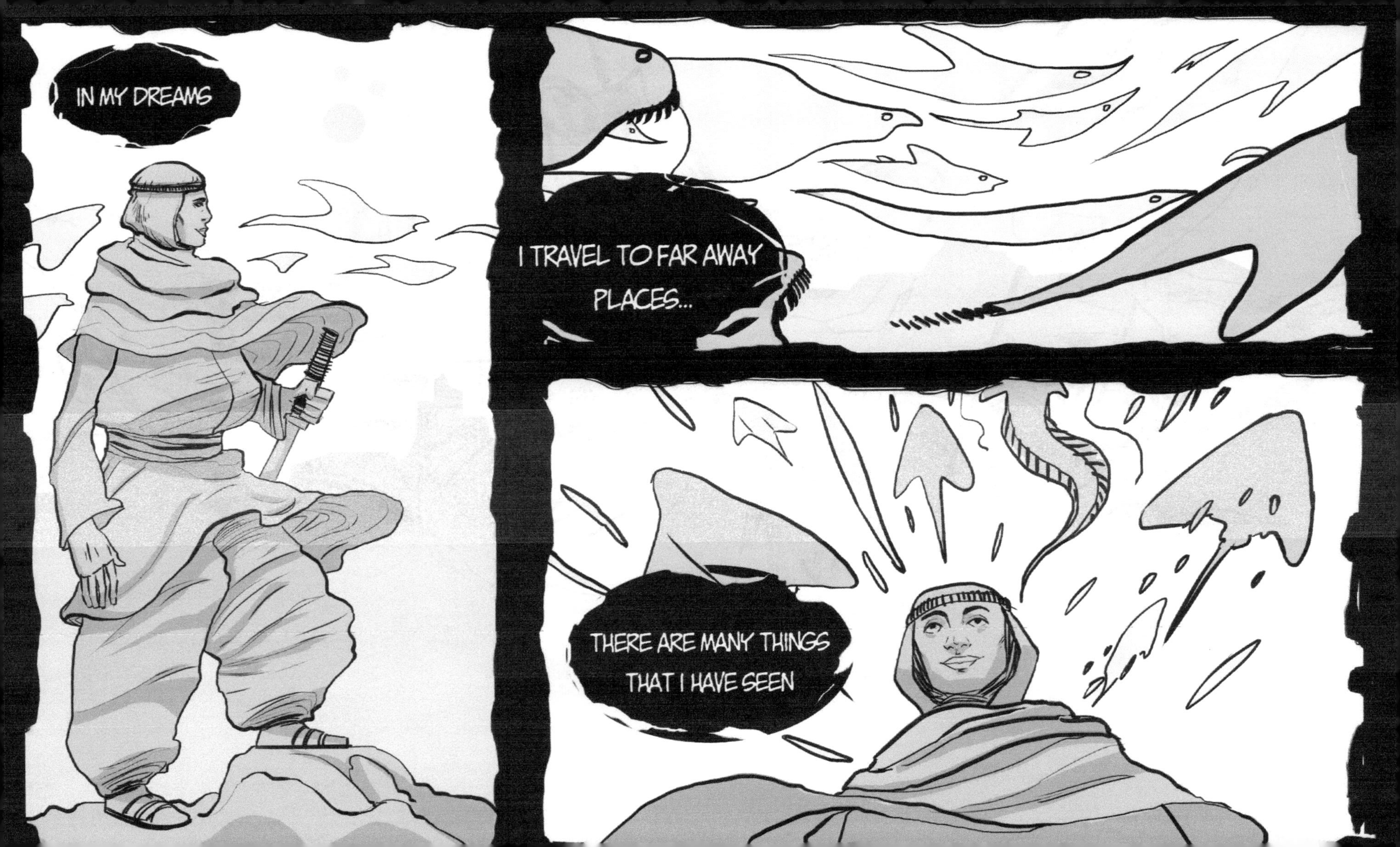
IN MY DREAMS
I TRAVEL TO FAR AWAY PLACES...
THERE ARE MANY THINGS THAT I HAVE SEEN

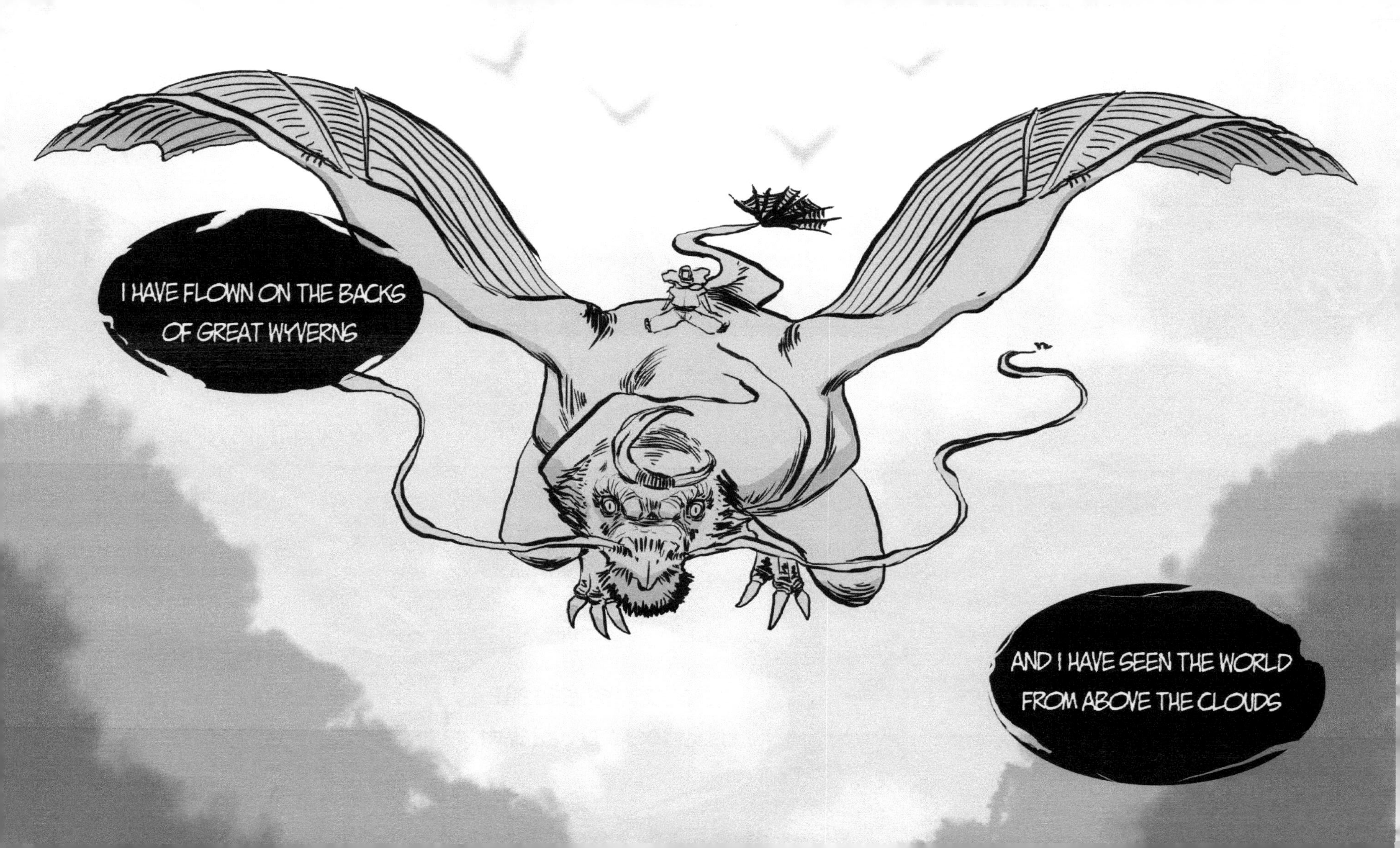
I HAVE FLOWN ON THE BACKS OF GREAT WYVERNS
AND I HAVE SEEN THE WORLD FROM ABOVE THE CLOUDS

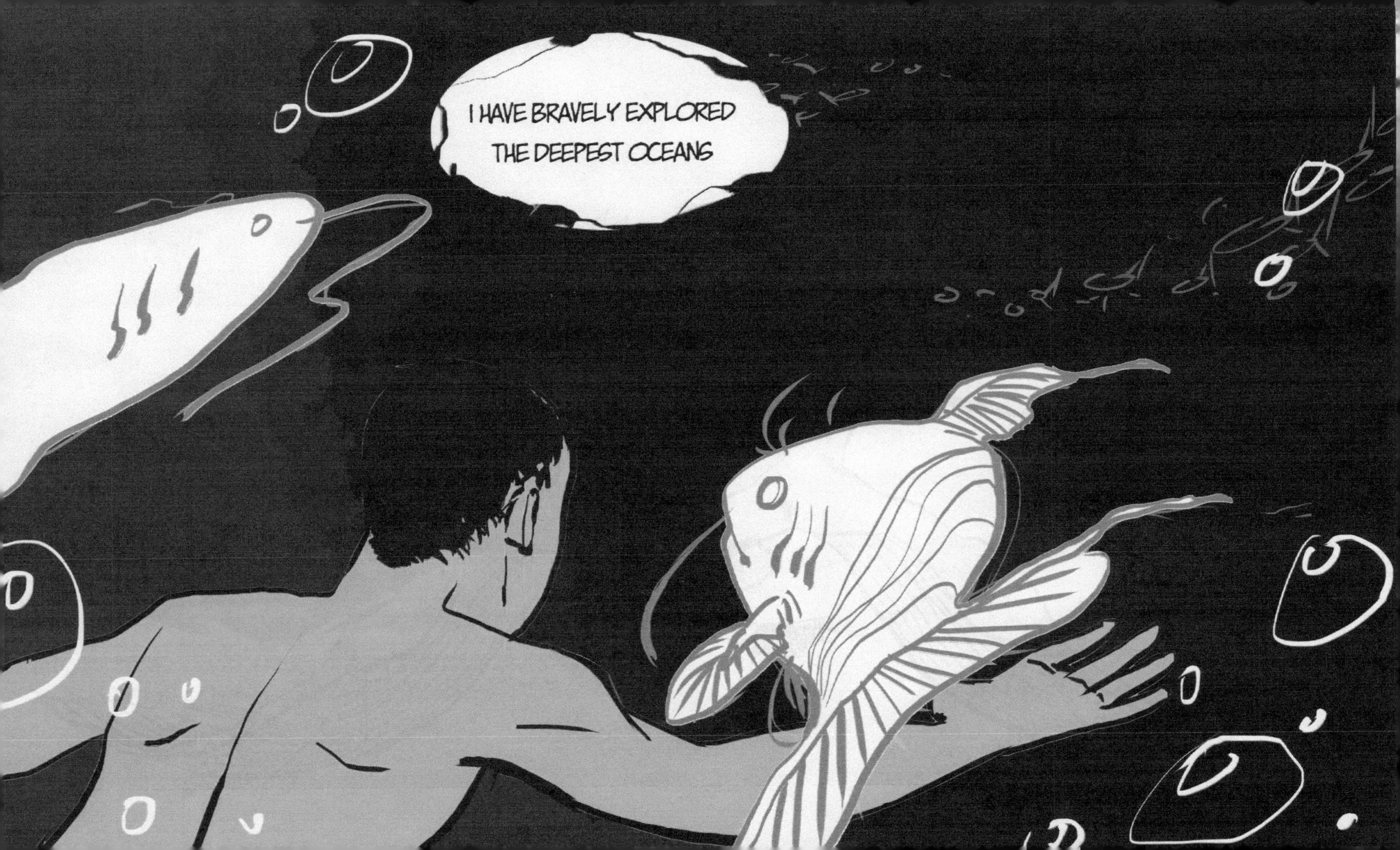
I HAVE BRAVELY EXPLORED THE DEEPEST OCEANS

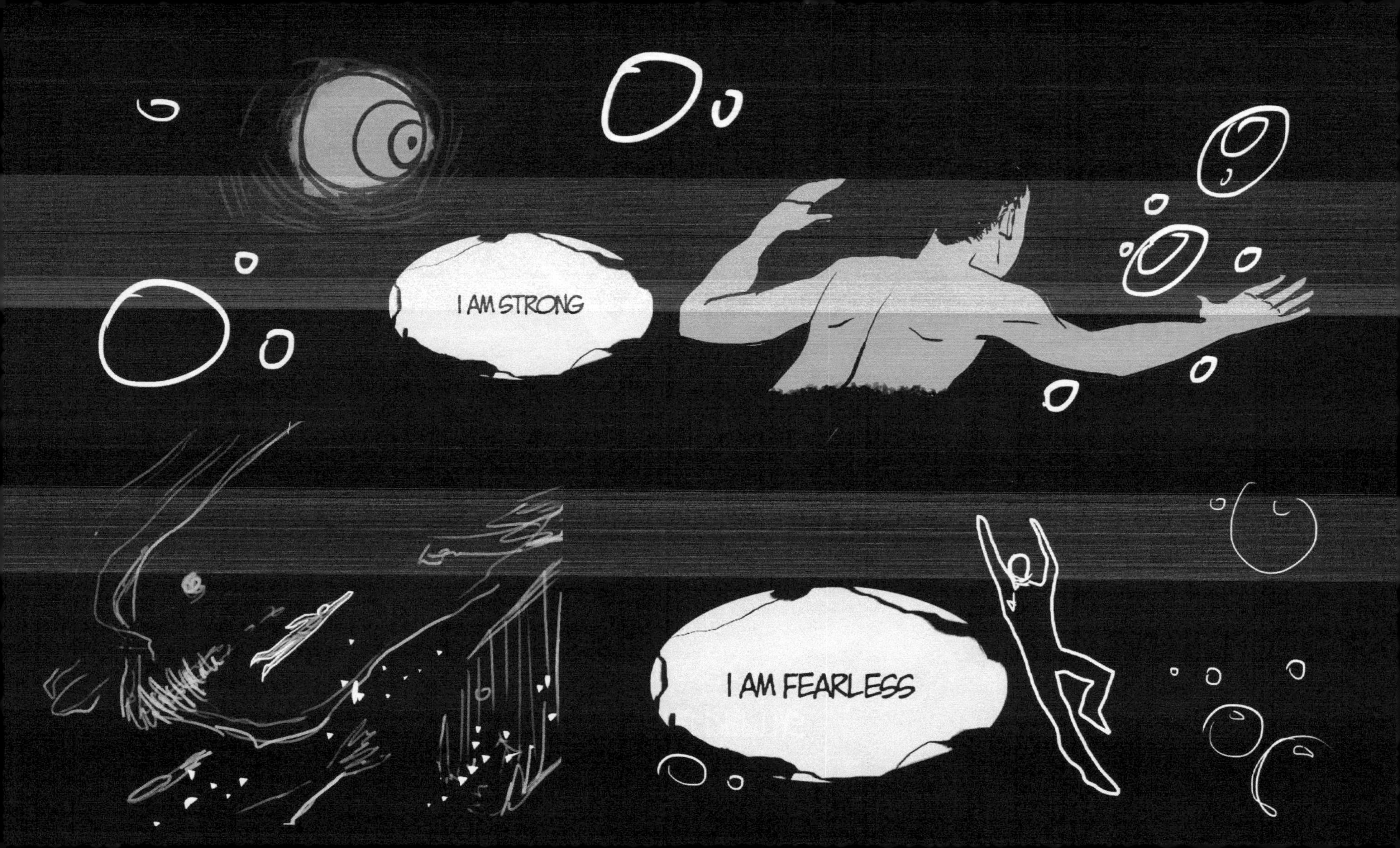
I AM STRONG
I AM FEARLESS

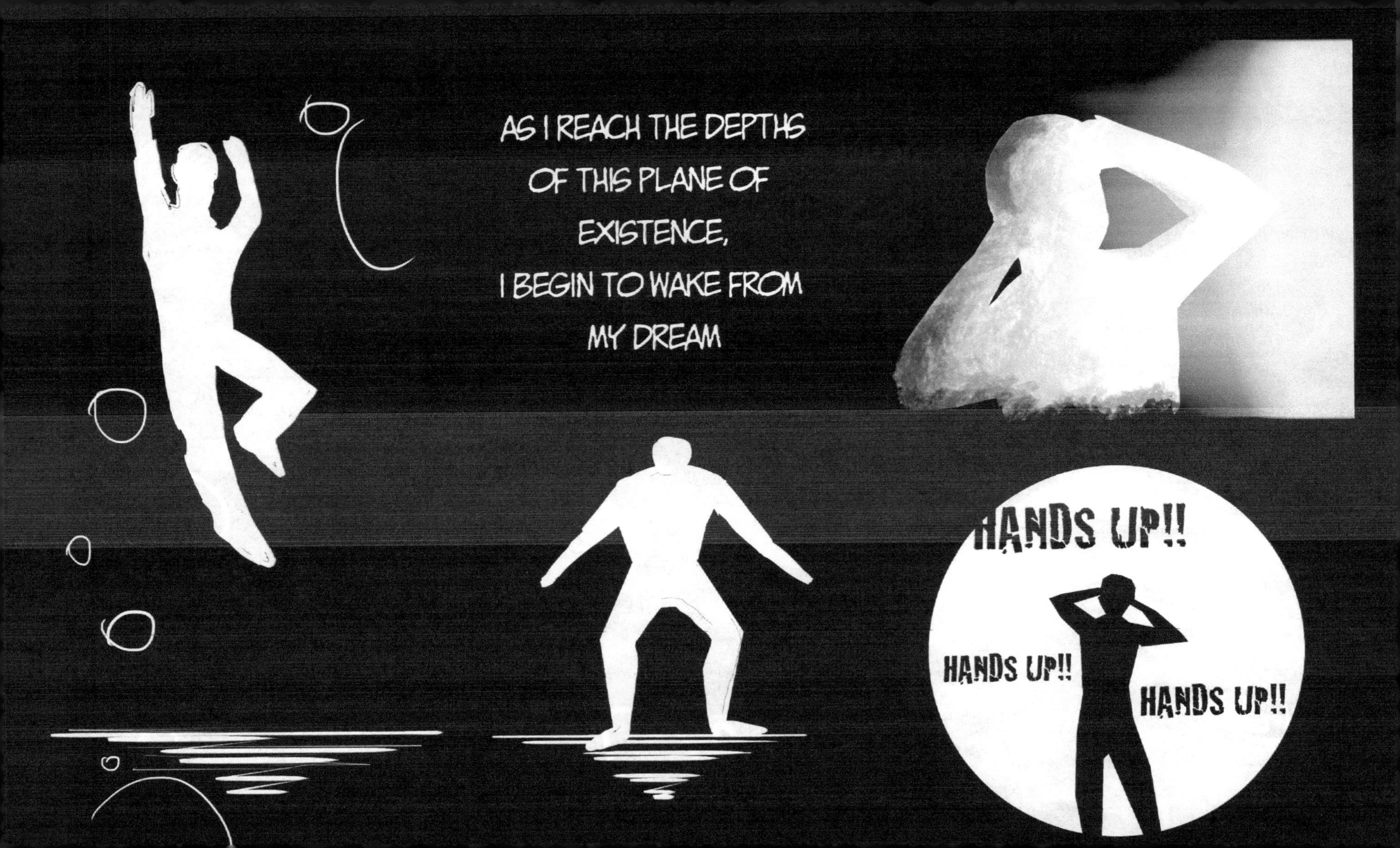
AS I REACH THE DEPTHS
OF THIS PLANE OF
EXISTENCE,
I BEGIN TO WAKE FROM
MY DREAM
HANDS UP!!
HANDS UP!!
HANDS UP!!

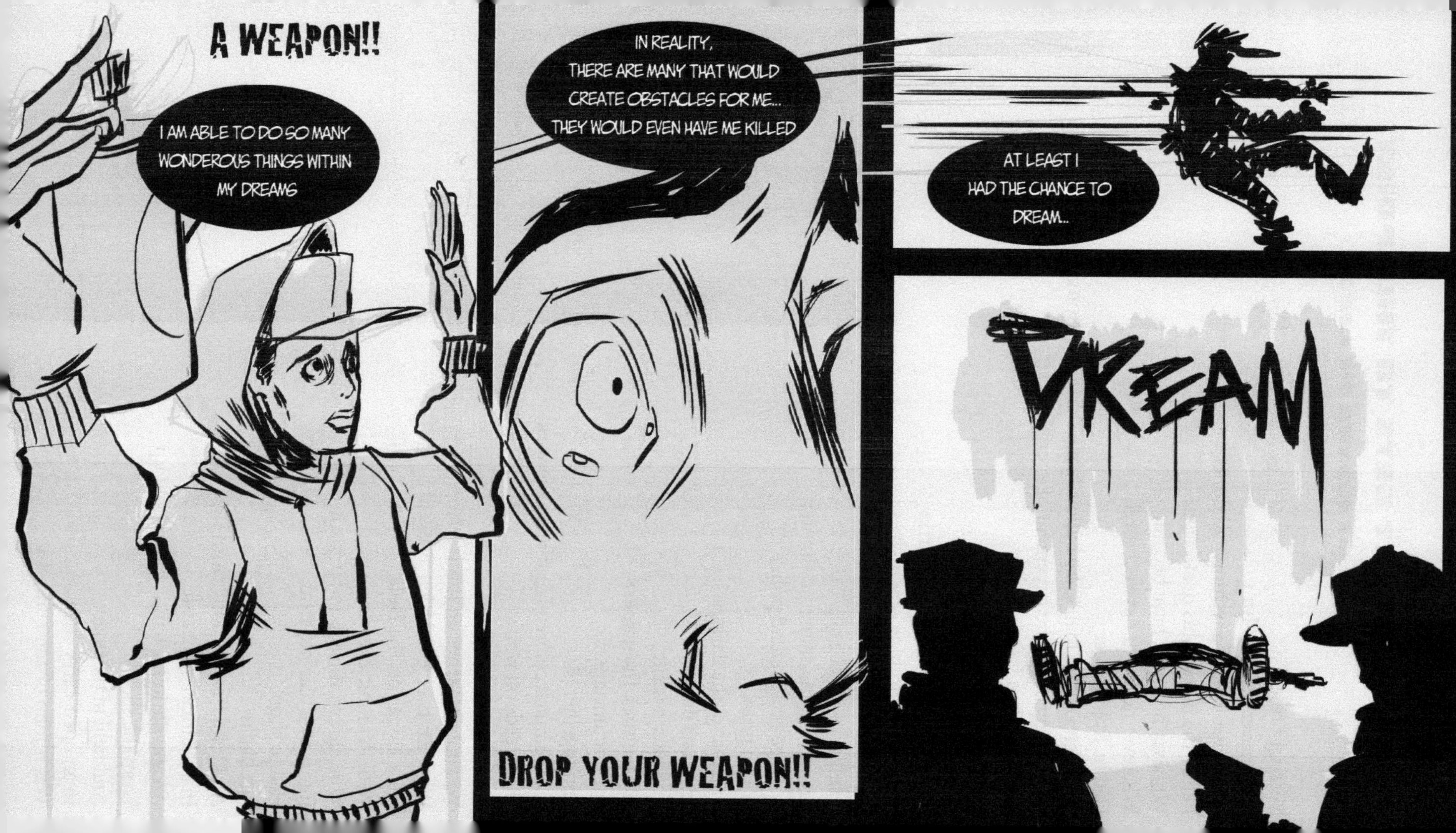
A WEAPON!!
I AM ABLE TO DO SO MANY WONDEROUS THINGS WITHIN MY DREAMS
IN REALITY, THERE ARE MANY THAT WOULD CREATE OBSTACLES FOR ME... THEY WOULD EVEN HAVE ME KILLED
DROP YOUR WEAPON!!
AT LEAST I HAD THE CHANCE TO DREAM...
DREAM

# WHEN IT GETS TO THIS POINT
## BY MONDO WE LANGA

Michael Brown?
I had never heard of him
Had never hear of anything he'd done
Before the news of his death came
Whoever he might have become
Whatever he might have achieved
Had he lived longer
Not been riddled lifeless by bullets from Darren Wilson's gun
And crumpled on the pavement of a ferguson street
For more than four hours in
The heat of that august day
And before
I never heard of Trayvon Martin
Had known nothing of who he was
Until I learned of his demise and cause of death
A bullet to the chest
George Zimmerman, the shooter
A badge-less pretend police
With a pistol
And fear of the darkness
Trayvon's darkness
And after a while
The pictures, the names,
The circumstances
Run together
Like so much colored laundry in the wash
That bleeds on whites

Was it Eric Garner or Tamir Rice
Who was twelve but seen as twenty
Hulk Hogan or The Hulk
With demonic eyes it was said
Who shrank the cop in ferguson
Into a five-year-old who
Had to shoot
Just had to shoot
And John Crawford the third
In a Walmart store aisle
An air rifle in his hands he'd picked up
From the shelf
And held in the open
In an open-carry state
Was it John or someone else

Killed supposedly by mistake
In a dark stairwell
I know Akai Gurley fell
I hadn't heard of him before
Nor of Amadou Diallo or Sean Bell
Prior to their killings
Which of these two took slugs in the greater number
I don't recall
My memory is too encumbered
With the names
Of so many more before and since
The frequent news reports of
Non-arrests, non-indictments,
Non-true bills
And duplicitous presentations by "experts in the field"
The consultants put out front
To explain away
That which is so often plain as day
To coax and convince us that we're the ones
Who can't see straight and
Can't hear clearly
Who are the ones replacing facts with spin
To mislead and mystify
As the beatings and the chokings and the shootings of
Our boys and men
By these wrong arms of the law
Proceed in orderly fashion
Before the sometimes sad
And sometimes angry faces of our uncertain
Our hesitant disbelief.

**LALO ALCARAZ** has been busy for over the past two decades chronicling the political ascendancy of Latinos in America and vigorously pushing the boundaries of Chicano art in the Post Chicano Art Era. He is the creator of the first nationally-syndicated, politically-themed Latino daily comic strip, "La Cucaracha," seen in scores of newspapers including the Los Angeles Times. Lalo has produced editorial cartoons for the L.A. Weekly since 1992 and also creates editorial cartoons in English and Spanish for Universal. His work has appeared in *The New York Times, The Village Voice, The L.A. Times, Variety, Hispanic Magazine, Latina Magazine, Mexico's La Jornada,* Germany's *BUNTE,* and many other publications. Alcaraz and his work have been featured on CNN, the CBS Evening News, ABC, NBC, Univision, Telemundo, PBS, Al-Jazeera TV, NPR, Air America Radio, and on Spain's Radio Nacional de España. Mi Ciudad Magazine named him "Best Latino Cartoonist in Los Angeles," and Lalo has also been featured by *Rolling Stone Magazine, Los Angeles Magazine, Associated Press, Editor & Publisher,* and profiled extensively in the *Comics Journal.*

**DR. REYNALDO ANDERSON** currently serves as an Associate Professor of Communications at Harris-Stowe State University. Reynaldo was recognized by Gov. Jay Nixon in 2010 for his leadership in the Saint Louis community and is currently a member of the executive board of the Missouri Arts Council. Finally, Reynaldo publishes research in regard to several dimensions of the African American experience, and the African Diaspora including Afrofuturism, Rhetoric, Cultural Studies, Africana Studies, globalization and world systems theory, and recently taught as visiting lecturer in Accra, Ghana. Finally, he is the co-editor of the forthcoming book *Afrofuturism 2.0: The Rise of Astro-Blackness* to be published by Lexington books in December 2015.

**STEVE ARTLEY'S** work in editorial cartooning has twice earned him the "Best Editorial Cartoonist of the Year" award from the Minnesota Newspapers Assoc. In 2009, he received First and Second Place from the Virginia Press Association News Contest and was honored with a "Best In Show" award and again took First Place in 2010, 2011, and 2012. His cartoons have been syndicated throughout the United States and Canada, appearing in publications such as *Newsweek,* the *Washington Post* and *New York Times.* His work has been included in online cartoon anthologies such as TIME "Best Cartoons of the Week" and NPR "Double Takes" and was among the "Best Editorial Cartoons of the Year," by the *Washington Post* in 2011. His editorial cartoons appear in *The Alexandria (VA) Gazette Packet* and are syndicated by ARTIZANS throughout the U.S. and Canada.

**DAVID BRAME** never wastes time combing his hair. All that extra time is spent making comics, telling stories and creating grand experiences. You can see his webcomics on splitlip.com and henbracomics.com, in numerous anthologies, and in the Action Lab original graphic novel, *The Trip.* Follow him on instagram @amazingdavidbrame

**BARBARA BRANDON-CROFT** became the first African-American woman to be nationally syndicated in the mainstream press in 1991. Her strip, *Where I'm Coming From,* featured nine opinionated black women and was distributed internationally for 14 years. A native New Yorker, she is part of an exclusive cartoonist dynasty. Brandon-Croft's father, Brumsic Brandon, Jr. is one of the nation's pioneer cartoonists with his nationally syndicated comic strip *Luther* which delivered a glaring view of what it's like to grow up black in America's inner-city. Both she and her dad are represented in the Library of Congress Graphic Arts Collection.

**JENNIFER MARIE BRISSETT** is a writer, artist, and former bookstore owner. She holds an MFA from the Stonecoast Program in Creative Writing at the University of Southern Maine. Her stories can be found in *The Future Fire, Halfway Down the Stairs, Morpheus Tales, Terraform,* and *Warrior Wisewoman 2*. Her debut novel *Elysium* (Aqueduct Press) won the 2014 Philip K. Dick Award Special Citation, was placed on the James Tiptree, Jr. Honor List, and was a 2015 Finalist for the Locus Award for Best New Novel. She lives in NYC.

**BILL CAMPBELL** is the author of *Sunshine Patriots, My Booty Novel, Pop Culture: Politics, Puns, "Poohbutt" from a Liberal Stay-at-Home Dad,* and *Koontown Killing Kaper*. Along with Edward Austin Hall, he co-edited the groundbreaking anthology, *Mothership: Tales from Afrofuturism and Beyond* and *Stories for Chip: A Tribute to Samuel R. Delany* with Nisi Shawl. Campbell lives in Washington, DC, where he spends his time with his family, helps produce audio books for the blind, and helms Rosarium Publishing.

**CHRISTA CASSANO** has a background in fine arts and began making comics in 2012 when she attended The Atlantic Center for the Arts. In 2013 she became a member of Hang Dai Studios in Gowanus, Brooklyn, where she wrote and drew *The Giant Effect*, and contributed to *The Hang Dai Comix Anthology*, and Seth Kushner's *Schmuck*. Christa recently co-adapted John Leguizamo's *Ghetto Klown*, coming out this fall from Abrams, and is currently working on her own graphic series, titled *Pawnland*. Check out: https://www.flickr.com/photos/ccassano/ and https://twitter.com/christa-cassano.

**KA YAN CHEUNG** was born in Hong Kong and grew up in NYC. She comes from a family of garment, restaurant, and homecare workers, and watching her family struggle each day moved her towards radical politics. Ka Yan spent eight years doing community and labor organizing in the San Francisco Bay Area. Comics is her favorite medium, because she considers it an art for the people. She is currently working on a graphic novel about three generations of women in her family. Connect with her at KaYanCheung.tumblr.com

**P. DJELI CLARK** (@pdjeliclark) is a writer of speculative fiction and a doctoral candidate in history. His historical work on the Black Atlantic has appeared in articles, essays, and interviews. His fiction has appeared in publications such as *Daily Science Fiction, Every Day Fiction, Heroic Fantasy Quarterly,* and genre anthologies. He will have a forthcoming novelette published by Tor.com in 2016 and is steadily working on a YA fantasy novel for the slushpile. A resident of Washington, DC, who dreams of returning to Brooklyn, he talks about "stuff" as the Disgruntled Haradrim on his blog pdjeliclark.com.

**JERRY CRAFT** has illustrated and written close to two dozen children's books and middle grade novels. One of his newest was co-written with his two teenage sons, Jaylen and Aren called *The Offenders: Saving the World While Serving Detention!* An adventure story that teaches kids about the effects of bullying. Jerry is the creator of *Mama's Boyz*, an award-winning comic strip that was distributed by King Features from 1995 - 2013. He also illustrated *The Zero Degree Zombie Zone* for Scholastic. For more info visit www.jerrycraft.net.

**RAFAEL DESQUITADO, JR.** is a freelance comic book illustrator based in San Diego, California. He has worked with several highly motivated (and patient!) independent creators tell their stories such as *Hope for Planet Random Comics*, and YA author Cody Stewart with his debut novel's companion comic book, *Shade*. Rafael continues to work with Stewart with the weekly science fiction webcomic series, *Constant*, and *Brian Hoover's* crime drama webcomic series, *Where The Light Is*.

The cartoonist **DAMIAN DUFFY** is a writer, letterer, curator, lecturer, teacher, Glyph Award winning graphic novelist, and PhD candidate at the University of Illinois Graduate School of Library and Information Science. His many publications range from academic essays (in-comics-form) about new media & learning to a forthcoming graphic novel adaptation of *Kindred* by Octavia E. Butler. He has given talks and lead workshops about comics, art, and education internationally.

**T. FOX DUNHAM** resides outside of Philadelphia PA—author and historian. He's published in nearly 200 international journals and anthologies. His first novel, *The Street Martyr* was published by Gutter Books and is being made into a feature film by Throughline Films. He's a cancer survivor. His friends call him fox, being his totem animal, and his motto is: Wrecking civilization one story at a time. Site: www.tfoxdunham.com. Blog: http://tfoxdunham.blogspot.com/. http://www.facebook.com/tfoxdunham & Twitter: @TFoxDunham

**GALLO FINO** doesn't matter. Only the work matters.

**MATTHEW FISHER** is a writer, podcaster, father, husband, and lapsed punk rocker living in Richmond, VA.

**AARON RAND FREEMAN** is the co-host and producer of "This Week in Blackness" and "We Nerd Hard" as well as the host of "Sportsball." Those shows cover the range of his interests of social issues such as race and discrimination, politics, comic books, video games, *Doctor Who*, and sports. Beyond being the perpetual sideman for Elon James White on all 7000 podcasts on the TWiB Network, he has also done stand up comedy. To see more of Aaron's work please visit www.twib.fm.

**CHARLES FETHEROLF** has been drawing since he was old enough to hold a pencil. Through his imprint, Giant Earth Press, he has self-published *Giants in the Earth* and *Sons of Cain*. More recently, Charles has contributed to *District Comics* (Fulcrum, 2012), the Harvey-nominated *Once Upon a Time Machine* (Dark Horse, 2012), two volumes of *Colonial Comics* (Fulcrum) and the Eisner winning *Little Nemo: Dream Another Dream* (Locust Moon Press). He lives in New Paltz, NY with his wife, two children and several annoying neighbors.

**GREGORY GARAY** is a Graphic/Web Designer with Comic Book Illustration skills. He was born in Brooklyn and raised in the Bronx (NYC). As a Pittsburgh transplant he looks to stretch his arms, start over and produce a multitude of projects, artwork, and memories. His current comics project is called *Jack B: Ride the Air*. For a look at this portfolio, visit http://gregorygaray.com/.

My name is **BRANDON L. HANKINS**, I'm a cartoonist and illustrator based in East Lansing, Michigan. I'm driven to seek artistic and spiritual growth through consistent practice, application and reflection. I've been an avid comic book reader since childhood, and I've dedicated my life to tell stories with this medium.

**SHOMARI HARRINGTON** is a Visual Artist born and raised in Chicago. From an early age, he has always been fascinated by the wonders of what a pencil and a sheet of paper could create. The desire and passion to create has helped him to become the artist that he is today. Shomari authored and illustrated a children's book, "Q Saves the Sun," and his art has appeared at the "Milestones: African American in Comics, Pop Culture and Beyond" gallery hosted at the Geppi Museum of Entertainment in Baltimore, MD. Shomari is an artist who enjoys working with others on a team, being productive, and creating thought provoking works of art.

**JASON T. HARRIS** is an emerging writer/futurist based in Baltimore, Maryland. He published his first book, *Redlines: Baltimore 2028*, a speculative fiction anthology, in 2012. His first novel, *Fly, Girl*, will be published this fall. He has participated in the Yale Writer's conference and is a 2015 Kimbilio Fiction Fellow. He has contributed to various publications both online and in print. He is the director of creative services at the Living Well Center in Baltimore, where he is engaged in community and diaspora art education projects.

Emmy award winner and Eisner Award nominee **DEAN HASPIEL** created *Billy Dogma* and *Beef With Tomato*, illustrated for HBO's "Bored To Death," was a Master Artist at the Atlantic Center for the Arts, is a Yaddo fellow, a playwright, helped pioneer personal webcomics with ACT-I-VATE.com and TripCity.net, and is a co-founder of Hang Dai Editions in Brooklyn, NY. Dino has written and drawn many comicbooks, including *The Fox, Spider-Man, Batman, X-men: First Class, The Fantastic Four, Wonder Woman, Deadpool, Godzilla, Mars Attacks, The Walking Dead,* and collaborations with Harvey Pekar, Jonathan Ames, Inverna Lockpez, Jonathan Lethem, Mark Waid, and Stan Lee.

**JOE HILLIARD.** Writer. Luddite. Teller of Tales. Grew up as a teen in Los Angeles on the fringes of 80s Hollywood. Graduate of the University of Michigan, where he first heard of Cynthia Scott. Marks time as a paralegal in California.

**WALIDA IMARISHA** is a writer, educator, public scholar, and poet. Through Oregon Humanities' Conversation Project, she has toured Oregon for six years facilitating programs on Oregon Black history, alternatives to incarceration, and the history of hiphop. Walidah is co-editor of two anthologies, *Octavia's Brood: Science Fiction Stories From Social Justice Movements* (AK Press, Spring 2015) and the 9/11 collection *Another World is Possible* (Subway Press, 2002). She authored the poetry book Scars/Stars (Drapetomedia, 2013) and the nonfiction *Angels with Dirty Faces: Dreaming Beyond Bars* (AK Press, Fall 2016). She currently teaches in Portland State University's Black Studies Department.

**JOHN JENNINGS** is an Associate Professor of Art and Visual Studies at the University at Buffalo-State University of New York. He is the co-author of the graphic novel *The Hole: Consumer Culture, Vol. 1* and the art collection, *Black Comix: African American Independent Comics Art and Culture* (both with Damian Duffy). Jennings is also the co-editor of *The Blacker the Ink: Constructions of Black Identity in Comics and Sequential Art* and co-founder/organizer of The Schomburg Center's Black Comic Book Festival in Harlem, MLK NorCal's Black Comix Arts Festival in San Francisco, and the AstroBlackness colloquium in Los Angeles at Loyola Marymount University. Jennings' current comics projects include the hip-hop adventure comic *Kid Code: Channel Zero*, the supernatural crime noir story *Blue Hand Mojo*, and the upcoming graphic novel adaptation of Octavia Butler's classic dark fantasy novel, *Kindred*.

**AVY JETTER** is the artist and creator behind the comic book, Nuthin Good Ever

Happens at 4 a.m. She lives and works in Oakland, CA, and is currently working on a portrait zine compiling drawings from her sketchbooks.

**JASON SCOTT JONES** is a Brooklyn born, American artist, filmmaker and producer of Caribbean descent. A comic industry professional who gained his start through an internship at Milestone Media, which he evolved into becoming a contributing artist, editor and department manager in the historic company. Jones comic art contributed to flagship characters and titles with DC Comics as well as a collaboration on the Wu-Tang Clan's *Liquid Swords* album cover. His artworks have been featured in the New York Daily News, exhibited in the Studio Museum in Harlem, Rush Arts Gallery and presented in across Japan and Spain. Currently Jones is at work on *Flatbush Yard* an original graphic novel to be published by Rosarium Publishing.

**BIZHAN KHODABANDEH** is a visual communicator who moves freely across the professional boundaries as designer, illustrator, artist and activist. He has received numerous international and national awards for his work, including a silver medal through the Society of Illustrators, placing in the Adbusters' One Flag Competition, the Good 50x70's poster project, The Green Patriot poster project, Poster for Tomorrow, and recognition by the American Institute for Graphic Arts. Khodabandeh has had work featured in publications such as Print, Creativity International, Adbusters, among others. Currently Khodabandeh freelances under the name, Mended Arrow and teaches at Virginia Commonwealth University.

**KEITH KNIGHT** is the world's foremost Gentleman Cartoonist and Star Wars prequel denier. www.kchronicles.com

**MONDO WE LANGA** is a poet, playwright, and a political prisoner of the Nebraska State Penitentiary since 1970. In the 45 years since his conviction, Mondo has created art, written short stories, poetry and journalism. He had five books of poetry published between 1973 and 1978 and has contributed poems and stories to such literary journals and magazines as *Prairie Schooner, The Black Scholar, ARGO, Black American Literary Forum, Shooting Star Quarterly Review, Pacifica Review, Obsidian, Black Books Bulletin*, and over 30 more. Currently incarcerated, Mondo has continued his education, and now in his 60s, is a mentor to young inmates just coming into the system. In all the years of his incarceration, he has not committed a single act of violence; he has, in fact, been an exemplary prisoner.

**DR. BETTINA L. LOVE** is an award-winning author and Associate Professor of Educational Theory & Practice at the University of Georgia. She is the founder of Real Talk: Hip Hop Education for Social Justice, an after school initiative aimed at teaching elementary students the history and elements of Hip Hop for social justice. Recently, Dr. Love was named the Nasir Jones Fellow at the W. E. B. Du Bois Research Center at Harvard University. She will begin her fellowship at Harvard in the Spring of 2016, where she will develop a multimedia Hip Hop civics curriculum for middle to high school students.

**ROBERT LOVE** formed Gettosake Entertainment with his brothers, Jeremy and Maurice in 1998, publishing their signature character, Chocolate Thunder. In 2004, Dark Horse published *Fierce*, written by Jeremy Love with art by Robert Love, followed by *Shadow Rock* in February of 2007. He was also the co-writer (along with David Walker) and artist on *Number 13*, which was also published by Dark Horse Comics in 2012. In 2013 he was the artist on *Never Ending*, another 3-issue miniseries from Dark Horse

Coimcs. His other credits include, *Alpha Girl* (Image Comics), The Blind Monkey Style (POPGUN, Image Comics), and *The Mad Mauler* (POPGUN, Image Comics), Outside of comics, Robert sold the rights to a movie to 20th Century Fox called *The Adventures of Venus Kincaid* and has optioned *Fierce* to Zucker Productions as well as *Number 13* with Legendary Pictures.

**TAKEIA MARIE** is an illustrator from Long Island, NY, currently living in NYC. She has done illustration and design work for rising small businesses under her Atomic Latte Studio brand. An avid Hip-Hop fan, she is also an editorial writer for *The Hip Hop Speakeasy.*

**MGRIVAS** is a lifelong lover of comics and the writer and illustrator behind two upcoming books, *Uncanny Cryptic 5* and *Murderers Of The World*. He became politically active when he was 20 in Chicago and believes that comics can be used as much more than a form of entertainment. Because of that, he considers it his duty to use whatever talents he has to bring the world stories that are relevant and socially responsible as a way to help change it for the better.

**KEITH A. MILLER** was born but not completely bred in Brooklyn, New York. When he's not busy corralling thirteen-year-olds (he's a teacher), he writes independent comics. He likes to play around in the science-fiction and urban fantasy genres but is not above a good slice-of-life graphic novel. He is the co-creator of *Triboro Tales* and *Insensitives*. His latest graphic novella, *Infest*, will hit the convention floors in 2015. He is currently producing the prison horror tale, *Manticore*, for Rosarium Publishing.

Brooklyn artist from the sunny suburbs of Los Angeles by way of Buffalo, Toronto, and Houston, **TOMMY NGUY-ENSMITH** started drawing with the intent of being an animator for Disney but then wanted to become an X-Man. The cheerful fantastic Americana mythology could not keep pace with his Queer Techno Orientalist social reality. Through community-focused performative installations to weirdo pop blazed events, he hopes for people to find their kink and enjoy that weirdness. Living in between cultures, comics, hip hop, technology, anime, clothes, and coffee is life.

Hello my name is **ANDREW NIEVES** and I lettered our submission. It was lots of fun working with Joe and Kevin. I come from Chino, CA and growing up around this town with a pencil and paper in my hands has definitely influenced my work. I hope our strip helps raise awareness about police brutality. Thank you.

**KEVIN NIEVES.** Upcoming artist, currently studying at Mount San Antonio College for 2D animation. From childhood, he has had an interest in sequential art.

Weaned on the images of Kirby and Steranko in comics, and Hammett and Himes in books, **GARY PHILLIPS** also draws on his experiences ranging from community organizer, union rep, teaching incarcerated youth, to delivering dog cages in writing his tales of chicanery and malfeasance. One reviewer said of his *Astonishing Heroes* collection, "It's a book for anyone who remains nostalgic for the golden age of Toei films, blaxploitation movies, and lusty grindhouse cinema." He has short stories in *Asian Pulp* and *Jewish Noir,* and his graphic novel *The Rinse* about a money launderer was optioned for TV -- he also co-edited the sci-fi anthology *Occupied Earth*.

**JOSHUA PLENCNER** completed his Ph.D. at the University of Oregon where he researched and wrote his dissertation project on the racial politics of origin stories in American superhero comic books. Working from an anti-racist, queer, and popular perspective, his writing on comics encompasses the major work of Fletcher Hanks, Steve Ditko, Alan Moore, Kyle Baker, and others.

**JASON A. QUEST** is a middle-aged cartoonist from a mid-sized city in the Midwest, who aspires to be a professional heretic and pornographer. He writes and illustrates religious satire under the "Holy Comics!" imprint, and produces queer erotica such as the serialized bio-porno-graphic novel *JAQrabbit Tales*. His art has been featured in Best Gay Erotica 2014, and his writing and art have been included in anthologies about bullying, bisexuality and transgender identity, and suicide awareness. http://JAQrabbit.com

**ANDAIYE REEVES** is a librarian, author, and poet currently residing in Georgia. She's written for Music Is Life Entertainment e-zine and Adonis Men's Magazine. Her poetry can be found online at gspoetry.com under the alias Nilla Bean.

**STACEY ROBINSON** is a recent MFA graduate at the University of Buffalo. His work examines the African-American form through various media. By comparing and contrasting pop culture aesthetics with AfroFuturism, he utilizes the African American experience to create narratives that construct a space of healing from Black trauma.

**JASON RODRIGUEZ** is a comic book writer and editor. The books he has edited or contributed to have been nominated for an Eisner Award and 10 Harvey Awards. Jason is currently editing a three-book series of anthologies about colonial New England and the Mid-Atlantic region for Fulcrum Publishing. His first sci-fi book, *Try Looking Ahead*, was released in May 2015 from Rosarium Publishing.

**SOFIA SAMAATAR** is the author of the novel *A Stranger in Olondria* and winner of the John W. Campbell Award, the Crawford Award, the British Fantasy Award, and the World Fantasy Award. She co-edits the journal *Interfictions* and teaches literature at California State University Channel Islands, where her interests include African and Arabic literature, Afrofuturism, environmental literature, and speculative fiction.

**SESHAT'S BRUSH** is a Baltimore based painter and martial artist whose work centers around Afrikan people.

**MELANIE STEVENS** is an Atlanta-based painter, writer and illustrator. She graduated from Yale University with a BA in Political Science in 2001, which she utilizes in the subtle and nuanced social commentaries within her work. She is the creator of the semi-autobiographical web comic, *Black Picket Fences*, which ran from 2010-2014. Currently, she resides in Portland, Oregon, where she is studying at the Pacific Northwest College of Art for her MFA degree.

**LANCE TOOKS** has been drawing all his life. A former assistant editor at Marvel Comics, his artwork has since appeared in more than 100 television commercials, films and music videos. He has self-published the comic books "Danger Funnies" (co-published with Cry For Dawn), *Divided by Infinity* and *Muthafucka*. He also illustrated *The Black Panthers for Beginners*, written by Herb Boyd. He has contributed to a Hurricane Katrina benefit comic, as well as to the Graphic Classics line of books, adapting the works of Edgar Allan Poe, Mark Twain, Robert Louis Stevenson and Ambrose Bierce. He co-edited and contributed to the acclaimed African-American Classics anthology, and to the Bohemians volume also. He wrote and illustrated the award winning "Narcissa", his first graphic novel for Random House/Doubleday (recently translated for publication in Spain) and a four volume series entitled "Lucifer's Garden of Verses" for NBM (a two time Glyph winner). He has also contributed to the Graphic Novel anthologies, The Beats (Hill and Wang) in collaboration with author Harvey Pekar, Studs Terkel's Working (the New Press) and The Graphic Canon (7 Stories). Lance Tooks lives in New York and Madrid. He merely exists everywhere else.

**TAK TOYOSHIMA** is the creator/illustrator behind Secret Asian Man Comics.

**JEROME WALFORD** is an award-winning writer and illustrator, as well as the founder of Forward Comix. Jerome is best known for his graphic novel series, Nowhere Man – winner of the Glyph Comics Award for Best Male Character. His other work includes Freeing Violet, Effect, Rambun-shialon-ctious, Moon's Ostrich, and The Scientist. Jerome is also the writer on the literary young adult series, Curse of the Griffin. Jerome continues to publish under Forward Comix and collaborate on projects that align with his belief that unique stories have the power to impact one's personal journey and encourage positive cultural movement.

Artist, Multi-Disciplinary Designer and Illustrator, **DAVID WHITE** draws inspiration from science fiction, pop culture, abstract impressionism and urban art. David White's artwork and design has been featured in a variety of publications including Stanford university's Black Arts Quarterly, Tha Global Cipha: Hip Hop Culture and Consciousness, Marcus Garvey, Jazz, Reggae, Hip Hop & the African Diaspora and The Souls of Poor Folk. White currently holds a corporate graphic design position in Delaware, and has previously held a number of such positions in New York and Pennsylvania.

A talented artist/creator and father of 6, **PHILLIP R WILLIAMS, JR.,** has been doing comics with a strong passion for many years and now has finally decided to get serious.

**YTASHA L. WOMACK** is an award-winning author, director and dancer. Her books include Afrofuturism: The World of Black Sci Fi & Fantasy Culture, the sci fi novel Rayla 2212, Post Black, and Beats Rhymes and Life: What We Love & Hate About Hip Hop. Afrofuturism is a 2014 Locus Awards Nonfiction Finalist. She is a frequent lecturer on Afrofuturism and showcases at Comic Cons. Her works have inspired conferences including Duke University's Race in Space Conference and Afrofuturism & Religion Conference at Vanderbilt. Her latest film, Bar Star City, an Afrofuturist work debuts in 2016. She's a Chicago native and a graduate of Clark Atlanta University.

Born and raised in Chicago, **ASHLEY A. WOODS** is an illustrator who got her start through self-publishing her action-fantasy comic series, "Millennia War", while attending the International Academy of Design and Technology. After earning her degree in Video and Animation, she traveled to Kyoto, Japan where she presented her work in a gallery showcase called, "Out Of Sequence". After returning to the states, her work from her comics were included in the "Black Comix" compilation table top book which was used in college courses at various universities internationally. When Ashley isn't working, she enjoys playing video games and studying Japanese.

**J. ANDREW WORLD** is the writer and illustrator of the progressive political webcomics Right About Now and Word Salad. He also designs eye-catching graphics highlighting inspirational, thought provoking, and sometimes controversial quotes. He is committed to using his talents for raising awareness of community challenges and for encouraging open and respectful debate.

List of people killed by police between the time we announced this book (12/15/2014) and the day before it's going to print (9/11/2015). Data taken from http://www.killedbypolice.net/, and represents news reports of people killed by U.S. law enforcement officers regardless of reason or method. Without getting into how many of these killings were justified, it is worth noting the number goes up significantly every year while crime continues to be on the decline.

We apologize for the small font. If we printed this list at 10-point font, it would have taken 8 pages.

1. 12/15/2014 - Cody Robert Healey, 28
2. 12/15/2014 - Xavier McDonald, 16
3. 12/15/2014 - Brandon Tate-Brown, 26
4. 12/15/2014 - Dennis Grisgby, 35
5. 12/17/2014 - Henry Castoreno, 48
6. 12/17/2014 - Julius L. Pinson, 48
7. 12/17/2014 - Adam Padilla, 34
8. 12/17/2014 - William R. Osterlind, 18
9. 12/17/2014 - Andrew Jay Worsfold, 25
10. 12/17/2014 - Johnathon Dean Mar, 18
11. 12/18/2014 - Sandra Simpson, 32
12. 12/18/2014 - Richard Fredrick Tis Mil Estrada, 17
13. 12/18/2014 - Brent Krout, 39
14. 12/19/2014 - Terrell Beasley, 28
15. 12/19/2014 - Joshua G. Dawson, 35
16. 12/20/2014 - Martin Sanchez-Juarez, 34
17. 12/20/2014 - Allen Locke, 30
18. 12/21/2014 - William Everett Corson, 53
19. 12/21/2014 - James Long, 52
20. 12/21/2014 - Nicholas Tyson Frazier, 28
21. 12/22/2014 - Timothy Rundquist, 62
22. 12/22/2014 - Jose Salas, 29
23. 12/22/2014 - Allen Berly Todd Jr., 27
24. 12/22/2014 - Austin Leake, 20
25. 12/23/2014 - James Arlen Monroe Jr., 61
26. 12/24/2014 - Khamis Shatara, 21
27. 12/24/2014 - Gregory Marcus Gray, 33
28. 12/24/2014 - Robert J. Jenkins, 55
29. 12/24/2014 - Antonio Martin, 18
30. 12/25/2014 - Francisco Manuel Cesena, 40
31. 12/25/2014 - Omar Rodriguez, 35
32. 12/26/2014 - Quentin Smith, 23
33. 12/26/2014 - Terrence Gilbert, 25
34. 12/26/2014 - John Hebebrand, 43
35. 12/26/2014 - Carlton Wayne Smith, 20
36. 12/27/2014 - Darren Robert Kindgren, 51
37. 12/28/2014 - Daniel Gray, 51
38. 12/28/2014 - Matthew McCloskey, 10
39. 12/28/2014 - Nicholas Ryan McGehee, 28
40. 12/28/2014 - David Andre Scott, 28
41. 12/28/2014 - Craig Schiffer, 54
42. 12/29/2014 - Thomas Monts Jr., 39
43. 12/29/2014 - Robert Battaglia, 28
44. 12/30/2014 - Joseph Anthony Pacini, 52
45. 12/30/2014 - Timothy Edward West, 48
46. 12/31/2014 - Kevin Davis, 44
47. 12/31/2014 - Mayra Cornejo, 34
48. 12/31/2014 - Ernest Lee Erwin 48
49. 12/31/2014 - Eric Tyrone Forbes, 28
50. 12/31/2014 - Kaileb Cole Williams, 20
51. 12/31/2014 - Jerame C. Reid, 36
52. 12/31/2014 - Robert Earl Lawrence, 30
53. 1/1/2015 - Garrett Gagne, 22
54. 1/2/2015 - Matthew Ajibade, 22
55. 1/2/2015 - Lewis Lee Lembke, 47
56. 1/3/2015 - Michael Kocher Jr., 19
57. 1/3/2015 - John Paul Quintero, 23
58. 1/3/2015 - Tim Elliott, 53
59. 1/4/2015 - Matthew Hoffman, 32
60. 1/5/2015 - Frank Jerome Smart, 39
61. 1/5/2015 - Andrew McIlvain, 39
62. 1/5/2015 - Michael Ray Rodriguez, 29
63. 1/6/2015 - Autumn Mae Steele, 34
64. 1/6/2015 - Patrick Wayne Wetter, 25
65. 1/6/2015 - Leslie Sapp III, 47
66. 1/6/2015 - Ned Womack, 47
67. 1/6/2015 - Kenneth Arnold Buck, 22
68. 1/7/2015 - Joseph Caffarello, 31
69. 1/7/2015 - Andre Larone Murphy Sr., 42
70. 1/7/2015 - Brian Pickett, 26
71. 1/7/2015 - Ronald Sneed, 31
72. 1/7/2015 - Hashim Hanif Ibn Abdul-Rasheed, 41
73. 1/7/2015 - Nicholas Ryan Brickman, 30
74. 1/7/2015 - Brock Nichols, 35
75. 1/8/2015 - Loren Simpson, 28
76. 1/8/2015 - Artago Damon Howard, 36
77. 1/8/2015 - James Dudley Barker, 42
78. 1/8/2015 - Omarr Jackson Sr., 37
79. 1/9/2015 - Andy Martinez, 33
80. 1/9/2015 - Jimmy Foreman, 71
81. 1/11/2015 - Salvador Figueroa, 29
82. 1/11/2015 - Brian Barbosa, 23
83. 1/12/2015 - Thomas Hamby, 49
84. 1/12/2015 - Tommy E. Smith, 39
85. 1/13/2015 - John Edward Okeefe, 35
86. 1/13/2015 - Richard McClendon, 43
87. 1/14/2015 - Louis F. Becker, 87
88. 1/14/2015 - Robert Edwards, 68
89. 1/14/2015 - Jeffrey R. Nielson, 34
90. 1/14/2015 - Talbot Schroeder, 75

91. 1/14/2015 - Marcus Ryan Golden, 24
92. 1/15/2015 - Quincy Reed Reindl, 24
93. 1/15/2015 - Jose Ceja, 36
94. 1/15/2015 - Donte Sowell, 27
95. 1/15/2015 - Nathan Massey, 33
96. 1/15/2015 - Michael T. Goebel, 29
97. 1/15/2015 - Mario A. Jordan, 34
98. 1/16/2015 - Rodney Walker, 23
99. 1/16/2015 - Christina Prestianni, 37
100. 1/16/2015 - Scott Wesley Hall, 41
101. 1/16/2015 - Zaki Shinwary, 48
102. 1/16/2015 - Howard Robbins, 69
103. 1/16/2015 - Phillip Garcia, 26
104. 1/16/2015 - Kavonda Earl Payton, 39
105. 1/17/2015 - Pablo Meza, 24
106. 1/17/2015 - Terence D. Walker, 21
107. 1/17/2015 - Daniel Brumley, 27
108. 1/18/2015 - Sinthanouxay Khottavongsa, 57
109. 1/19/2015 - Carter Ray Castle, 67
110. 1/19/2015 - Johnathon Craig Guillory, 32
111. 1/19/2015 - Paul Campbell, 49
112. 1/20/2015 - Dewayne Carr, 42
113. 1/21/2015 - Miguel Anguel de Santos-Rodriguez, 36
114. 1/21/2015 - John Ballard Gorman, 45
115. 1/21/2015 - Andrew Toto, 54
116. 1/22/2015 - Kristiana Coignard, 17
117. 1/22/2015 - Todd Allan Hodge, 36
118. 1/22/2015 - Isaac Holmes, 19
119. 1/23/2015 - Jose Antonio Espinoza Ruiz, 56
120. 1/23/2015 - Demaris Turner, 29
121. 1/23/2015 - Robert Francis Mesch, 61
122. 1/24/2015 - Daryl Myler, 45
123. 1/24/2015 - Darin Hutchins, 26
124. 1/24/2015 - Tiano Meton, 25
125. 1/25/2015 - Orlando Jude Lopez, 26
126. 1/25/2015 - William Campbell, 59
127. 1/26/2015 - Raymond Kmetz, 68
128. 1/26/2015 - Alvin Haynes, 57
129. 1/26/2015 - Joshua Omar Garcia, 24
130. 1/26/2015 - David Garcia, 33
131. 1/26/2015 - Jessica Hernandez, 17
132. 1/27/2015 - Nicolas Leland Tewa, 26
133. 1/27/2015 - Chris Ingram, 29
134. 1/27/2015 - Jermonte Fletcher, 33
135. 1/28/2015 - Larry Kobuk, 33
136. 1/28/2015 - Alan Lance Alverson, 44
137. 1/28/2015 - Matautu Nuu, 35
138. 1/28/2015 - Cody Karasek, 26
139. 1/29/2015 - Wendell King, 40
140. 1/29/2015 - Ralph W. Willis, 42
141. 1/30/2015 - John Barry Marshall, 48
142. 1/30/2015 - Tiffany D. Terry, 39
143. 1/31/2015 - Victor Manuel Reyes, 31
144. 1/31/2015 - Edward Donnell Bright, Sr., 56
145. 2/2/2015 - Francis Murphy Rose III, 42
146. 2/2/2015 - David Anthony Kassick, 59
147. 2/2/2015, Hung Trieu
148. 2/3/2015 - Dewayne Deshawn Ward Jr., 29
149. 2/3/2015 - Anthony Purvis, 45
150. 2/3/2015 - Ledarius Williams, 23
151. 2/3/2015 - Yuvette Henderson, 38
152. 2/3/2015 - Kenneth Brown, 18
153. 2/4/2015 - Izzy Colon, 37
154. 2/4/2015 - Paul Alfred Eugene Johnson, 59
155. 2/4/2015 - Markell Atkins, 36
156. 2/4/2015 - Jimmy Ray Robinson Jr., 51
157. 2/4/2015 - Salvador Muna, 28
158. 2/4/2015 - Joaquin Hernandez, 28
159. 2/4/2015 - Kevin Demetrius Garrett, 60
160. 2/5/2015 - Wilber Castillo-Gongora, 35
161. 2/5/2015 - Jeremy Lett, 28
162. 2/6/2015 - Herbert Hill, 26
163. 2/6/2015 - John Sawyer, 36
164. 2/7/2015 - Alan James, 31
165. 2/8/2015 - Joseph Paffen, 46
166. 2/8/2015 - Natasha McKenna, 37
167. 2/8/2015 - Sawyer Flache, 27
168. 2/8/2015 - James Howard Allen, 74
169. 2/9/2015 - Dean Joseph Bucheit, 64
170. 2/9/2015 - Vincent Cordaro, 57
171. 2/9/2015 - Desmond Luster, Sr., 45
172. 2/9/2015 - Larry Hostetter, 41
173. 2/10/2015 - Anthony Bess, 49
174. 2/10/2015 - Antonio Zambrano-Montes, 35
175. 2/10/2015 - Brian P. Fritze, 45
176. 2/10/2015 - John Martin Whittaker, 33
177. 2/11/2015 - Phillip Watkins, 23
178. 2/11/2015 - Fletcher Ray Stewart, 46
179. 2/11/2015 - Kenneth Kreyssig, 61

180. 2/12/2015 - Jonathan Paul Pierce, 37
181. 2/13/2015 - Matthew D. Belk, 27
182. 2/13/2015 - Jonathan Larry Harden, 23
183. 2/13/2015 - Richard Carlin, 35
184. 2/13/2015 - Andres D. Lara-Rodriguez, 21
185. 2/14/2015 - Jason C. Hendrix, 16
186. 2/15/2015 - Roy Joy Day, 51
187. 2/15/2015 - Howard Brent Means Jr., 34
188. 2/15/2015 - Daniel Mejia, 37
189. 2/15/2015 - Bruce Lee Steward, 34
190. 2/15/2015 - Lavall Hall, 25
191. 2/15/2015 - Cody Evans, 24
192. 2/16/2015 - Jacob M. Haglund, 17
193. 2/16/2015 - Daniel Lawrence Caldwell, 56
194. 2/16/2015 - Michael K. Casper, 26
195. 2/17/2015 - Pedro Pete Juan Saldivar, 50
196. 2/17/2015 - Betty Diane Sexton, 43
197. 2/17/2015 - Matthew Lundy, 32
198. 2/17/2015 - Doug Sparks, 30
199. 2/18/2015 - Anthony Dean Marino, 58
200. 2/18/2015 - Michael Steven Ireland, 31
201. 2/19/2015 - Chance Dale Thompson, 35
202. 2/19/2015 - Janisha Fonville, 20
203. 2/20/2015 - Rubén García Villalpando, 31
204. 2/20/2015, Alejandro Salazar
205. 2/20/2015 - Stanley Lamar Grant, 38
206. 2/21/2015 - Terry Price, 41
207. 2/21/2015 - Jason Moncrief Carter, 41
208. 2/21/2015 - Kent Norman, 51
209. 2/22/2015 - Bradford Samuel Leonard, 50
210. 2/23/2015 - A'Donte Washington, 16
211. 2/23/2015 - Robert Kohl, 47
212. 2/23/2015 - Anthony Giaquinta, 41
213. 2/23/2015 - Michael Wayne Smashey, 37
214. 2/23/2015 - Jerome D. Nichols, 42
215. 2/24/2015 - Calvon A. Reid, 39
216. 2/24/2015 - Joseph Biegert, 30
217. 2/24/2015 - Daniel A. Elrod, 39
218. 2/25/2015 - Alexander Phillip Long, 31
219. 2/25/2015 - Francis Spivey, 43
220. 2/25/2015 - Glenn C. Lewis, 37
221. 2/26/2015 - Crystal Lee Miley Harry, 34
222. 2/26/2015 - David Cuevas, 43
223. 2/27/2015 - Russell Edward Sharrer, 54
224. 2/27/2015 - Chazsten Noah Freeman, 24
225. 2/27/2015 - Ernesto Javier Canepa Diaz, 27
226. 2/27/2015 - Rodney Biggs, 49
227. 2/27/2015 - Amilcar Perez-Lopez, 21
228. 2/28/2015 - Stephanie LeJean Hill, 37
229. 2/28/2015 - Ian Sherrod, 40
230. 2/28/2015 - Cornelius J. Parker, 28
231. 3/1/2015 - Darrell "Hubbard" Gatewood, 47
232. 3/1/2015 - Jeffrey C. Surnow, 63
233. 3/1/2015 - Jessica Uribe, 28
234. 3/1/2015 - Donald Lewis Matkins, 49
235. 3/1/2015 - Charly Leundeu Keunang, 43, Africa
236. 3/1/2015 - Thomas Allen Jr., 34
237. 3/1/2015 - Deven Guilford, 17
238. 3/3/2015 - Shaquille C. Barrow, 20
239. 3/3/2015 - Matthew Metz, 25
240. 3/3/2015 - Fednel Rhinvil, 25
241. 3/4/2015 - Derek Cruice, 26
242. 3/5/2015 - Tyson Damian Hubbard, 34
243. 3/5/2015 - Sergio Alexander Navas, 35
244. 3/6/2015 - Andrew Anthony Williams, 48
245. 3/6/2015 - Tony Chance Ross, 34
246. 3/6/2015 - Bernard Moore, 62
247. 3/6/2015 - Tony Terrell Robinson Jr., 19
248. 3/6/2015 - Naeschylus Vinzant, 37
249. 3/6/2015 - Tyrone Ryerson Lawrence, 45
250. 3/7/2015 - Adam O'Neal Reinhart, 29
251. 3/8/2015 - Monique Jenee Deckard, 43
252. 3/8/2015 - Michael L. McKillop, 35
253. 3/8/2015 - Aurelio V. Duarte, 40
254. 3/9/2015 - James Brent Damon, 46
255. 3/9/2015 - Lester Randolph Brown, 58
256. 3/9/2015 - Anthony Hill, 27
257. 3/10/2015 - William Russell Smith, 53
258. 3/10/2015 - Cedrick Lamont Bishop, 30
259. 3/10/2015 - Christopher Mitchell, 23
260. 3/11/2015 - Aaron Valdez, 25
261. 3/11/2015 - Benito Osorio, 39
262. 3/11/2015 - Jamie Croom, 31
263. 3/11/2015 - Terry Garnett Jr., 37
264. 3/11/2015 - James Greenwell, 31
265. 3/11/2015 - Hue Dang, 64
266. 3/11/2015 - Terrance Moxley, 29
267. 3/11/2015 - Edixon Ivan Franco, 37
268. 3/11/2015 - Theodore Johnson, 64
269. 3/12/2015 - Jonathan Ryan Paul, 42

270. 3/12/2015 - Bobby Gross, 35
271. 3/12/2015 - Ryan Dean Burgess, 31
272. 3/13/2015 - Salome Jr Rodriguez, 23
273. 3/13/2015 - James Richard Jimenez, 41
274. 3/13/2015 - Fred E. Liggett Jr., 59
275. 3/13/2015, Antonio Perez
276. 3/14/2015, Andrew Driver
277. 3/14/2015 - Aaron Siler, 26
278. 3/14/2015 - Clifton Reintzel, 53
279. 3/14/2015 - Richard Castilleja, 29
280. 3/15/2015 - Troy Ray Boyd, 36
281. 3/15/2015 - David Werblow, 41
282. 3/16/2015 - William Dean Poole, 52
283. 3/16/2015 - Justin Todd Tolkinen, 28
284. 3/17/2015 - Sheldon Haleck, 38
285. 3/17/2015 - Roberto Jose Leon, 22
286. 3/17/2015 - Alice Brown, 24
287. 3/17/2015 - Declan Owen, 24
288. 3/17/2015 - David P. Watford, 47
289. 3/17/2015 - Eugene Frank Smith II, 20
290. 3/17/2015 - Andrew Charles Shipley, 49
291. 3/18/2015 - Kaylene Stone, 49
292. 3/18/2015 - Askari Roberts, 35
293. 3/18/2015 - Jeff Alexander, 47
294. 3/19/2015 - Robert Paul Burdge, 36
295. 3/19/2015 - Justin Fowler, 24
296. 3/19/2015 - Jamison E. Childress, 20
297. 3/19/2015 - Adam Jovicic, 29
298. 3/19/2015 - Kendre Omari Alston, 16
299. 3/19/2015 - Brandon Jones, 18
300. 3/19/2015 - Shane Watkins, 39
301. 3/19/2015 - Garland Lee Wingo I, 64
302. 3/19/2015 - Brandon Rapp, 31
303. 3/20/2015 - Richard White, 63
304. 3/20/2015 - Gilbert Fleury, 54
305. 3/21/2015 - Jason L. Smith, 42
306. 3/21/2015 - Gary Page, 60
307. 3/21/2015 - Tyrel Wes Vick, 34
308. 3/21/2015 - James J. Ellis, 44
309. 3/22/2015 - Enoch Gaver, 21
310. 3/22/2015 - James Moore, 43
311. 3/22/2015 - Devin James Gates, 24
312. 3/22/2015 - Phillip Conley, 37
313. 3/23/2015, Mychael J. Lynch
314. 3/23/2015 - Denzel Brown, 21
315. 3/23/2015 - Christopher Ryan Healy, 36
316. 3/24/2015 - Jeffrey L. Jackson, 47
317. 3/24/2015 - Steven Timothy Snyder, 38
318. 3/24/2015 - Joseph Tassinari, 63
319. 3/24/2015 - Nicholas Thomas, 23
320. 3/24/2015 - Walter Brown III, 29
321. 3/25/2015 - Jeremy Lorenza Kelly, 27
322. 3/25/2015 - Victor Daniel Terrazas, 28
323. 3/26/2015 - Scott Dunham, 57
324. 3/26/2015 - Adrian Solis, 35
325. 3/27/2015 - Meagan Hockaday, 26
326. 3/27/2015 - Adrian Hernandez, 22
327. 3/27/2015 - Angelo West, 41
328. 3/27/2015 - Gary Kendrick, 56
329. 3/27/2015 - Douglas Harris, 77
330. 3/27/2015 - Carl Lao, 28
331. 3/27/2015 - Jamalis Hall, 39
332. 3/27/2015 - Neil Seifert, 40
333. 3/27/2015 - Deanne Choate, 53
334. 3/28/2015 - Harvey Ellis Oates, 42
335. 3/29/2015 - Robert Rooker, 26
336. 3/30/2015 - Gregory Thomas Smith, 39
337. 3/30/2015 - Dominick R. Wise, 30
338. 3/30/2015 - Byron Herbert, 29
339. 3/30/2015 - Ricky Shawatza Hall, 27, known as Mya
340. 3/30/2015 - John Allen, 54
341. 3/30/2015 - Jason Moland, 29
342. 3/31/2015 - Jeremy James Anderson, 36
343. 3/31/2015 - Phillip White, 32
344. 3/31/2015 - Benjamin Quezada, 21
345. 3/31/2015 - Brian Babb, 49
346. 4/1/2015 - Robert Washington, 37
347. 4/2/2015 - Aaron Marcus Rutledge, 27
348. 4/2/2015 - Donald J. Hicks, 63
349. 4/2/2015 - Eric Courtney Harris, 44
350. 4/2/2015 - Donald S. Ivy Jr., 39
351. 4/3/2015 - Christopher A. Prevatt, 38
352. 4/3/2015 - Darrin A. Langford, 32
353. 4/4/2015 - Justus Howell, 17
354. 4/4/2015 - Paul Anthony Anderson, 31
355. 4/4/2015 - David Cody Lynch, 33
356. 4/4/2015 - Walter Scott, 50
357. 4/4/2015 - Ethan Noll, 34
358. 4/5/2015 - Ken Cockerel, 51
359. 4/6/2015 - William J. Dick III, 28
360. 4/6/2015 - Jared Forsyth, 33
361. 4/6/2015 - Desmond Willis, 25
362. 4/6/2015 - Richard August Hanna, 56
363. 4/6/2015 - Alexander Myers, 23
364. 4/7/2015 - Keaton Farris, 25
365. 4/7/2015 - Erick Rose, 32
366. 4/7/2015 - Tyrell J. Larsen, 31
367. 4/8/2015 - Michael Earl Lemon, 41
368. 4/8/2015 - Roberto Fausto Rodriguez, 39
369. 4/8/2015 - Dexter Bethea, 42
370. 4/8/2015 - Douglas Faith, 60
371. 4/8/2015 - Joseph Jeremy Weber, 28

372. 4/9/2015 - Gordon Talmage Kimbrell Jr., 22
373. 4/9/2015 - Don Oneal Smith Jr., 29
374. 4/9/2015 - Phillip Michael Burgess, 28
375. 4/9/2015 - Mark Smith, 54
376. 4/10/2015 - Jess Leipold, 31
377. 4/10/2015 - Angel Cresencio Corona Jr., 21
378. 4/11/2015 - Donald W. Allen, 66
379. 4/12/2015 - Richard Dale Weaver, 83
380. 4/12/2015 - Mack Long, 36
381. 4/13/2015 - Isaac Jimenez, 27
382. 4/13/2015 - Celin Nunez, 24
383. 4/13/2015 - Jason Lee Evans, 32
384. 4/14/2015 - Karl Taylor, 52
385. 4/14/2015 - Colby Robinson, 26
386. 4/15/2015 - Sean Clyde, 36
387. 4/15/2015 - Joseph Slater, 28
388. 4/15/2015 - Ernesto Flores, 52
389. 4/15/2015 - Tevin Barkley, 22
390. 4/15/2015 - Donte Adaryll Noble, 41
391. 4/15/2015 - Frank Ernest Shephard, III, 41
392. 4/15/2015 - Stanley Watson, 72
393. 4/15/2015 - Christopher Grant Finley, 31
394. 4/16/2015 - David Kapuscinski, 39
395. 4/16/2015 - Rodolfo Velazquez, 47
396. 4/16/2015 - Mark W. Adair, 51
397. 4/17/2015 - Jeffery Kemp, 18
398. 4/17/2015 - Elias Cavazos, 29
399. 4/17/2015 - Darrell Lawrence Brown, 31
400. 4/18/2015 - Erik Tellez, 43
401. 4/18/2015 - Grover Zeno Sapp Jr., 45
402. 4/18/2015 - Thaddeus McCarroll, 23
403. 4/19/2015 - Richard Brian Reed, 38
404. 4/19/2015 - Norman Cooper, 33
405. 4/19/2015 - Freddie Gray, 25
406. 4/19/2015 - Michael Foster, 40
407. 4/20/2015 - Santos "Cuate" Cortez Hernandez, 24
408. 4/20/2015 - Dana Duwane Hlavinka, 44
409. 4/21/2015 - Luis Molina Martinez, 29
410. 4/21/2015 - Daniel I. Covarrubias, 37
411. 4/21/2015 - Daniel Wolfe, 35
412. 4/21/2015 - Stephen Gene Davenport, 40
413. 4/22/2015 - Jose E. Herrera, 27
414. 4/22/2015 - Carlos Saavedra Ramirez, 51
415. 4/22/2015 - Lue Vang, 39
416. 4/22/2015 - William L. Chapman II, 18
417. 4/22/2015 - Kimber Key, 59
418. 4/22/2015 - Reginald McGregor, 31
419. 4/23/2015 - David "Levi" Dehmann, 33
420. 4/23/2015 - Samuel D. Harrell, III, 30
421. 4/23/2015 - Joseph Potts, 51
422. 4/23/2015 - Andrew George Valadez, 26
423. 4/23/2015 - Terry Lee Chatman, 48
424. 4/23/2015 - Jonathan Efraim, 30
425. 4/24/2015 - Mark Cecil Hawkins, 49
426. 4/24/2015 - Karen Jenks, 46
427. 4/24/2015 - Todd Jamal Dye, 20
428. 4/24/2015 - Hector Morejon, 19
429. 4/25/2015 - Daniel Howard Davis, 58
430. 4/25/2015 - David Felix, 24
431. 4/25/2015 - Gary Timmie Collins, 63
432. 4/26/2015 - Albert Hanson Jr., 76
433. 4/26/2015 - Billy Joe Patrick, 29
434. 4/26/2015 - Brandon Lawrence, 25
435. 4/26/2015 - Dean Kristian Genova, 45
436. 4/27/2015 - Terrance Kellom, 20
437. 4/28/2015 - Bryan Rashod Overstreet, 30
438. 4/28/2015 - Joshua Green, 27
439. 4/28/2015 - Jared Johnson, 22
440. 4/28/2015 - David Parker, 58
441. 4/29/2015 - Andrew Jackson, 26
442. 4/29/2015 - Joshua Deysie, 33
443. 4/29/2015 - Luis Martin Chavez-Diaz, 27
444. 4/30/2015 - Erick Emmanuel Salas Sanchez, 22
445. 4/30/2015 - Alexia Christian, 25
446. 4/30/2015 - Jeffery O. Adkins, 53
447. 4/30/2015 - John D. Acree, 53
448. 4/30/2015 - Fridoon Rawshan Nehad, 42
449. 5/2/2015 - Kenneth Mathena, 52
450. 5/3/2015 - Billy Grimm, 44
451. 5/3/2015 - Elton Simpson, 30
452. 5/3/2015 - Nadir Soofi, 34
453. 5/3/2015 - Kevin Vance Norton, 36
454. 5/4/2015 - Roark K. Cook, 36
455. 5/4/2015 - Michael Asher, 53
456. 5/5/2015 - Thong Kien Ma, 32
457. 5/5/2015 - Robert Frost, 46
458. 5/6/2015 - Nuwnah Laroche, 34
459. 5/6/2015 - Jason Champion, 41
460. 5/6/2015 - Brendon Glenn, 29
461. 5/7/2015 - John Paul Kaafi, 33
462. 5/7/2015 - Nephi Arriguin, 21
463. 5/7/2015 - Michael G. Murphy, 35
464. 5/7/2015 - David Johnson, 18
465. 5/7/2015 - Joseph Roy, 72
466. 5/8/2015 - David A. Schwalm, 58
467. 5/8/2015 - Dedrick Marshall, 48
468. 5/9/2015 - Sam Matthew Holmes, 31
469. 5/11/2015 - Kelvin Antonie Goldston, 30
470. 5/11/2015 - Justin Edward Way, 28
471. 5/11/2015 - Sean Johnson, 35
472. 5/11/2015 - Michael Tyrone Gallacher, 55
473. 5/11/2015 - Lionel Young, 34
474. 5/11/2015 - Stephen Cunningham, 47

475. 5/12/2015 - Dajuan Graham, 40
476. 5/12/2015 - Bruce Zalonka, 46
477. 5/12/2015 - Alec Ouzounian, 40
478. 5/12/2015 - D'Angelo Reyes Stallworth, 28
479. 5/13/2015 - Lorenzo Hayes, 37
480. 5/14/2015 - Sean Michael Pelletier, 37
481. 5/15/2015 - Mark T. Farrar, 41
482. 5/15/2015 - Denis Reyes, 40
483. 5/16/2015 - Matthew Coates, 42
484. 5/17/2015 - Austin Goodner, 18
485. 5/17/2015 - Ronell Wade, 45
486. 5/17/2015 - Timothy Jones, 27
487. 5/17/2015 - Dennis Richard Fiel, 34
488. 5/19/2015 - David Gaines, 17
489. 5/19/2015 - Anthony Quinn Gomez Jr., 29
490. 5/19/2015 - Alfredo Rials-Torres, 54
491. 5/20/2015 - Marcus D. Wheeler, 26
492. 5/20/2015 - Jonathan Colley, 52
493. 5/20/2015 - Jonathan McIntosh, 35
494. 5/21/2015 - Cary Lloyd Martin, 53
495. 5/21/2015 - David Alejandro Gandara, 22
496. 5/21/2015 - Markus Clark, 26
497. 5/21/2015 - Javoris Reshaud Washington, 29
498. 5/21/2015 - Elvin Jesus Diaz, 24
499. 5/21/2015 - Nikki Jo Burtsfield, 39
500. 5/21/2015 - Jerome Thomas Caldwell, 32
501. 5/21/2015 - Chrislon Talbott, 38
502. 5/21/2015 - James Anthony Cooper, 43
503. 5/22/2015 - Alan Edward Dunnagan, 68
504. 5/22/2015 - Michael Lowrey, 40
505. 5/23/2015 - Caso Jackson, 25
506. 5/23/2015 - James Horn Jr., 47
507. 5/24/2015 - Eric Robinson, 40
508. 5/25/2015 - Thomas R. Ramey, 64
509. 5/25/2015 - Barbara V. Ramey, 64
510. 5/25/2015 - Anthony Dewayne Briggs, 36
511. 5/25/2015 - Cassandra Bolin, 31
512. 5/26/2015 - Jessie Nicholas Williams, 24
513. 5/26/2015 - Dalton Branch, 51
514. 5/26/2015 - Millard James Tallant III, 62
515. 5/27/2015 - Simon D. Hubble, 33
516. 5/27/2015 - Garrett Sandeno, 24
517. 5/27/2015 - Randall C. Torrence, 34
518. 5/27/2015 - Scott McAllister, 39
519. 5/28/2015 - Kyle Baker, 18
520. 5/28/2015 - Kenneth Joel Dothard, 40
521. 5/28/2015 - Darrell Morgan, 60
522. 5/28/2015 - Feras Morad, 20
523. 5/28/2015 - James Edward Strong Jr., 32
524. 5/28/2015 - Harry Davis, 57
525. 5/29/2015 - Coy Wayne Walker, 41
526. 5/29/2015 - Bin Christopher Williams, 46
527. 5/29/2015 - Kevin K. Allen, 36
528. 5/30/2015 - Alexander Tirado Rivera, 39
529. 5/30/2015 - Ebin Lamont Proctor, 19
530. 5/30/2015 - Robert Box, 55
531. 5/30/2015 - Nehemiah Fischer, 35
532. 5/31/2015 - James Anthony Morris, 40
533. 5/31/2015 - Richard Gregory Davis, 50
534. 6/1/2015 - Billy J. Collins, 56
535. 6/1/2015 - Joseph M. Ladd, 23
536. 6/1/2015 - James D. Bushey, 47
537. 6/2/2015 - Kamal Dajani, 26
538. 6/2/2015 - Usaamah Rahim, 26
539. 6/3/2015 - Ronald Neal, 56
540. 6/3/2015 - Unidentified
541. 6/3/2015 - Miguel A. Martinez, 18
542. 6/4/2015 - Curtis David Jordan, 45
543. 6/4/2015 - Rudy Baca, 36
544. 6/4/2015 - Lorenzo Garza Jr., 46
545. 6/4/2015 - Sherman Byrd, 24
546. 6/5/2015 - Donald J. Pinkerton-DeVito III, 23
547. 6/5/2015 - Jesus Quezada Gomez, 50
548. 6/5/2015 - Andrew Ellerbe, 33
549. 6/6/2015 - Christie L. Cathers, 45
550. 6/6/2015 - Joe Don Nevels, 42
551. 6/6/2015 - Alejandro Campos Fernandez, 45
552. 6/6/2015 - Demouria Hogg, 30
553. 6/7/2015 - Damien James Ramirez, 27
554. 6/7/2015 - Gene Marshall, 58
555. 6/7/2015 - James Smillie, 53
556. 6/8/2015 - Richard Warolf, 69
557. 6/8/2015 - Mario Ocasio, 51
558. 6/8/2015 - Rene Garcia, 30
559. 6/8/2015 - James Johnson, 54
560. 6/8/2015 - Matthew Wayne McDaniel, 35
561. 6/9/2015 - Ryan Keith Bolinger, 28
562. 6/9/2015 - QuanDavier Hicks, 22
563. 6/9/2015 - Unidentified
564. 6/9/2015 - Ross Anthony, 25
565. 6/9/2015 - Jeremy John Linhart, 30
566. 6/10/2015 - Isiah Hampton, 19
567. 6/11/2015 - Mark Flores, Jr., 28
568. 6/11/2015 - Raymond Peralta-Lantigua, 22
569. 6/11/2015 - Raymond K. Phillips, 86
570. 6/11/2015 - Charles Allen Ziegler, 40
571. 6/11/2015 - Fritz Severe, 46
572. 6/12/2015 - Shelly Lynn Haendiges, 17
573. 6/13/2015 - Anthony W. Hodge, 46
574. 6/13/2015 - Deng Manyoun, 35
575. 6/13/2015 - David Eugene Munday, 50
576. 6/13/2015 - James Lance Boulware, 35
577. 6/14/2015 - Zane Terryn, 15

578. 6/14/2015 - Kenneth Garcia, 28
579. 6/14/2015 - Candace L. Blakley, 24
580. 6/15/2015 - Kris Jackson, 22
581. 6/16/2015 - Jermaine Benjamin, 42
582. 6/16/2015 - Christopher DeLeon, 28
583. 6/16/2015 - Tamara Seidle, 51
584. 6/17/2015 - Joe Charboneau, 31
585. 6/18/2015 - Kenneth Lanphier, 48
586. 6/18/2015 - Oleg Tcherniak, 58
587. 6/18/2015 - Wendy Michelle Chappell, 40
588. 6/19/2015 - Santos Laboy, 45
589. 6/19/2015 - Louis Atencio, 50
590. 6/19/2015 - Trepierre Hummons, 21
591. 6/20/2015 - Zamiel Kivon Crawford, 21
592. 6/20/2015 - Kevin Bajoie, 32
593. 6/21/2015 - Adrian Simental, 24
594. 6/21/2015 - Charles David Marshall, 49
595. 6/22/2015 - Tyler James Wicks, 30
596. 6/22/2015 - Robert Kenkel, 38
597. 6/22/2015 - Tyrone Harris, 20
598. 6/22/2015 - James Monroe Barrett, 60
599. 6/23/2015 - Allen K. Hernandez, 23
600. 6/23/2015 - Randall Waddel, 49
601. 6/23/2015 - Joshua Dyer, 34
602. 6/23/2015 - Jonathan P. Wilson, 22
603. 6/23/2015 - Eduardo Reyes, 35
604. 6/24/2015 - Damien A. Harrell, 26
605. 6/25/2015 - Gilbert Jake Vanderburgh, 61
606. 6/25/2015 - Spencer Lee McCain, 41
607. 6/26/2015 - Joe Angel Cisneros III, 28
608. 6/26/2015 - Richard W. Matt, 49
609. 6/26/2015 - Alfontish Cockerham, 23
610. 6/27/2015 - Joshua P. Crittenden, 35
611. 6/28/2015 - William Dale McIntire, 60
612. 6/29/2015 - Alan Lee Bellew, 29
613. 6/30/2015 - Jimmy Payne Jr., 51
614. 6/30/2015 - Clay Alan Lickteig, 52
615. 6/30/2015 - Richard LaPort, 51
616. 7/1/2015 - Kevin Lamont Judson, 24
617. 7/2/2015 - Brian Johnson, 59
618. 7/2/2015 - Victo Larosa III, 23
619. 7/2/2015 - Julian Joseph, 40
620. 7/2/2015 - Kaleb Landon, 35
621. 7/2/2015 - Douglas Buckley, 45
622. 7/3/2015 - Arturo Lopez, 46
623. 7/3/2015 - Christian Siqueiros, 25
624. 7/3/2015 - Ton Nguyen, 60
625. 7/4/2015 - Michael Shannon Gaby, 37
626. 7/4/2015 - Bryan David Bauer, 36
627. 7/4/2015 - Robert Elando Manlone, 42
628. 7/4/2015 - Cesar A. Limon Juarez, 27
629. 7/4/2015 - Kawanza Jamaal Beaty, 23
630. 7/4/2015 - Oscar Camacho, 33
631. 7/5/2015 - Neil Van De Putte, 25
632. 7/5/2015 - Johnathon Patrick Deming, Jr., 19
633. 7/5/2015 - Richard Munroe, 25
634. 7/5/2015 - Michael McGregor Holt, 35
635. 7/6/2015 - Jason M. Hendley, 29
636. 7/6/2015 - Adam Edward Dujanovic, 33
637. 7/6/2015 - Maximo Rabasa, 52
638. 7/6/2015 - David Oliva Sarabia, 27
639. 7/6/2015 - John Leonard Berry, 31
640. 7/6/2015 - Tyler Rogers, 20
641. 7/6/2015 - Johnny Ray Anderson, 43
642. 7/7/2015 - Nicholas E. Booth, 35
643. 7/7/2015 - Jose Graciano Lopez, 39
644. 7/7/2015 - Daniel Hernandez, Jr., 47
645. 7/7/2015 - Unidentified
646. 7/7/2015 - Joe Cody, 59
647. 7/7/2015 - Hagen D. Esty-Lennon, 42
648. 7/7/2015 - Unidentified
649. 7/8/2015 - Jonathan Sanders, 39
650. 7/8/2015 - Michael T. Westrich, 59
651. 7/8/2015 - Joshua S. Blough, 28
652. 7/9/2015 - Jimmy Lloyd Washington, Jr., 53
653. 7/9/2015 - Robert Hammonds, 68
654. 7/9/2015 - Dallas Shatley, 62
655. 7/10/2015 - Javon Hawkins, 21
656. 7/10/2015 - Unidentified, 38
657. 7/10/2015 - James Michael Todora, 54
658. 7/10/2015 - Cyrus Hurtado, 17
659. 7/10/2015 - Rocco Joseph Palmisano III, 50
660. 7/10/2015 - Martice Milliner, 27
661. 7/11/2015 - Anthony Dewayne Ware, 35
662. 7/11/2015 - George Mann, 35
663. 7/12/2015 - Matthew Watson, 24
664. 7/12/2015 - Freddie Blue, 20
665. 7/12/2015 - David Allen Lepine, 62
666. 7/12/2015 - Frederick Farmer, 20
667. 7/13/2015 - Bruce Dean Stafford, 55
668. 7/13/2015 - Matthew Graham, 23
669. 7/13/2015 - Shane Gormley, 30
670. 7/13/2015 - Billy Maine, 31
671. 7/13/2015 - Christopher Charles Benton, 27
672. 7/13/2015 - Salvado Ellswood, 36
673. 7/13/2015 - Elbert G. Piolo, 38
674. 7/13/2015 - Nyal "Bud" Brown, 77
675. 7/13/2015 - Paul Castaway, 35
676. 7/14/2015 - Charles Crandell, 70s
677. 7/14/2015 - Rafael Suazo, 23
678. 7/14/2015 - Chacarion Avant, 20
679. 7/15/2015 - Eugene Kailing, 43
680. 7/16/2015 - Saige Dell Hack, 23

681. 7/16/2015 - William Dale Jeffries, 57
682. 7/16/2015 - Antonio Gonzales, 29
683. 7/16/2015 - Edward Foster III, 35
684. 7/16/2015 - Mohammod Youssuf Abdulazeez, 24
685. 7/16/2015 - Patrick Stephen Pippin, 30
686. 7/16/2015 - Jason Davis, 41
687. 7/16/2015 - Anthonie Smith, 25
688. 7/17/2015 - Jose Roman Rodriguez, 24
689. 7/17/2015 - Albert Joseph Davis, 23
690. 7/17/2015 - Sam Toshiro Smith, 27
691. 7/18/2015 - Troy Goode, 30
692. 7/18/2015 - Charles Dewey, 65
693. 7/18/2015 - Kevin Thomas Snyder, 46
694. 7/18/2015 - David Wheat Jr., 22
695. 7/18/2015 - Darrius Stewart, 19
696. 7/19/2015 - Samuel DuBose, 43
697. 7/19/2015 - Estevan Andrade Gomez, 26
698. 7/19/2015 - Billy Ray Davis, 59
699. 7/20/2015 - Pierre Gabriel Koellner, 29
700. 7/20/2015 - Joshua LeBoeuf, 35
701. 7/20/2015 - Heriberto Godinez Jr., 24
702. 7/20/2015 - Jackie Brand Jr., 50
703. 7/20/2015 - Unidentified
704. 7/21/2015 - Darren Billy Wilson, 47
705. 7/21/2015 - Joseph Fuller, 24
706. 7/21/2015 - Stephen Ray Brown, 54
707. 7/22/2015 - Michael Todd Sabbie, 35
708. 7/22/2015 - James T. Bush, 20
709. 7/22/2015 - Jerrod Tyre, 35
710. 7/22/2015 - Andre Dontrell Williams, 26
711. 7/22/2015 - Devon Guisherd, 26
712. 7/23/2015 - Robin George Welsh, 55
713. 7/23/2015 - Tamala Anne Satre, 44
714. 7/23/2015 - Brian Stortzum, 32
715. 7/23/2015 - Derek R. Wolfsteller, 31
716. 7/23/2015 - Robbie Lee Edison, 47
717. 7/23/2015 - Unidentified, 25
718. 7/23/2015 - Dontae L. Martin, 34
719. 7/24/2015 - Lee Aaron Gerston, 33
720. 7/24/2015 - Seth Raines, 44
721. 7/25/2015 - Earl Jackson, 59
722. 7/25/2015 - Bryan Keith Day, 36
723. 7/25/2015 - Roger Braswell, 50
724. 7/25/2015 - Christopher Olmstead, 60
725. 7/26/2015 - Zachary Hammond, 19
726. 7/26/2015 - Khari Westly, 33
727. 7/27/2015 - Timothy Milliken, 56
728. 7/27/2015 - Jean Paul Falgout, 45
729. 7/28/2015 - Timothy Johnson, 41
730. 7/28/2015 - Samuel Forgy, 22
731. 7/28/2015 - Allan F. White III, 23
732. 7/29/2015 - Michael Malone, 34
733. 7/30/2015 - Ryan Daniel Vrenon, 25
734. 7/30/2015 - Filimoni Raiyawa, 57
735. 7/30/2015 - Wilmer Delgado Sobá, 38
736. 7/30/2015 - Roger Darrin Barker, 53
737. 7/30/2015 - Oscar Lotari Romero, 47
738. 7/31/2015 - Jeremy Hatch, 34
739. 7/31/2015 - Rafael Molina Jr., 33
740. 7/31/2015 - Philip 'Flip' Vallejo, 30
741. 7/31/2015 - Mark Perkins, 48
742. 8/1/2015 - David Lane Cook, 52
743. 8/1/2015 - Joseph Sheldon Hutcheson, 48
744. 8/2/2015 - Antonio Clements, 49
745. 8/2/2015 - Armando Serrano Jr., 29
746. 8/2/2015 - Virgil Lee Reynolds, 63
747. 8/3/2015 - Shawn Michael Ruble, 35
748. 8/3/2015 - Joshua Malave, 18
749. 8/4/2015 - Darius D. Graves, 31
750. 8/4/2015 - Daniel Robert Avila, 55
751. 8/4/2015 - Franklin M. Short, 71
752. 8/5/2015 - Jason Galaviz, 40
753. 8/5/2015 - John H. Dieringer, 51
754. 8/5/2015 - Raymond Hodge, 39
755. 8/5/2015 - Tyler Alexander Dattilo, 18
756. 8/5/2015 - Keshawn D. Hargrove, 20
757. 8/5/2015 - Vincente David Montano, 29
758. 8/6/2015 - Gustavo Ponce-Galon, 42
759. 8/6/2015 - Troy Robinson, 32
760. 8/7/2015 - Derrick Lee Hunt, 28
761. 8/7/2015 - Abel Correa, 24
762. 8/7/2015 - Aaron Marchese, 30
763. 8/7/2015 - Charles Bertram, 22
764. 8/7/2015 - Christian Taylor, 19
765. 8/8/2015 - Unidentified
766. 8/8/2015 - Kevin Lee McDaniel, 40
767. 8/8/2015 - Matthew Russo, 26
768. 8/8/2015 - Tsombe Jashon Clark, 25
769. 8/8/2015 - Mark Keckhaser, 53
770. 8/8/2015 - Shamir Terrel Palmer, 24
771. 8/9/2015 - Robert Patrick Quinn, 77
772. 8/9/2015 - Edrian Rivera, 22
773. 8/9/2015 - Andre Green, 15
774. 8/9/2015 - Eric Keith Tompkins, 41
775. 8/9/2015 - Jeffrey Clyde Wilkes, 58
776. 8/10/2015 - Richard Tyler Young, 24
777. 8/10/2015 - Taylor Culbertson, 32
778. 8/11/2015 - Roger Dean Shull Jr., 24
779. 8/11/2015 - Randall Lance Hughes, 48
780. 8/11/2015 - Casey George Alarcon, 34
781. 8/12/2015 - Reginald Marshall, 27
782. 8/12/2015 - Anthony Lorenzo Vallejo, 27
783. 8/12/2015 - Redel Kentel Jones, 30

784. 8/12/2015 - Nathaniel Wilks, 27
785. 8/13/2015 - William Smith, 49
786. 8/14/2015 - Hector Rene Soriano Gonzalez, 26
787. 8/14/2015 - Garland Tyree, 38
788. 8/15/2015 - Jonathon Pope, 30
789. 8/15/2015 - Benjamin Peter Ashley, 34
790. 8/15/2015 - Allen Matthew Baker III, 23
791. 8/15/2015 - John Unsworth, 43
792. 8/15/2015 - Asshams Pharoah Manley, 30
793. 8/16/2015 - Jonathan Velarde, 23
794. 8/16/2015 - Matthew Castillo, 29
795. 8/16/2015 - Oscar Ruiz, 44
796. 8/17/2015 - Richard Jacquez, 40
797. 8/17/2015 - Frederick Roy, 35
798. 8/17/2015 - Christopher T. Anderson, 53
799. 8/17/2015 - Steven B. Norton, 47
800. 8/19/2015 - Mansur Ball-Bey, 18
801. 8/20/2015 - David Scott Coleman, 38
802. 8/20/2015 - Tyler James Gerkin, 19
803. 8/20/2015 - Pablo C. Tiersten, 38
804. 8/20/2015 - Raul Herrera III, 17
805. 8/20/2015 - Jeffory Ray Tevis, 50
806. 8/20/2015 - Wade Allen Baker, 44
807. 8/20/2015 - Deviere Ernel Ransom, 24
808. 8/20/2015 - Jason Hale, 29
809. 8/21/2015 - Troy Francis, 54
810. 8/21/2015 - Timmy L. Walling, 57
811. 8/22/2015 - Thaddeus Faison, 39
812. 8/22/2015 - Unidentified
813. 8/22/2015 - Adam Russell Schneider, 31
814. 8/22/2015 - Alan Joseph Rushton, 38
815. 8/22/2015 - Charles S. Hall, 30
816. 8/23/2015 - Christopher Ray Tompkins, 36
817. 8/23/2015 - Richard Francis Compo Jr., 36
818. 8/23/2015 - William Lee Snider, 57
819. 8/23/2015 - Kenneth Henry Morgan, 64
820. 8/23/2015 - Nicholas Garner, 26
821. 8/23/2015 - Jason Lee Alderman, 29
822. 8/24/2015 - Julian Hoffman, 21
823. 8/24/2015 - Bobby Troledge Norris, 53
824. 8/25/2015 - Shane Randolph, 45
825. 8/25/2015 - Todd Tomlinson, 53
826. 8/25/2015 - Curtis Smith, 34
827. 8/25/2015 - Marvin Maestas, 30
828. 8/26/2015 - Brent Pickard, 46
829. 8/26/2015 - Marvin Orlando Arroliga, 22
830. 8/26/2015 - Steven Dodd, 22
831. 8/27/2015 - Bertrand Syjuan Davis, 43
832. 8/27/2015 - Yonas Alehegne, 30
833. 8/28/2015 - Michael James Tyree, 31
834. 8/28/2015 - William Evans, 28
835. 8/28/2015 - Gilbert Flores, 41
836. 8/28/2015 - Wendell L. Hall, 50
837. 8/28/2015 - Manuel Soriano, 29
838. 8/28/2015 - Robert Arthur Hober, 54
839. 8/29/2015 - Roger Albrecht, 43
840. 8/29/2015 - Rafael A. Cruz Jr., 29
841. 8/29/2015 - Felix Kumi, 61
842. 8/29/2015 - James Marcus Brown III, 25
843. 8/30/2015 - David Moreno Leon, 40
844. 8/30/2015 - Shawn Allen Hall, 20
845. 8/31/2015 - Nicholas Tanner Dyksma, 18
846. 8/31/2015 - James Carney III, 48
847. 8/31/2015 - William Rippley, 45
848. 9/1/2015 - Charles Robert Shaw, 76
849. 9/1/2015 - Michael Todd Evans, 47
850. 9/1/2015 - Tyree Crawford, 18
851. 9/1/2015 - Cedric Maurice Williams, 33
852. 9/1/2015 - Devin Brian Dial, 23
853. 9/2/2015 - Arthur Edward Bates, 45
854. 9/4/2015 - Lucas Markus, 33
855. 9/4/2015 - Harrison Lambert, 23
856. 9/4/2015 - Sully Lanier, 36
857. 9/4/2015 - Richard Keith Kelley, 27
858. 9/4/2015 - Jose Ramon Damiani, Jr., 49
859. 9/4/2015 - Curtis James Meyer, 37
860. 9/5/2015 - Manuel Ornelas, 47
861. 9/5/2015 - Luis Guillen Wenceslao, 32
862. 9/5/2015 - La'vante Trevon Biggs, 21
863. 9/6/2015 - Patrick D. Ennis, 50
864. 9/6/2015 - Ben A. C de Baca, 45
865. 9/6/2015 - Mohamed Ibrahim, 28
866. 9/6/2015 - Richard Cosentino, 63
867. 9/6/2015 - Carlos Yero, 59
868. 9/6/2015 - Angelo Delano Perry, 35
869. 9/6/2015 - India Kager, 28
870. 9/7/2015 - Wayne Wheeler, 41
871. 9/7/2015 - Casimero Carlos Casillas, 45
872. 9/7/2015 - William Verrett, 42
873. 9/9/2015 - Vincent Perdue, 33
874. 9/9/2015 - Tyrone L. Holman, 37
875. 9/9/2015 - Dustin M. Kuik, 25
876. 9/10/2015 - Eddie Tapia, 41
877. 9/10/2015 - Austin Wilburly Reid, 32
878. 9/10/2015 - Brandon Foy, 29
879. 9/10/2015 - Unidentified
880. 9/10/2015 - Tian Ma, 31
881. 9/11/2015 - Unidentified